SHADES OF AURA

PHASE 1: TOTERRUM TRILOGY

BOOK 1

THE WALLS OF TOTERRUM

BOOK 2

THE CALAMITIES OF TOTERRUM

BOOK 3

THE HOPES OF TOTERRUM

SHADES OF AURA

PHASE 2: GAIA CYCLE

BOOK 4

SERENDIPITOUS SIGHT

BOOK 5

COMING SOON...

BOOK 6

COMING SOON...

Shades of Aura

Serendipitous Sight

Benjamin Kamphuis

BENGAR PUBLISHING

CONTENTS

This book is dedicated to my Grammy,
the inspiration for wanting to heal a loved one.
Your unconditional love and support to my messy,
creative mind has meant the world to me.
I love you with every corner of my mind.

This book is also dedicated to Amelia,
the inspiration for Isabella, and William.
I would do ANYTHING to protect you.
You ARE and WILL always be loved.

REMEMBER
SURVIVE
COALITION
HUSK
SOLARA

THE BATTLE OF THE FERTILE LANDS
BLANCHE
CORNIA
MAIZE
AMAR
ISLE

PART I

CONSCRIPTION

CHAPTER I
THE TALONHOUND

The worst part of owning a pet was cleaning up its shit. I wandered my yard haphazardly as the clumped mounds clung to the green grass and stared up at me. They were never in one pile, always scattered. At twenty-seven, was this my life? Cleaning up Talonhound shit?

As much as I hated it, it distracted me from the war entering our country.

I glared over at Harper, who stared back at me without blinking, letting out a soft whimper. Her latest nest, a deep hole, held the hoard of sticks and rocks she enjoyed collecting. Black and white patches covered her long, furry body. Rigid arches curled up and down her spine. Four legs with claws like talons scraped at the ground, perfect for digging deep. Her beady black eyes and droopy ears reached for the ground like her long lips. A cute Talonhound, in her own way.

"You could poop in one area," I said as if she understood.

Harper yawned and curled up in her hole, sticks crunching below. Clouds filled the sky in gray fluff, rare for the country of Maize.

I sighed and continued pulling my metallic rake across the ground, watching the feces slide into the shovel. A weekly routine, for the weeks I cared enough to do it. When the scooper was full, I poured the little bastards into a plastic bag and continued my journey.

As I neared the last pile, I came across something peculiar. I paused, staring at it. A pile covered in...white. Unique. It shivered as if alive, almost like white fur covering a small beast. My gaze moved across my yard. The remaining piles were coated in the same white fluff, something I had not noticed before. Inside the plastic bag, the droppings were covered in the same thing—white fluff.

"How'd I miss that?" I whispered to myself, a soft buzz ringing in my ears. I had the urge to touch it. As I reached my hand forward, the fluff shivered and seemed to shift like an odd form of energy.

"I hear they're holding a meeting today," a deep voice snapped me back to reality. A pair of Maizeans walked by my yard, the person speaking sparing me an uneasy smile. "Do you think they'll make people go to war?"

Was their question valid? How could I be fretting about Harper's feces when war threatened our land?

Weariness covered the faces of Cornia's citizens, heavy lines etched into the brows of people young and old. The impending war and the need for more warriors threatened our land. I tried not to dwell on it. Dwelling on something wasn't me—I focused on enjoying my life with my family and friends.

I hesitated, then scooped up the last of the white-covered feces, then tied the bag and brought it to the trash, letting my victims fall to their demise. Harper fixated on me and wagged her tail. I patted her head, and we walked into the kitchen.

"Did you accomplish everything you wanted?" Valeria asked.

My wife wore a skintight black shirt and pants with a red shawl draped over her shoulders and arms. A braid of silky black hair hung in front of her right shoulder. Her bronze skin glistened like warm embers in the kitchen light, brightening her fiery brown eyes. Though her fire could burn me, I had always been drawn to it, seeking the flame's warm embrace.

"Very funny," I replied with a snarky tone and a smile.

For some reason, the white fuzz on Harper's feces bothered me. Had it moved? Did I imagine it? I was about to say something, but hesitated. It was just feces.

"Ciro, is something wrong?" Valeria narrowed her eyes.

"Nothing," I lied.

"It's the war again, isn't it? If I could get involved, I would—"

Valeria stopped as my daughter ran into the kitchen, which connected to a small dining room and living space. Blue tiles made of turquoise slate native to Maize's shores shimmered from their sparkly sheen. Windows let in sunlight across the wall to the backyard. Essential oil burned from the counter, filling the room with a floral, spiced aroma.

"Daddy, banana," Isabella requested with a smile. Though her hair shined black like her mother's, it didn't hold quite the same silkiness. It was more of a frizzy mess, loosely tied back and not yet brushed. A twinkle in her honey-brown eyes brought ferocity to her little frame, like a spark ready to ignite into a blaze. I burned every time I fell into her blaze. The tension in my back released at her smile. Such glorious warmth grew in my chest at that smile of hers.

I grabbed a banana from the counter and peeled it.

"Now, make sure you throw this away when you're done."

"Okay, Daddy."

She smiled and stuffed her face. I touched her soft hair before moving my hand to her cheek and tickling behind her ear. Her little giggle warmed my heart as stray banana chunks fell to the ground. Harper licked them up as fast as they fell.

Isabella just turned three, the age of growing ferocity and constant energy. She exhausted my wife and me. Trouble followed wherever she went, as did the unrelenting want for more. She demanded something every waking moment of the day...and night.

"That is her second banana today," Valeria said. "Ella sabe como traba-jarnos."

"It's better than candy," I said, winking at Isabella.

"La fruta no es dulce." Isabella grinned and took another bite.

"You're right." I kissed Isabella's head. "She's already speaking better native Maizean than I ever will."

"Maybe if you'd listen to your maestra." Valeria smirked, twirling her hand in the air before placing it on her chest. "I'm a pretty good teacher."

I chuckled and recalled all the times Valeria tried to teach me the native language. Although I came to Maize at a young age, I wasn't taught the native language. My whole body relaxed as I reminisced about those simple times. A time when war didn't threaten us.

"It's wild. Ten years ago, you barely heard the old language except with you and a few others. Now, even the Stena sprinkles it into speeches."

"Stena Mezca is our first native leader in...what, five decades?" Valeria crossed her arms and looked out the window again.

I basked in the light reflecting off Valeria's face. Her loyalty to Maize didn't always make sense to me, but I respected it. My heart fluttered, lost in the warmth of her beauty. For a moment, I recalled the hugs my father used to give before he passed.

"*The Stena wants, and the Stena gets,*" I echoed old wisdom passed down to me. "At least that's what my father's cousin told us all those years ago when my father and I first came here from Solara."

Valeria's eyes didn't move from the window.

"Maybe the rules were never really ours to make." With an exasperated sigh, she turned to me. "I wish people would just relax about the war. As the daughter of a warrior—"

"—You know that fighting for your country is necessary to keep free-dom." As I finished her statement, she shot a glare at me, the warmth gone from her eyes. Walking forward, I put my arm around her hip and pulled her close, fragrant floral essential oils wafting off her hair.

"I know how strong you are." I kissed her soft lips. "You don't need to tell me. I see it in your eyes."

To that, she grinned and patted my chest.

"Well played, esposo."

Though Valeria seemed confident in our country fighting a war, the idea made my stomach twist. My father died during the war. I didn't want the same for my family. Taking on crop delivery as my occupation kept me away from trouble. I trusted our leadership to keep things at bay. Stena Mezca captivated the country, well respected by both the native people and the immigrants. This respect proved especially important due to the impending war with the Coalition, another neighboring nation. About five years ago, the leaders of Maize chose to focus on creating and sustaining its own energy. In doing so, coal, the driver of the Coalition's economy, was cut as an energy source. The Coalition retaliated by stopping the import of crops, Maize's economic driver.

"I just wish they'd stay away from our land," Valeria said. "Proteger la tierra."

"Our land has the crops, and theirs has the coal. They want what we have."

"The Coalition may try, but they won't take away our fertile lands, no matter how many border territories they threaten."

A knock on the door drew my attention.

"Wonder who that could be..." Valeria said with a playful smirk and raised eyebrows.

I answered the door to exactly who I expected—Aameen.

He had a dark appearance: black hair, black beard, dark eyes, all counteracted with a bright, white smile. This smile was not limited to just his friends, but to everyone he met, evoking quick, trusting bonds with even strangers.

"My brother, Ciro," Aameen said, embracing me for a hug.

"Aameen," I said. "I just saw you yesterday."

"And the day before that, and the day before that…" Valeria added.

"Valeria, you know you love my visits," Aameen said. "I have to maintain my best friend title."

Valeria simply raised an eyebrow toward him before picking up Isabella and going upstairs.

"We'd better get to the meeting," Aameen said.

"Shit, that meeting was today?" I palmed my forehead. "V! I'm leaving with Aameen for—"

"The governmental meeting!" Valeria called from upstairs, finishing my statement. "I know."

"I need my—" I started.

"Notepad," she yelled. "It's on the counter."

"Thank you." I grinned at her attentiveness. "¡Te amo!"

"Te amo más." Her voice echoed down the stairs.

"What would you do without your best friend and wife?" Aameen asked with a sly look.

"Never make it to a meeting." We both laughed.

Harper barked at us as I shut the door, the city stretching before me.

Cornia, the capital of Maize, had been my home for so long, specifically in the western center of the city. Most buildings stood no taller than two stories in residential areas, but the city stretched as far as I could see. Tan stucco plastered most of the walls, with bright orange, teal, or yellow shingles covering the roofs.

As we walked across the compacted dirt streets, roads branched off into more neighborhoods and businesses. If we followed the main street, we would hit the marketplace to the east and the government buildings to the north.

The clouds broke up early for the day, releasing a sweltering heat. It shouldn't have surprised me—it was always hot in Maize.

The people of Maize scurried on their different routes. Laughter and friendly conversation filled the city on its normal days, but recently, people moved with more haste and less interaction. I tried to smile at all who passed by, but most wouldn't give me the time of day. They were worried about the war. I worried about the war. But I had to be positive.

"How's your family?" I asked Aameen.

"Amir lost his first tooth today."

"He is growing up way too fast."

"The twins slept the whole night for the first time," he said. "I caught Dani writing a letter to a boyfriend." I laughed. "Hey. You too will have a teenager someday."

"You are too protective." I knew he had taken the letter from her.

"Maybe I am. Layla and I went out last night. My mother-in-law watched the kids."

"I don't even know the last time Valeria and I had a date night."

"You need to have one." He smirked. "Maybe we can have Dani babysit for you."

"Think she is up for the challenge? Isabella is fierce."

"That she is." Aameen's cackle echoed throughout the street.

We turned the corner to Pastel Castle, the capitol building.

The building was named for its resemblance to a tiered cake—each level was narrower than the last. The first floor widened as the stucco walls curved to the left and to the right. Turquoise shingles angled upward toward the second level. Stucco walls followed the same pattern, but this floor was narrower than the first floor. Orange shingles topped it toward the next floor. Then, purple shingles topped the last floor.

At the very peak of the building sat a copper weathervane, forged in the shape of corn. The tip of the corn faced whichever direction the wind blew.

"What flavor do you think the meeting will be on today?" Aameen asked.

Most people referred to the capitol building's floors as "flavors," with each flavor named for the colors of its shingles.

"Hmmm...I'm going clementine today."

"Clementine...that's new." Aameen grinned.

"I didn't want to say orange..." I admitted. "I felt like adding variety today."

"Naming a kid a child still makes it a kid."

Aameen always liked his wise sayings.

There were four entrances to Pastel Castle: the turquoise doors, the orange doors, the purple doors, and the yellow doors. We faced the orange doors.

My wife's culture said the door you entered decided what attitude you would carry that day. If my memory served, orange meant timid. Too many people focused on the negative side of timidity, especially in a country that valued warriors. But sometimes being timid gave further room for respect. Bold people weren't the best listeners. Bravery had its place, but not everywhere.

As always when attending important meetings with Maize's leaders, I decided on the orange doors.

The orange clay doors creaked open to the main floor, the public meeting space. Only certain citizens were invited each time, rotating in and out. We never knew how many people would be there until we arrived at the meeting.

"Prominent people are here today," Aameen whispered to me.

He was right. It would be a serious meeting.

Stena Mezca's five-person council attended most meetings. The Counts were chosen by Stena Mezca and each oversaw a different part of the city. One of the council members, our least favorite, stood near our door—Count Ariba. Her height commanded a presence, a head taller than Aameen and me. She had slim cheekbones and wore her seasoned gray hair tied tightly. Though her skin was tan like many Maizeans, it appeared gray. She wore her usual purple suit, but today had an unusual scarf on, fluffy and somewhat transparent. I couldn't pinpoint the color—it was a combination of green and light blue.

"Count Ariba," I said. "Lovely afternoon."

Ariba pressed her lips together in a thin smile. "Ciro. Aameen. Lovely afternoon."

"What flavor are we enjoying today?" Aameen asked.

"Flavor?" Ariba asked. "Ah, yes. The ridiculous way the citizens refer to the floors. Floor two."

Ariba always had a lofty attitude, thinking herself higher than everyone else. It was off-putting, but Stena Mezca trusted her. She had held her position for ten years since he took over.

We simply smiled and made our way to the staircase. I nudged Aameen since my flavor guess ended up correct. He chuckled while I looked back at the scarf around Ariba's neck.

"Count Bebida," Aameen said, my attention turning back to the staircase.

Bebida drew anyone's attention, an exceptionally beautiful native woman of Maize. Her family and my wife's family had always been close. Straight black hair, silky like Valeria's, hung to near her waist. Each time she moved, her hair shimmered in a wave. She wore a native tunic covered in geometric shapes and pastel colors.

"El dia es brillante," Bebida responded. "The meetings you two are invited to are always the best."

"You flatter us," I said. "How are the conversations going with the border?"

Her face stiffened. "They could be going better. I'm afraid the Coalition is going down a path from which they will not recover."

"That's disheartening," Aameen said. "Part of me wonders if compromising some of our land would prevent the war from continuing."

"The Hoggara who takes food from the Shapple has an unsatisfiable hunger," Bebida said.

"But the Shapple without a fence will wander away from the flock," Aameen rebutted.

I wondered at their analogy, picturing the great, fat Hoggara eating the grass the slender Shapples pick at while the Shapples wandered out into an open field. Why Bebida picked such an ugly beast to represent the Coalition and a herding beast to represent Maize struck me as peculiar. And did Aameen think Maizeans needed boundaries?

"Wise words from a wise man," Bebida said, much more satisfied with Aameen's analogy rebuttal than I was. "You would make a wonderful councilperson when the next position is open."

"If that ever becomes an option," Aameen said. "Pretty sure a council person serves until death...or involuntary dismissal."

"Or voluntary forfeit," Bebida added. "El futuro no está claro. You never know what the future holds."

"Lucky we have a young council." Aameen scratched the back of his head and smirked. The oddest twinkle danced in Aameen's eyes. I hadn't witnessed it before with my friend.

Before I pressed Aameen with more questions, Count Ariba loudly scolded someone nearby for who knew what.

"And a passionate council," Bebida said with a hum. "At least the Stena has control."

With a curt nod, Aameen pounded his chest. "At least we have that."

"Well, if the position ever does open, you will have my endorsement," Bebida said.

"You would have to earn my support." I elbowed Aameen.

"Welcome."

A strong voice sounded from above. It came from a brass megaphone attached to pipes weaving across the ceiling. Megaphones were positioned throughout the space. They all connected through a hole in the ceiling, the original announcement mechanism Pastel Castle had used since its construction.

"Please make your way to flavor orange for today's meeting."

Everyone chuckled, except for Count Ariba. We all knew the voice to be Stena Mezca.

The crowd of about twenty people gathered for the meeting migrated toward the rounded staircase encased in the colorful tiles. Our migration reminded me of the way livestock at the edge of Cornia moved during their feeding time.

What sustenance would Stena Mezca provide us?

Once on flavor orange, a longer table sat in the center of the floor's common space. Stena Mezca sat at the head of the table in a grand golden chair. He wore the cultural headpiece of the Stena, made of copper. The piece mimicked husks of corn, woven in a circle. Ten feathers feathered out of the top, each an assorted color representing the ten birds important to Maize's ecosystem. Each time I saw the headpiece, the white feather stood out the most, representing a primary food source in Maize, the Maizean Chickaroo. It was the least grand of the birds, but still sat upon the crown.

Count Ariba sat to the right of Stena Mezca, where she always sat. Count Bebida sat next to Ariba.

The rest of the council came from the other portions of Maize. I didn't know them well. Count Juan, a burly man with a black beard, wore matching black clothes. To the left of Stena Mezca sat Count Pepe, slender and tall. Count Margarita sat last, shorter, broad, and often smiling.

"Welcome to today's focus group," Stena Mezca said. "Today, I would like your input on the upcoming war. Unfortunately, we are at a point where we will need to protect our land with firmer forces. Wise words are falling on deaf ears. Our army has not been reinforced for quite some time, and we need to gather and train new forces. My first question is this: How can we gather additional troops?"

The group was silent, fear heavy in the room.

"Will the other cities provide troops?" a woman near the back asked, breaking the silence.

Stena Mezca looked over at Count Pepe.

"Husk is providing one thousand, Blanche is providing two thousand, and Amar is providing two thousand five hundred," Pepe said. "The smaller towns total about seventy-five. With these additions and our army, we are still about three hundred people short of the Coalition's estimated army size."

"Our warriors are better trained," a man said.

"That is far from true," Count Bebida retorted. "We may have a strong maritime fleet, but the Coalition will only be attacking by land. I cannot say the last time Maize was at war on land."

"Solara will come to our aid," another woman said.

Solara was another neighboring nation, directly southwest of Maize, a large country with tall buildings bleached by the sun.

"Solara remains neutral—bound to both the Coalition and us by treaty," Count Ariba said. "They've asked us to avoid dragging them in unless absolutely necessary."

"We have provided aid to them in the past," another man said.

"We have," Stena Mezca replied. "Time and time again. Do I believe they will help us if needed? I do. But they have requested that we help them avoid this, if possible. They will remain on standby. The Coalition does not know this.

"Now, I need you all to answer the question I originally asked. How will we gather more warriors?"

"Financial motive," I said.

"We already provide this," Count Ariba snapped.

"I know," I said. "Perhaps more of an incentive that normally offered for them and their families who stay here."

"Can this be done quickly enough?" Stena Mezca asked.

"Maybe." I swallowed, mouth dry.

"We need more than a maybe," Stena Mezca said.

"Correct me if I'm wrong, Stena Mezca. But it feels like we're dancing around the decision that the council has already made," Aameen said.

"And what is that?" Stena Mezca asked.

"Drafting citizens," Aameen said. "A mandatory duty."

The room broke out in chaos, everyone speaking at once. Count Ariba leaned over to Stena Mezca and whispered something into her ear.

"Enough!" Stena Mezca yelled.

The room quieted. Stena Mezca surveyed the room.

"Aameen is correct."

The room erupted again.

"I said enough!" Stena Mezca's voice boomed, his features rippling with intensity.

"You must understand that our nation is in dire need of support. Our citizens are not volunteering. We wouldn't do this if we thought there was another option."

"How will it be decided?" Aameen asked.

"Completely random," Stena Mezca said. "Those under eighteen and over fifty-five will be excluded. Both men and women are eligible. A household will always remain with one caretaker of children."

"How long until this occurs?" Aameen asked.

Silence filled the room.

"A couple of days from now," Stena Mezca said. "We would like for this group to spread the word."

The room went into an uproar again.

"The Stena has spoken!" Count Ariba yelled, her scarf flashed bright for a moment, seeming to catch the light coming in through the window. She coughed, looking at her hand for a moment. Her face twisted before refocusing on the crowd. "Let us have time."

The crowd began to move out of the room, scowling at the council. Though it upset me, I understood it to be the only option. Bebida smiled at us as we left. I saw Ariba wipe her hand on a white cloth she pulled from her pocket, specks of blood on it.

As we walked down the stairs, a man and woman I recognized but didn't know well were complaining.

"They put us out there to die over their inability to govern," the man said. "This is why the indigenous shouldn't—"

"Shouldn't what?!" Aameen yelled, forcing himself into their conversation. "Lead? This war has nothing to do with this. Actually, the *natives* kept peace in this land longer than any other nation has. This war is happening because of the Coalition's greed. Nothing else. We are in dire need of help and have a strong and plentiful population to aid this cause."

"If you say so," the man said as Aameen pushed past him outside.

"I do say so," Aameen spat. "Now, have a good night and remember all Stena Mezca has done to keep you safe."

Aameen stormed down a route that wasn't our normal one.

"You know we don't live in this direction," I said.

"I know," Aameen said, his temper flaring. "I just didn't want to walk next to those idiots."

"They're just scared. We are all scared."

"I know." He took a deep breath. "I know you're right."

"Did you see Count Ariba cough toward the end?"

"Yes, what about it?"

"I saw her wipe her mouth with a cloth, and it had blood on it. It was odd. Kind of like her scarf."

"That is strange...but I don't remember a scarf."

"You must have missed it."

Aameen sighed. "I hope my wife can handle the kids once I'm gone."

"Gone?"

It hit me.

He is going to draft himself. What about me? What about my family?

Valeria came from a family of warriors. She would want to fight. My father died during a war. What if Valeria died?

Clenching my sweaty palms, I tried to slow down, but my heart was pounding in my ears. I had to keep my family safe. Neither of us could die. I grew up without my father. I wanted it to be different for my daughter. How would this work?

How would I keep my family safe?

Be positive. Be positive. You will figure something out. It will all work out.

We rounded the corner and walked toward my house. My wife paced near the front door.

"Ciro!" she yelled as she saw us. "Come here quickly! Something is wrong with Harper!"

Aameen and I raced to the house. Valeria opened the door and I rushed past. Harper lay on the ground, unmoving. White fluff pulsed and vanished along her leg like a living beast.

The white fluff made no sense to me, but Harper whimpered. Whatever it was, my beast was in pain, and I needed to help.

CHAPTER 2
THE SURGERY

"What happened?!" I leaned over Harper. The white fluff around her leg flickered before fading, as if it had never been there.

"She was making a weird noise before she laid down," Valeria said. "¿Qué te pasa? Her stomach has been gurgling since you left."

"We need to get her to the vet," I said.

"I can watch Isabella," Aameen said.

"Are you sure?" Valeria asked.

"You're both family to me." He squeezed my arm before pushing me forward. "I've got this. Go."

"Thank you." I lifted Harper up, my arms straining to carry her bulky, round body and raced out the door. Our veterinarian was about two blocks away. I tried running, but Harper whimpered louder if I bounced too much.

"I'm worried," Valeria whispered.

I wanted to roll onto the floor and sob. War. A sick Talonhound. Too much was going on. I swallowed hard.

"I'm sure it's nothing," I lied. The white fluff covering her feces and now her leg lingered in my mind.

Our veterinarian Victor tilted a watering can toward flowers in front of his office as we approached his house. As soon as he saw us, his face shifted. *Clang.* The canister bounced on the ground. He flung his door open, a burst of wind pushing my hair back.

"Come inside." His shaggy brown hair bounced as he pointed to a steel table. I placed Harper on the surface. Lining up his square face to Harper's tense snout, Victor tilted the dog's head in both directions before turning back to us, his gray eyes searching ours.

"What happened?" he asked.

"She started acting funny about thirty minutes ago," Valeria said. "Since then, only whimpers and constant gurgling have come from her stomach."

Victor put his stethoscope to Harper's stomach.

"Nothing odd before this?"

The white fluff filled my mind, begging me to confess what I saw. Uncertainty continued to make me doubt myself. Was I hallucinating? Would they think I was crazy?

Again, the white fluff appeared on Harper's leg for a brief moment before fading. I rubbed my eyes and gave up on keeping my secret.

"Her poop had this white fluff on it earlier today," I said, my voice cracking.

Victor's head perked up. "White fluff?"

Valeria whipped her face toward me. "You never said anything about this."

"I didn't think it was worth mentioning," I said. I debated bringing up the fluff on Harper's leg that didn't stay visible for more than a second at a time.

"I have never heard of white fluff—" Victor began.

Harper let out a sharp whine, and poop sprayed out of her butt, covered in the white fluff.

"There," I said, pointing. "There's the fluff."

I wasn't losing my mind. The fluff was there. I looked up from Harper and saw Victor and Valeria looking at each other with furrowed brows.

They didn't see it.

I looked back at my Talonhound. The white fluff was as clear as day, wriggling across Harper's mess on the floor. Recoiling my pointed finger, my back arched as my finger and the muscles in my arms and legs clenched all at once. The tension begged for release. Any confidence I had faded until Harper's chest fluttered in a sharp whine. Whether the fluff was real, my beast needed help.

"Can you help her?" I asked.

"I'm going to run some tests," Victor said. He took a syringe and injected liquid into Harper's body. She let out a small yelp, then her breathing calmed and her eyes fluttered shut. "That'll help her rest."

The rancid smell of the feces finally hit me, forcing me to cover my nose. Victor took a towel and threw it on top, unfazed by the stench. I breathed a sigh of relief when I saw the peace across Harper's face.

Valeria reached over and squeezed my hand. "What now?"

"I'll figure out what's going on," Victor said.

"Is it okay if we stay?" I asked. Victor nodded.

As we waited, Valeria paced, hands above her head. My gaze drifted between her and Harper. Valeria's impatience often irked me, but it could be controlled in less stressful situations. I tapped my foot while tapping my knee at the same beat, trying to distract myself from Valeria's incessant pacing. But I knew better than to tell her to go. The tension built as my worry built.

Before I erupted, Valeria let out a deep sigh, stepped forward, and squeezed my hand. "I should get back home," she said. "Isabella was scared."

Valeria leaned over Harper's head and kissed her. "Se fuerte mi perro."

"I'll come home soon," I said before kissing Valeria's cheek.

"Take care of our perro, Victor." Valeria paused at the door, looked at Harper once more, and left.

"I will," Victor replied. He pointed at a stool near his table. "You can sit there while I work."

Victor began an array of tests using needles, blood samples, fecal samples, and microscopes. With each test, Victor's face tensed more, and his grunts became louder. My stomach twisted into knots. According to Victor's thermometer, Harper's temperature continued to rise.

Victor came and went from the room, leaving me alone with my beast. The silence was cut only by the ticking of a clock. The vein inside my head pulsed in a treacherous beat. I fixated on Harper, her black, purple, and white fur moving up and down as she breathed.

"My poor pup," I whispered, gripping the fabric of my pant leg tightly. I worried that if I let go of the fabric, I'd somehow lose Harper.

A terrible pain in my chest with each agonizing heartbeat I focused on Harper.

Suddenly, a bubbly moss began to spread over her leg. No, a green fluff. Just like the white fluff from earlier, it held no real shape. Just a mass of green bubbly clouds shivering across her limb.

My hand lifted from my leg as I reached toward the green mass. My heart pounded like a war drum, in sync with each tick of the clock. I tried to touch the fluff, but I only felt Harper's fur. My hand passed right through the green fluff as if nothing were there. Just the slightest buzz tickled my fingertips. For a moment, I thought I could grab—

"Ciro," Victor said as he walked back into the room. I pulled back my hand. With a long, defeated breath, he tilted his head. "I'm afraid I don't know what's going on. Her temperature keeps rising and her other vitals aren't looking good. I'm running out of options."

I waited, hoping for him to say more, but a terrible shadow crossed his face. The face of defeat.

"What does that mean?" I asked.

"We have to think about her comfort." He crossed his arms and tilted his head in the other direction. "She may need to be euthanized."

"No." My breathing sped up. "We can't lose her."

Death slammed itself into my reality. War and death.

Victor leaned on the table, shoulders slumped. "I think it's our best option. I don't know what else to do."

I looked back at my Talonhound, across her body, and fixated on the green fluff. A burst of hope invigorated me. It was now or never.

"What about her leg?" I pointed at the green fluff. "What's the green fluff right here?"

He scrunched his eyebrows and walked over to her leg. I nodded forward. Reaching his hand through the fluff, he touched her leg. For a moment, I swore he saw it. Then he just looked up at me.

"What green fluff?"

His fingers found it. How could he not see it? I nodded and pointed right where he was. "Right there. Your hand is right on top of it."

Glancing back down to her leg, he moved his hand around before looking back up. "What are you talking about?"

"There's something there. I swear."

His eyes shifted between Harper and me, eyes searching my face. He didn't believe me.

"Maybe it's inside her." I didn't know what I was saying, but panic outweighed rationalization. "Just look."

"Ciro—"

"Please." My cheeks tightened as I tried to hold back tears. "For Harper's sake."

Whether he realized I wasn't going to back down or felt the same hope I did, he grabbed his scalpel, paused, and cut right where the green fluff sat.

Blood seeped out in a viscous wave, a red sheen flickering in the light. He took some gauze and blotted it away while he examined the area.

More blood rushed out. I stepped back, preparing for some kind of nausea or fear to overtake me.

Instead, nothing happened. No tension in my muscles. No pain in my chest. Just the sound of my heart pounding in my ears.

A metallic scent filled the sterile office air. A rush of energy filled my veins.

Victor hummed and moved the gauze before he stopped. His brow furrowed as he wiped more blood, revealing a thick black residue covering stark white—Harper's bone.

Looking closer, a black residue coated the bone.

"It's infected," Victor said. "The hip bone is very infected." His head dipped down. "This isn't good." With his other hand, he frantically pushed around tools until he found a narrow object with a sharp point at the end. "I'm going to need you to leave."

He was wrong; I needed to stay. "But—"

"Leave *now*," he said. "I don't want you to see what I have to do." I just stood there. "Trust me, Ciro. Leave. I have more hope than I did before. Please trust me."

Looking at Harper one last time, I nodded and walked out the door. The door clicked shut behind me.

It was dark outside and no one else was around. The nighttime air cooled my burning body. With each attempt to breathe in, my rapid heartbeat punched at my lungs. I couldn't breathe.

Should I go home? Do I stay?

I paced mindlessly around for what felt like hours. The stars shimmered above, but all they did was irritate me. Dust kicked up from the ground.

My focus switched back and forth between the stars and the ground. They were the only distractions, and I clung to them.

"Ciro!" Victor stood in his doorway. "Come quickly!"

In a blur, I ran back inside to Harper, covered in blood. More blood than I'd ever seen before.

The drumming in my ears turned into a sharp ringing.

Large patches of fur drenched in blood sat on the table. The metallic scent in the room was even greater than before.

The ringing intensified.

Then, I realized the large patch of fur wasn't just fur—it was her leg. Harper's entire leg sat on the table, separate from her body.

A harsh pain pressed at my sinuses as the ringing became deafening.

Victor pressed large pieces of gauze in the space her leg used to be. His lips moved, saying something to me.

"What..." I whispered.

His lips moved again, the ringing fading. He wanted me to hold something.

"Hold this gauze!" he yelled.

I couldn't move.

Victor had amputated her leg. Her entire leg.

"Ciro!" Victor screamed.

Shaking my head, I ran over and held the gauze. Thick blood warmed the fabric and coated my hands. My fingertips stuck to the gauze in a sticky mess. It seemed wrong to have so much blood touching me.

Victor ran to the counter and grabbed a long needle and what looked like thread.

"What's that for?" My voice shook as I tried to process everything that was going on.

"She is bleeding more than I planned. The clotting should resume soon." He unraveled the thread and stuck it through the needle. "I want to stitch the areas with less bleeding."

With methodical precision, he began sticking the needle through Harper's bloody flesh, bringing the skin together and pulling it taut. Each movement was so fast and exact that it left me in a trance.

He asked me to clean the already stitched flesh with the gauze. With one last stitch and snip of a small pair of scissors, it was done.

"There," he said, taking a deep breath. "She should be stable now."

I stared at the zipper-like scar covering the stub where her leg used to be. For some reason, I moved my hand through the empty space where her leg and the green fluff had been. All I felt was a slight breeze.

"Is her leg...?" I looked over at her rogue leg set casually to the side, also not covered in green fluff anymore, unable to form further words.

"Amputated?" He wiped his hands on a towel, not entirely answering my question. "Yes." He leaned on the table and cracked his neck. "The bone was rotted, and the infection was moving up her body. It was my only choice." He threw the crimson-stained towel to the side and grabbed another to continue wiping his hands. "Now, I just need to apply antibiotics and hook her up to an IV. I'll clean up. You should go home."

"But..." I still couldn't talk.

"Come here tomorrow. You need rest, and so do I. The sink is over there." He nodded to the right.

I floated over to the sink and put my hands under the running water, though I felt nothing except the numb sensation of the water's force against my hands. The blood splashed into the sink, swirling down the drain. The scent of floral soap clashed with the scent of iron.

"Is...is she going to be okay?"

"Yes, I think she will." Victor smiled. "Now, please, get some rest. I have a lot of questions for you, but not now."

Numbly, I moved toward the door and, somehow, made it home. My mind was going a million miles an hour.

The blood, her leg, and the in-between replayed in my exhausted mind, but I wasn't focused on the scene. Whatever I saw on Harper's leg saved her life, and Victor didn't see it. Green fluff.

What was going on? I had to be losing my mind.

CHAPTER 3
VICTOR'S OBSERVATIONS

When a nightmare becomes your reality, sleep becomes nearly impossible. With each toss and turn, I tried to rid myself of torturous thoughts.

War, the possibility of being drafted, the green fluff on Harper's leg, all the blood, and the amputation haunted my every thought. I could scream. I could cry. Anything to release the torture. Instead, I held it in. Valeria had always been the strongest one in our family. I needed to embody her courage.

While my fears tortured me, Harper's health tortured Valeria.

"What do you mean you helped find the infection?" she pressed the next morning.

"I noticed this lump," I lied in one conversation.

"Harper's leg shook as I held it," I lied in another.

None of it made sense to me. How would it make sense to her? All that mattered was Harper.

"Victor says she will heal," I tried my best to convey Victor's confidence in Harper's recovery.

I needed that confidence to ooze into all the other areas of my life.

"So," I gulped, "what are we thinking about for the draft?"

"I'm from a long line of Maizean warriors," Valeria said each time we discussed the topic. "It's my *duty* to fight for Maize."

Such boldness exuded from my wife. I knew her history. I believed her words. But something tightened in my chest and made me second-guess her confidence. The tighter it squeezed, the more I realized what it was—dismay.

"What if we had other options?"

"I said it's my duty—"

"I'm not saying you won't fight." I raised my hands, trying to keep her fury at bay. Her wild eyes made me cower. "I'm just saying we need to be smart with it."

I took her hands into my own, watching the fire in her eyes.

I pushed forward before I backed down.

"If we can ensure that we're both safe, that means Isabella will always have two parents. We need to keep our family intact. Let's just consider our options."

Lips pinched tightly together, her eyes narrowed. She marched away from me, mumbling to herself in the native tongue. I couldn't understand a single thing she said. Here and there, she stopped and faced me.

A pounding resounded in my chest, consuming any space my lungs once had for air. As she turned and marched away, my body remembered how to breathe.

Every time she came closer to me, I lost all memories of basic bodily functions. Every time she moved away, I watched her like prey being stalked by a predator.

Without a doubt, her ferocity would be an asset in the war. Respect and honor were hers to obtain. But death paid no mind to either. One mistake or attack and I could lose her. My warrior wife. I couldn't handle it. I needed her. Isabella needed her.

With a few swift steps, she stepped right in front of me. Her eyes shifted around my face as she analyzed me. Did she know how afraid I was of losing her? I needed to come up with something fast. Then her face softened.

"Bien." She clicked her tongue. "Fine."

The deep tension riddling my abdominal area released at her concession. The sensation overwhelmed me, forcing up an unwanted bubble from my gut, nearly turning into a burp. I swallowed it down.

Eyelids fluttering, Valeria smirked at the control she had over me. Her one-word answers never meant she was convinced; it just meant she processed her real thoughts at a slower pace. For now, that was enough for me.

"But don't think for one second that you'll do better than me just because you're a man." Valeria raised a finger and narrowed her gaze. "If you think this, I will never speak to you again. Silencio para siempre." She pressed her index finger and thumb together near her lips, sealed them shut, and flicked away an invisible key.

I flinched, attempting to dodge the nonexistent projectile, but only looked like a fool. She patted my chest, whispered another inaudible comment in the native tongue, then walked into the kitchen.

Did she think *I* would draft myself? Aameen would draft himself to keep his family safe, but the same gesture didn't work for our family. I feared my wife too much, which proved her point. As soon as Valeria entered the war, she would do everything she could to protect those she was loyal to. And the more she fought, the higher the likelihood she could be killed.

And the alternative? I go to war and most likely cower in a corner until I either made it through the war unscathed or an enemy found me. I gulped hard, imagining my death. One of us would have to serve while the other kept Isabella safe. Was it better to throw in the warrior or the coward?

Were those the only options?

I needed to think through all potential scenarios. That was something I was good at.

With our conversation set to simmer, I went to check on Harper. Maybe my beast held the answer I searched for…if she was still alive. I stopped in front of the veterinary office, my arms shaking at my sides. What if she were dead? I shut my eyes and clenched my fists. There was no room for negative thoughts. I needed positivity. If I didn't manifest her health, there was no way it could be.

With a deep breath, I pushed the door open. Scanning the quiet room, my heartbeat pounding at my eardrums, I found a purple mass resting on a bed. Harper raised her head for a moment, her eyes bloodshot, wagging her tail. After a long, quivering breath, I almost burst into tears.

She was alive. She was moving.

White bandages wrapped tightly around her leg—or lack thereof—with no signs of the bloody massacre from the night before. Had I dreamed it all? A chemical smell wafted in the air and the counter shimmered brightly in the morning light. The smell reminded me of all the blood and the reality I had witnessed. Visions of the green fluff flickered in my mind before jolting away.

Pushing myself forward, I squatted next to Harper and spoke in the voice I often used when speaking with my Talonhound and babies, a pitch higher than normal. "My good girl looks so much better. Daddy is so happy you're alive." I petted her head tenderly. She didn't lean into my hand like she normally would, but she panted, droopy lips curling up like a smile, and wagged her tail. I searched her body for any other signs of green fluff. Only her blotted purple fur and a few brown and red stains of dried blood covered her body.

"I'm happy as well," Victor said with a chuckle. I stood straight up. "Don't stop your Talonhound voice just because I walked in."

"I didn't see you there." I scratched the back of my head.

Arms crossed, Victor's laughter faded before his eyebrows furrowed. "Speaking of seeing things…" He paused. "Tell me about yesterday."

My entire body stiffened. Maybe if I didn't move, he'd forget I was there. I didn't know what happened. I barely had time to think about it. The green fluff saved my beast's life. That was all that mattered. A little tickle formed at the base of my skull and rippled across my brain. But what was it?

"What about yesterday?" I asked, trying to remain coy.

Head tilted and eyebrows high, he gaped at me.

"Oh, the leg thing?" I let out a thin, uncertain snicker. "It was a lucky guess." Trying to avoid his gaze, my eyes gravitated to him like a magnet. I wanted to know as much as he did.

Victor shifted his stance, arms still crossed. "Is that the story you're going with? Drop the ruse."

Mouth agape, I couldn't come up with anything to say. The truth? He wouldn't believe me.

The absurdity of what I saw contradicted all logic. Yet, I saw it. I saw the white fluff on Harper's droppings. My eyes glossed over as I recalled the scarf around Count Ariba. Could that have been something? Could it have been trying to warn me like it did for Harper?

Victor listened to me. He saved Harper because of the chaos in my mind. I watched Victor, waiting for him to show any sign of thinking I'd lost my mind. But he kept a firm gaze, warm tan eyes waiting for an explanation.

"You sure you want to know?" I swallowed hard as he nodded. "Well, you had left the room during one of the tests. I kept looking at Harper, hoping for her safety."

The scene replayed in my mind. Harper's frail body was on the table. A harsh chemical scent stung my nose. Uncertainty swirled around me.

"Then, I saw something I hadn't seen before." I swirled my hand toward Harper's missing leg. "It was green fluff on her infected leg. I tried to touch it, but I didn't feel anything." My lips snapped shut. I had said too much, but at the same time, I needed to give him more. Maybe he could help. "Maybe a little fuzz, but I figured that was her fur. Then, I told you about it."

My heartbeat thundered in my chest. I waited for Victor to break out into laughter. I braced for the humiliation. Victor stood there, relaxed as could be. A smile curled up his cheeks.

"And then I found the infected bone that ended up saving her life." He paused. His truth set into me like a spade into dirt. "Nothing pointed to the infected bone, except what you examined within seconds. You saw something that I didn't see." He fell silent again, no laughter following.

As his gaze remained fixed on me, I shifted my eyes back and forth like Harper did when she was in trouble. Was I in trouble? Tension rippled across my body.

"And?" I asked.

Victor squinted and abruptly turned to leave for the back room. I lowered my head, stress weighing on me. The sun streamed into the room through skylights. As I waited for Victor, I looked around the room. A wall filled with shelves and cages rose to the ceiling. One squeaky ceiling fan teetered in a haphazard spin. The space where Harper's amputated leg had sat was clean.

Victor came back into the room holding a Capynx. The hairless rodent beast scrunched its flat nose above its long mouth. White fur shivered while its two long, pink tails whipped around. Its matching pink face looked up at me with two beady eyes. I'd seen a Capynx a few times growing up, a pet for some, but this beast wore what looked like bright pink shoes, something I'd never seen one wear before. Each shoe pulsed like a heart.

Placing it on the table, Victor gestured to the beast. "Tell me what you see."

"Well, I see a Capynx." I smiled. He raised his eyebrows and dipped his head in my direction. He wanted me to look for an abnormality. "With bright pink slippers that are...pulsing."

Victor lifted each of the Capynx's feet, analyzing the beast. "Fascinating."

"What is?"

"This beast came to me a week ago because it was 'acting weird', according to its owner. They insisted I keep the Capynx for observation, with a financial incentive, of course." He grinned. "I obliged. Until this morning, I couldn't figure out what was wrong with it. Then, I found small fungal infections below each of its toenails. It was something I was unable to see without a microscope." He lifted one of the beast's feet. "Just a regular foot to the naked eye." He placed the foot back down. "Now tell me, how did you manage to figure out something was wrong with its feet within seconds, but it took me nearly a week?"

A great pounding resounded in my chest. A quivering shake moved across my chest and along my arms and legs.

"Maybe I'm a better vet than you?" An innocent smirk bloomed across my face, to which he frowned. "Because of the pink slippers I saw."

"*Slippers* I don't see. I'm trying to convince myself it's all circumstantial, but you have correctly identified unidentifiable health issues twice now. Even before anyone else noticed that something was going on. How is that?"

What did he want me to say? That I was magical? There were rumors of such things far overseas. Did I believe in tales about the Descendants of Gaia? Could I be magical like them? Blinking, I shook my head.

"I have no idea," I admitted, though the words didn't sit well across my tongue. My gaze drifted down to my fingers and I recalled the sensation of the fluff grazing against them. The green fluff had moved across Harper's body, begging me to touch it. To interact with it. Nothing about what I saw felt fake. It felt real. So real.

With his arms crossed and right hand raised to scratch at his chin, he pressed his lips together. "This might sound wild, but I think you can see sickness somehow."

My eyes widened, a hollow pit growing inside my head. He voiced the paranoia clouding my thoughts. I saw something Victor didn't. I felt it. I shook my head before the thoughts festered into delusion.

See sickness? How can that be? Delivering crops to homes is all I'm good at. I've accepted this identity.

Was Victor truly insinuating I had special powers of some kind? The absurdity made me scoff.

"That is *ridiculous*," I echoed my thoughts. "How would that even make sense?"

"I don't know, but I want to test you more another day." He grabbed loose papers across his desk and stacked them. "I want to see if I'm right." With a soft tap, he straightened the pile in his hands.

I stepped back. "I don't know."

"What do you have to lose?" He shrugged and scooped up the Capynx.

What if he was right? What did I have to lose if I tried?

"Fine. But mention this to no one. I don't want people to think I'm crazy."

"Fair." He leaned forward, Capynx held tightly to his chest. "But Ciro. I'm serious. The tales of people like Gaia's descendants across the sea and their abilities...This could be *big*."

An electricity moved across my body, making each fingertip tingle. The idea made my stomach flip. So much of me longed to stay and keep asking more questions, but my body retreated back toward the door.

"It could be... I should go."

He stepped toward me. "Okay. But please come back."

"You have my Talonhound." I rubbed Harper's head. She licked my hand before I left.

What in the world is going on? Is Victor losing his mind? Am I losing my mind? Am I dreaming? What if he's right?

I pushed the door open, morning sunlight striking me across the face and forcing me against a wall. I tried to understand my situation. Instead, a throbbing headache overtook me. I needed a distraction. Anything.

Something caught my eye—signs. So many signs. They lined the street, showing corn husks shaped into a giant shield.

Draft Day is near. Serve and Protect Maize.

My headache became irrelevant. A new tightness gripped my chest. Draft Day was only one day away. One day.

Each person who passed me looked at the signs, dipped their heads, and marched forward at a faster rate. The city was tense. Worry hovered above every person's head like a dark storm ready to thunder. Either you drafted yourself or your assigned Count for your city section would randomly draft an adult from your family.

A chilly mass swirled in my gut, climbing through my veins each second I thought about death. To add to my anxiety, the idea of being...magical ate at me. I surveyed every living thing around me for some kind of abnormality. Birds flew overhead, nothing of any interest across their bodies. City beasts, from rodents to pets, all appeared normal. Each person who passed by showed no signs of...sickness. If that's even what I saw. What was I supposed to look for?

Doctors can find diseases because they have medical training and know what to look for.

The thought occurred randomly in my head. I stopped walking. An idea hit me.

What if I were trained in the medical field? Maybe this could be used as an opportunity to keep my family safe. Maybe I could volunteer for a role where I wouldn't see battle. This would keep Valeria away from war and me in a position of safety. What about being a medic?

With a soft chuckle, I rubbed the bridge of my nose. The absurdity of the idea tickled my forehead. But this seemed like my best option. Raising my head, I quickened my pace again.

Pushing the front door of my house open a little too hard, it hit the wall and knocked over a picture frame.

"Sorry." I scooped up the photo and placed it back on the table.

"Daddy." Isabella raised her head from her toys.

"Is something wrong with Harper?" Valeria asked, voice squeaking.

For a moment, I forgot who she was asking about. Then, I remembered where I had just come from.

"She's great. Nothing's wrong." Surrounded by the people who loved me, my heart rate finally slowed. They made me feel normal. "Harper raised her head when I walked in. She's on a lot of pain medication."

"She's a fighter," Valeria said. "I'm proud of her."

"You should go see her this afternoon." The base of my head throbbed just thinking about Victor and all his questions. I didn't need any further stress from his inquisition. "I'm sure she would love to see you."

"Great idea. I was going to start making dinner soon." Before I raised an eyebrow at the earliness of her cooking, she held a hand up and grinned. "I was thinking carnitarias tonight in case one of us has to go to training right away."

"That sounds wonderful." I smiled, thinking of her food. "I'll take Isabella on a walk to give you some space."

Valeria walked over and kissed me. "That would make my day great. Take a few hours. I'll visit Harper after I get the meat going. You should make flanesta tonight."

"I'll grab the ingredients while we're out." I leaned forward, hands on my knees. Isabella's honey eyes were mixed with flakes of gold. They stole my heart every time I gazed into them. "Isabella, want to go on a walk?"

"Yay, walk!" Isabella flung her toys in the air and ran over to me.

"Adios mis encantadores," Valeria said as we zipped out the door.

I followed Isabella's haphazard path. She knew the way to the market. More importantly, she knew I'd buy her a snack once we got there.

The citizens of Cornia scurried around, loading up on basics. Why people felt the need to gather supplies before Draft Day went beyond my understanding. The stress was palpable, but a surprising tranquility rushed across me like a cool breeze as Isabella darted by. She said hi to everyone we passed. Her joy was contagious—just like a sickness, her smile spread from one passerby to the next.

A dark mass approached, a stark contrast to Isabella's sunshine. A man with long dark hair, a thick black mustache, and very tan skin moved closer and closer until his eyes locked in on me. His face was covered with purple blotches, each in a peculiar shape that matched the next. The purple that filled each blotch was a color of purple I had never seen before.

Isabella approached the man, naive to his dark energy. All the air rushed out of my lungs and refused to come back.

"HI!" my daughter yelled.

The man glared down at her. He seemed to be immune to her joy. Was he about to do something to her? I stepped forward, hand stretched forward before the man replied, "Hi."

That was it. With a soft smile, the purple spots disappeared, and his face lit up.

"Morning," I said with a nod.

As he passed by, I stared at him, trying to find the spots again, but they never showed. Almost as if they were never there.

Could that have been—?

"Isabella!" Aameen yelled as I turned to find him scoop my daughter up and toss her lightly, pulling me out of my thoughts.

She giggled. "Uncle Aam!"

She couldn't say Aameen's full name. I wondered if the nickname would stick.

He lowered her to the ground as she hurled her body toward a few birds eating crumbs off the ground.

"Why are we staring down Antonio today?" Aameen asked, nodding his head toward the purple blotched man.

"Did he look...odd to you?"

Aameen tilted his head. "The mustache is questionable, but nothing different."

I opened my mouth and hesitated. "What about the spots?"

"Spots?" He looked back and forth between Antonio and me.

"Nothing." I swiped my hand through the air. "Never mind."

"This is not the first odd thing you've said lately. Seeing things that others are *not* seeing." He placed a hand on my shoulder. "What's going on with you?"

"I'm just stressed." I lied. I wanted to tell him what was going on, but for some reason felt like I should keep it secret.

"Whatever you say." Aameen stared me down. "Are you nervous about tomorrow?"

"Not as much as I should be. Are you?"

"Well, I'm going to go. No matter what."

Someone from our house was going to have to go as well. I wondered if Aameen thought my medic idea could work.

"I was going to talk to Valeria tonight, but I think I may declare as well." Holding my hand up before he could respond, I waved. "Not for combat, though." I swallowed hard. "For medical."

"For what?" Aameen stared for a moment before he started laughing. My face didn't move. "Ciro, since I've known you, you haven't *once* shown any interest in medicine." Palms up, he moved his hands in exaggerated circles, like he often did when excited. "Remember the time you made me put on that bandage for Isabella's cut when she was bleeding?"

"I had *just* gotten over the flu." I waved my hand in the air before he retorted. "But that I know. The idea is a bit...off script..." My brain started churning, trying to look for a logical response. "*But* it may be an opportunity to make something of myself when we return."

My lie even convinced me.

As his hands lowered to his sides, his eyes narrowed. "You're serious?"

"I am." I aggressively nodded. "I know Valeria would be an excellent warrior, but this could be a way to keep us both safe while helping our family prosper. Plus, I don't exactly want to risk Isabella having one less parent. You know my father did that to me."

My brain catapulted me to the past, to the pounding at our door when the news of my father's death was delivered. Those dark words started a major shift in my life. I never wanted Isabella to live through that.

"You still turned out okay." He squeezed my shoulder and released me. "I just don't know..."

Aameen had been there for so many wild moments in my life. The time we accidentally released a herd of stampeding Shapple through the streets of Maize. The time he begged me to jump into the city's fountain during that day of extreme heat only to get a bacterial infection from the unclean water. If Aameen told me to jump, I'd ask how high. I needed him.

"You trust me, right?"

"To the ends of the sky and the depths of the dirt." With shrugged shoulders, his body language didn't mimic trust. "But I can trust you while questioning your intelligence. I guess being a medic could work. I still don't quite understand the inspiration."

"It's a smart idea. You'll see." If I kept talking to him, I knew I'd slip and tell him what I saw on Harper. "Just like releasing the Shapple was."

A flash of his bright white teeth eased the tension between us. "Well, if you're bringing up the Shapples..." He let out a boisterous laugh. "I just hope you have this thought out."

"I do." I stepped away before he could ask any more questions. "But I have to go and get the ingredients for flanesta. Isabella! Who wants a chocolate!"

"Me!" Isabella exclaimed as Aameen waved, going the other way.

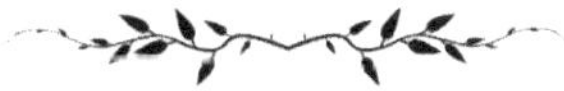

After a successful market visit, Isabella and I returned home to a house smelling of spices and meat. My mouth instantly watered. Valeria nowhere to be found, I opened the pot as the meat bubbled in a red and brown sauce. I stirred it before returning the lid to its base.

Isabella yawned, so I took her upstairs and put her on the daybed for a nap. She refused to let me leave, so I rested my head. Her honey eyes fluttered shut, and a symphony of soft, sleepy breaths blew at my face. The sweet aroma of chewed-up chocolate made me grin. No matter how much energy Isabella had, she always melted in my arms when we rested by one another. I cherished her spunk, but I adored her soft peace. Just being near her gave me such solace. Enough for my mind to drift into endless bliss.

When I lifted my head later, I realized I had napped as well. Isabella still snored as I left the room and tiptoed down the stairs. Valeria sat at the kitchen table reading a book, the pot lowered to a simmer. She glanced at me with soft, amber eyes and a warm smile.

"How was your nap?" she asked.

"It was good." I stretched my arms. "Unintended but necessary. Harper looks great, doesn't she?"

"More than great. We have so much to thank Victor for."

"I agree." Still unsure about Victor's sanity. "I wanted to talk to you about Draft Day tomorrow."

With a snap, she closed her book and placed it on the table. No longer soft and welcoming, her fiery eyes locked in on me. "If you say you are drafting yourself, I swear—"

"There's something I didn't tell you about last night," I interrupted, hands raised in caution. "Something about Harper."

"What could—" She stopped and rolled her eyes. "Is this about her poop being fluffy and white again?" She scowled and began mumbling in the native tongue.

"I saw something else." I cut her off, keeping my hands flat and still in front of me, worried that if I flinched, I might shatter something fragile between us. "Victor couldn't figure out what was going on and was worried about Harper's pain level. He suggested we put her down." Valeria put her hand over her mouth.

"But then I saw a green fluff on Harper's leg." Her judgmental glare returned. "I told Victor about it. He didn't see it. I pleaded he check there. He did an incision and found out her bone was rotted from an infection. V, *I'm* the reason that Harper's life was saved."

She opened her mouth and shook her head. "Estas loco."

"I thought so too, but Victor told me today that he doesn't think I am."

"You're both loco." She stood from the table and walked to the pot to stir the sauce.

"V, listen. Victor brought in a Capynx today and wanted to see if I noticed anything about it. I saw something on its feet he didn't see, and he said the beast had a fungal infection in its toenails that was only visible via microscope."

With the pot lid in her hand, her side glare made me worry she might throw the lid at my head. "Ciro, what are you getting at?" She slammed the pot lid back on the pot instead of throwing it, but I still winced nonetheless.

"Please don't freak out as I say this or think I'm out of my mind." I cowered as she stepped forward, the fire now blazing in her eyes. "But Victor thinks I might be able to see...sicknesses or something."

Valeria stared at me as I held her gaze. The fire faded and her face scrunched together. Deep laughter rolled out of her, the exact reaction I expected Victor to have. My confidence wavered with each laugh she let echo throughout our kitchen.

"You're funny." She pointed at my frozen frame that showed no sign of joking. "You aren't joking?" Hands thrown in the air, she shook her head. "Hombre loco. You must be joking."

"What if he's right?"

Hands on her hips, her mouth hung open, inaudible for a moment. "What does this have to do with tomorrow?"

Now was my time.

"I want to volunteer as a medic." I stood up straight. "For the war."

"No, absolutely not." Her face contorted, giving me a judgmental look. The pride of her father flared in her eyes. I knew this would happen. Maybe the logic I used with Aameen would help.

"V, what if I can pull this off and could maybe use this for future opportunities when I return? Something in the medical field." I stepped closer, falling for my own arguments and imagining an occupation where I no longer delivered crops. "This means we would get a bigger house." I slowed down my words. "Buy new things."

"Loco." She emphasized the word slowly, mocking me. "You've never shown an interest in medicine."

Just as logic failed to impress Aameen, the same fate occurred with Valeria.

"Now I am. I have good reason to. Plus, it'll keep us both safe, and you know I don't want Isabella to lose either of us."

"But you would be going to *war*!" Her lip curled up, and she pointed at her chest. "Being a warrior is part of *my* family line. Not yours."

"Away from the frontline," I defended my declaration. "Away from danger. You would be away from danger. Isabella's parents would both be safe."

She stared at me. Her quietness normally meant I was persuading her. I had a passion for safety, as she did for glory.

"I don't know," she said.

"I think it could be something big." I moved closer to her. "For both of us."

"I have a duty to protect." She grunted.

I placed my hand just above my heart. "We both have a duty to protect our family." I moved my hand from my chest to hers and touched her pounding chest. "We both love our family." The pounding slowed as my hand rested.

"It feels like you've made this decision already. I don't want anyone to think I'm not strong and fierce."

"No one will think that." I wrapped my hands around her waist and pulled her close, kissing her cheek. "This will be good for us." I patted her lower back, heat warming my fingertips and goosebumps forming along her skin. "But please don't tell anyone else about it."

She stepped back five steps. "Absolutely not. I don't want the whole city thinking you're loco." Arms crossed, she narrowed her gaze. "I may understand this would be best for Isabella, but how do you expect to be drafted for medical?"

"I believe a certain Count owes you a favor…" The little dance my eyebrows began made my forehead hurt, but it was worth rubbing in my point.

Count Bebida, her family friend on the Stena's council, owed Valeria a favor. I didn't know what the favor was for; I just knew it was something. Valeria would never tell me what it was. She said that would void the favor.

"Bebida? You expect me to use *my* favor on *this*?" She scowled.

I battered my eyelashes. "Maybe…" I mused, embracing her for a kiss. She hesitated at first, but after the second kiss, she returned my passion. Everything about her warmed me up. Her skin, her eyes, her touch, her smell. All of it. I ran my hand up her back, pulling her shirt up just a little so my other hand moved across her skin, which bubbled with goosebumps. No matter how tense she was, she melted in my touch as I melted in hers.

As we moved away from each other, she grinned. "Fine. But now *you* owe me a favor." She jabbed her finger into my chest.

"Whatever you wish," I promised, kissing her again and releasing her body, both of us nearly collapsing from our effect on one another.

"Now, go make your flanesta." She stopped moving and furrowed her brow. "But this is *not* my favor!"

"Too late." I scurried away as she chased me around the kitchen. Isabella walked into the kitchen and watched us running around. "Ah! She's awake!"

Isabella screamed and ran away from me as I chased her. While I ran around the kitchen with my small family, pride overwhelmed me. Not just pride, but a newfound desire to protect them. I had to protect our structure. This family belonged to *me*.

After coming together as a family and enjoying the prepared meal, we read a book together while snuggling on the couch. The next day would come fast, and I wanted to enjoy this moment before things changed. I hoped I was making the right decision.

Valeria and I stayed up talking to each other as Isabella fell asleep with my arm around her. I yawned, exhaustion taking over, but the anxiety of the upcoming day counteracted it. We sat in peaceful silence, Valeria's head resting on my shoulder. The symphony of our wooden wind chimes clinked in the backyard. No matter what happened during this war, the moment before me would drive my every decision and every movement. I needed to maintain my lovely life.

I lifted a prayer:

Gaia, our Light, you've blessed me with these women I love.

My fingertips tingled like they did when I moved them through the green fluff. I had the power to protect them, and I would do just that.

CHAPTER 4
ENLISTING

The crop storage buildings within the western portion of the city marked our quadrant's draft stage. Normally filled to the brim with crops, the one-story buildings sat empty. It was outside harvest season, and their dark, open doors looked like mouths begging for food. A small burst of wind made the doors shudder as stale dust battered against my face.

A large crowd stood together just outside the storage buildings, avoiding eye contact and conversation. The quiet sent a shiver down my spine, as if Death ran its cold fingers across each vertebra.

As I approached the crowd with Isabella, Count Bebida and Valeria finished a conversation. Valeria had left our house early to discuss her favor with the Count. Bebida smiled in my direction.

"So?" I asked once Valeria found us

"Beyond her shock and confusion at the request, she will make it happen," Valeria said, arms crossed. "But you have to make the formal declaration during the event."

"Of course." I touched her arm.

I would be a medic. Everything was working out. In the midst of terror, I smiled.

What's wrong with me? I shouldn't be happy right now.

But I was.

"My favorite family," Aameen said, patting my back from behind. "What a pleasure to see you all."

At least I'm not the only person basking in inappropriate happiness.

"Where's your family?" Valeria asked.

"They stayed behind," Aameen replied. "The younger ones were having a rough morning and didn't need to be here watching me declare myself."

Valeria grumbled in the native tongue. I squeezed her hand. She glared at me, but then her eyes softened. She had pride. Loads of it. But she knew this decision was a smart one for Isabella.

"Hello, citizens of Maize!" Count Bebida yelled. "This is my least favorite thing I have had to do as a Count, but our nation needs this more than ever. I know fear floats over the city." She placed her hand on her chest. "My fear joins yours. But the more help we have, the better chance of victory. The Coalition will not only drain our land of its life. They will raid our fields and cause an imbalance in our crops. As one Maize, we can protect our country and keep the life force strong."

The crowd stood silent. I could feel the tension and uncertainty about how to respond. Some in the crowd furrowed their brows or let out low grunts. Others shook with fear.

In the silence, Aameen grinned at me.

"For Maize!" he yelled.

After a beat, a man to our right echoed Aameen.

"For Maize!"

More and more people echoed the chant.

Valeria and I looked at each other as we yelled, "For Maize!"

Isabella yelled, "For Ma-za!"

Bebida's posture shifted into a comfortable stance. She had delivered the speech necessary to evoke pride and confidence. Whether we wanted to fight in this war, our country needed us.

"Now then," she said. "I will start with voluntary declarations. You may make your way up to the stage and sign your declaration. Now, please step up."

About twenty men and women made their way up to the stage and formed a line. Aameen looked over and raised his eyebrows before moving forward. I leaned over and kissed Valeria.

"This will all work out," I said.

"Danos sabiduría, Gaia," Valeria whispered and kissed my cheek.

"It's the wise thing to do," I whispered back, squeezed her hand, and followed after Aameen.

Aameen's confident stride left me behind in his shadow. As I walked toward the stage, I pictured arrows flying around me, striking down my people. Glimpses of orange fluff appeared and disappeared on some around me. I forced my eyes shut and took a deep breath.

"Just walk, Daddy," a soft voice said from behind.

I turned to find Isabella's bright smile. She didn't know what was happening, but her belief in me made me move my heavy feet. One step after the next, my body gravitated toward Aameen.

You won't even see a battle.

I wanted to believe my thoughts, but fear made my stomach twist. Finally, I came to the end of the line, and Aameen patted my shoulder. We inched closer and closer to Bebida. Rather than stare at the line, I looked across the crowd. The citizens nodded with pressed lips and folded hands, silently thanking us for our service. No, our sacrifice. Utter gratitude radiated from them and warmed my chest. At least twenty more people joined the line, encouraged by our strength.

A surge of vigor found me. I bravely looked toward Bebida. Only two people were in front of Aameen. The time grew near. My heartbeat pounded in my ears, drowning out the sounds of the crowd. I kept drifting between confidence and terror. I didn't know what to feel.

Aameen turned back to me. "Remind me that this is the right decision." His normal energy faltered. Seeing just a tinge of worry in his eyes somehow empowered me.

I placed my hand on his shoulder and squeezed tightly.

"This is the right decision." I paused. "Or possibly the wrong one." I grinned.

He glared before we both laughed. The inappropriate sound echoed in the silent crowd. Confused looks shot in our direction. I looked toward Valeria—she was shaking her head and placing her hand on her forehead. We quickly reigned in our laughter and faced Bebida again.

With one more deep breath, Aameen stepped up to sign the tan scroll Bebida had rolled out on a table. Aameen signed the scroll with an ornate feathered pen. He passed Bebida, smiling at her. She reached out, squeezed his forearm, and gave him a warm look. Then she turned her attention to me.

This is it.

Before I could second-guess myself, I forced myself forward and stepped up to Bebida, wood squeaking below. My time had come.

I eyed the scroll staring up at me. So many names I recognized danced across the page. Alejandro, my old neighbor. Julia, my first girlfriend. Mira, my old babysitter. They were all willing to risk their lives for Maize. Some I remembered from classes growing up. I remembered sitting next to them. Faces flashed across my memory. The weight of their commitment pulled at my heart. I looked over to Valeria, sensing her stare. Her eyes widened and she gave a look of *just do it already.*

I picked up the pen and wrote:

Ciro Sinsal—Medic.

I was still getting used to using my wife's last name, but the more I wrote it, the more it fit me. I glanced up at Bebida.

"I will keep my promise to Valeria," she whispered.

"Thank you." I descended the stairs back to my family, numb.

I wrapped an arm around Valeria's waist and hoisted Isabella up in my other, hugging them both tightly. The hardest part was over.

Or was it?

All the air left my lungs. My chest ached as I panicked and gasped for air.

"Did it just hit you?" Valeria asked, hands moving across my back.

"Un poco," I replied. Within each of her strokes, I found more and more air.

"Sé valiente," Valeria reassured me.

She was right; I needed to be brave. The last person signed their name and stepped off the stage. Bebida picked up the document and reviewed the list. Once she finished, she took out another list and began crossing names off. The more she crossed off, the fewer names she would have to draft. The crowd watched her, analyzing her every move in complete silence. Each time she crossed a name off, the pen let out a dull scratch. People in the crowd shook with fear and anticipation.

With a solemn glance, Bebida lowered the first list and held the remaining list in front of her.

"I know it may seem like I made these choices, but they were truly random," Bebida announced. "With the already declared, here are the names that remain..."

As she announced the names, my brain disassociated, a sweet release from the screams around me. Focusing on the floor, I anxiously tapped my right foot. Isabella tapped her toe next to me at the same rhythm, a warm smile covering her face. I was grateful for her ignorance.

My mind stuck on all the families caught in the tragedy of the draft. The younger adults would have their lives changed forever. They may never find love or start a family. They may never see their homes again.

Isabella twirled in circles while looking up at the sky, oblivious to the nightmare surrounding her. No matter the suffering others felt, my job was to protect my daughter. As much as I wanted to rid the other families of their sorrow, Valeria and Isabella were my priority. They would always be.

Aameen nudged me. I looked up and saw the crowd dispersing. The final group of people approached Bebida to sign their names in the scroll, as was required to finalize their contract to serve. Some cried. Others wouldn't, or couldn't, move toward her. Though we wouldn't go to war right away, the scroll made the enlistment real. The bold marched confidently forward, while others walked together, arms slung around each other for support. This was something we were all living through. Not just individually, but as Maize.

It inspired me. Yet, the responsibility and reality struck me. I'd be going to war.

I forced down a pocket of air with a firm gulp. "Did she say when our service would start?"

"Tomorrow morning," Aameen responded.

My body went weightless and my brain foggy. "That soon?" My voice drifted. I didn't know if I was asking him or asking something greater.

"We should go and pray to Gaia," Valeria said.

"Yes." I looked over at her, relieved. "We'll need it."

"And I will pray for your family as well," Aameen added. "Agma be with us."

Aameen worshipped Agma, the one God of Isle, where he had immigrated from. Isle fell twenty years before, another victim of the Coalition.

"Hopefully, some of Isle's tenacity will transfer here," Valeria said.

"I still can't believe it's been this many years since my country fell," Aameen said. "I try my best to keep its memory and culture alive, but I was so young when it all happened."

"The Coalition will pay." I held out my hand toward Aameen.

With a grin, he gripped my hand. "That they will, my friend."

He smiled before tears welled in his eyes. It was rare to see Aameen cry. He said nothing as I pulled him in for a hug.

"Stay strong, old friend," I said.

He chuckled, shoulders making my arms shake as he pulled back and wiped the tears from his eyes. "*Old*? I'm only a few years older than you." He joked.

"A *few*?" Valeria scoffed. "More like ten."

"Numbers are irrelevant." Aameen swiped his hand in the air. "But I must go to my family." He took a deep breath. "One night left with them."

Valeria pushed him forward. "Go. Hug your kids and kiss your wife."

And just like that, Aameen nodded and ran the opposite way down the street, leaving just me and my family.

With Valeria's hand in my left and Isabella's in my right, we walked down the street toward the Iglesia de la Gaia to spend some time praying. Though daylight still burned above, the streets held a darkness.

I tried to remember the liveliness of Maize's citizens before the war, but the streets were empty. I could hear the wails from various houses. Some people walked the streets like us, making their way to the church.

The church shone in the afternoon sun. The stucco building, covered in abstract shapes painted in pastels, was an important social pillar in our city. The roof was flat on top, with sides curved like a dome. You couldn't see it from our view, but one clear window sat in the center of the dome.

The belief in Gaia had withstood many generations. Some said the religion came from ancient Maize. Others said it came from overseas. All of it was up for debate. I grew up with the stories of Gaia's descendants, women picked by Gaia to hold special abilities. They lived across the sea. Valeria grew up knowing Gaia blessed the fields before journeying across the sea to bless women. Others say one of Gaia's descendants had come to Maize and blessed the land here. No one I knew had ever witnessed their powers, but I had been taught it was true.

I found the specifics of the stories irrelevant. We viewed Gaia as the Mighty One. The Light we all strove for. The Light we would enter upon death. In that moment, we all needed Gaia's strength, peace, and wisdom. I fixated on the building as we approached.

Like Pastel Castle, the church had four doors. Turquoise doors, orange doors, purple doors, and yellow doors. Every time we entered the church, Valeria picked the purple doors. Her family believed them to be the doors of courage.

The church opened into a wide circular space, where rows of stone pews formed concentric rings, large rings on the outer edge of the room, smaller as the pews neared the center. In the center of the space was a clear view of the dome's window. Mirrors on the floor and walls amplified the sunlight, illuminating the entire room.

For a midweek day, the space was crowded, but we knew the reason they were all here. Mumbled prayers to Gaia buzzed. People prayed on their own. Families prayed together. Though unsure about my beliefs, I found the prayers beautiful and empowering. I always went to the ceremonies and rituals because of Valeria. She believed in Gaia with every essence of her soul. Her family did, so our family had to.

Valeria kneeled about three rows back from the front. Isabella raced next to her and did the same. I kneeled next to Isabella.

I surveyed the room while Valeria began her prayer in the native language. She talked so fast, I could only comprehend fragments of her overall message. Isabella mumbled with her, but she seemed to speak gibberish, or maybe she knew the language of Gaia better than us all. I absorbed every bit of it.

The light flickering off the ceiling drew my gaze upward. A sense of power rushed into me. It could've been the mix of emotions going through my mind. It could've been the heightened awareness of potential death. In that moment, courage engulfed me. Maybe the purple doors were working.

I prayed.

Gaia, protect my family. Protect Maize. Give me courage to do what I fear. Help me make a difference. And whatever this new sight I have been blessed with, let it continue to aid me during this war. Let this sight bring safety to Valeria and Isabella.

I looked at my wife and daughter. Love pulsated from my prayer. I could do this. I would serve Maize and do amazing things. I would heal people. It would be my purpose during the war.

I carried my prayer into the night and the next morning. Time moved faster than I wanted it to. The knock at my door startled me, even though I expected it. Aameen stood there waiting at the door.

"Just a moment," I said to him.

"Take your time." He smiled back.

I turned to find Valeria wearing a purple shawl and a skintight black dress. A tight braid hung down her side and smelled like fresh flowers and honey. Everything about her pulled me in. She came to me as if floating on air and held my face. Her eyes sparkled like fireworks, tears filling them before she shook her head and wiped them away. Valeria rarely cried. She always kept her emotions in check. She had to be strong.

"Watch out for arrows. They will catch you by surprise. And make sure to keep your hygiene on track. I don't want your teeth to rot. They are important to your health. I packed some sweet cookies in your bag. I know they won't last long, but I wanted you to have something you loved for the journey to Husk." She pressed her quivering lips together and paused. "We will keep everything together. Don't worry about us. Even as much as I want to fight for Maize, I will hold my place for as long as I can. My mother will help. You know she will."

"Valeria—" I said.

"And I put your favorite socks in your bag. And I will walk Harper every day."

"Valeria—"

"And I will—"

"Valeria!" She stopped and looked at me. "Thank you for being the best esposa a man could ask for."

Glistening teardrops flickered in Valeria's eyes. A genuine smile covered her face, and two tears fell down her proud cheeks. No more, no less. Just two tears. She kissed me. I kissed back. The electricity flowing between us astounded me. It reminded me of the night we shared just before. Our naked bodies intertwined. Most of the time, we just sat and stared at one another late into the night. Few words were exchanged. My mind returned to the room with her and Isabella.

"El más grande amor," Valeria said. She kissed me three times on the cheek. She hugged me again.

"The greatest love," I echoed. Isabella began pulling on my pants. "My greatest loves." I bent over and picked up Isabella, throwing her in the air before hugging her tightly. Her little body was so soft, especially her little cheek as it brushed against mine.

"Isabella." I pulled her back and gazed into her sparkling honey eyes. She was bold, just like her mother. "I want you to listen to Mamá. As much as you can."

"Daddy," Isabella said. "Mamá is mean."

I laughed. "I know, but she only wants you to listen and be safe." I knew she didn't understand that I was leaving for as long as I would be. She smiled and touched my cheek. "Hija. Don't forget your daddy. I will think of you every day. Grow nice and strong. But don't grow too fast." Brushing just the tip of my nose onto hers, she giggled, making my cheeks warm. "I love you, Isabella."

"Love you." Isabella's bright smile illuminated the room as she reached out and hugged my neck. "Here." She forced a folded piece of paper into my hand.

Holding my breath, I unfolded the paper to find a drawing. In all red, she had drawn a tilted box with three figures of different sizes positioned across it. One additional figure was drawn on the ground with four sticks and a scribbled tail. The drawing made me release all the air in my lungs. My shoulder slumped, and I pulled Isabella in tight.

"That's you." She squirmed out of my arms and pointed at one of the larger figures on the right of the drawing. "That's Mamá. And that's Harper." She grinned broadly.

"Is that Aam?" I pointed at the smallest figure on the couch.

Her body shivered in little giggles. "No." She shook her head and pointed at her chest. "That's me, Daddy."

"Oh, of course!" I squeezed her with all my might, never wanting to let go. A chill moved down my cheeks in teary rivers. Pressing my face against Isabella's, I kissed her little soft cheek, hugged her one last time, and handed her over to Valeria before I could stop myself from doing it. "Don't forget to keep drawing, my love."

Looking down at her cheeks, Isabella put her right hand into her mouth and batted her eyelashes, little honey eyes glistening in the light.

"Te amo mas que al mundo," I said. I realized only Harper was missing. "Be sure to tell Victor I'm sorry we couldn't meet more. And give Harper extra scratches at night. I will write to you. Please write to me."

"Goodbye, Ciro," Valeria said as Isabella waved. "Te veré en mis sueños."

"I will see you in my dreams," I echoed.

I walked out the door, and Valeria hugged Aameen. She whispered something to him, and he nodded. I was sure that she asked him to watch over me. I turned one last time and waved to my family.

"Are you ready for our journey?" Aameen asked.

Just the other day, I was cleaning up Harper's droppings in my yard, not knowing how much my life would change over the course of a few days. Somehow, a strange confidence forced me to enlist as a medic for our war with the Coalition. Me, a normal man. The choice was made and I had to live with it. But would I ever be ready for this leap?

"No, not at all." I turned away, looked at Isabella's drawing one more time before folding it into my pocket, and took a deep breath. "But I don't have much of a choice."

CHAPTER 5
HUSK

We were two weeks from Cornia on foot. A week and a half by Mountiff. Corn stretched endlessly before us. Still a few hours away, Husk waited for us at the far northwestern edge of Maize. The city perched at the very edge of the outer crop line, a border between cultivation and whatever lay beyond.

Between here and there was more of the same—green stalks reaching toward the sun, whispering leaves waving in the wind. On clear days, they blended into the horizon, lost in the sun's bright light. The air smelled like dust and fresh air.

Though I had never been, I imagined being at sea felt similar. I pictured water as far as the eye could see. Waves instead of stalks. Little islands instead of small houses and barns.

Aameen and I spent most of our time talking about how we expected our families to cope without our presence, how long we thought we would be at war, what food we would eat.

I learned nothing new, except that Aameen's confidence in his family's welfare superseded any worry he had about being away from them. I didn't feel the same. It wasn't that I didn't think Valeria could handle it—I was afraid of missing out on so much.

Or that my family would get used to functioning without me.

Or worse, that Isabella would forget about me.

Isabella's laugh and her floral scent took over as I closed my eyes. Their spirits revived me before my mind returned to my conversation with Aameen. I replayed the farewell every hour, afraid the details might fade.

But living in memory felt dangerous. Like choosing a dream over the ground beneath my feet.

Aameen laughed about something he said, so I laughed as well. I had no idea what it was, but it brought me back to reality, back to the drafted marching all around me. It reminded me of our destination—war.

Fixating on my conversation with Aameen was a distraction from my growing fear. With every step I took, the weaker the distraction became.

Even though I wasn't fighting, I didn't know how to be a medic. Once the commanders figured this out, would they send me to the battlefront to fight instead?

Would this walk be my last walk?

Would anyone remember it?

I shut the thoughts down, shaking my head. Whatever waited for me beyond this moment didn't exist, at least not yet.

I fixed my attention on the backs of the men and women marching in front of me. My fear felt so unfamiliar—normally, I tried to focus on the good things in life. I needed this stress to go away.

We approached Husk in the evening. About a quarter or less the size of Cornia, Husk consisted of mostly one-story buildings, with a few two-story buildings dotting the skyline. Loose dirt covered the streets, and we kicked up billows of dust as we marched in. Dust coated every building we passed. My heart longed for the pastel roofs in Cornia. Husk's dull visage paled in comparison.

With us, chaos marched into Husk, now the epicenter of Maize's war camp. Families departed the city as we entered. Embraces of melancholy accompanied cries of grief, with each family leaving behind their drafted hero. I wondered if Husk had ever witnessed such fear before. Their city wouldn't be their home for who knew how long. And would Husk still feel like a home to the Huskan warriors left behind?

I hoped it was only for a brief period. I needed it to be only for a brief period.

I would serve and leave. I would make it home.

By the time we were assigned lodging, dusk surrendered to night. Sleep proved difficult. Too many bodies. Too many thoughts. The house I was assigned to belonged to one of Husk's warriors who had stayed behind. Newly married and expecting their first child, the warrior welcomed us as if family.

A crib had been pushed against the far wall to make room for us. I asked his name at some point, but I couldn't remember it. Juan or Tomas. Something ordinary and easy to forget.

Though I appreciated his hospitality, I felt like an invader, not family.

From a lone chair behind the modest house, I watched crimson and copper rays reach across the field as the sun crested the horizon. For a moment, the world looked peaceful—untouched and calm.

The peace belonged to no one in Husk.

I closed my eyes and thought about Isabella. The crib inside the house reminded me of hers. I could almost smell the scent of warm bread and vanilla that wafted off her hair as I held her close to me during those late nights. Such exhaustion overcame me then. I wrapped my arms around myself as I leaned back against the chair and took a deep breath.

My mind replayed my goodbye with them. Isabella's little nose tickling my own. The flowered perfume coming off Valeria's neck as I brushed my lips against her cheek. The memories made me—

A horn sounded from the west. My eyes flashed open.

"Arise, Maizeans!" a man yelled. "Today's training begins in twenty minutes! You are expected to be dressed and ready in the town center!"

Is this what my life is like now?

"Luckily, I was just coming to look for you," Aameen said, walking up to me. "Could you imagine if *that* noise woke me instead?"

"It still beats a three-year-old waking you up at five."

"Without…a…doubt…" Aameen and I snorted in unison. "Do you think we will be training together?"

"I would hope, but I don't know." I continued to watch the rising sun.

"Probably not." He placed a hand on my shoulder. "Some of us have to do all the fighting…"

"Some of us will have to save your ass when you get hurt…" I smirked, patting his hand.

"Dr. Ciro has spoken." He bowed.

"Oh, shut up." I shoved him. My gaze drifted past him toward the town center. "We should probably head over."

"Probably."

More dust billowed with each step I took on the streets. My hope that Husk would be more appealing in the sunlight failed. The array of browns and tans shone in the daylight. I sighed, again remembering Cornia's vibrancy as we made our way to the town center.

"I hope this war is short," Aameen said, as if reading my mind.

"Me too." A new thought came to me once I realized how close to Maize's border we were. Our enemy had to be close to Husk. Too close. "What are the Coalitionists like?"

"Harsh." Aameen shrugged. "I don't know. It has been so long. They were never kind to Isle. Why?"

"I was just thinking about how close they are."

Facing north, Aameen pointed. "Most likely not too far that way." Lowering his hand, he puffed out his chest. "And they'll be facing me soon. Retribution for Isle." Each of his muscles flexed, visible even in his baggy shirt. Hauling hay from one part of Cornia to another built up his physique over time, making him a prime candidate to fight for Maize.

Both Valeria and Aameen displayed a ferocity I wish I had. Volunteering for this was the only courage I'd ever exhibited, and even now I'd be far away from the frontlines.

Aameen locked his gaze into my own. The intensity in his brown eyes transferred over to me. The Coalition hurt him. I wanted to help my best friend.

"They have no idea what's coming." I squeezed his muscular shoulders. "From what I have read, Isle put up a good fight. Maize is much larger than Isle, so there shouldn't be an issue."

"Let's hope." We turned the corner, approaching the town center. Pausing, he eyed me. "Before things get a bit chaotic, something's been bothering me."

"What?"

"Are you going to tell me why you wanted to be a medic? I keep trying to figure out what actually inspired this, but nothing makes sense."

I froze, not knowing what to say. Telling Valeria the truth was necessary for me to draft myself. Telling Aameen the truth didn't hold the same weight. I wanted to tell him, but the fewer people who knew, the better.

"I told you. I saw this as an opportunity for myself and also a way to keep my family safe. Why else would I do this?"

That was the right response—reflect a question back at him. This would make him stumble. If I evade his question, I don't have to answer with the truth.

"Are you trying to ask me another question in order to make me avoid the first?"

Shit.

"No..." I fell silent for a moment. "You just don't seem to believe me."

"Ciro, I'm your best friend. Don't you think I know you well enough to know when you are avoiding a question?"

I was already in deep. "Aameen, don't worry about it. You'll see, I'll end up being the best medic here."

"Did I hear your name is Ciro?" someone asked from behind me. I turned to a shorter woman with a wide stance. Curly dark brown hair with a few gray strands was tied tightly to her head. Bushy eyebrows arched downward. She stood with perfect posture and looked me up and down. Her face was tense.

"Yes," I said, crossing my arms. "Why do you ask?"

She pulled out a sheet of paper. "So, you are going to be *the best medic here,* yet you come with no experience?"

Next to me, Aameen stifled laughter.

"Who are you?" I asked.

"Kernel Ofelia Herrera." She stood up even straighter, though nowhere near my height. "I'm the head medic."

Shit again.

"And you seem to be starting off on the wrong foot with me," she added. "I don't take to arrogance when dealing in the art of healing and saving people."

Triple shit.

"I'm sorry," I said, voice cracking. After clearing my throat, I tried to stand up straight, but I wanted to crumble to the floor. "I was only joking with my friend."

She stepped up close to me while maintaining eye contact. "Do you think this war is a *joke*?" I shook my head back and forth. "You, señor, are in for a shock. I will be sure to work you harder than any other medic. I will not let your carelessness lead our injured warriors to death." In a cloud of dry dust, she turned and marched away.

A dark wave clouded my mind and made me dizzy. I didn't understand anything about the medical field. The most I'd done was point out my Talonhound's infection before Victor had to put him down. I couldn't just point at things and tell others to fix them. A sharp pain pierced my stomach and made me clench my gut. I lied my way into this situation. Would lying get me any farther, or would I finally be caught?

Aameen put his hand on my shoulder. "That was rough. I guess my training will be easier."

"Yeah…" I regretted ever enlisting as a medic.

More and more trainees filled the town center. Some stood tall. Some wrapped their arms around bodies in an effort to hide their shaking. Some spoke too loudly, and others stared ahead in complete silence.

"Maize salute!" a man yelled somewhere in the crowd.

Several recruits near me stood erect with their arms at their sides, facing the voice. Worried about what would happen if I didn't do the same, I straightened my posture like the others. Aameen mimicked me. Many others caught on.

"MAIZE SALUTE!" the man yelled louder.

A shorter man stepped on the ledge of a fountain located in the middle of the town center.

He had a burly frame and the only hair on his head was a thick black beard that frilled away from his face, looking like a storm cloud. Black paint surrounded his eyes, making the whites pop. His faded armor bore a bright gold symbol on the breastplate—the Maizean crest. The sides of the armor were covered with the pattern of black corn husks. The crest shone with dots of golden kernels covered on its sides with black husks.

His ferocity was unsettling.

The man scanned the crowd with a slow, deliberate gaze. Rushing footsteps came from behind me. Another woman next to me turned to look at the incoming people.

"DO NOT MOVE UNTIL COMMANDED TO DO SO!" a woman soldier next to the shorter man yelled.

Out of the corner of my eye, the woman next to me whipped her head back forward. My gaze darted back to the fountain where the shorter man hopped off the fountain and marched toward the latecomers.

"We are sorry, Commander," a woman said from behind me.

"We overslept," a man echoed, breathing heavily.

The short commander laughed. "Please, come up front. I want a good look at you."

Shuffled footsteps moved past me. I recognized the individuals. The man was Diego, and the woman was Elena. He worked as a farmer in Cornia, and she owned a bakery. As a deliveryman for crops, I recognized faces even though they often didn't recognize me. They walked up to the short man who looked at them with no words.

Elena looked over at Diego as Diego said, "We're sorry, Commander. It won't happen again."

The commander smirked, turning away from them. He pulled an iron hammer from his belt and looked at it. The hammer's head was as large as the man's broad chest.

He held the handle with two hands and swung the hammer toward Diego's side, abruptly stopping before making contact. Diego stumbled backward, his body slamming against Elena's, who fell and hit her head on the side of the fountain. Diego's shoulder hit the fountain.

"Sorry?" Spit flew off the commander's mouth as he yelled. "Sorry means nothing in war! Tardiness means your fellow warriors face death or capture!" He crouched next to them, Chloe cradling her bloody head. "Consider this a warning to those who do not do what is expected. Next time, I won't be so gracious with my swing." Slowing down his speech, he popped out each word. "I do not miss."

He stepped over them and back up onto the ledge of the fountain. One of the recruits in front of me gripped their shirt as they shook. Only then did I realize I was doing the same thing. The commander looked back down at Diego and Elena.

"Well, get up!" the woman commander next to him yelled as they scurried to their feet and joined the recruits near them.

"My rules are few and simple," the commander announced with calm but firm words. "One: Never be late. No matter what it takes. Two: Know your role and stick to it. Three: You will refer to me as my title—Krown Kernel. And lastly, never leave our troops behind. Does everyone understand?"

"Yes!" some yelled.

The Krown Kernel sighed. "I will ask again: Does everyone understand?"

"YES!" more yelled.

"AGAIN! DOES EVERYONE UNDERSTAND?!"

"YES, KROWN KERNEL!" everyone yelled in unison.

"Good." He looked calm, as if nothing had happened. "I'm your head commander, Krown Kernel Fernando. My role is to achieve victory through superior training. Next to me is Kernel Selena. She will train you in melee."

The woman, muscular and tall, nodded her head. Her skin was deeply tanned. A black and gold helmet sat atop her short, frizzy hair. The helmet had haphazard etchings scattered across the helm. I had a feeling they were for a dark reason.

"Next is Kernel Chaco, who is busy preparing our training field," Krown Kernel Fernando stated. "He is a specialist in ballistics and archery. Those who find his favor will become supreme markspeople. Even with our short timeline." Extending his hand to the left, he gestured downward. "And lastly is Kernel Ofelia. She healed half of our army during the Battle of the Shore, when she was only a teenager."

"I look forward to meeting our medics." Kernel Ofelia glared at me. "No matter how unskilled they may be."

My shoulders caved in toward my chest. I wanted to hide behind the other warriors surrounding me and disappear into the ground. How could I have been so stupid to think I could be a medic without any training? Kernel Ofelia would eat me alive.

"Now, we will divide to start our training," Krown Kernel Fernando announced. "Medics know their roles already. Please join Kernel Ofelia at the fountain. The rest of you, follow Kernel Selena and me. We will do some preliminary testing to see where your strengths lie. Maize compress!"

People started scurrying in different directions. I turned to Aameen. "Good luck today."

"I think you'll need luck more than I will," he replied before walking toward Krown Kernel Fernando.

I faced Kernel Ofelia. Swallowing hard, I searched within myself for confidence. I had to be more serious. As if gripping my own heart, I attempted to slow my heartbeat. As I approached the fountain, seven others stepped up.

I have to gain their respect. I have to protect myself and my family.

"Welcome," Kernel Ofelia said. "I want to be as clear as the Maizean sky when I say this. *Your role will save people.* Your role will win this war. Without our role, the warriors will have no crutch to fall upon. You will have to be ready to support the weight, because a lot will be coming to us."

We all just stared at her. "Train us and we will be," I said.

Like a knife, she sliced me with an abrupt scowl.

"Now, I know our best medics will come from Amar. This will allow us to get a head start until they arrive. We will start with some wounded Shapples in the barn. Follow me."

She marched away. We all followed like a Shapple to its shepherd.

I walked next to a woman I recognized from the medical center back in Cornia, one of the doctors. She stitched my arm one time when I cut myself on a piece of wood.

"I'm Florencia," she said. "What's your name?"

"Ciro. You stitched me one time a few years back." I showed a faint scar on my left arm.

"That looks like my work." She leaned over and slapped my bare arm, just above the faint mark. "Barely a scar to show."

"I can see it," a man in front of us stated without looking.

"Quiet, Miguel," Florencia hushed the man. "You aren't even looking."

With the slight turn of his head, his chiseled jaw shifted into a sparkling smile. "I saw it the moment we all met," he said.

"Don't mind him." She rolled her eyes. "He runs the cardiac unit and thinks himself Gaia."

I laughed, but my laugh mixed with nervousness and politeness and sounded like a squawk. No matter how hard I tried, I'd never fit in with this group. Kernel Ofelia saw me as inadequate, and, more and more, I agreed with her.

"Forgive me, but I don't recognize you. What's your role in Cornia's medical community?" Florencia asked.

Kernel Ofelia laughed, glancing back at me. I eyed the path that led out of Husk. If I just ran toward it, would anyone stop me?

"Me?" I said. "Well, I am new to this area of expertise."

"Did you just complete training at the medical school?" Florencia asked.

"Not quite. I'm currently working in farming." For some reason, I thought that sounded more interesting than saying I delivered crops that farmers gathered, not me.

"So, you must be good at healing livestock?"

"There have been a few cases." It wasn't a total lie. I *had* helped Victor.

"Hopefully, our group will make your training easy, Kernel Ofelia," Florencia said.

"We will only know once in the medical tent," Kernel Ofelia said. "That is when the true test will occur."

A stable stood before us. The structure was made with four brown wooden posts covered with a hay roof. Every stable in Maize looked the same. Because our weather stayed so consistent, walls proved unnecessary to keep our beasts safe from the elements. All that the Shapple needed was access to shade from the intense sun.

About thirty Shapples milled around the stable as we stopped and watched them. They paid no attention to us, chewing hay in the field. They were fluffy beasts with blueish white fur densely curled across their midsections, legs, and necks. Their heads and hooves were blue, rough with scalelike callouses, and their snouts were long and pointed, with two patches of fur covering their nostrils. The Shapples' scaly ears drooped to each side, swaying as they sauntered.

When they needed more hay, the wool from their midsections came together and extended to the ground, scooping up hay and bringing it to their mouths. The fur above their nostrils moved and caught hay that fell out of their mouths. It impressed me every time the Shapple did that with its fur—that it could be moved like a limb but still be shed, sheared, and grown back.

"Shapples are an integral part of Maize," Kernel Ofelia announced. "They provide wool, food, milk, and much more."

"You are telling us things we already know," Miguel assured us with his vast knowledge of the obvious.

Kernel Ofelia smiled at him. "I see the cardiologist knows everything already. Tell me, what are these Shapples doing?"

She pointed to three Shapples standing very close to one another. The one in the middle looked different—it had yellow bubbles along its front left leg. It stood still while the ones on its sides moved their hooves back and forth. Another Shapple came up as it pushed the left Shapple forward from behind. It did the same movement, shuffling hooves back and forth, as the one it took over for.

"How am I supposed to know?" Miguel asked.

"Shapples are a community creature," Kernel Ofelia said. "When one is hurt, the others will support it as a herd until it heals. This little guy has been like this for weeks. He doesn't seem to be getting better. What's wrong with him?"

Before I could say something about the yellow bubbles, Miguel spoke up over me. "Obviously, something is wrong with its legs. It cannot stand."

Kernel Ofelia walked over to the injured Shapple with slow steps and pushed the others away. As soon as she did, the Shapple in the middle collapsed as it stuck its legs to the sides, the yellow bubbles intensifying.

"Please, Miguel, fix the problem." Kernel Ofelia gestured.

Miguel, whom I now had a good look at, was very handsome. His perfect white teeth were complemented by his golden skin and chiseled jaw. A purple shirt hugged his muscular body. I knew of him in Cornia—he was well respected and desired by many, both because of his status and his looks.

He walked over to the fallen Shapple and began inspecting each of its legs. He moved them. He bent them. The Shapple showed no reaction to the movement, which seemed odd. He paused for a moment and then lowered the Shapple to its side, observing its abdomen by pushing on it.

Then I saw it. The yellow bubbles. They moved along its bare belly, traveling through its fur. I didn't notice how much of the Shapple it covered before. Miguel flipped the Shapple back over, and I saw the bubbles stop at the arch of its back.

"Well?" Kernel Ofelia asked.

"The legs are not broken," he said. "The muscles are not torn. There is not a hernia or any other noticeable rupture in its abdomen. I...I don't know."

"Splendid," Kernel Ofelia praised him with sarcasm. "Well, I can say none of us know what is wrong with the beast. It is simply unknown. He will most likely be euthanized within the next week if he doesn't get better. This brings me to my first lesson. Some people will not be curable. We must know when to move on."

"Kernel Ofelia," I said before I stopped myself.

She cocked her head. "Yes?" Her look intimidated me.

"If I may..." I stepped forward to the Shapple. What had come over me? I kneeled and looked into the beast's beady eyes. "Hey there, buddy." I felt its side and followed the yellow bubbles up its ribs until I came to the spot where the bubbles disappeared. The ridges of its spine pushed my fingers up and down. Then, I felt a small bump. I pushed deeper, and something hard pushed back. The Shapple groaned.

"Here."

Kernel Ofelia was kneeling next to me in the blink of an eye. Eyes squinted, her brows were raised so high they nearly collided with her hairline. She stared me down, then pushed me to the side and felt the area I pointed at. I reached out and took her hand and placed it on the bump. Her eyes lit up.

"How..."

She looked back to me, eyes of amber and saffron full of question.

"What is it?" Miguel asked.

"Well, it's a cyst," Kernel Ofelia said. "In the Shapple's spine. It is firm. An aneurysmal bone cyst. It isn't too large." She pulled a knife out of her cloak. "I should be able to just..."

She took the knife and poked the skin. The yellow bubbles flared up as the Shapple's skin folded back. The beast groaned louder and tried to move away but failed with its failing legs. At the incision, a small mass appeared. It held tightly to the Shapple's spine. I could tell the Shapple wanted to move away, but it couldn't move its legs. It flailed around its feeble body.

"Hold still." I held the Shapple's soft body as it relaxed, its puffy fur extending and wrapping around my wrist like a hand.

With the knife, Kernel Ofelia cut the mass from the bone, pushing it out of the Shapple's skin. "There we go." It plopped to the ground, and the yellow bubbles popped along its body. She began sewing the wound shut with thread from her pack while I held the Shapple. The delicacy and swiftness she moved with mystified me. Before I knew it, the wound was fully stitched. She stood up.

"That was amazing," I said, letting the beast go.

The Shapple groaned as it tried bending its knees, slowly regaining mobility in its legs. It pushed its knees off the ground and stood up, with wooly crutch extensions on each side.

Everyone began clapping, except for Kernel Ofelia, who just stared at me.

"How did you know?" she whispered.

Florencia came behind me and took my hand to shake it. "That was spectacular. How quickly you diagnosed this was shocking."

Miguel slapped me on the back. "I'm impressed. I'm not easily impressed."

The others gave me small congratulations. Kernel Ofelia continued watching me. "Everyone, take a break." Kernel Ofelia stuck her hand in front of me before I could move. "Ciro, stay with me."

My spine stiffened.

"Yes, Kernel Ofelia?"

"Please tell me how you figured that problem out."

"Well, I saw its legs weren't moving, just like everyone else saw. Then, I saw Miguel inspect the Shapple. He checked everything I would've. Then, I saw..." I gulped. "I saw the bubbles."

Should I be telling her this?

"Bubbles?" She looked down at the Shapple.

"Yes, yellow bubbles." The opportunity to lie passed. "They started at the legs and traveled up the sides of the animal until they stopped at the spine."

Kernel Ofelia opened her mouth, then closed it. She opened it again, but nothing came out. I didn't know if I should say something or not.

"We had better get to our next training portion." She turned and walked away.

I stood there...shocked. That was it.

"Um, okay."

I followed her until something brushed my legs. The Shapple we had helped looked up at me. Extending its puffs of hair out, it wrapped its fur around my fingers, which tickled a little, and caressed each fingertip before pulling its fur back. I pet its head and made my way out of the stable.

We spent the rest of the morning practicing sewing. The medical professionals found this quite easy. It took me a while to get it, but Kernel Ofelia patiently taught me. Our overall relationship changed after the Shapple incident. I felt like she didn't see me as a joke anymore.

I dare say, she seemed to respect me.

When it finally came to lunchtime, the sun had reached its highest point. Though not too far away from Cornia, it was hotter here—the closer we got to the desert, the warmer the land became.

I looked out at the horizon, at the fields of corn. It seemed smaller here than in Cornia. The stalks stood taller, but the cobs of corn seemed shorter, more petite. Perhaps the temperature had something to do with it.

The other troops had already begun eating. Aameen laughed with some people I didn't recognize. He saw me and waved.

"It feels good to get a break from this morning." Florencia walked with me, herding me like a Shapple. We moved toward a table where Miguel and the other medics sat. "Did you find the sewing to be a bit overkill?"

"I don't know if you saw, but I needed the practice," I said.

"You will get the hang of it quickly. With how skilled you already are at diagnosing, you already have a clear understanding about the more difficult parts of our job."

We sat down at the table.

Are these my new friends?

"The food could be better," Miguel said, picking up his stuffed tortilla and taking a bite.

He wasn't wrong. The corn tortilla, rolled and stuffed with cheese and dry meat, sat in the center of my plate. No sauce, no seasoning. Dry and bland. I took a depressing bite. I missed home.

"Have any of you served as a medic in this type of setting?" I asked the group.

The group went silent, mostly shaking their heads. Miguel spoke up. He seemed to always have something to say.

"My father was a medic in the Battle of the Shore. He told me many stories of what he saw and tried to teach me a lot about trauma treatment. He's the reason I went into emergency care."

"And now you just boss people around instead of treating them," Florencia muttered next to me.

"Hey," Miguel said. "Someone needs to make sure our facility runs smoothly. I'm that guy."

"Do you think what you've seen so far back in Cornia will be anything like what we will soon see?" I stared north toward the war zone.

"Yes...or no. I don't know. I'm sure the warzone cannot be that bad." Miguel looked up as his eyes grew.

"You have no idea what's coming," a voice from behind said.

I turned to find Krown Kernel Fernando. His presence was even more intimidating up close. His warm breath pushed at my hair. I stood up and went to the side as fast as I could, worried he may try to scare me like he did the late warriors.

"Simmer down." He opened one eye wider toward me. "I didn't mean to startle you."

"Yes, Commander...Kernel..." I fumbled out.

"What our warriors will see on the battlefield will be gruesome, but what you all will see will be terrifying," Krown Kernel Fernando said. "Kernel Ofelia's training is important to get you prepared for when your minds don't work as well as you wish them to. No matter what skill level or trade you come from, you can all improve." He paused, assessing the people before him. "And…" He drifted off into silence for what seemed like a full minute.

"Yes, Krown Kernel?" Miguel asked.

Krown Kernel Fernado dipped his head and made a circular motion with his hand. "War is a fickle beast, relentless and harsh." He nodded, proud of what he had just said, though it didn't come off all that profound.

He fixed his eyes on me.

"Ciro, is it?"

How did he know my name? A rush of air filled my lungs.

"Yes, Krown Kernel." I stood as straight as I could.

"You have impressed Kernel Ofelia, and she doesn't impress easily. Keep up the good work." He sauntered away. Without looking back, he spoke again. "I expect big things from you, Ciro of Cornia."

My cheeks warmed. Maybe coming to the war wasn't as bad a choice as I thought it'd be.

CHAPTER 6
SHIFTING PERSPECTIVES

Here we are. Here we are. Maizeans from afar.
Here we are. Here we are. From field, to sea, to star.
Fight for the land. Fight for the crop.
Hoe the ground. We are on top.
We are Maize and Maize empowers.
A country where there are no cowards.
Fight for the land. Fight for the crop.
Hoe the ground. We are on top.

"Woo!" the group yelled all at once.

The song was a traditional war song Maizeans passed from one warrior to the next. The words had been translated from the native language, and now sounded vexatious and clunky. If it were meant to be inspiring, it didn't make me feel ready to charge into battle, screaming for Maize and glory and all. But it became normal to me after the last couple of weeks of singing it every night by the fire.

The size of our army had increased substantially during the first week. Recruits from the city of Blanche arrived first, many of whom brought purple-feathered Zapas, a bird beast large enough to ride. The Zapa had a long neck with feathers and a lean body, allowing the Zapa to fly quickly and quietly. Its wings were large, casting a lavender-hued canopy from its purple feathers. Its claws were a darker purple, with talons large enough to grasp a human.

Though unsure if they were strong enough to lift another human and drop them, I liked to imagine they could. Stories said the beasts contained the ability to heal any wound when mounted. I hoped the tales were true. The people of Blanche specialized in riding the beasts, providing an aerial approach to the war. The Stena's headpiece included the Zapa's purple feather on it because of the city's wartime contributions.

Amar arrived a couple of days after Blanche. Kernel Ofelia was right about Amar in their skill and knowledge of medical procedures. They told us stories of the war they served in, emphasizing the importance of practicing the tedious tasks. Just as Kernel Ofelia and Krown Kernel Fernando said, stress from the war would overcome our senses.

Then came someone I didn't expect—Count Ariba. She stared at me from across the fire, the same odd scarf around her neck. The fire's shadows on her sharp cheekbones made her look like a skeleton. It wouldn't surprise me if she were death's representative.

Though Count Ariba was tasked with informing the Stena on the training's progress, all she seemed to care about was watching my every move.

According to Kernel Ofelia, the report the Krown Kernel gave to Count Ariba referenced me, saying I progressed with my medical training at an alarming rate. "A hope for Maize's future" was one direct quote that baffled me. Without prompting, Ofelia promised that nothing out of the ordinary made it on the report, just a standard account of personnel. Nonetheless, it made Count Ariba suspicious. I didn't know why it mattered so much to her. After Count Ariba coughed into her cloth again, I found myself watching her every move.

"She hasn't taken her eyes off you," Kernel Ofelia said, sitting next to me.

"I hadn't noticed." I laughed.

"She is smug. Even her cough comes off condescending."

Glancing over at Ofelia, I smirked. "I'm glad you noticed it, too."

"Her smugness is rampant." Ofelia's eyes widened as she spoke.

"Well, that too, but I meant her cough." My gaze drifted back over Count Ariba. "And that scarf. She keeps wearing that odd scarf."

Kernel Ofelia squinted and looked over at me. "Scarf?"

"Yeah. Around her neck..."

"If you say so..." Ofelia had stopped questioning me when I spoke about things no one else could see. After the Shapple incident and a few other instances of discovering invisible illnesses, Ofelia always wondered but never pushed. The other medics were always impressed.

My confidence in my abilities had grown, but Ofelia's lack of questions left me questioning her intentions.

Aameen walked past where I sat with Ofelia, chatting with his new friends. As expected, he had many. We hadn't spoken to one another much since coming to training. It only made sense—he trained in combat and I trained in medicine. I smiled at him and looked back at the fire.

"Oh, shit," Kernel Ofelia said.

I looked up, and there stood Count Ariba, smirking down at me.

"Kernel Ofelia," Count Ariba began. "I hear your training with the medics is going splendidly."

"Indeed, Count Ariba," Kernel Ofelia responded. "Enough for you to *grace* us with such a compliment. It serves our hearts well."

Count Ariba smiled before turning her attention to me. "And you." She paused. "You have made quite an impression. Your achievements in healing have proven...curious."

"It serves my heart well to hear this." I grinned. Her kindness shocked me, and it seemed genuine. For the first time, I saw Count Ariba as a person.

Count Arbia coughed and brought the cloth to her mouth. The scarf around her neck vibrated. She pulled the cloth away, and little crimson dots revealed themselves. A couple of areas in the middle of her scarf grew brighter before it pulsated through the rest of the scarf.

"Excuse me for noticing, but is that blood on your handkerchief?" Kernel Ofelia asked.

I glanced at Ofelia. What was she doing?

Count Ariba gaped, eyes wide, and pulled the cloth close to her chest. "Yes. It is a little bug I am dealing with."

How could she have been sick with a little bug for almost a month?

"You had it back in Cornia," I said before almost throwing my hand over my mouth, trying to stop the words. I clenched my fists to stop myself. Even though Count Ariba shot a glare at me, I kept talking. "I noticed then. I don't think it's a bug."

The moment was the bravest I had ever been with Count Ariba.

"It may be worth some attention," Kernel Ofelia said.

With a soft smile to Kernel Ofelia and a glance at me, Count Ariba looked at her bloodied cloth.

"It could warrant some concern," she admitted. "I have noticed it hasn't become any better."

"Do you mind?" Kernel Ofelia extended her hands.

Count Ariba nodded, holding her chin high. Kernel Ofelia felt her neck. She hovered over where the scarf shone the brightest. I coughed before Kernel Ofelia moved past it.

Kernel Ofelia glanced toward me, and I raised my eyebrows at her.

"Here." She pressed on Count Ariba's neck. "There are some hard lumps where your lymph nodes are."

"There are?" Count Ariba's eyes widened.

"Yes," Kernel Ofelia answered. "They may be the reason for the bloody coughs. Come find me tomorrow so I can run a couple of tests."

Count Ariba's face went pale as she nodded tightly. She walked away without any further words.

Kernel Ofelia sat back down next to me. "I assumed your little cough was the right spot?"

"Yes..." I found myself trusting Kernel Ofelia more and more. She knew what I could see and hadn't told anyone else.

"There were tumors there. They seem to be rather new, but prominent. I'm afraid of what she has."

I knew what she leaned toward. Cancer. A close neighbor of mine died of the same thing. My heart sank. I disliked Count Ariba, but not enough to wish ill upon her.

"Are you sure?"

"I am." She lowered her voice. "I haven't said anything about some of the odd things you have noticed. Don't go and question me now."

"Odd things?" I gulped.

Leaning closer to me, she looked around to make sure no one else was within earshot. "Ciro, you can see things that others cannot. I doubted it at first, but you're too consistent with it. I think you know it as well." She placed a hand on my shoulder, gripping it tight. "Don't worry, your secret is safe with me. I suggest you keep it this way as well. If the wrong person heard about it, your gift could be used the wrong way."

I wrapped my arms around myself, suddenly anxious. Hearing her voice it made it seem...real.

"You haven't told anyone?"

"No, and I don't plan to. But, please keep me in the loop on things you notice." She looked around the fire. "Has your gift highlighted illnesses in other humans before?"

"Just Count Ariba."

"Curious…" She gazed into the fire. "I expect more will come. And Ciro, this is good for us. I imagine you will save a lot of lives with this gift." She looked back at me and smiled before walking off.

My eyes shifted to the fire. I couldn't help the smile covering my face. I knew I had come to serve as a medic, but hearing the Kernel of medicine tell me I would save a lot of lives felt good. Maybe my intention to come and stay under the radar wouldn't work.

A man stepped in front of the fire. It was the post person who traveled between Cornia and Husk delivering letters.

"Ciro?"

"Yes, that's me."

He handed the letter to me. I recognized the handwriting on the envelope. It was Valeria's. My heart skipped a beat.

"Mail for you."

I grabbed the letter and smiled at him. "Thank you."

"De nada." He nodded and walked away.

I ripped the envelope open in excitement, accidentally ripping the top corner. My hands slowed down as I unfolded the paper and saw my wife's writing scrawled across the page. It smelled like her cinnamon soap. My heart fluttered.

Ciro, mi alma,

It seems like ages, yet it has only been weeks since I held your face against my own.

I tried to write to you sooner, but we were told letters would only distract you from training. I fervently shared my mind with Count Bebida on this matter. No puedes retener a una mujer salvaje.

Isabella asks for your hugs every day. I try to hug her even more, but she says they aren't the same. She isn't wrong.

Harper is such a strong bestia. Her legs move as if she has been missing the front leg her whole life.

We have been told that your training will soon end. Letters will be even more difficult to get back and forth. Please write to me. Let me see your words so I can hear your voice in my mind.

Con amor y pasión,
Valeria

Tears trickled down my face. To say I missed my family was an understatement. I longed for them. The post person had more letters to deliver, so I wanted to write her back and get it to him before he left. It could be my only chance for a while.

I ran back to my room and grabbed some paper and a pen. My hand moved as fast as possible without scribbling.

Mi amor y luz,

Thank you for writing this. I know you aren't happy that I enlisted for our family, but your words give me strength and courage to keep pushing forward.

The warriors are going to war soon, which means we will see patients at any moment. My head medic is Kernel Ofelia. She was apprehensive of me at first, but I gained her trust. I'm proving to be much more valuable than anyone expected.

Tell Isabella how much I love and miss her. I keep reminding myself I did this to keep our family safe, and more importantly, to keep her safe.

I have so much more to say to you, but I wanted to get this letter to the post person before he leaves.

Think of me when you walk. Dream of me when you sleep. Close your eyes and hold yourself tightly when you feel lonely. Mi deseo y fuego.

Love,
Ciro

P.S. Pet Harper for me and tell her she's a good girl.

I folded the letter and ran back to the fire. I found the post person heading back toward the town center. I raced to him and tapped his shoulder.

He turned. "Hello. Did I forget something?"

"No." I panted as I handed him the letter. "I wanted to get this to you before you left."

He laughed. "I wasn't leaving until tomorrow afternoon. I always like to give opportunities for people to respond to their loved ones."

I laughed. "Oh. Now I know for next time."

He pulled an envelope from his bag with a pen and handed it to me. "Better put their name on it."

After printing Valeria's name with a heart, I licked it shut. It tasted of bitter glue.

"Thank you. You are a great post person."

"Estoy aquí para servir a aquellos que necesitan servicio." He ran two fingers across his forehead.

"Gracias, mi amigo." I bowed a little as he turned and walked away.

I took a deep breath and glanced up at the night sky. I imagined Valeria and Isabella looking at the same sky. If only for a moment, we were connected.

Our couch appeared vividly in my mind, my family sitting with me. Isabella was laughing, up well past her bedtime, and enjoying every minute of it. Valeria was telling me about how much her family drove her mad. Harper had her chin resting on my lap. I wanted to be home so badly, but my purpose was to protect moments like these.

My eyes fluttered open, and I noticed a silhouette sitting alone on the ledge of a nearby garden's stone wall, away from the fire's light. The person took deep breaths in between what sounded like silent sobs. I slowly approached them.

"Are you okay?" I asked.

The person coughed into a cloth before turning to face me. My brain registered who it was just before I saw their face and scarf—Count Ariba.

In her typical fashion, she gave me a harsh glare, but this time with reddened eyes.

"You again? Just leave me alone. Your ignorance and attitude are not desired here."

Any compassion I held moments before transformed into disgust. As I geared up to curse her out, she sniffled again.

I took a deep breath, letting my heart calm. "I can leave you to cry alone."

"I wasn't crying." She raised her chin and closed her eyes.

"If you say so." Her eyes opened, rimmed in red, and I recognized the fear I saw in them. "I would be scared right now, too."

"Scared? Scared of what?" she scoffed.

"What Kernel Ofelia and I told you."

Her mouth hung open before she shut it. I expected critical words to be stated. Instead, she turned and looked at the horizon.

"I have given my entire life to Maize." She took in a deep, shaky breath. "Every single moment."

I thought about all the distress she had caused me. She was never kind, nor did she make my life any easier. "You've been unkind to so many people, including me."

"The other Counts get to be nice. They get to bring good news. They get the task of keeping others happy. They get all the praise from the citizens. But someone must deal with the ugly. Someone must deal with Maize's issues that no one else wants to deal with." She swallowed hard. "I have to deliver bad news. I have to address problems within the city. I have to enforce change to make Maize stronger."

Everything she said confused me.

All my life, the only feelings I had for Count Ariba were anger and frustration. No, utter loathing. She was arrogant, egocentric, and superior. She represented everything I hated.

But as I listened to her, I felt my heart softening.

"What do you mean?"

She turned her entire body to face me. Her ghostly eyes looked into mine. "My role has always been to deal with the worst parts of Maize. This meant I would not have friends. I would not find love. I would not have a family." With a deep sigh, she gestured to the space around her. "All for *Maize*."

My damn empathy continued to grow. "You don't have friends?"

"Stena Mezca is my friend." She smiled while saying it. "Well, at least for the moments we get to relax. Which is not a lot."

"I'm sorry. I didn't realize—"

"Do not pity me." She turned away from me again. "I did not ask for it." She coughed and looked at the blood on the cloth. "I just feel like my life is crashing. I may be sick. I may be at Gaia's edge. I did all this just to die *alone*?"

Her scarf glowed brighter than ever, especially in the two spots at the base of her throat. A turquoise iridescence shrouded her face and softened her harsh cheekbones. She looked...beautiful, if only for a moment.

"Well, I'm your friend now."

Count Ariba glanced over at me. "What?" She laughed. "You?"

"Yes, me."

"I do not need your pity." She tried to turn away from me, but something piqued her curiosity.

"Then leave the pity and take the friendship." I smiled.

She waited, analyzing me. "You are annoying."

"And you're rude."

Her analytical gaze took me in. Shifting her mouth side to side, I knew she was trying to figure out how to respond. Her mouth curled up a little before her brows arched in the harshest way possible. "Fine. I will accept your offer, as if it will mean anything."

"I'm serious. Once I am back in Cornia, I will treat you like a friend. If you need anything, all you have to do is ask. And I hope you will show kindness in return."

"Kindness?" She laughed.

A puzzled expression took over, which I merely nodded and smiled at. Her mouth warped in an odd way until it set into a menacing grin.

"Is that supposed to be a smile?"

"No." She recoiled.

A warmness developed in my core and forced its way up my body until it morphed into a smile.

"I'll take it," I said. "Now, I must get some sleep. You should, too. You have some important tests tomorrow."

Count Ariba's face relaxed, and she nodded. "Goodnight." The glow of her scarf shimmered into a soft hue.

"Goodnight, Count Ariba." I bowed before walking away.

"I'm sorry I have seen you as...less," she said to my back. "You are truly a hope-inspiring person. Keep this up. Maize needs you."

Hope. That is a good word.

She was right. We would need more hope for the war.

CHAPTER 7
THE BATTLEFRONT

Count Ariba left Husk very early the next day, right after her meeting with Kernel Ofelia. All Kernel Ofelia told me about the results included two words: "Not good." When I asked more about it, she wouldn't say anything more.

"Doctor-patient confidentiality," she said. I rolled my eyes. "By the way, Count Ariba left this for you."

Kernel Ofelia gave me a folded piece of paper with my name written on the front. When I unfolded it, one sentence stretched across the paper.

I look forward to our friendship.

The note made me chuckle. It had been a few weeks since leaving home, and I had already made friends with one of my worst enemies.

Kernel Ofelia raised her eyebrows in a silent question—she wanted to know what the letter said.

"Doctor-patient confidentiality."

"Ass," she replied with a raised chin.

I shrugged with a cocky smile.

That afternoon, the warriors were told they were being sent to the frontline.

I found Aameen outside his lodging. We embraced in a hug and exchanged a few empty-feeling words. It wasn't like our normal friendship. He looked different—though he still had facial hair, it was more rugged, wild. His skin looked dusty as it often did nowadays, but he still smiled and had bright eyes, positivity never wavering.

"You look like shit," I said to Aameen.

"And you look pampered." He smiled back. "Be careful while I'm away."

"Don't get yourself killed." With one final hug, he was off.

For the first time in my life, I had none of my closest friends or family around. A certain grief pressed against my chest. Maybe it was loneliness. Maybe it was fear. No matter what it was, I couldn't let it pull me down.

The medical team could be my new family. For now.

Within days of the warriors' departure, a new structure was erected at base camp: the medical tent.

Great poles held up heavy white fabric that cascaded down from the highest points to the lowest. The interior was protected from the elements, with only two doors allowing for entry and exit, positioned at the front and back.

Kernel Ofelia instructed us to bring in cots. So many cots. Row after row of cots were arranged in a grid.

"Nope." Kernel Ofelia walked in and lifted a cot, moving it even closer to another cot. "We need to fit as many people in here as possible. At least twenty more cots should be brought in."

"There is no way this tent will be filled with that many people," one of the medics said.

Kernel Ofelia picked up another cot to move it and let out a loud laugh.

"We can hope for this, but my job is to be realistic. There will be times this tent will be too full, and we will have to discharge some people who probably shouldn't be discharged."

"What about more serious cases?" I asked. "An arm's length from one cot to the next can't be enough room to properly treat someone."

Kernel Ofelia pointed to the middle of the tent. "We will have ten cots placed there for intense procedures. But the patient will also be moved, when possible, to another cot once things die down. Our job is to heal as many warriors as possible. Is that understood?"

"Understood, Kernel Ofelia," we all replied in unison, as expected of all warriors.

Once the cots were mapped out and placed, it hit me. Soon, I would spend most of my time in this tent. It looked so empty. I tried to imagine what it would be like when the war truly started, but I had a hard time comprehending.

"Now," Kernel Ofelia began, "it's time for a field trip. We will be making our way to the edge of the front lines."

One of the medics slammed down their cot as silence filled the tent. Low grumbling came from the medics deeper in the tent. Two medics near me backed away from Kernel Ofelia as if she were a feral beast.

"What?" I asked, breaking the silence.

"Calm down." Kernel Ofelia waved both hands up and down. "I want you all to get some practice treating smaller cases and see and hear how some of their injuries occurred. Rather than sit and wait, I want us to *really* start learning."

"Will it be safe?" a male medic asked.

"It is war; nothing is safe about it. But we will be kept away from any weapons. There is a small station set up there."

The group fell silent. None of us was excited to go into the war zone.

"When are we leaving?" I asked.

"Now," she said. "It is about an hour's hike there. This will give us ample time to practice before heading back tonight. I imagine the troops handling the first few waves of Coalitionists will be happy to have us there."

"Like now, now?" I asked.

"Like now, now." Kernel Ofelia turned and started walking. No one followed. She topped and waved us forward. "On we go!"

The group reluctantly followed Kernel Ofelia. Among the medics, panic and terror ran rampant. A couple of medics behind me started complaining in soft whispers. I grunted and moved away from them—too much negativity for me. I sped up to Kernel Ofelia and walked with her.

"The team isn't excited about this," I said.

"I know," Kernel Ofelia said.

"And they're scared."

"I know." She sighed. "They should be. *You* should be. This isn't a light task we will be doing. War is dark and scary. It will haunt you. It will make you weary. But this is our role—to heal. We need to break the ice at some point. I would rather have the shock in a smaller setting where I can oversee every single one of you. Before the real fighting starts."

Kernel Ofelia tapped her right hand on her leg as she marched. The sweat beading her forehead glistened above her shaking eyes. My commander was scared.

"Hope will get us through it." Reaching over, I patted her shoulder. "Hope that the war will be short. Hope that we will know what to do."

"That's very optimistic." She patted my hand, then lifted it with her index finger and thumb before tossing it back to me. "You will need that."

I glanced at her. "Sounds like you do as well."

"Sounds like it." A singular laugh erupted from her and echoed ahead. "I'm also *hoping* for you to lean into your abilities in the war zone. I know you can see ailments in people. Let's see if you can do it in a stressful situation."

"I don't know. The only human I've seen it on is Count Ariba."

"You're sure about this?" After adjusting the strap of her sack, she tilted her head toward me. "You can't think of anyone else?"

I scanned my memories and only remembered Count Ariba. After the first meeting, I saw it. I went home, talked to Valeria, and then took Isabella to the market. Then it hit me. I thought of the man in the marketplace with the purple dots across his body. But the dots were so temporary and gone so fast. They were probably nothing.

"No, nothing else." I scratched the back of my head. "Just the stuff with the other beasts, saving my Talonhound and all."

"I believe great things will come from you if you can figure out how to see this in other people. The more warriors we heal, the more that can return to battle and win this war."

War had always been such a weird concept to me. I had a hard time understanding why compromise involved more violence rather than conversation.

"War..." I released so much air out of my mouth that my lips vibrated with an awkward noise.

Kernel Ofelia mimicked my noise, followed by a boisterous laugh. "War has that kind of effect."

I was becoming more comfortable with Kernel Ofelia every day.

I cleared my throat. "Can I ask you something?"

"Absolutely," she replied, weakening any leftover discomfort I had with her.

"Why even put us in a position where people need to be healed from violence? Why does war always seem to be the answer?"

With widened eyes, I worried she'd scold me for a moment before her expression softened.

"Because people cannot agree sometimes." She glanced over at me with an uneasy look. "This is my second war, though this one is much larger, and I struggled with this idea the first time around. Then, I saw that our enemy often wanted to gain something of ours at whatever cost. War is fought because we are trying to protect our people and land from those who wish to harm them." Her uneasiness changed to confidence as she spoke.

"Just like Maize was originally taken from the natives?" Something came over me. My wife's native pride guided my words. "Though they lost the war and their land was taken."

"Fair point." She shrugged. "I cannot speak for the past, but I can speak for the present. We are trying to keep this from happening again. The way Maize has recently changed things and lifted the native people is astounding. I mean, our leader is native. This gives great hope for the future of Maize, and we don't want to lose it. Therefore, we fight. We wage war on the Coalition, who will take our land and cease any progress made."

"La tierra que protegemos es la tierra que nos protégé." I heard my wife's words as clear as day as I repeated them out loud.

"The land we protect is the land that protects us," Kernel Ofelia hummed. "This is why we go to war."

"My wife would say the same thing. But it still troubles me."

"You are a healer. It would be wrong if it didn't trouble you."

For the remainder of our hike, Kernel Ofelia told me about her family. She grew up in Blanche. Her family ran a small restaurant that made the best chiletentas in all of Maize, at least according to them. She described the food in the greatest detail. The corn tortilla was filled with seasoned pork and peppers, and soaked in a hot white and green cheese made from Shapple milk. The tortilla would cook until the cheese cooled to room temperature. My mouth watered as she described the food.

Kernel Ofelia broke away from her family's restaurant when she was fifteen, worked at the medical facility in Blanche, and became a doctor. Quickly after, she was recruited to the Battle of the Shore, a short war with a rogue island nation—the United Islands—along the Mar Azul.

Ironically, the United Islands wanted Maize for its fertile lands. Our naval forces quickly extinguished the threat. The United Islands did have one strong push on the southern coast of the Amarian Peninsula. Kernel Ofelia was appointed the Head Medic after her great success in managing the medics there.

"More lives were saved that day than on any other day in Maize's history," Kernel Ofelia gloated.

I told her about my family, about how young I was when my father died. I told her of my mother dying shortly after my birth. Most of my time focused on Valeria and Isabella. Confessing my dedication to my family's protection gave me such pride.

"You are a good husband and father," Kernel Ofelia said, smiling. "I admire you."

"And you're a good leader. I admire you and am glad to call you my friend."

Her smile suddenly fell. I followed her gaze to rising smoke in the distance. A few steps further, I began to hear the sounds of war—low screams and the zing of arrows piercing the air.

Kernel Ofelia turned around to face the group. "Stay tight and follow me. We are out of range of most arrows, but be alert."

She began running. Following her pace, my heart raced like a pup following its pack, panic overtaking my senses.

Injured Maizeans were everywhere.

One man screamed in pain as an arrow stuck out of his left leg. A bright green spot formed just above the piercing. The green spots shifted. A new shape formed. It drew me in like a bug to a light.

"Keep up!" someone yelled ahead.

I shook my head and regained focus. As I ran faster to catch up, my eyes drifted away from the green. Great barricades made of wood lined the battlefront. The grass underfoot lay trampled. Arrows stuck out of the ground like flowers. An archer grabbed one of the arrows from the ground, notched it, and let it fly for enemy territory before I understood what was happening.

Unmoving warriors covered the trampled terrain. Two arrows stuck out of a nearby body like the arrows in the ground. One arrow stuck out of her chest and another out of her neck, blood spurting out like a fountain. I averted my eyes from the scene and hurried to catch up.

Kernel Ofelia stopped in front of a small white tent. The tent opened on the side away from the battlefront, and had two small cots inside. Two warriors approached, carrying a wailing man. It was the same man I saw moments ago with the arrow sticking out of his left leg, surrounded by green dots.

"Right here," Kernel Ofelia said as the man was lowered onto a tan and white cot. A wave of extreme heat overtook the tent and amplified the stale musk of metallic body odor.

Kernel Ofelia raised her voice. "This is the type of thing medics will see on the battlefront. Can anyone tell me what I should do with this case?"

I looked at the man's leg and observed the bright green, which weren't spots anymore but ribbons extending off the man like a present, waving in the air. The ribbons began at the bottom part of the puncture.

"You need to get rid of something right here," I said, pointing. The other medics looked at me in confusion. Kernel Ofelia did as well. I had to say something else. "There is...an...infection there."

"Infection..." Kernel Ofelia trailed off as she looked at his leg. "This early..." Kernel Ofelia handed over a piece of cloth to the man screaming. "Put this in your mouth and lie back."

He took the cloth and stuck it in his mouth. Biting down and leaning back, the man held onto the sides of the cot.

Kernel Ofelia pulled the arrow out, as a muffled scream followed. She then took a knife from her pocket and cut his leg where I had pointed. Her eyes widened. A yellow, goopy substance seeped out. A sour scent followed.

"An infection already." Kernel Ofelia flashed a glance at me.

She pulled out a small bottle and poured it on the yellow substance. It bubbled as the man screamed louder.

She wiped up the pus and then poured the bottle on again. Fewer bubbles formed the second go around.

Then, she pulled out a needle and medical thread and stitched the wound. Just as fast as she stitched, her other hand pulled out gauze and covered the wound.

"Wow." My mouth hung open.

Kernel Ofelia grabbed a hypodermic needle from a nearby cart with a vial. She filled the needle and injected it into the outside portion around the wound.

"Can anyone tell me what two things I did to deal with the infection?" Kernel Ofelia asked the group.

One of the medics next to me responded, "Antibiotics. Fernelic acid to treat the open wound and penicillin injected for further antibiotic involvement."

"Precisely," Kernel Ofelia confirmed. "When an infection is found, it is very important that we not only treat it but also prevent any further infections from growing. Great job." Turning to me, she nodded. "And Ciro, fantastic job noticing the infection. They don't normally occur this quickly. This makes me think there was a prior infection that we found from this wound." She turned to the warrior. "You are lucky you were hit. If not, you may have had your leg amputated."

The warrior looked at Kernel Ofelia with exhaustion and laid his head down. His eyes opened and closed slowly. I couldn't help but think about Harper at the mention of amputation. I'd never wish that upon any person or beast.

"Once your leg feels better, your Kernel will tell you your next steps." Kernel Ofelia stood up.

The group patted me on the back and congratulated me on my discovery.

The next warrior came in with an arrow sticking out of her arm. I didn't see anything unique to her. Kernel Ofelia stared at me. I realized she was waiting for an acknowledgment of some kind. I was taken aback, but I shook my head.

"Lucky for all of you, this first arrow is a field point arrow," Kernel Ofelia announced as she grasped the shaft. She yanked the arrow out in one pull as the warrior screamed in pain. She held the arrow up. "The point of this arrow is sharp and simple. It goes in easy, and it comes out easy. Please, pass it around." Each person examined it. "The arrow didn't puncture too deeply into this warrior."

"My name is Selene," the warrior said, grasping her arm.

Kernel Ofelia looked over at her and smiled. "Warrior *Selene*. My apologies." She turned back to us. "With this type of arrow point and a shallow wound, you just need to firmly grab the shaft and pull straight out."

The bloody arrow made its way to me, bits of residual connective tissue hanging off the lower left corner. I shook it away before squinting to observe the triangular point. A dull metal absorbed all light, or maybe the blood just made it seem that way. Either way, only the point seemed to cause damage.

The shaft was a rough texture—parts of the wood curled off. It pricked my finger and a small sliver burrowed into my skin. The end of the shaft opposite the arrowhead was covered in red feathers. Someone told me it was called a fletching, but I found the name silly. I preferred to view it as a flower. Maybe my desire for ignorance with such a serious weapon overcame my sensibility...or maybe it was just immaturity. No matter, I enjoyed viewing it as a flower.

"Can anyone tell me what should be done if the point is all the way through to the other end, or close to it?" Kernel Ofelia inquired of the group.

A silence filled the tent, broken only by the sounds of whizzing arrows and screams. Then, Selene, the wounded warrior, responded, "You make sure the point is all the way through the other end before you break the shaft and pull each end out quick and smooth."

"Precisely, Warrior Selene." Kernel Ofelia smiled. "Maybe we should have you become a medic. The less distance a pull has, the better." Putting her fists together, she gestured breaking an invisible shaft before pointing at Warrior Selene's wound. "Pull out any visible slivers within the flesh. Then, treat it with Fernelic acid and stitch the wound."

Kernel Ofelia had one of the medics come over and stitch the wound as she watched over his shoulder. Warrior Selene thanked her and made her way back into the battlefield. Her wound wasn't too damaging, and she could still move her arm well.

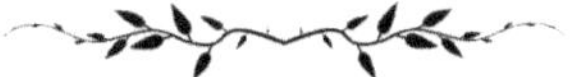

More warriors came in over the next few hours. Kernel Ofelia began having each of us practice diagnosing, taking an arrow out if present, disinfecting, and stitching the wounds. A new arrow eventually made its way into the tent. It was a broadhead arrow, rarer than a field point arrow.

It had a clean point, but a broader triangle. This allowed the arrow to wedge into the flesh easily but hold on to more when pulled out. We were told to push all the way through, if possible. Otherwise, we had to make further incisions on each side of the arrow to help pull it out. If the incision methodology became necessary, it was a very important step to avoid arteries or veins when doing so.

The most important thing we learned was the use of a tourniquet. If we noticed severe bleeding or pulled the arrow out and caused excessive bleeding, a tourniquet needed to be applied to stop any heavy blood loss from an artery. Kernel Ofelia instructed to always have them handy and even use them before pulling an arrow to play it safe. Stitches weren't to be applied until the blood clotted from the arterial injury. At all costs, bleeding out needed to be prevented, and it would be with proper procedures.

When not involved with the treatment of a warrior, I used my time to observe the battlefront.

Large barricades crafted with wood and stones drew my attention. Some were about as tall as a person. Others were about the height of two people stacked atop one another. Our warriors hid behind these walls as they took turns peeking around them to shoot arrows. Other warriors pushed past the barricades in waves. They held hammers and swords. The warriors from Blanche rode their winged Zapas in aerial attacks. Wielding bows and arrows flowered with Zapa feathers, they shot the projectiles with death growls. Arrows rained down from the Zapa's quick and quiet flights.

For as much color was scattered across the battlefield, my eyes painted it all in red and brown. Gruesome and dark. Nothing beautiful came from the death I witnessed, even using my imaginative arrow flowers to decorate the landscape. A pit formed in my throat and worked its way down to my gut. It made me want to vomit. I made my way back into the medical tent. Seeing the blood in the healing tent made the pit dissipate, an odd thing since it was blood that made me feel sick in the first place. I at least understood blood in a place of healing. On the battlefield, it painted a different picture. War morphed into a stranger and stranger beast.

The sun met the horizon, and Kernel Ofelia called it a day. We all walked back to the base in silence. Some whispered the smallest prayers, breaking the silence at random moments. We were all exhausted. I was overwhelmed—at the same time, the weight of the day cast a shadow on my heart while the healing we learned and practiced lightened my steps.

Once we arrived back, everyone exchanged tired pleasantries and went to bed. Kernel Ofelia said our real day would start in the morning and not stop until the war was over.

"How long will this war go on?" I asked her after everyone else had wandered to their beds.

"Hopefully, a few months to a year."

"You think it could be a year?" I nearly screamed. I thought of Valeria and Isabella. I couldn't bear not seeing them for that long.

"I'm hoping we will make a swift victory." She let out an exhaustive, deep sigh. "Goodnight, Ciro. Good work today. It seems like you are seeing more and more each day."

"Goodnight, Kernel Ofelia."

I had made good progress with my gift. I saw more, and was expecting to see even more in my upcoming days to a year.

A year. I looked up at the night sky and thought again of Valeria and Isabella looking at the same sky.

My delirious state believed it would be only a few months until I was back home in my bed. Back with my wife curled up beside me, my beautiful daughter sleeping in the room next to us, and Harper stretched out at the end of my bed.

It had to be only a few months. That was all.

Right?

PART 2

THE WAR

CHAPTER 8
THE FRAGILITY OF TIME

Abrupt pounding on my door startled me. I sat in my bed, heart racing and eyes wide open. You would think after a few years of this routine, I wouldn't be so alarmed, especially since it was how Kernel Ofelia often caught my attention. It didn't matter—my heart pounded just the same.

Three years in Husk. I still couldn't believe it.

My room was awash in darkness—neither the sun nor I was ready for the day. Though I could only see the silhouette of my bed, a lounging chair, and piles of my clothes, the slight stench of unwashed clothes finished painting the rest of my room's image in my mind. I never had time to wash my clothes, so they sat crumpled around the room.

"Ciro, we have another wave coming in," Kernel Ofelia said through the door.

The same pattern. The same routine. Every month Maize came close to ending the war, the Coalition took over the momentum. Month after month passed. Month after month Kernel Ofelia woke me from my limited sleep.

"Just a minute," I cracked out.

I threw on a shirt, pants, and shoes. They passed my smell test. I nearly made it to the door before remembering to brush my teeth, something I often forgot to do. Valeria made me promise to keep good hygiene, so there had to be some part of me not reeking of sweat and gunk.

My room was the only one in medic housing with an attached bathroom. It felt unfair, but Kernel Ofelia did all she could to give me better amenities. Once I began brushing my teeth, I took in my reflection. The oval mirror, outlined in worn bronze, looked just as tired as I did. Dark bags weighed down my eyes. Patchy facial hair formed islands across my chin and cheeks. My hair hung long and ratty.

I slapped my cheeks a few times and made my way out of my room and house toward the medical tent. The houses boarding the medical team were quaint. I'd heard many complaints about the lack of space to sleep and live, but it was much better than sleeping in tents or outdoors. For the most part, the medics remembered this. Almost everyone else fighting this war had been living on the battlefield in tents for more than three years. Keeping the medics rested was important to military leadership.

Rested. That was funny.

The medic house was a two-story adobe arch. Adobe arches were a style of house in Husk that were covered in white stucco with an arched tiled roof. A plain house but at least the roof lit up the dull horizon in a dark turquoise, the most colorful roof in the dusty city. The house smelled moldy. The owners were some of the first people killed when the Coalition crossed the border. Maize took ownership of their house afterwards but did nothing to strip the house of its prior owners' history. Walking through their house was like walking through a museum. Pictures of their wedding day, the building of their home, and other family members lined the walls. Living here felt like violating their legacy, in a way, even though they weren't around anymore. They had been middle-aged native citizens. They didn't have any children, at least from what I could tell based on the photos. They had little furniture. The house, divided into small rooms, was perfect—me and the three other medics I lived with each had a space to sleep.

Outside, the sun had yet to rise. I pulled out the drawing Isabella drew for me all that time ago, as I did every morning. The red ink had lost its vibrancy, and the paper was on the brink of ripping, but the drawing of my family on our couch lifted my spirits and gave me all the energy I needed to face the day. Folding the artwork back up with meticulous care, I stuck it back in my pocket.

A soft brush tickled my hand. Glancing down, the Shapple I had saved three years before greeted me like it did each day. At first, the beast's relentless push to touch my hand with its wooly extensions confused me. But as time went on, I found myself looking forward to the beast's comforting touch. I felt like the beast wanted to keep my worry at bay, like it sensed my distress.

I stopped about halfway between my temporary housing and the medical tent to take a deep breath. "To another day," I said to my Shapple friend. The beast grunted in return.

The white medical tent glowed from within, shadows dancing along the walls. It reminded me of when I used to cast shadows on bedsheets using a lantern to entertain Isabella. Instead of fantastical creatures and stories, the tent held chaos. Ten new warriors were carted in as I entered. Any bit of tiredness was blown away by the tent's abrasively bright lights.

The tent's scene was the same it had been every day, just different people—a bloody mess. The heat in the tent could almost bake meat in the oven. The tent's white walls contrasted with the brown and red gore covering the floors. And the smell. I never wanted to smell this smell again in my life. It was a mix of salt, sweat, and shit.

"Another early morning," Eduardo said from the bed near the entrance.

I smiled. "At this point, early mornings are just normal mornings."

Eduardo put me in a good mood. In the short three weeks I had known him, he had quickly become one of my favorite people to be around. He was bedridden, healing from an infected leg. The stitched wound didn't allow him to move his limb at all without ripping the stitches back open, which had happened twice already.

"Over here!" Kernel Ofelia yelled from across the tent.

"That's my cue," I said.

"Good luck today," Eduardo said.

I ran over to Kernel Ofelia and grabbed a pair of nearby medical gloves. I snapped them on, and the latex immediately dried out my hands. At first, the gloves didn't bother me much. After three years of wearing gloves every day, great cracks covered my hands like the cracked ground of a desert. I pushed past the terrible sensation each day.

"Patient Clea is the worst case arriving with this group." Kernel Ofelia pointed at a female patient with her bloody, gloved hands. "Arrow wounds in the right shoulder and left leg. The bleeding isn't too bad, which is why they kept her out there for longer than they should have." The patient shivered while sweating. "She is sick with some type of infection."

Patient Clea looked pretty, even in her terrible state. I observed the scabbed wounds on her shoulder and leg, expecting to find some kind of infection indicators near the wounds. When others saw nothing, my gift showed me green ribbons as a clear sign to me of infection in patients. Because of this, I would always show Kernel Ofelia where the infected portions were. Either she would cut them out or, if it was easy enough, I would do the procedure myself. No green ribbons decorated Patient Clea.

So, I kept searching her body for something else. There had to be an infection somewhere. Then I discovered something odd. A red ball on her stomach.

"How long has she been feverish?" I asked.

"Clea," Kernel Ofelia said to the patient, who just groaned in return. "Clea," Kernel Ofelia repeated. "I need you to focus."

Patient Clea's head shook as her eyes cracked open. "Yes?"

Kernel Ofelia looked over at me. "How long have you been feverish, Clea?" I shouted.

"It…" Clea started. "It began a few days ago. I was fine."

"Does your stomach hurt?" I asked.

"Yes!" Clea exclaimed as she clenched her stomach. "It hurts so bad."

"Stomach?" Kernel Ofelia asked.

"Peritonitis," I stated. When I wasn't in the medical tent, I read medical books Kernel Ofelia gave me. "I don't think there is any infection from the wounds. She has another infection in her stomach."

"Peritonitis?" Kernel Ofelia asked. "Did you see something?"

I observed Clea's stomach and watched the red ball shiver.

"Red ball," I simply stated. "Stomach." We tried to keep our language short and vague.

"Interesting." Kernel Ofelia walked over to the drawers and cupboards filled with antibiotics. She came back with a bag and IV drip equipment. "Clea. Your stomach lining is infected. We aren't sure why, but this should be a simple fix. These antibiotics will help kill off the infection."

"Ow!" Clea clutched her stomach and moaned.

Kernel Ofelia took the bag and hung it on a nearby metal rod. With the apparatus set up, she took Clea's arm and brought over the long tube with a needle on its end and poked it into Clea's vein. Kernel Ofelia grabbed a glass of water and two pills.

"Take these," Kernel Ofelia said. "They will help with the pain." The pills were gone in seconds.

"Thank you," Clea squeezed out.

"Our pleasure," I said.

Kernel Ofelia and I walked over to the cleaning station. We threw out the gloves and washed our hands and arms. As the water washed away the soap, my hands felt so dry. The continual washing had long removed any natural oils that could provide a semblance of moisture.

"I don't know what I would do without you," Kernel Ofelia said.

"You are a great medic," I said. "You would be fine without me."

"The amount of time we save on diagnosis is astounding." Rotating her head around, her neck cracked. "Seriously, whatever gift you have is remarkable."

She offered the same compliments often. The hostile relationship we began with seemed so long ago. Now, we talked every day. Over the past three years, Kernel Ofelia had become my best friend, and I became hers.

"I'm going to check on the other medics." She touched my shoulder. "Stay nearby in case I need you."

"Yes, Kernel. I will be by—"

"Eduardo, I know." She patted my shoulder and walked away.

I walked back to Eduardo. The other medics were treating other patients. Most injuries just needed to be stitched and disinfected. There were a few mild cases of infection, but those were easy removals. Each medic smiled and nodded to me. They respected me, and I respected them. They had become my family here.

"Another quick treatment by Dr. Ciro," Eduardo cheered. "The best of the best."

"Stop it." I sat down next to him.

"You saved my life. And you just saved another life. You are a holy person. Dios de la curación."

"You are dramatic." I tried to hold back a smile.

"I'm grateful. So is the lady you saved and all the others. Stop selling yourself so short."

My eyes drifted to one of the empty beds next to him. It was the only one left, which meant Eduardo would be moved soon. We needed the space, and his stitches were finally holding together. I was happy for him, but I didn't want him to leave.

"They are going to discharge you tomorrow," I said.

"Oh, to see the sun and breathe fresh air again." He grinned. "Que terrible."

"I'm going to miss having you around."

"Visit me in Blanche." He wasn't only going to be discharged from the medical tent but sent home. He ended up being more of a liability than an asset, according to the Krown Kernel's standards. "You can meet my daughter and wife."

"Then our daughters can become best friends."

I thought of Isabella. Valeria last wrote to me a few weeks before. They had celebrated Isabella's sixth birthday just before she wrote the letter. She had an art party where Isabella covered the house in portraits and paintings with her friends. I felt for my daughter's drawing in my pocket. I had missed three of her birthdays.

The lack of a new letter made me worry about Valeria's state. She typically responded more quickly. I figured the post person was moving slowly this week.

Three years had passed since I last held my daughter. I tried to imagine what she looked like, but the image I had changed every time. Most of the time, I imagined she looked like a younger Valeria. Striking eyes, a bright smile, thick black hair, and sass galore. My mood teetered between sadness and happiness when I thought of present-day Isabella. A smile forced its way through my depressed state.

"Thinking of your daughter again?"

Eduardo placed a hand on his chest and tilted his head. I shook my head, snapping back to reality.

"Yes. I don't know how to feel anymore. I want to see my family again. I want to snuggle with my daughter. I want to kiss my wife."

"Me too." Eduardo's eyes grew so large. "Not your wife, though. Of course." His nervous chuckle made me laugh. "I feel bad that I will soon see my family while you remain here."

"I'm saving lives." My words carried little emotion.

"You are." He gestured around to the patients filling the tent before wincing at the pain from his side, "Maybe don't sound so uninspired." Rubbing his side, he repositioned himself on his cot.

"I'm happy to do it." I put more emotion into my response. "I really am. I'm just tired today."

"You're human, Dios de la curación." His eyebrows bounced up and down.

"You're right, I'm human. Still not a god."

The other end of the tent's flaps whipped open as someone yelled, "Hurry! We need help!"

I stood up and found Aameen pushing a body through the tent entrance. At least I thought it was him. It had been a year since I last saw him. A long, rugged beard covered his whole face. His familiar eyes fixed on me.

Kernel Ofelia raced to his side.

"Aameen?" I yelled across the tent. He just kept staring.

With Kernel Ofelia's help, Aameen pushed the cart with a body sitting on it to an empty bed next to Eduardo.

"Ciro..." Aameen said, the cart stopping in front of me. "She needs your help."

Tears riddled his cheeks and beard.

"Help me," Kernel Ofelia said to Aameen. They turned toward the body and lifted her onto the bed. "Ciro, help now. It looks bad."

Aameen grabbed my arm and locked eyes with me. The chaos in the medical tent slowed down. His gaze put me in a trance. "Keep your head clear. She needs you."

What an odd thing to say.

He let go of me, and I began looking over our patient.

Time stopped. The air rushed out of my lungs.

How? How is this possible?

"Va..." I tried to say, but my voice wavered. "Valeria?"

My wife's body contorted in pain. An arrow had pierced completely through her right leg. A garment was tied tightly around the wound, trying to stop the bleeding.

Warring emotions filled my head. The joy of seeing her for the first time in so long. The fury with the fact that she wasn't supposed to be anywhere near the war. The alarm in her current, wounded state.

I shook my head, smiled, let out a whimper, and threw my hand over my mouth.

Valeria's lips trembled. "Ciro." She panted. "I'm...I'm so sorry." With a deep groan, she reached for her leg.

I had so many questions. I wanted to launch myself at Aameen. He knew why she was there. I wanted to pummel him.

Forming fists, I pushed past the rage. My wife needed me.

"Do you know her?" Kernel Ofelia asked me. "Actually, don't answer that. I need you to be in the right headspace."

"Right." I wanted to cry.

"Patient..." Kernel Ofelia began.

"Valeria," I finished.

Kernel Ofelia looked at me and back toward my wife. She knew. "Patient Valeria, I'm going to pull the arrow out and begin my work. Ciro is going to inspect the rest of you while I do this. Okay?"

Valeria took a deep breath and yelled, "Okay, Kernel!" She was still fierce, even in her current condition.

Kernel Ofelia grabbed the arrow and pulled it straight out, a clean pull. Blood started spraying as she quickly began stitching and bandaging the wound.

I searched for an infection. No green ribbons surrounded the wound. Instead, purple flowers pulsed near the arrow's entry, something new to me.

"Purple flowers," I said. "Wound."

"Nearby?" Kernel Ofelia asked. "I'm not sure what to treat it with."

Something different about the purple flowers drew me to them. They moved in little spirals before splitting in two and migrating away from the wound.

They are spreading. They are spreading quickly.

"They're moving. They're growing across her body." My heart pounded.

"Growing?" Kernel Ofelia stopped the bleeding and stitched the cut. "What do you mean, growing?"

I started hyperventilating. "Ofelia, they're *spreading*."

"That's not good." Searching Valeria's body, Kernel Ofelia performed any test she could think of, using blood pressure cuffs, small blood samples, temperature checks, and whatever else she could.

The world went fuzzy. I backed up and fell into the chair next to Eduardo.

Kernel Ofelia tried to say something to me, but I couldn't hear her.

My worst nightmare was coming true. My wife was about to die right in front of me and I couldn't do anything. I had helped so many people, but with the most important person, I didn't know what to do.

A hand touched my shoulder, making me jump. I turned to Eduardo. He talked, but I heard nothing. I focused on his mouth, and his voice sounded over the buzzing in my ears.

"Ciro, they need you. Save her. I know you can."

He was right. I nodded and stood back up.

"Ciro!" Kernel Ofelia yelled. "How is it spreading?"

I looked back down at my wife's leg at the purple flowers. They filled every area from her feet to her thigh.

"Nearly her whole leg is covered," I said.

"Necrotizing fasciitis," Kernel Ofelia stated without hesitation.

Serendipity at its finest; I had just read the chapter about disease the night before. Necrotizing fasciitis was a bacterial infection that attacked the connective tissue and spreads like wildfire. The death rate was significant for those infected by it. The only treatment I knew of was to—

"We need to amputate her leg before it spreads further," Kernel Ofelia finished my thought.

"Are you sure?" I looked at Valeria, her eyes widening and her arms trembling.

Was this what Harper felt like?

"Yes, or it *will* kill her." Kernel Ofelia grabbed a bottle of morphine, dabbed it on a cloth, and held it to my wife's nose and mouth. Before I knew it, Valeria's eyes fluttered shut. Her body went limp. Kernel Ofelia grabbed a saw. "Hold her down."

As I moved to Kernel Ofelia's side, I watched the purple flowers. They moved into her hip.

"Ofelia, they are in her hip now," I said.

Kernel Ofelia dropped the saw. "No..."

"What? Why are you stopping? Do what you were going to do. Save her."

"Ciro…"

"Grab the saw! Cut her leg off! Save her!"

"Ciro, there is no—"

An inopportune rage pulsed through me. I reached out toward the purple flowers in anger, trying to push them off.

"She cannot die!" I kept pushing. Then, I felt something. I felt the flowers. "She cannot die." My voice faded. Like thin paper, the petals moved along my fingertips.

Why can I feel the flowers?

Instinctively, I began grabbing them, picking them like flowers in a field. As I did this, they kept filling in the empty spots I picked from with not only more flowers but double the amount. It aggravated them.

For some reason, I started swirling my hands. The flowers started floating up into the air, toward my hands. They formed a purple mass hovering above Valeria's body. I looked at her. She had no more flowers on her. Every single one of them was gone.

The soft petals forming a mass sharpened like knives, cutting at my hands. The mass suddenly felt hot, burning my hands.

What am I supposed to do with them?

The heat became so unbearable that I flicked my hand trying to get rid of the flowers. They flew in the air and were gone. I didn't care where they went, just as long as they were gone.

Taking a deep breath, my heart steadied as I looked down at my wife. My healed wife. The purple flowers were gone. My burning hands touched her cool body, sending a shiver across my skin.

"What just happened?" Kernel Ofelia asked.

"I…I saved her." A smile formed on my face. I grabbed and kissed Valeria's cheek. "I saved my wife."

"How did that happen?" Aameen quietly asked from behind.

Instead of responding, I began crying. It turned into joyful sobbing.

"She's okay," I whispered amidst my cries.

I was so mad at her for being there. I had so many questions about why she was there. But all that mattered in that moment was that she was alive.

A sharp cry came from behind.

"Ciro," Kernel Ofelia said.

I spun around to Eduardo, screaming and pushing at his legs.

"What's going on?" I rushed to his side.

Bulbous beads of sweat raced down his face. His leg had turned bright red, covered in purple flowers. After a quick inspection, I realized they weren't just on his leg, but all over his body.

"His fever spiked," Kernel Ofelia said, grabbing an antibiotic bag and injecting him with a needle.

"It's on him now." I stared at him. "It's everywhere." I held up my trembling hands and looked back at this body. "The purple flowers."

"What?" Kernel Ofelia exclaimed. "How?"

Without thinking it through, I tried swirling my hands again. The purple flowers pulled up a little toward me but snapped back. My arms ached. I was exhausted. I kept trying, but nothing worked. The flowers were everywhere.

"No, no, no." I kept trying to pull, but nothing happened. "Eduardo, stay with us."

Eduardo's breathing shortened into long, heavy breaths. Dark brown eyes vibrated as they pleaded with me to save him. The heat radiating from his body warmed my own body. He burned from the inside out.

Then, his eyes softened. It was as if he had realized something. His eyes linked to my own as he cracked out, "Tell my family I love them."

"Stop it," I said. "You're going home."

The brightness in his eyes wavered before dimming. I screamed and started trying to remove the flowers again, one by one. But two more took the place of every flower I pulled. In a last-ditch effort, I twirled my hands again, but my arms burned and did nothing.

Eduardo's arms went limp.

One last breath left his lips before his chest stopped moving.

All the purple flowers across his body faded to gray.

Then, the flowers faded to nothing.

His eyes closed.

"NO!" I screamed so loud my throat burned.

I slammed my head into his chest and let my shrieks fall into intense sobbing.

"Ciro..." Kernel Ofelia said, touching my shoulder.

I didn't move. I only clung to my friend Eduardo.

Whatever I did to save my wife just killed my friend.

I wasn't a healer.

I was a murderer.

CHAPTER 9
THE CURSE

A chilly air blew over Husk, a peculiar thing for Maize. The moon illuminated the ground in shimmering grays. Based on how brightly the ground lit up, I knew the sky had to be clear, though I dared not look up at it. Witnessing my vomit on the dirt was all I deserved. A sheen from its moisture reflected the moonlight in streaks. I vomited again. I just couldn't handle it. He was dead. He was dead because of *me*.

I swished water in my mouth and spat it out. The bitter taste of bile made my stomach twist. I deserved it. My Shapple friend continued to stroke my back as I switched between sobbing and vomiting.

Stumbling back into the tent, I looked at Eduardo's old cot, now positioned immediately next to my unconscious wife. It was the second night since his death. When I wasn't vomiting, I slept in Eduardo's cot next to Valeria, whom I had saved in exchange for his life. I had fought hard when they pulled his body from the bed, but my energy was so low at that point. I couldn't put up much of a fight.

"Ciro," Aameen said, sitting next to me on the cot. "You need to get some good sleep back in your own bed. You need to rest."

Instead of going back to the battlefront, he spent his time with me. His support reminded me of the best friend he was to me. But was he anymore? He knew my wife had been fighting in the war behind my back. Who was watching Isabella? Did he not care about my family's safety?

It all left a bittersweet taste in my mouth.

"We need to talk about everything that happened." For the tenth time that day, he brought the same concern up. "You need to process it."

Process it.

I stared ahead, numb. Avoiding the subject had been easy if I didn't speak to anyone. Each time he brought it up, a little hammer hit my brain. Pounding, pounding, pounding.

"I killed someone." The faint taste of vomit lingered. I took another drink of water, swished it around, and spat it on the ground behind me. "I killed someone who was my *friend*." Eduardo's radiant smile flickered in my mind before it disintegrated into a skull. I gasped for air. "He was about to go home and see his family."

Aameen sat forward. "You didn't *kill* him. You were saving your wife."

I sat up and looked Aameen straight into his brown, speckled gold eyes. "You act like you know what I was doing." Whipping my hand around, I gestured to the rest of the tent. "No one here knows what happened. You can't *see* what I *see*."

As if my eyes came into focus for the first time, the green fluff sharpened into flowing waves. Ribbons danced around patients behind Aameen, taunting me.

Were the diseases becoming easier for me to see? I could see every detail, every movement.

I shook my head and rubbed at my temples. What did it matter?

Green fluff or ribbons or whatever, no one saw what I saw. They all could see the bright lights of the tent, but they didn't see the ribbons slithering across their bodies. Since seeing the purple flowers move across my wife's body, the movement of the green fluff across patients' bodies became more vivid. Either I hadn't noticed it before, or my gift just continued to torture me with more gruesome detail.

Aameen pressed his lips together and placed a hand on the side of my bed. "I still don't quite understand what you see. I don't know what you mean. But I know you. I know you aren't someone who would kill another person."

At one time, I believed this to be true, but *my* hands caused death. Just as Aameen said, I didn't mean to do it. Of course I didn't. But did that make it okay?

"Just leave me alone."

Every other time I told him to leave, he respected my wish. This time, he sat staring.

"No. I'm not leaving my best friend. You need to process everything. Just tell me what happened."

"Why didn't you tell me about Valeria fighting?"

With a great sigh, he sat up straight. "I should've told you, but she begged me not to. She promised she would tell you soon."

I scoffed. "*That* went well." Sweat beaded on the back of my neck. The heat filling the tent was stifling.

"And I can't change it." He leaned forward. "Ciro, I am so sorry. I never thought *this* would happen." Pointing at Valeria, he scrunched his brow. "Now, can you please tell me what happened?"

"What happened..." I ran my fingers through my hair as the stress transcended all other emotions. It was too tiring to keep my secret. I didn't know why I had waited this long to tell him what was going on with me. I turned to face him and lowered my voice.

"I can see...disease." The rest came pouring out. "I can see sickness. I have been able to since Harper's leg was amputated. I can see things others can't."

"What do you mean?" Brow furrowed, he stared at me with bright eyes. I couldn't tell if my confession excited him or filled him with fear.

Still whispering, I replied. "I see colors and shapes on those who are sick. Colors and shapes that other people can't see." I looked past him toward an infected patient about ten feet away from us. "Her." I pointed at the patient. "Where you see a wound, I see green ribbons covering the area. That tells me she has an infection from the wound."

Aameen turned, observed the patient, and turned back to nod. "I only just the wound."

"Our medics will now remove the space surrounding this wound and treat it with antibiotics. It's a simple treatment. But not all cases are like this."

"Like Valeria's."

Looking past him at Valeria, I gripped the bed. My jaw ached from my clenched teeth.

How dare he mention her name.

"Valeria had necrotizing fasciitis. They were purple flowers. They spread faster than anything I'd ever seen before. It's extremely deadly. I did what I had to so I could save her."

Paying no mind to the anger in my voice, he gaped. "You...moved it? That doesn't make sense."

"I know. I don't understand it. It just happened that way." I felt disconnected from my words. I should have felt something at the revelation, but my body was calm, numb.

The brown depths of Aameen's eyes reflected the harsh lights of the tent. But instead of the compassion I expected him to extend to me, his face hardened. Dramatic creases formed across his forehead and cheeks, his eyes shadowed. It wasn't the face I had recognized all these years.

"If this is true, you have to tell the Krown Kernel."

"No." I grew angry, some emotion returning to my voice. "Why would I do that?"

"It could help Maize. If we tell the Krown Kernel about this, he can use it to help us."

Help Maize?

What did that even mean? I didn't recognize my good friend. He wasn't the Aameen I had known all these years. He wanted to give up my secret to the Krown Kernel to help himself.

"Who are you?"

The creases on his face dissolved, a softness returning to his gaze. "I'm your best friend, Ciro. And I believe what you're saying. I know you only came here to protect your family. This is how you can do that."

My brain rattled. Anger scorched the inside of me.

"Don't you *dare* tell me how I can protect my family!" I didn't even notice I stood until I looked down on Aameen. "I have done more than anyone expected me to. I have saved countless lives. I have given up my sanity and sleep to make sure those who risked their own lives could live another day. I have missed watching my daughter grow up and learned that my wife, who I expected to be there at her side, joined a war she wasn't supposed to. *Now*, my wife lies next to me in a deep sleep. *Now*, I'm looking at my friend who kept this secret from me. I sit in this disgusting, death-filled tent only to be told I can do *more* to protect my family."

I spat on the floor before him, bitter bile returning to my mouth. "Espero que puedas dormir por la noche por lo que has dicho," I muttered my veiled insult, wondering how he did sleep at night.

Keeping perfect posture, Aameen looked up at me. He may not have understood a thing I said in the native tongue, but my tone showed how deeply he had offended me. The sad part was that I believed my insult, knowing well enough that he would find sleep no matter the damage this conversation would have on our relationship.

Keeping intense eye contact, he pressed his lips together.

"Fine," he said. Pushing up from the bed, he stood, his face close to my own. "I fear you forget all I have done for you. I know you are emotional. I know you have had a lot thrown at you. But don't *forget* what I have sacrificed for your family. Not just mine."

He stormed off. I fell onto my cot in exhaustion. It was the longest conversation I had attempted in a few days.

"That was rough," Kernel Ofelia said from behind me.

"Were you here the whole time?" I asked without turning to face her.

"Every minute. I take it you just told some important information to your friend. Information I *thought* you were afraid to share. Are you okay?"

Am I okay?

I should have been worried about telling Aameen of my abilities—I had promised myself I would keep them a secret. But I wasn't worried. Kernel Ofelia seemed okay with my confession. Maybe I was too. Aameen had changed, but he was still my lifelong friend, even if he did recommend telling the Krown Kernel. Aameen would never do something to hurt my family or me. Well, besides lying about Valeria, but Valeria insisted on that.

I sighed, staring at the poles lining the tent. "Do I look okay?"

She laughed harshly, and I jumped at the sound.

"Not at all."

I knew her banter was an attempt to make me feel better, but it only felt like another exhausting interaction.

"How is Valeria?" I changed topics.

Kernel Ofelia shifted her stance. "Her vitals are getting stronger. I'm a bit surprised she hasn't woken up."

"I wouldn't wake up if I were her." I raised my head for a moment before it fell back down toward Kernel Ofelia.

"I don't think I would either." Gesturing around, she shrugged and grinned. Another attempt to lighten my spirits.

"How are the patients?"

"Good. Nothing too severe. I do miss having your help."

Part of me missed helping. "I'm sure you're doing okay without a *murderer* helping you."

Two medics caught my eye as they passed by, nodding. All the medics stole glances at me when they could, confusion and concern plastered across their faces. Everyone had seen what I did. No one understood what happened. Only Ofelia knew. And now Aameen. I ran my fingers through my hair and stared back up at the ceiling. If I stared at the ceiling all the time, I never had to see anyone's concern.

Kernel Ofelia touched my rigid shoulder. "Don't mind them." She seemed to always know what I felt. A real friend. "They are only confused by what they don't understand."

"And you understand?"

"Eres una buena persona. You have always been a good person. That I know. Something terrible happened that you didn't plan on." She leaned closer to me. "I know this isn't what you want to hear, but you can learn from it."

Is she right?

I ran my hands through my greasy hair. I hadn't showered in days. "Maybe someday I'll remember I'm a good person. Today, I feel like the complete opposite. Me siento como una mala persona."

"Si." She moved her jaw side to side and stepped away with a sigh. "I have to keep checking on patients."

As she walked away, I heard a familiar voice from the cot next to me. Valeria stirred in her bed, moving her hand to her head.

She moved. She was waking up!

"Valeria?" Tears filled my eyes.

"Ciro..." she whispered, her eyes fluttering open. Copper eyes dotted with gold flakes made my heart jump. For a moment, I forgot all that had happened. It was just her and me sitting beneath the moon the first night she kissed me.

I launched myself forward and wrapped my arms around her. I never wanted to let go.

"Ow..." She winced in pain. Her body was still weak from the trauma.

"I'm so sorry." I held her and kissed her lips. Her lips quivered, but not from pain. Her hands reached for her leg. I pulled away. "I'm happy you're awake...and alive."

Her eyes held mine for a moment before they darted around, surveying the tent. They widened.

"How...why..."

"Calm down." I touched her face. "You went through a lot."

"Where are the other warriors? Are they okay?"

"You were the only one who came in after we received the first wave of patients. They came from a different front. No one else came from yours. Just Aameen."

"They're safe?" Her large eyes searched mine before softening. "They're safe." She reassured herself. Her eyes shifted as mine did the same. We knew the next part of our conversation. "I know you're angry with me."

I recalled my fury when she first came into the tent. The purple flowers across her leg ripped that away and hadn't come back.

"I was angry when I first saw you, but it disappeared the first night. I was mostly shocked to see you after so long. Now, I would say disappointment is the correct feeling." I searched for a reason to look past her selfish decision to join the war, but it ate at me. "How could you do this? We agreed to keep Isabella safe by having only one of us go to war while the other stayed. *I'm* here as the medic."

"It wasn't an agreement." The fire I remembered blazed in her eyes. "It never was. You made the decision. Not a joint decision, your own decision. You expected me to fold to it. And you said it would only be a year." She reached down to her leg with tension in her face before relaxing again. "Ciro, it's been over three!"

My resentment came flooding back as I remembered the drastic actions I made to protect her. It was her tone. She had planned it. A deep burning began in my heart and moved up to my brain, demanding release. I wanted to yell at her. I wanted to scream. But that wasn't me. I didn't like yelling at her.

"What about Isabella?" I kept my voice calm, but it was strained. "Is she safe?"

"She's with my mother. Of course, she's safe. I'm not reckless."

Slamming my hands on my thighs, I gripped my pants tightly, willing away my building anger. "Reckless? Really? I'd say this is pretty reckless."

"Our country needed warriors! It isn't reckless when you know how to fight."

I took a deep breath, unsure if I could keep my voice down. "This isn't the right time for this conversation. You're still recovering. You just woke up."

No matter what pain she felt, she still managed to roll her eyes. "Another decision made on your own." Her words felt like a knife stabbed into my heart and twisted. "Hombre egoista."

"Selfish?" I yelled. My plan to stay calm backfired. After all my sleepless nights, long shifts, and sacrificing my sanity, she called me selfish. "I've done *everything* for our family."

"Nuestra familia no es importante para ti." Her mouth moved so fast, the native fire I often feared within her raging. "Tu eres estupido y descuidado y egocéntrico y—"

"Stop!" Our eyes locked into one another's. For the first time ever, I matched the fire in her eyes. I understood the fury, but I didn't like it. My wife was alive.

"You're—"

"Stop..." My voice weakened. "Stop..." Tears filled my eyes.

"Mi amor..." Her eyes doused the fire within them as the gold specks returned.

We paused for a moment, the tension between us like a barrier.

"How long have you been fighting?" I asked.

"About a month..." She squeezed her lips together as I winced. "I know. I know. I messed up. You were right. I endangered myself. I almost died." She looked down at the ground. "I almost died. How did I...I saw you...then I..." With her mouth hanging open, she reached down and touched her leg. Not in pain, but she touched it to feel if what she remembered was real.

"I saved you," I whispered.

With a twist, she pulled her hand back and flashed her eyes upward. "How? I thought my leg was going to be amputated. Then, I was knocked out. Now..." she looked at her leg, "...I still *have* a leg. I'm *alive*. I'm *healthy*. How?"

With the way my wife pieced things together, I couldn't lie to her.

"You know how I figured out Harper's sickness?"

"Yes." Her eyebrows arched upward, and she lowered her voice. "How you said you could see sickness on animals?"

Leaning in close, I whispered, "I started seeing disease on people as well. I use that here to help heal. We have saved so many warriors from death." A sense of pride washed over me until I recalled the tent flapping open and Aameen walking in. "Then you came in. It was something that we couldn't fix." With each word, my heartbeat quickened and my breath shortened. "I was overcome by fear. I couldn't lose you." A soft ache pulsed in my eyes as I tried to hold back the tears. "Then I touched it." I gasped for air, tears trickling down my cheeks.

"Touched what?"

I got closer to her, whispering in her ear.

"Touched the...disease. I could grab it. But it wasn't enough." My throat dried, forcing me to swallow hard. "I found I could swirl and capture it. I was holding it in my hands. It was so hot. It was burning me." My hands warmed just like they had. "I had to get rid of it. So I just...threw it." A great wave of relief made my whole body relax, if only for a moment. "You were okay. Everything was okay. Then, I realized I threw it at another person. Eduardo..." I started shaking.

A breathless pressure made my whole body give in, sudden exhaustion overtaking me, no motivation to move. I thought of Eduardo's life fading from his eyes in that last moment. The torture he went through because of me. My cheeks cooled as the tears poured down.

"Eduardo?"

"My friend." I blubbered. "He had a daughter the same age as Isabella. He was about to go home. And now..." I sobbed. It hurt so much. I slammed my face into my hands, trying to stop the tears.

With soft hands, Valeria brought me in. I buried my head into her shoulder, both of us shaking.

"Ciro..." Valeria's light words lifted my chin like a hand. "Whatever you did, whatever happened...don't think you killed your friend. You did something amazing that no one may ever understand."

"That doesn't change the fact that he is still dead." I pounded my hands on the side of my head. "Soy malo."

"Tu eres bueno." Her response came as fast as the words left my mouth. Gripping my wrists, she pulled my hands down. "You have always been a good person. You care deeply for everyone you know. You even care for people you don't know. Don't forget this."

The same thing Kernel Ofelia said to me.

"It doesn't change how much it hurts."

A feeble breath trembled out of my mouth. My tears subsided. My stomach turned, and I darted out of the tent to vomit in the bushes again, but nothing came out. With each dry heave, I tried to breathe. Instead, mucus hung from my lips and reached for the ground. Too cold, as gravity pulled it down until it snapped and fell. I took a deep breath, stood up, wiped the dirt off my knees, and reentered the tent.

The water jug by my cot allowed me to clean my mouth out. After spitting just outside the tent, the last bit of warm mucus expelled from my mouth, I took three big gulps of water. No matter how terrible I felt, the rush of cool water refreshed my mouth and my heart.

Valeria watched me as her eyebrows arched up toward the middle of her forehead. "Please, sit back down. I want to touch you and I can't stand yet."

Following her command, she placed her hands on each side of my head and held it just like she did with our daughter. My neck relaxed in her soft grasp.

"Is Isabella okay?" I asked.

"She is, and she is *vibrant*." Flashing her teeth, my wife's smile lit up the space around me. "To be truthful, I already miss her deeply. Con todo mi corazón." A singular tear trickled down her cheek. "And it looks like my little stupid adventure will be cut short, and I will see her again." She paused, struggling with her words.

"All the undermining remarks from the natives became too much to handle. It was continuous and became worse each week. *You have a duty to Maize and your family* was said so often. I tried my best to ignore it, but..."

She glanced at the ground. "It got to me. I wanted to live out my family's legacy. I promised myself only for a little while. My mother promised to keep Isabella safe. And now?" She covered her face with one hand. "I've accomplished nothing except for nearly dying and disappointing the most important man in my life."

I didn't agree with what she did. I didn't know how to feel about it.

But I did understand that the war had lasted longer than we planned. And the way the natives spoke to her was different than how they spoke to me. I understood that. Did it make up for what she did? No. Was Isabella still safe? Yes.

Taking her hand into mine, I gripped it like my life depended on it. "V, I'd be lying if I didn't admit the disappointment I feel, but my joy in seeing your beautiful, living face far outweighs it." I kissed the back of her hand, a salty sweat lingering on my lips. "Tu eres mi fuego y mi latido del corazón. Just promise to never do anything like this again.

"I promise. My dedication is to you and Isabella." She smiled with teary eyes and puffy cheeks. "You are too good to me."

"You are too good to *me*." Bringing my lips to hers, our normal passion, absent from earlier, coursed between my lips and hers. One of my favorite things about Valeria was when the fire in her eyes made it to her lips. My body tingled...a feeling I hadn't felt in *so* long. I wanted her body against mine. To feel her skin, her curves, her existence.

Someone walked by, dousing our ecstasy in the cold waters of reality. We were in the absolute worst place to display our affection, but I didn't care. Pulling away from one another, our noses stayed close enough that the tip of her nose tickled me. I explored the faint freckles lining her cheeks as they somehow connected to my own freckles, her soul connecting with my soul.

"I've missed you. I have missed you *so* much. I miss Isabella. I miss our house, our bed. I miss Harper." With a light kiss to her nose, I grinned. "I even miss your mother."

Laughing and rolling her eyes, she placed her forehead against my own one more time before pulling away. "I'll let that slide only once." She held up a finger.

"I love your mother." I used a somewhat convincing tone. She glared. "You know I do!"

"I know." She surveyed the tent and took in the scene. "This place is...depressing."

I observed the tent that had been my home for the past few years. "The lighting is rough, the colors are grim, and the smell is terrible. But I have started seeing more light than darkness in this space." I shrugged. "Well, until they carried you in."

"I don't know how you do it."

"Nor do I understand you being in the field." I squinted. "Have you had to...never mind. I don't want to know."

She put her hand on my forearm.

"War is a game of life or death. You either play the game of life or lose in the game of death." With a deep sigh, her face went dark. "I only took a life when needed to protect my fellow warriors or myself."

"That doesn't make it pleasant."

"I don't think I said it was." She stared ahead. "I won't lie...it has been tough."

"Um, excuse me?" someone asked from a few cots away.

"Yes?" I asked, standing to move toward them, though they looked fine. "Did you need a medic?"

"No." The young warrior shook his head, looking past me. "I wanted to say thank you to the Hero of Husk."

Perking up, I turned to face my wife, who looked around.

"Who? Me?" Valeria pointed to her chest.

"Yes, you." The young warrior smiled. "I owe you my life. You took over when the Kernel fell and kept us from dying." Pointing at Valeria, the warrior faced me. "We were outnumbered five to one with so many injured. She empowered those that could fight and took down over half the Coalitionists herself." Gesturing to the surrounded tent, the warrior continued, "If not for the Hero of Husk, the Coalition would've broken the line and destroyed this place."

A crimson flushed across Valeria's cheeks. She sat up a little straighter as a smile curled up her cheeks. "I'm sure you would do the same."

Sitting as straight up in his cot as he could, he nodded to her. "To the Hero of Husk." The young warrior pounded his chest with his fist and raised it in the air.

Valeria repeated his movement and stared at the warrior as a medic came up to check his vitals. The last time Valeria's face lit up like that was when Isabella was born. Whether coming to Husk was the correct call, the warrior pride within my bride went unmatched. She did something good, and I knew the pride would carry her on, even if it meant going back home.

Widening my eyes, I stared at Valeria, a tension moving up my back. Had she really fought that many Coalitionists? Had she killed them?

Noticing my gaze, Valeria's smile faded. Before her confidence wavered, I said, "I'm proud of you." I patted my fist against my chest and raised in the air. "To the Hero of Husk."

Fluttering her eyes, Valeria looked back at me. "I can't believe that just happened. I have to tell Aameen about it."

The strangest jealousy crept into my chest. "Were you stationed with Aameen?"

"Si. He has emerged as quite the commander. It is said he may get the role of Kernel soon."

"He has certainly become close with the Kernels." My eyes shifted to the side.

"You have to. They are in charge of us." She eyed me. "Why do you sound so...irritated with him?"

I sat back down on the side of her bed. "He approached me right before you woke up. I told him what I did to save your life, and he immediately wanted me to tell the Krown Kernel about my abilities, to use them as a weapon."

"A weapon?"

I lowered my voice. "I...killed someone with it. Remember?"

"Hm..." She observed me. "Do you think you could?"

My mouth fell open. Aameen surprised me with his intentions. But Valeria?

"V, even if I could, I would never."

She noticed my discomfort and touched the side of my arm. "Ciro, I admire your heart and desire for healing, but the amount of death happening out there is significant." She bit her lip. "There is word that the Coalition may have the numbers to cut east and then south to attack Cornia. That could endanger so many more." Squeezing my arm, she tilted her head. "What if this could be prevented?"

I stared back at her, unsure about her response.

Is she the same Valeria I married? Has the war changed her? Or am I being callous? What if they're right? What if I could prevent more death?

"I need to think about it," I said. "I don't know if I could even do it again."

Kernel Ofelia walked up as soon as I said this. "But we can practice it."

"Practice?" I asked.

"Yes, practice," Kernel Ofelia answered. She looked over at Valeria and held out her hand. "Hello, my name is Kernel Ofelia. I have heard so much about you. The Hero of Husk." She placed a fist on her chest and raised it up. "It's an honor. You two are a powerful pair. You have quite the amazing husband here."

A soft blush radiated from Valeria. "I'm Valeria. Ciro has written high praises about you. Mucho gusto."

They smiled at one another before Kernel Ofelia turned back toward me. "I have thought about it. It may be a little sketchy, but I think we can practice on beasts. Then, work our way...up."

"Practice on beasts?" I exclaimed. "That's terrible." When had everyone become so grim with their intentions?

Kernel Ofelia leaned forward and whispered, "Would you rather practice on people?"

"This is becoming dark so fast," I said. "I don't think I can do it." My head ached from the pressure put on me.

"Ciro," Valeria began, "our goal is to protect Isabella. I don't want to pressure you into something you don't want to do, but think about it. This could help prevent the Coalition from making a move against the capital. You said you would do anything to protect her."

I felt Isabella's folded-up drawing in my pocket. My entire existence was dedicated to Isabella's safety.

I was confused. I tried to be as wise as I could, but it seemed like either scenario resulted in death. I craved who I was a few days ago—just a healer.

"It still might not work," I said.

"But you will try?" Kernel Ofelia asked.

"I don't know," I admitted. "This is going against who I am and who you trained me to be."

"I understand," Kernel Ofelia said. "Can you at least try tomorrow and see how you feel afterward?"

The question gave me great pause. Kernel Ofelia only suggested I try. It wasn't like I was joining the war as a warrior. I wasn't agreeing to anything.

Groaning, I stood up. "Fine. I will try."

"Great," Kernel Ofelia said. "Tomorrow."

I looked around the tent again, at the hope in all the healing. Kernel Ofelia and I lived in this same environment together, helping people. What could make her want to inflict pain on others? Was war only about hurting and killing?

I thought I had only come to the war to heal and keep myself and my family safe. Maybe they were goals that couldn't be obtained all at once.

Maybe I had to do some things I didn't want to.

CHAPTER 10
THE PRICE OF WAR

I'd finally had too much of the cot. Whatever it did to my back that night, the pain was too much for me to manage.

How do patients sleep on these things? Sleeping on the ground would've been more restful.

I stretched, releasing some of the tension with a loud crack, and sat up. The medics performed their morning runs. A symphony of pens writing on paper echoed throughout the tent. Most nights, we were too exhausted to make long notes, so the mornings were a brief time to catch up. Note-taking proved important in case the assigned medic became unavailable during other parts of the day.

Valeria yawned next to me. I turned to my side, fluttering my eyes open while rubbing, and jumped at an unexpected sight. Kernel Ofelia leaned over my body, her face inches from mine.

"Morning," she said with a glowing smile. "I was just about to wake you. What convenient timing. We need to train, and they need this cot for an incoming warrior."

"What in the Maizean hell?" I rubbed my eyes further and rose from the cot. Ofelia laughed.

After I changed my shirt, I looked down at the cot that had held both my body and Eduardo's. Placing my hand on the cot one last time, I vowed to find his family someday and tell them about his last words.

A chill rushed across my skin as I thought about the patient who would fill the bed next. I hoped we would do better for them. I hoped I would do better.

"I think that was the most you've slept since I've been here," Valeria said, making my heart nearly leap out of my chest.

"It's depressing to think I slept so well the night before I learn how to hurt people," I said.

"Your body needed it," Valeria said.

A little hum escaped me and warmed my chest. I leaned over and kissed her cheek. "You're a wise woman, V. Don't get too bored without me."

"I don't know how anyone could ever be *bored* in this tent." Pulling me close, she kissed me, letting her lips linger just enough to tease me as she pushed me back and patted my chest. "Stay true to yourself today."

Outside the tent, the sun peeked over the horizon, a mist covering the ground. The morning humidity coated my skin in sweat before the air cooled it. The dew invigorated the local scents, a mixture of fresh crops and the pungent odor of war. Maize, the beautiful.

"Ready?" Kernel Ofelia asked.

"I guess." I breathed in the strange air. My core relaxed with unexpected gratitude to be outside of the medical tent. "You don't need to come with me."

"The medical team can handle the tent. It's a slower day. Plus, I think having an outside perspective while navigating your newfound ability could be useful. I've observed you for a few years. Let me help."

"As you wish." I half-smiled. "Where are we going?"

"The small forest over there." She pointed southeast at a treeline. "I'm hoping to find more wildlife further from the battlefront."

The forest appeared ablaze, but I realized no fire existed, just the sun. Its orange light hit the forest, reflecting off the green leaves like fire. I hadn't noticed the forest before. The only times I looked in that direction were when I took a break, which wasn't often. It surprised me to have missed it, especially for how large it was—about fifty to one hundred trees scattered the area. Then again, I spent all my time in the tent or sleeping, not exploring the surrounding landscape.

I thought about the last few days. Death haunted my every action while life begged for my help. Looking back at Husk with a frown, I moved my gaze forward to the forest. An inappropriate smile forced itself past my glower. An odd energy pulsed through my veins, urging me toward the forest. I thought about Husk and the medical tent. Ofelia marched ahead of me, humming a song.

"What made you so callous with death?" I asked Ofelia, who glared back at me and shook her head. "Sorry, that came out harsh. I'm sleep-deprived and honestly overwhelmed. It's just...you seemed readily apt to use my ability to attack other people, which is the opposite of healing. This seems counterintuitive to both our natures."

She rubbed her neck.

"Give me a second to recover from the whiplash you just gave me." She kept rubbing before peeking through closed eyes and witnessed my lack of laughter. "Tough crowd." She grinned. "You're right, it does sound counterintuitive." She paused. "I'm a healer. I want to help others, no matter who they are. But I'm not *callous to death*. Sometimes, you're a bit dramatic. I do sit up at night, so many scenarios running through my mind. What if I healed the wrong person? What if I fought instead of running the medics? What if I could stop this war? What if it hurts other people? What if it could stop more Maizeans from being hurt and killed? Would I do it? Could I do it?"

Her vulnerability made me lose my breath. "I didn't realize you thought like this. I don't think about these things. I just think about my family."

"And I'm happy you have a family to worry about. I don't. I only think about Maize."

It was similar to the conversation I had with Count Ariba a few years before. I did everything for my family. Itching at my neck, I smirked at the thought.

"What would you do for Maize?" I asked.

"I would do what is counterintuitive to my nature...which is why I want to help you. I think we can both overcome our nature to ultimately help more people than we hurt."

"And what if we're wrong?"

"I cannot see how we would be."

"What if something worse happens from it?" The steady drumming of my heart intensified. I looked over at her. "I meant to save my wife when I moved the disease, and it ended up killing Eduardo." My stomach tied up again. "We're messing with fate and nature when we change or move disease. I'm not Gaia."

"You aren't, but what if Gaia gifted you for a reason?" She kicked at the ground, causing a burst of dust to go up into the air. "What if, with one movement, you could change the course of the war? What if you were given this ability to stop the war?"

I watched as the dust settled back to the ground. My posture relaxed and my shoulders slumped. "Gaia should have picked someone different then."

She huffed a laugh, leaning her head back. "You have to be more confident in yourself. Gaia picked you because you are strong. You have a good heart. You are a true healer." With a swift glance at me, she nodded. "But I hope I'm not forcing you into something you don't want to do. I trust your wisdom with this, but I think we should try."

"I guess." Kernel Ofelia respected the silence that followed as we walked under the rising sun.

Before I knew it, the distant treeline became a tall forest. The trees stood taller than most buildings in Husk. The trunks were large, covered in white bark. Birds and small beasts scurried in and out of the forest, unaware of the war nearby. The peaceful setting gave me great pause. Part of me just wanted to live in the forest and not go back. They wouldn't miss me. Kernel Ofelia closed her eyes and took a deep breath. I wondered if she thought the same.

"Now what?" I asked, a little ashamed to end the peace.

"Well…" she responded before dropping into silence, searching for something. Her face lit up. She ran over to a Furrowburrow. The little ball of fluff stood on four arched legs covered in short, white fur, with long ears flopping to each side. With its beady black eyes atop a flat whiskered nose, it darted its little head around. It stood no taller than my knees and gazed at Kernel Ofelia with a panicked face. Normally, these animals scurried away before you had a chance to catch them. The one before us breathed heavily. Bright green ribbons weaved through one of its arms, which was bent at a terrible angle. "This little beast seems to be sick."

"It has an infected arm," I confirmed. "I see bright green ribbons running along its arm."

"Wow." She squinted at the arm and sighed after she saw the leg. "I'm always shocked by the things you see."

"It's an infection I often see, though this one is quite a bit smaller."

She licked her lips. "Can you…move it?"

With my arms close to my sides, I glanced down at my hands. My fingertips tingled as I recalled the burning sensation with the purple flowers. Forming fists, I shook my head.

"I don't know…"

"Just try." She looked over at another beast. "And try to move it to another Furrowburrow."

"Last time I tried this, I moved it to Eduardo." I moved my hands behind my back. "I don't want the same thing to happen to you."

"I will move away." She backed up about ten steps, stopped, and crossed her arms. "Walk me through what happened with your wife."

The last thing I wanted to do was relive that moment. It had destroyed my mentality and still wreaked havoc on my confidence, scraping at my insides like a caged beast and forcing me to the ground, gasping for air.

"Well, I first tried to pull the purple flowers off one by one, but they replaced themselves each time right away." The little purple flowers grew across Valeria's leg in my mind. A brutal pain pierced my diaphragm, making it hard to breathe. I closed my eyes and took a steady breath. "I tried doing something different and swirled my hand to gather the disease into a ball." I mindlessly moved my hands like I did that night. "Each flower gravitated toward me." Purple flowers floated around in my head. "Once it was in my hands, it warmed up. The more and more I tried to hold on to it, the hotter the ball became. Until it was too hot to handle. So, I threw it to the side. And...you know the rest."

Arms still crossed, she raised her right hand and scratched at her chin. "It heated up?" I nodded. "Curious. Well, do the same thing, but this time focus on where you're throwing it. And maybe don't hold it as long?"

"Are you sure?"

"Sort of." She laughed. "I honestly have no idea what I'm doing, and I cannot do it myself. Let's just give it a shot."

"Okay." After committing to her request, my hands refused to move. An unrelenting tension made my joints stiff.

Ofelia just stood there, staring at me. I widened my eyes and tilted my head to the side. Her eyes brightened, realizing I waited for her to get farther away. She ran far enough from any crossfire but close enough to observe.

I focused on the Furrowburrow. It was so small and shook as I stared, eyes tightly shut and wincing in pain. No fear, just pain. It needed to be healed. The bright green ribbons shone even brighter as I approached the animal. I forced my hand forward despite the stiffness and swirled my fingers. The green ribbons danced off the beast's body and over to me much more easily than the purple flowers had.

A little ball formed until there were no ribbons left on the Furrowburrow. Its eyes brightened. My hand heated up, bearable at first. I searched the area and had to put the disease elsewhere. Another Furrowburrow drank water by a pond. I threw the ball at the new beast. The green ribbon ball darted to its new host in one quick streak, hitting the Furrowburrow. The green ribbons latched onto its front leg.

"I did it!" I exclaimed as Kernel Ofelia ran over to me. My heart fluttered, making me feel as if I floated above the ground.

The original, diseased Furrowburrow walked, using its once-infected arm to move across the ground at its normal speed. The arm stretched out as if never broken. Only then did I realize the infection caused the bend, not a fracture. It chirped in delight and ran off.

"Wow!" Kernel Ofelia yelled. "That is amazing!"

As I grinned at my accomplishment, I heard sharp chirps and groans from the pond. My eyes drifted to the new Furrowburrow, chirps morphing into agonizing screams. Any happiness I felt seeped out of my body.

"Where did you throw it?" Kernel Ofelia asked.

I raised my right hand and pointed to the new, sick Furrowburrow. My hand shook in the air and my chest tightened as I recounted what I had just done.

"It was healthy moments ago." My words felt cold.

"This means it worked." Her words came off just as cold.

Kernel Ofelia joined me as we stared at the suffering beast, my heart aching with each scream of pain.

"Now what?"

"I guess you keep practicing."

A cold silence fell between us. The chirps of agony filled the quiet void.

"This doesn't feel right."

Kernel Ofelia shook her head, trying to refocus. "But it worked and will save lives." Her voice brightened. "You will do a lot of good with this. You just have to believe it!" I tried, but all I wanted to do was vomit. As if noticing my physical discomfort, she reminded me of my primary purpose. "It's to save your family. To save your daughter. We need this, Ciro. Push past your guilt. Try again."

An internal pressure formed while I held my breath. It was best to push away the guilt, but a pit curled up in my throat. After I could no longer hold my breath, I gasped for air, and the pit dissolved.

Without hesitation, I swirled my hand, taking the infection from the new host. The ball sat in my hand, and I shot it toward another Furrowburrow and then another. The infection grew hotter and hotter the more I repeated the exercise. After ten shifts, it landed upon a Furrowburrow, but this time the bright green ribbons turned a deep red. As soon as it latched onto its new host, the animal went limp. The infection faded. The animal's eyes shut.

Hand still burning, I fell to my knees and gasped for air. My ears buzzed as I stared at the limp beast. A voice echoed around me, but sounded muffled. It became clearer and clearer.

"Ciro!" Kernel Ofelia yelled. "Where did it go?"

Raising my still burning hand, I pointed at the limp Furrowburrow. "That one. The...dead one."

"Oh..." Kernel Ofelia's voice faded again as the buzzing took over.

I gripped my leg and pinched myself, trying to distract myself from the terrible pit in my gut. Maybe it was all a dream. Maybe I'd open my eyes and still be in the medical tent, lying on that cot. Forcing my eyes back open, the dead beast still lay before me.

"The beast is dead." All the emotion left my voice. "I don't see another infection. I don't want to keep doing this."

Kernel Ofelia looked over at me like I looked at Isabella when she was upset. "This is enough for now. We should get back and help the medic tent anyway."

I said something in return, but didn't remember what. A coldness lifted me and moved my body outside the forest, Ofelia at my side.

We walked back to the medical tent in silence. Recalling the green ribbons and the way the disease moved at my command perplexed me. The pit in my throat returned, but it shifted to my stomach and morphed. An odd sensation transpired. Nothing to do with vomiting or wanting to fall over. It transformed into a surge of confidence. Though not happy about it, I felt...powerful.

"I did that," I said.

Kernel Ofelia looked over at me but said nothing. She just patted my shoulder and kept walking.

Once we arrived back at the tent, Kernel Ofelia stepped in front of me. "Listen, I'm proud of what you just did, but keep yourself grounded."

Was she envious of me? The warning caught me off guard, reminding me of all the terrible things that had occurred from my gift. "I will. I promise."

"Okay, good. I think tomorrow we will try—"

A boom came from the west. A small group of soldiers charged toward the medical tent.

"The Coalition!" Kernel Ofelia yelled. "Ambush!"

CHAPTER II
THE AMBUSH

The medics poured out of the tent, wielding hammers and shovels.

Kernel Ofelia ran over to one of the several hidden garrisons she had scattered throughout Husk. Sword in hand, she charged toward the Coalitionists.

The black and dark brown leather tunics of the Coalitionists were stark against the white tent. Their black sticks with spiked balls on the end whipped in the air with each swing.

We collided with the attackers in a clanging barrage of metal on metal. I counted at least a dozen Coalitionists. Though a small group, it was trained warriors against medics who didn't see combat.

Planned protocol called for eight medics to leave the tent and defend. The rest protected the interior in case of a breach.

Two Coalitionists made it past our eight defenders and into the tent's entrance opposite the one I stood at. I ran into the tent as fast as I could.

Bones crunched as the Coalitionists attacked the healing warriors. Blood sprayed against the white tent. Shrieks echoed all around.

The medics within charged forward. The Coalitionists moved faster. With one swing, one of the medic's necks snapped. Another medic was stabbed in the throat. The jugular artery sprayed blood like a fountain while the medic tried to contain it.

I ran to Valeria as she screamed, "What's going on?" She tried to stand but winced and grabbed her leg.

"Sit down!" I pushed down her shoulders. "You're in no shape to fight."

"I can't just sit and watch them slaughter us." She grunted. "I'm the Hero of Husk!"

Her words echoed in my head. I can't just sit here and watch.

As if beckoned, the bright green ribbons shone brighter than ever, dancing among our bedridden warriors. Nothing too severe, but enough to work with.

I ran forward and swirled each of my hands at my sides. The green ribbons rushed to each hand, forming two small balls. I hurled them at the Coalitionists. One ball struck the first in the head. My target gripped at his eyes, screaming.

"I can't see!" the Coalitionist exclaimed. "My eyes are burning!"

A medic to my right struck the now-blind Coalitionist across the head with a metal rod normally used to hold bags of antibiotics. With a dented head, the enemy toppled over.

The second ball struck the other Coalitionist in the left leg. It swelled like a balloon. Another medic used this opportunity to stab the Coalitionist in the head with a scalpel. The medic continued to stab, blood spraying on their face, until the enemy stopped moving.

I ran to the other end of the tent, past the Coalitionists' bodies.

Exiting the tent, I found only four of our medics, including Kernel Ofelia, standing against six remaining Coalitionists. I pulled at green ribbons from a nearby patient behind me. Instead of throwing one big ball of green ribbons, I shot out tiny balls of disease at the Coalitionists.

My little green balls of destruction struck each Coalitionist in the head. A white film covered each of their eyes. Green ribbons weaved in and out of their eyelids.

The remaining medics attacked my targets with swords and shovels.

A Coalitionist to my right took a spear and hurled it straight at me. I swirled my hands as if it'd do something, but the spear didn't stop. My body tensed, ready for impact.

Out of nowhere, a stretch of white streaked from behind and smacked the spear to the ground.

Gasping for air, I found a Shapple holding the spear and hurling it back at the Coalitionist, striking them in the chest. The Shapple let out a groan, nodded to me, and walked off.

My morning Shapple friend saved me.

The medics surrounded the two remaining panicked Coalitionists. They were easily captured and tied up.

I pivoted around, scanning the buildings for any stray enemies. My heart pounded so loud, I worried it might explode. I found no one else. Releasing little quick breaths, my heart rate slowed, but my fingers still tingled.

Kernel Ofelia marched over to me. "Was that a Shapple?" She shook her head. "Never mind that." Leaning in close, she whispered, "Did you just attack them with...disease?"

I took a deep breath, blood rushing to my head. "I...I did." My voice shook like my body. "I took them all down."

She looked over at the medics staring at us. "There are going to be a lot of questions. Let me do the talking."

The pit formed in my throat again and made its way to my stomach. I toppled to my knees, staring at the bodies in front of me. Turning away to avoid the weight, I watched the Shapple walk past the tent entrance. Inside, the other two bodies lay in pools of blood.

What did I just do? Why...why did it feel so natural?

Kernel Ofelia helped me to my feet, walked me into the tent, and brought me over to Valeria.

"Are you okay?" Valeria asked. "What happened?"

"Keep it down," Kernel Ofelia whispered. "Any questions are to be directed my way. Ciro, sit down next to your wife. Take a breather."

Sitting on the edge of Valeria's cot, I avoided eye contact. If I looked into her eyes, it'd make it all real. My wife had been the first person I moved disease away from. Now, I was a—

"Ciro." Valeria touched my cheek and guided my face. "Look at me. Are you okay?"

Copper eyes pulled my own eyes in. As soon as our gazes locked, tears released.

"Valeria..." I said between sobs. "I...I..."

"Shh," she said, leaning forward. My head collapsed into her chest. She patted me on the back of the head and whispered, "It's okay. Tranquilo tu mente. Keep your mind still."

With each pat on my back, she grazed her fingernails along my spine. Her movements slowed until they stopped.

"Ciro," she said. "Did you just kill those Abolitionist attackers??"

I forgot how to breathe. Trying to steady my chest, I forced out air to let more in. "I...I did." I cried more.

"Más tranquilo," she whispered. "Quieter voice."

She was right. I replied in a panicked whisper. "I just took the infections and threw them. It happened so fast. It came so naturally. I killed them."

She took my head from her chest and held my cheeks. "Listen to me. You saved so many lives just now. They were attacking the injured and weak. You are supposed to heal, but you are also supposed to protect. You did everything right today."

She was right. They were the enemy, and they attacked defenseless warriors while they slept. With terrible acts come terrible consequences.

Aameen was right. How long would it be until they did this type of thing to Cornia? What would stop them from attacking defenseless citizens? Defenseless children? Isabella?

"We have to stop them!" I exclaimed. She put a finger to her mouth. "You're right," I whispered. "Aameen is right. I must do what I can to stop this war as soon as possible."

Her eyes softened. "Calm down. You're running on adrenaline."

My veins pulsed at each rapid heartbeat slamming at my sternum. I sat up, energized. "I'm running on the desire to protect. It's the right thing to do."

"Ciro..." She let go of my cheeks. She looked at me like she didn't recognize me.

Kernel Ofelia walked up before any more could be said between Valeria and me. Ofelia crouched down and whispered, "I have curbed many of the questions."

"How?" Valeria asked.

"I said that Ciro is part of the Gaia family line," Kernel Ofelia said.

"What?" Valeria exclaimed.

"Quiet..." Kernel Ofelia reminded her.

How did my life become part of a story? The Gaia family line lived in Conifera, Avi Ahi, and other areas across the sea. The story said that some sisters were blessed with gifts, giving them supernatural abilities that passed down to their descendants. Some believed it to be true, but most of the family's history seemed more of a tale.

"You're saying Ciro is part of a children's story?" Valeria asked in a quiet yet firm voice.

"Would you rather I say he can move disease?" Kernel Ofelia pushed back.

Valeria fell silent.

"So now people think I'm special, and I can...what? Throw mind tricks?" I asked.

"Cause temporary blindness," Kernel Ofelia answered.

"That's absurd," I rebutted.

"Everything you have done is absurd," Kernel Ofelia said. "I needed to tell a lie to protect what you can actually do."

Running my fingers through my hair, I pressed my lips together and tried to suppress the pressure building on my forehead. I understood keeping things a secret before, but saying that I have another gift to keep my real one hidden?

"But why? Why can't we just tell the truth at this point?"

"Ciro, we need to protect you. There are many people seeking greater power in Maize," Kernel Ofelia said. "Your gift can cause irrevocable damage if guided down the wrong path."

My head ached as I shook my head. "I would never."

"Earlier today, you said you would never kill," Valeria said. I glared over at her. "Now what?"

She's right. I'm causing damage. Is this the wrong path?

"This will all settle," Kernel Ofelia said. "We need to get this mess cleaned up. I'm planning to bring you to the battlefront tomorrow."

"You're what?" Valeria slammed her hands on her cot. "It's too soon."

Though hearing it said shocked me just as it did Valeria, I knew it'd be the next step. My skin cooled and my muscles relaxed. What other choice did I have? If I wanted to protect Cornia and my family, I had to protect Maize's border.

I took Valeria's hands and looked into her deep, fire eyes. "V, you said I have to do everything I can to help end this war. Kernel Ofelia is right. It's time for me to fight. The medical team is looking at me in terror. I just want to get this over with and go home. I want to hold Isabella."

Valeria blinked away tears. "But what if you get hurt? The point of all of this was to *stay safe*."

I laughed. "Funny, coming from you." Though it came off harsh, I didn't intend it to. I held Valeria's hands. "What this attack just showed me is that the Coalition will hurt anyone in any way they can. It's only a matter of time before they send soldiers to Cornia. They could hurt children." I paused and cried a little. "They could hurt Isabella. I will go and end this war. You need to go home and heal."

"I was going to say you were ready to leave tomorrow anyway." Kernel Ofelia stood up. "We can get you on the next cart to Cornia." Valeria smiled her thanks at my Kernel, tears still lining her eyes. Ofelia patted me on the shoulder and walked away.

"Ciro..." Valeria said, squeezing my hands. "I can't leave you. I must protect you."

"You've always protected me. You're the backbone of our family. You hold us all together. You keep us strong and have made me stronger." I patted my chest with a fist and raised it in the air. "It's now my time to do something. Please let me do this, Hero of Husk."

Valeria leaned forward and kissed me. The passion flowed between us, carried by breath and heat. We continued to kiss. As she moved her lips away from mine, she lingered for a moment before fully pulling away.

"Okay. I'll go home. I'll hold Isabella. But you *will* come home as soon as you can."

"Prometo. I promise I'll come home as soon as I do all I can."

She pulled me close. Though terror of the future haunted us, the excitement of the next steps made my skin tingle. Her body so close to mine only enhanced the sensation. I wanted to make love to her. Once again, the medical tent proved an inappropriate place for our union.

The medics finished cleaning, repairing, and moving the bodies out of the tent area. Kernel Ofelia assured me I just needed to rest. I wanted to help, but she was right.

Valeria and I didn't talk much. We only sat in each other's company. The sun set, and we shared a meal together. I spent every moment I could absorbing her beauty and her copper eyes. I wanted them to haunt my every moment until the next time I saw her. It reminded me of our couch back home, sitting quietly next to our daughter and Talonhound. If it went the way I expected, I would be back in that scene soon enough. I patted Isabella's drawing in my pocket, willing her art into existence.

Real war approached us. It had changed me so much already, but darker decisions lay on the horizon. I hoped I would still be the same man Valeria had loved all this time. A man who could move disease.

CHAPTER 12
THE RAINBOW FLOWER

Eight, nine, ten, eleven...

I watched the diseases dance over to their bodies.

Twelve, thirteen, fourteen, fifteen...

Legs collapsed in sudden weakness. Eyes became cloudy as they lost their sight.

Sixteen, seventeen, eighteen, nineteen...

They were either shot dead or escorted off by other Coalition soldiers.

The number of deaths I caused grew by the day. After the first week, the numbers shocked me. After a month of fighting, I grew numb. Aameen told me not to count, but I kept counting. It was the only way to keep me present and aware of what I was doing. Because what I was doing wasn't me.

I have to protect my family. I have to protect my family.

I continually reminded myself why I did what I did. I even began poking at my pocket with Isabella's folded drawing to remind myself of my motives. It still didn't make it feel right. Nothing about it felt right. The Maizean warriors who fought alongside me were taking lives. That was what war was—continuous death and fighting. Why should I feel like what I did was worse than what others did? The Coalition soldiers were doing the same thing. We were all doing the same thing.

That didn't make it feel right.

The lie Kernel Ofelia made up had sped across the battlefront. She called me one of Gaia's descendants, given a gift from the goddess herself, a lie we could use to our advantage. Our initial lie, that I could cause blindness, faded as our warriors saw me kill Coalitionists in other ways. What my gift was remained unknown, and no one dared to ask me. Instead, our warriors looked at me with admiration. It also meant they protected me at all costs.

No matter how much I missed having Kernel Ofelia around me every day, I needed to keep fighting and keep the medical tent clear of victims.

Being right on the battlefront next to the wooden blockades, it gave me an ample amount of disease to use as a weapon. New colors and shapes taught me about illnesses I hadn't run into before, diseases most seemed unaware they had.

There was an orange bell that spiraled around the chest. I had to pull all this disease off in one attempt. If I didn't, the portion I held would just snap back to its host. When I threw it at a target, a long, flat orange piece would stretch out and often hit two or three warriors at once, infecting each. I didn't know exactly what the disease was, but it limited the ability to breathe. No longer in the medical tent, I just had to throw the disease, not learn about it. The victim would gasp for air and fall forward. The curious part was that the original host didn't seem to have trouble breathing like the victims did. Part of me thought they were already used to its symptoms.

Another disease appeared to me as a red, serpent-like shape. This disease slithered around the waist. It seemed to always be moving, but never ventured away from the waist. I could pull the red worm off in chunks and shoot it at new enemies. Intense vomiting followed infection. Maybe an intestinal disease?

Besides the normal green ribbons from basic infections, the most common disease consisted of tiny pink dots. They formed around ears, noses, eyes, and other areas—common in the medical tent. I tried moving the dots, but they seemed to have little impact. Almost as if they dissolved during transit.

After every ten to fifteen minutes of attacking, I had to take a break. My endurance became better, but being the master of disease and death was an exhausting role. Though moving the diseases in smaller doses allowed me to do more, the action still depleted my energy.

"I'm going to take a break," I said to one of the warriors assigned to me.

"I shall escort you, Co-Kernel Ciro," the warrior announced.

Another new thing was my title: Co-Kernel, or a step below Kernel. The funny thing was that there were no other Co-Kernels. Though no one said it, I believed the title was made up for just me.

Once the warrior brought me to the war tents off the battlefront, I entered to find Aameen looking over letters and maps. After barely seeing him for a few years, I now saw him every day. His armor was dull in the dim tent. A few torches blazed in the cramped space, and a table and chairs sat in the middle of the tent. Sheets of war plans were scattered across the table.

"It's busy out there today."

"It is, *Co-Kernel Ciro.*" Aameen nodded.

My best friend had become obsessed with titles. Especially when it involved pointing out his own, which he expected every warrior to use when addressing him.

"*Kernel Aameen*, I'm sorry." I entertained his ego. "I'm still getting used to your new position."

One of the war Kernels had recently been killed in battle. In fact, the Kernel was killed in the breach that had allowed the Coalitionists to ambush the medical tent. It was the biggest breach Maize had seen yet. To make matters more stressful, the Coalitionist army continued to replenish every soldier they lost. Our army couldn't keep up.

Aameen had remained the only troop leader not to lose warriors at the rate of the others. Thus, the title of Kernel was well earned and fit his personality better than I expected.

Aameen smiled. "How has the first week in the war zone been?"

Gravity and fatigue weighed my head down. I wanted to collapse, but there was no time to rest. The warriors needed me—it was said that the line assigned to me, the main battlefront, had the largest spike in Coalition fatalities. My triumph was important to our cause, but the deaths weigh on my conscience.

"It's still draining," I confessed. "If it weren't for how tired my mind was, I feel like my head would consume itself."

He glanced up. "You are still counting deaths."

I sighed. "I can't stop doing it."

"How many?"

I resisted the urge to cry by pursing my lips together with every muscle in my face.

"Ninety-four."

Aameen's eyes widened before they returned to their regular size. "You are doing good work for Maize."

"Very good work," a deep voice said from behind. I turned to see Krown Kernel Fernando entering the tent. He was dressed in the same armor as Aameen, but his glistened with a better polish. His presence sent a shiver down my spine. "You've taken down an impressive number of enemies."

I stood erect, my spine snapping into place, and saluted. "Krown Kernel. My duty is to serve Maize."

"Relax." Krown Kernel Fernando patted me on the back, which felt more like a punch. "Your new status gives extra perks, Co-Kernel. You only have to be formal when we are around the big group. In this tent, you can view me as somewhat of an equal."

The first time Krown Kernel Fernando recognized me, a new fire of confidence burned inside me. But now, the same fire didn't burn inside of me. A sharp chill coated my veins and made my head hurt.

"An equal?" I asked.

"More or less." Krown Kernel Fernando patted my back again and snorted. He was so jolly for being at the battlefront. I think it gave him joy. "How is your line holding, Kernel Aameen?"

"Their numbers are still strong," Aameen responded. "I know my warriors will hold, but I'm not sure what we will do if their numbers keep increasing."

"Very true," Krown Kernel Fernando acknowledged. "They must be pulling in more soldiers from the desert tribes. Which is why I am sending you to Solara's capital."

"Sol?" Aameen looked shocked. "For what reason?"

"To plead for Solara's assistance," Krown Kernel Fernando said. "As much as your leadership and Co-Kernel Ciro's talents are proving effective, we need our allies to support us. The Coalition's numbers keep increasing, and we cannot match the growth. It is most problematic."

I recalled glimpses of my home country of Solara, of tall buildings reaching high into the sky, and the sun statue sitting atop the highest tower, reflecting sunlight in every direction. I had heard rumors that the sun statue shined brighter than ever before, according to rumors.

Nothing had changed since the war began—Solara had an alliance with both the Coalition and Maize. We both neighbored Solara, Maize to the east of Solara and the Coalition to the north. Though the Sun Tower may have changed, the Solareons wouldn't change their mind. But Krown Kernel Fernando had a grin on his face.

"Has something changed that I am unaware of?" Aameen asked, glancing over at the Krown Kernel's odd grin. "My understanding was that the Sol monarchy was staying out of this war."

"That is why you will be talking to Kuraka Amaru," Krown Kernel Fernando said.

"Who?" Aameen asked.

"The head of foreign affairs," Krown Kernel Fernando said. "We have been writing. His twins, who were born during an eclipse, have some...interesting abilities. It is said they are powered by the sun and moon."

"Interesting abilities?" I asked.

"Yes," Krown Kernel Fernando responded. "Gifts that are...similar to the gift of another person I know." He nodded to me. "Kuraka Amaru would like to align our powers together."

"You mentioned me to them?" I asked. Krown Kernel Fernando just smiled.

When did I become an object used in bartering?

"Why would we inquire with Kuraka Amaru instead of with the Sol monarchy directly?" Aameen asked. "And why send me? It seems the leaders should meet with one another, not their lower commanders."

"Second in command meeting with second in command," Krown Kernel Fernando said. "It raises fewer flags and fosters communication with a strong ally."

Aamen squinted. "You are talking treason within Sol."

"I'm simply talking about getting an ally we desperately need," Krown Kernel Fernando said.

"Stena Mezca should be the one making this call," Aameen said. Krown Kernel Fernando chortled and handed a letter to Aameen. Aameen glanced over the letter. "I see. Maize sees this as an opportunity."

"To win a war we are losing," Krown Kernel Fernando said. "Whatever happens in Sol after this isn't our concern. Their inner dynamics are shifting. We will benefit and push the Coalition back. They cannot handle two armies. We all know Solara is much larger and more powerful than us both."

Aameen sighed. "When do I leave?"

"Tonight," Krown Kernel Fernando said. "Co-Kernel Ciro will be able to handle this area. He has already proved it. And Kernel Aameen..."

"Yes, sir?"

"Remember: What you do in Sol will prove you're up for higher positions back in Cornia," the Krown Kernel said. "A position may be opening soon. I have received word that Count Ariba's sickness has taken a turn for the worse. I can put in a good word with Stena Mezca."

"Yes, Krown Kernel." Aameen stood up, looked over at me, and nodded. He tripped on one of the chairs before exiting the tent, an uncharacteristic, clumsy mistake by my friend.

"Now, I must pay visits to the other battlefront sectors," Krown Kernel Fernando said. He gripped my shoulders and held me in front of his gaze, his brown eyes piercing me. "If my sources are accurate, there is a strong push coming soon. The Coalition plans to overwhelm one portion of our fronts to finally break us down. If it comes your way, remember to do *everything* you possibly can to protect the battlefront. Your friends, your family, and your country need you to hold. Am I clear?"

"Yes, Krown Kernel."

He smiled and let go of me, then left. I released a breath I didn't realize I was holding.

I thought of Count Ariba. Her sickness had taken a turn for the worse. I remembered our conversation about her loneliness. It had been a few years since our last interaction, but I had truly looked forward to a friendship with her.

Gaia, please protect her.

I hoped my prayer would do something.

Exiting the tent, I found a different warrior stationed outside. He began to follow me.

"Co-Kernel Ciro, what should the front be doing now?" the warrior asked me. I turned to the young man, about nineteen or twenty years old. He stared at me, waiting. "I will inform the other lieutenants of your orders."

That's right, I'm in command now.

"Right, yes... We will keep the same positions. Our goal is to hold this front as long as we can. We have a good position. I don't want to lose it."

"Yes, Co-Kernel." The warrior saluted and marched off.

I went back into the frontline and continued my normal actions: Move disease, infect Coalitionists, and keep count of my victims. Rinse and repeat.

Before I knew it, another week had passed. Then another. My routine stayed the same, but eventually I lost count. I gave up or became too numb to keep track.

The Coalition was relentless. They pushed harder to take our fertile land. But the more I thought about it, the more the bloodshed didn't make sense. The more I thought about it, the more I thought they had other motives than simply taking our land.

My battlefront continued to stand strong as Coalitionists seemed to sprout from the ground. They pushed our front back with their increased numbers, but we were able to regain ground. If the push was what Krown Kernel Fernando mentioned, it wasn't too bad. It made me think the war would be over soon. We were handling the situation.

Though my troops were fighting well, I was facing a new problem, something I didn't know how to handle. The number of diseases I had to work with diminished. It made sense since I pulled them from our warriors. Each time I took a disease away, I healed them. Healed soldiers didn't have diseases. It was a bit of an ironic problem to have. In the medical tent, my accomplishment would've been a great achievement, but the warrior version of myself needed more. I resorted to using the pink dots from ear, nose, and eye infections to at least distract our enemy, an ineffective strategy.

What good am I if I can't do the only thing that I'm good at?

Every time I tried something else with the pink dots, nothing new happened. I grew angrier and angrier with my lack of results. One day, my frustration took over, and I held the pink dots in my hand for longer than I normally did. They grew hotter and hotter as I decided which Coalitionist would be my next target.

What's the point? This ball isn't going to do anything.

I held the pink dots until I couldn't take the pain anymore. I chucked the mass into the air. It arched across the sky like a falling star, then struck my target in the head. His face blistered and turned bright red.

He screamed and screamed while pulling at his face in horror. Before I knew it, he scratched the skin off of his face. The terror continued until he dropped to his knees, his hands limp at his side, and fell face-first onto the ground. The pink dots swarmed his head like flies on a dead animal until they flickered away.

Then I realized it...he was dead.

What did I do?

My body shook with terror. My hands still felt like they were on fire, burning away every living thing they came into contact with.

"Co-Kernel!" a warrior yelled and yanked me to the ground. An arrow zipped past my head and lodged into the barricade just above me. "Sir! You have to watch out. You can't just stand there."

"I'm sorry." I stared at my hands again.

The warrior rose from the ground and shot an arrow at the soldier who had nearly shot me.

What just happened? Did I just amplify the disease?

Curiosity overtook the disdain I had for myself. I stood back up and found another pink dot infestation. I swirled my hand, the ball formed, and I let it sit as my hand as it warmed up. Instead of throwing one big ball, I split it up and tossed it at several enemies. The balls struck five of them.

Like the first target, the Coalitionists screamed and clawed at their eyes. A barrage of arrows from my warriors flew toward the Coalitionists, and the screaming finally ceased. An unexpected smile formed on my face.

That's new.

Leaning on my toes, I bounced from side to side, a new desire to count my victims sprouting again. It barely took any energy to use the pink dots. Not only did I have a newfound weapon in my arsenal, but I could be more efficient. I could kill more Coalitionists with less work.

Will this be the final push?

Hope and confidence returned. The war would be won.

From the north, a great horn sounded, interrupting my excitement.

A herd of hooved beasts appeared on the horizon, charging in our direction. Countless soldiers in brown uniforms stampeded toward us. The wave Krown Kernel Fernando warned of.

What am I going to do? I can't just sit here and wait. We need help.

"The four of you!" I yelled to the warriors surrounding me. "Come here at once!" They all ran over. I pointed at the two warriors always closest to me. One was a young man with a scar running down his right cheek. The other was a woman around my age, slender and lanky. "The two of you, run down the battlefront and tell as many of our warriors as you can that a large wave is coming toward us. They must fall back to our main battalion and form a line. Go! Now!" One ran in each direction, jumping onto Mountiffs and speeding off. I looked at the two remaining warriors and knew the younger boy ran fast. "You, run to the Krown Kernel's battalion. Tell him the wave is here. Run as fast as you can!" He grabbed a Mountiff and sprinted south.

"And you," I said to the last warrior. "Tell the northern battalion to send all they can our way. Go!" He ran off with another Mountiff.

For the first time since arriving, I was alone and vulnerable, peeking around the barricade at the incoming charge. Based on a very rough estimate, the Coalition wave would reach us in ten to twenty minutes. The warriors I sent to gather more aid wouldn't be back in time. My mind was blank, and my body stood idly, waiting for impact.

You can't just sit here, Ciro. You at least need to fight.

Rounding the barricade's corner, I grabbed more pink dots from surrounding warriors and Coalitionists and held them tightly, chucking them at my enemy once they warmed. I continued this pattern, striking down the enemies near me before they were fortified.

"Shoot them!" I yelled to the Blanche warriors flying above.

Arrows rained down on the infected Coalitionists. One by one, their bodies fell to the ground. One by one, the pink dots flickered away.

The Coalition charge came closer and closer. Impact was imminent. Panic took root. My eyes surveyed the battlefront, and I grabbed more pink dots and threw them when hot enough. No matter how many more Coalitionists I struck down, we were severely outnumbered.

Valeria and Isabella's faces flickered in my mind. Valeria smiled with fiery eyes. Isabella giggled and twirled around.

Will I see their faces again? Is this the end?

Then, I saw the last thing I wanted to see—purple flowers. Eduardo appeared lying on the ground behind a barricade, but it couldn't be. His body flickered into Valeria's, covered in the blooms.

Am I losing my mind?

I rubbed my eyes, hoping to wipe away the insanity. When I reopened them, there was a Coalitionist hiding behind the barricade. His body was covered in purple flowers. He held his side where the purple was deepest.

Hyperventilating, I turned away. My eyes shifted to the right at the incoming Coalition wave. There were so many of them. I couldn't breathe.

"Co-Kernel," a warrior said next to me. My eyes were blurry. I tried to focus on the warrior. "Co-Kernel. Another warrior met me on my way. The Krown Kernel received intel just before and is moving as fast as he can. He told me to tell you Sol is on its way."

The warrior appeared before me in pieces, like a puzzle coming together. "What...what did you say?"

"Sol is on its way."

"It can't be." Hope came flooding in again. I stood up with my new-found strength. "Warriors! Hold the line! We need more time!" I looked over at the warrior who reported to me. "How long?"

"Thirty minutes out," the warrior responded. "Maybe?"

Thirty minutes? We would need a miracle to hold that long. What if...

My gaze drifted to the purple flowers, a dark creation made of terror and grief. Whatever I did to the flower last time killed Eduardo almost instantly. I could do that again.

That would only take down one soldier.

A dark thought came to me.

What if I mixed as many diseases together as I could?

I shook my head.

I couldn't do that.

The Coalitionists were closing in.

I have to. I have to protect them. I have to protect my family.

My attention shifted to every disease in front of me. Pink dots drew into my swirling hands, forming into the familiar pink ball. New diseases covered the soldiers of the attacking army. Green ribbons, orange bells, and red worms. My hands were already burning, but I kept swirling them. The new disease joined the pink ball. Every disease before me now sat in my burning hands.

All but one—the purple flowers. I pulled the source of my nightmares into the multicolored ball. Static zapped in my hands from the growing heat. I screamed in pain. The ball felt so heavy, too big to throw at my distant enemies. I had to get closer. I started running toward the incoming army, the large ball pulling me back.

"Co-Kernel!" one warrior yelled.

"Stop, sir!" another yelled.

I kept running forward, carrying the enormous disease boulder. An arrow came hurling at me and struck me on the shoulder. I fell to the ground. The pain pulsing in my shoulder, the fire burning in my hands, and the shocks of the ball collided into one agonizing, deep atrocity.

It's now or never.

I screamed and pushed the giant boulder forward. It flew through the air, smoother than I expected, making its way toward my enemy. Arrows whipped past my head. I watched the multicolored mass begin to transform. The shapes all morphed into the flowers, covering the entire mass.

They crystallized, reflecting purple light in every direction. The purple faded as each petal became a different color. The gem-like casing covering each flower shattered, revealing rainbow flowers.

Free of the ball of disease, the pain pulsing through me faded and was overtaken by a cooling awe that relaxed every one of my muscles. Pure joy crashed in my mind. Then, a rush of ecstasy began numbing all pain, all fear. I forgot where I was. I wanted to stay in this ignorant state.

The flower ball lit up the sky and exploded like a firework. The rainbow flowers shot in every direction. They fell from the sky like shimmering, colorful comets.

Was this the end of the war? Were we setting off fireworks to celebrate?

The ecstasy faded. My spirit darkened. Melancholy overtook the joy. I watched the rainbow comets fall onto people, binding to their new hosts.

The Coalitionists were knocked back by the explosion. The impact pushed my hair and shot beyond me as I fell on my back. I pushed myself up.

Maizeans had fallen as well.

I had infected my own people.

I tried to swirl my hands and pull it away, but I had no energy left.

"No..." I gasped for air.

The Coalitionists now turned their attention to our small army.

I tried to stand, but I fell over. I used my uninjured arm to push myself up. The rainbow flowers were painted across the charging Coalition army. I swirled my hands and pulled the rainbow flowers off in small pieces and threw them as far back as I could. Each time I did this, I furthered the spread. They landed on as many Coalitionists as I could hit. I kept doing this and became dizzy.

A great battle cry came from the southwest. An army charged in our direction. They were covered in the yellow of Maize. Then I saw glistening gold—Solara.

My eyes rolled back into my head. The world spun as I fell over to my side, reaching down to my pocket to hold Isabella's art. My head struck the ground. I blacked out.

CHAPTER 13
THE DISEASE

A familiar song echoed around me, but I couldn't find the source. The piano, guitar, and drums came together in an upbeat rhythm as I started tapping my foot. Light streaming in from a nearby window blinded me. I recognized the room. I was back in Cornia. The light came from the window above the sink in my kitchen. I saw our crisp, white counters, void of any mess. I saw our shimmering silver sink, and smelled the wonderful aroma of spices and meat. I closed my eyes, took a deep breath. I could almost taste the smell.

The music's rhythm overtook my body. My toe tapping escalated to dancing. I smiled while moving my feet from side to side. My hips swung while my arms flailed. I loved dancing to this song. But what was it?

"Daddy!" a little voice yelled. I turned to find my daughter, my beautiful Isabella, grinning ear to ear. Her black hair, bright face, and little pointy teeth spaced apart from one another fixated on me. Hair tied into two ponytails on the sides of her head bobbed as she moved. "Daddy, dance!"

Without hesitation, I ran over to her, took her hands, and we danced together. She laughed while spinning in circles, occasionally stopping to touch the ground with her hand before rising again. She moved the world like it was all hers. It was her show, and everyone was a spectator to her wonder.

Then, something caught my eye. I looked over at the wall covered in textured tan wallpaper. A bright color blotched the wallpaper like a stain on a shirt. The colors formed different shapes, expanding, contracting, and shifting around.

The mass molded into a familiar shape.

A terrible shape.

A rainbow flower.

Another flower appeared next to it. Rainbow flowers grew across the walls and continued to the floor and the ceiling like weeds in a garden. They consumed everything they touched, a tidal wave of iridescence.

"Pretty," Isabella danced toward the incoming flowers.

I reached for her, but she moved out of my grasp. The rainbow flowers crept up her leg. She smiled and twirled as they covered her body piece by piece. My body, frozen in place, forced me to watch my daughter be consumed. The music faded away, and only then did I hear the sound the flowers produced, like leaves bustling in the wind.

The flowers consumed my daughter's body. Only her honey eyes were visible. The terrible noise of the flowers' movement terrorized me, as they slowly covered her eyes.

"No." Only a whisper came out as I reached for her, her face disappearing in a rainbow swarm.

Whatever kept me from moving ceased, and I fell to my knees, my heart ripped out of my chest.

"Ciro..." a quiet voice echoed all around. "Ciro." It was louder. "CIRO!"

Jolting up from my bed, I opened my eyes. It was just a nightmare. With each heavy breath, Kernel Ofelia sat next to me, holding my shoulders. Her eyes caught my attention, but something seemed odd about them. They didn't shine with life and vigor like they normally did.

Kernel Ofelia also shouldn't have been at the war front. Her duty remained with the medical tent back in Husk.

"Is this a dream?" I asked.

"No, you're awake." She wrapped her arms around me.

I didn't hug her back. I was in the medical tent, not on the war front. Medics rushed around in a panic. My eyes felt fuzzy as I leaned back from Kernel Ofelia and rubbed them.

"What happened?" I refocused on her face.

"A lot." She stood up, her foot tapping on the ground, beads of sweat on her forehead and neck. "I've heard a lot of stories. I'm trying to decipher what's true and what isn't." Staring at me with a brief pause, I noticed the bags under her eyes. "The warriors say they saw you knock over a whole army with your hands."

The battle came flooding back to me. I remembered the big ball of rainbow flowers exploding with great force. So many people fell to the ground in the explosion's wake. A cold sweat coated my back, and my chest throbbed with a sharp pain.

I nodded. "But then I passed out. What happened after that?"

Her lips moved for a moment before stopping. She squinted, then pinched the bridge of her nose. With each movement, my stomach twisted into a terrible knot.

"Solara arrived with the rest of the Maizeans. They took out the remaining troops. Ciro, the war is likely to be over soon." Instead of smiling or showing any bit of joy, she crossed her arms. "But I have a bigger problem on my hands." She turned and looked at the tent, overfilled with patients on cots, the floor, and even standing. Rainbow flowers covered so many of them. "A new sickness has been infecting the incoming warriors. It's like necrotizing fasciitis but slower. The disease drains a person's energy as it takes over the entire body. We have tried amputation, but it seems to have spread further than the site of infection." Her voice cracked as she cleared her throat. "Ciro, I don't know what to do about it. We've already had over twenty deaths this past week just from the disease."

"Week?" I gasped for air. I looked at my right arm, where an attached tube drooped down and up to an IV bag. "How long was I out?"

"A week, like I just said." An uncharacteristic sharpness came with her response. Shaking her head, she forced out a small smile. "Sorry. I'm tired." She lowered her voice. "Where did this disease come from?"

I leaned back and put my hands behind my head. A heaviness weighed on my heart before it dropped into my stomach and forced up bile that I swallowed back down. A sour taste dried out my mouth.

Whatever disease this is, I created it. How was I out that long?

Pinching the upper bridge of my nose, I closed my eyes. A terrible pressure built up in my forehead. I analyzed the room, my heartbeat speeding up at a rapid rate. The frantic medics, the stench, the brightly colored flowers dancing across the victims without a care in the world collided into my worst nightmare. It was colorful and bright, but harsh screams, oozing wounds, and motionless bodies tainted the flower's beauty. Medics threw their hands in the air out of helplessness before moving onto their next patient. Beauty and horror melded into one.

I looked back at Kernel Ofelia, her eyes still squinting. She suspected me of something, triggering my tears without breaking eye contact.

"Ciro..." she said. "What happened?"

I whispered, "I...I...I didn't mean to. I tried to keep the incoming army from destroying us. It came so naturally. I held it for longer." Holding out my hands, they shook with such violence. "Longer than I ever had. It hurt my hands. Then I threw it. It changed." Throwing my hands forward, I gestured all around. "It's everywhere."

"You...you made this?" she whispered. She covered her mouth in a muffled gasp. "Ciro..."

The absolute worst feeling formed within me, a combination of airless breathing, a rapid heartbeat, extreme nausea, and a pounding head. I was no longer a healer. I was a monster. A monster who tried to be Gaia and created an abomination.

I was an abomination.

Attempting to focus on the patients surrounding me, blurred circles of many colors forced my eyes away. Instead, I focused on the dirt below. If I just fell forward, I could escape this horrendous place. Gasping for air, I coughed, not noticing I had slumped so far forward, I cut off my trachea.

Patting my back until I sat back up, Ofelia removed her hand. "Tell me everything you know about it." Kernel Ofelia leaned forward. "I need some guidance."

"I don't know anything. I didn't mean to do it."

She grabbed me by the shoulders and lightly shook me. "Ciro..." She paused and took a deep breath. "...get it together. I need you to help and stop feeling sorry for yourself. I can't handle any more deaths."

Her eyebrows furrowed, the bags under her eyes sagged, and her mouth hung open. Though she said no more, her face and body pleaded for my aid. She was desperate. Everyone in the tent looked desperate. What good could I do? My hands only created evil.

"It's a rainbow flower," I said. "It looks like necrotizing fasciitis's purple flower but isn't focused in one area."

"Can you move it?"

I recalled the battlefront when I first created it. "I tried to pull it off the infected on the battlefront. It doesn't move easily and flies back to its host after a failed attempt. I know nothing else."

She let go of me and sighed. "Well, keep observing it. I know you need to recover, but I need your help. Please."

A sharp pain in my right arm pricked. Kernel Ofelia had yanked out my IV needle. A small pool of blood formed before she took gauze and put pressure on it, before strapping a bandage on. Patting my thigh, she returned to the other patients.

I was a patient now.

I rubbed the sides of my pounding head.

"Co-Kernel Ciro?"

The voice came from the bed next to me. I turned to a warrior with a wrapped-up leg. She looked to be about my age, with brown hair and a bruised, tired face. I took a deep breath of relief when I saw no rainbow flowers riddled across her body. She was dressed in plain tan clothing. I recognized her as one of the warriors who had been assigned to protect me.

I searched my mind, trying to remember her name. "Melia," I almost yelled. She smiled at my correct guess. "It's good to see you healthy."

"Thanks to you." Melia nodded. "This whole tent is alive because of you."

I looked around and only saw rainbow flowers across the room. "I wouldn't go that far."

"You're a hero," she said. "The Hero of Maize."

A man lying in a bed across from me echoed, "The Hero of Maize!" He had a patch over his eye and an arm hoisted by a sling.

"The Hero of Maize!" a few more people repeated.

Joy covered each of their faces, but what they said was wrong. They would have looked disgusted if they knew what I had done. Weeks before, my wife held the title of Hero of Husk. She was a real hero. I was an abomination.

I couldn't take it. I got out of my bed, stumbling as my legs remembered their purpose, and left the tent for some air. The night sky glistened above me. My breathing quickened, and I gasped for air, hands on my knees. A pool of poured water sat on the ground, reminding me of my vomit after Eduardo's death. Another example of my failure.

"SON OF A BITCH!" I screamed at the sky.

I just want to go back home. I want to lie in my bed with my wife. I want to play with my daughter. I want to pet my Talonhound.

I fell to my knees and started sobbing. My body felt so heavy. I closed my eyes and thought of Valeria. She was so much stronger than I was. She wouldn't be outside feeling bad for herself; she would be helping. She was the real hero of this war. I needed to emulate her heroism. I would help others just like she would have.

What am I doing?

My arms shook in violent tremors. I clenched my fists to contain them, but it only made the rest of my body join the shake.

What good am I? I was a coward who wanted to run away from training on day one. How did I let things get this far?

Slamming my fists onto the ground, dust billowed away in a mushroom cloud. The trembling stopped. A cool wave moved across my mind and raised my head. I needed to get up.

The crescent moon caught my eye, lifting me from the ground back to my feet. It was the same sky my wife and daughter looked at. We were still connected. This connectedness gave me a burst of energy. I turned around and marched back into the medical tent.

The tent's harsh lights slapped me across the face. I needed that. Kernel Ofelia watched me walk in and nodded to me, drawing me in her direction.

"Are you back?" she asked.

"As much as I can be."

"Good." She looked down at the male patient before her. His skin was covered in dust mixed with sweat. He held his side where a melon-sized mass had formed. The mass was infested with rainbow flowers. "He started showing symptoms of the disease two days ago."

"Two days?" I exclaimed. "And there is a mass this large already?" Kernel Ofelia nodded. "Holy shit. What are the symptoms?"

"Fever, profuse sweating, sharp pain, and then the tumors form. They take so many different forms, but the masses start as the body fights it."

I touched the mass before the man winced in pain. An unexpected softness surprised my fingertips. Cancerous tumors were hard and often painless.

"It mimics a benign tumor," I said.

"They're strange, but I think they're related to the disease."

"They are." I paused. "There are lots of flowers."

Masses covered his body in multiple spots. His obliques, his left shoulder, and his right leg had masses surrounded by rainbow flowers. The flowers appeared in a few other areas on his body, less dense but still glowing.

A guttural groan climbed out of my mouth. "I don't know what to do. I don't want to risk an Eduardo situation."

"We should try something. This is phase three of five." Kernel Ofelia glanced at me.

"Phase?"

"Next, the tumors will...burst." She shivered. "Then, the organs shut down. Then...death. The remaining phases come very fast."

The man alternated between crying and screams of pain. Pure terror filled his eyes.

What am I supposed to do?

"I don't know what to—"

"Ciro," Kernel Ofelia interrupted me, "I'm tired. I'm tired of your excuses. Try something. I trust you, now trust yourself."

My eyes ached, wanting to shut. Kernel Ofelia kept eye contact with me. I had to try something. I searched my mind for ideas, but what?

An abrupt sizzling noise came from a few beds away. One of the medics cauterized a small wound, which was sometimes practiced if bleeding didn't stop. I watched the patient's flesh burn.

Burning? I know I feel heat when holding a disease. What if I burned it from within?

"I have an idea."

"Good," she said. "Now try it."

I brought my hands close to the tumor and grabbed the rainbow flowers. Then, I just held them. I sat there, my hands warmed up. They became hotter and hotter. The rainbow flowers flared within my burning hands. The man began flailing his arms and groaning, so Kernel Ofelia grabbed his hands to allow me to concentrate.

"Look," Kernel Ofelia said, nodding down to the tumor as it shrank.

Was it working? The burning on my hands intensified, becoming unbearable. I had to keep pushing since it produced results. The rainbow flowers shrank near the tumor, even to the point that they disappeared. The agonizing pain in my hands hit a breaking point. I let go and violently shook my hands like I had been holding a burning log, yet they looked untouched. Not a scratch or blister.

Kernel Ofelia's face brightened. "You did it. You pulled it off!"

A grin covered my face. I did something right. I made the tumor shrink.

But then, my smile faded. The rainbow flowers in the other areas of his body rushed to the spot I had removed the flowers from. Just like in my nightmare, they infested him like weeds in a garden.

"No." I started shaking my hands, hoping to make the burning sensation dissipate. "No, no, no."

"What is it?" Kernel Ofelia asked.

Without any other options, I grabbed the incoming flowers with my scorched fingers. There were too many flowers rushing to the area I had healed. My hands hurt so badly, but I had to try again.

The tumor grew rapidly. I tried to hold them back, but the rainbow flowers pushed at me. I squeezed my eyes shut, started screaming, and pushed back at the flower stampede. An unusual sensation came over my hands. The actual tumor pushed my hands, even though my hands were an arm's length away from the patient.

I opened my eyes to a heaping, veiny tumor blowing up like a balloon. Someone knocked me to the ground. The burning stopped.

Kernel Ofelia stood over me, her attention locked on the tumor. She took a plastic sack and tied it around the giant mass before shielding her face with her hands.

A loud pop sounded ahead of me. Yellow, white, and red gunk splattered the walls of the bag. The colors mixed into one of the ugliest I had ever seen—rotted gray mangled in vomit green.

"Why did you stop me?" I yelled.

"Because I can't afford for you, me, or anyone else to get infected!" she yelled back. "That pus is extremely contagious. That is how I lost Medic Hernandez." So much fire filled her eyes. "I can't lose any more of us!"

I stood back up, watching the rainbow flowers cover his entire body. With more screams, the man flailed until he breathed one last time. The light in his eyes flickered into nothing, just as the rainbow flowers lost their color and faded.

He was dead.

"It didn't work..." I whispered.

"That was the quickest phase five has come yet," Kernel Ofelia sighed.

A darkness clenched my heart and made my stomach twist. "It was my fault."

"Oh, just shut up." She stamped her foot and raised her hands to her sides.

Despite her annoyance, the pressure within me kept pressing at my insides. "What? It is."

She pointed at my chest and jabbed her finger with each statement said. "You had a golden record before this. Sometimes things don't work out the way you want them to. If I let every death bring me down, I would lose my mind! Stop feeling bad for yourself and just keep healing!" She screamed as the whole tent looked at her.

All the eyes on us only amplified the pressure in me. My muscles ached as I drew into myself even more. How long would it be until I just curled up into a ball and fell into the dirt?

"I'm sorry..."

Kernel Ofelia grunted and spun around, glaring at the tent. "Everyone back to work!" She marched out of the tent.

The dead patient lay before me with the pus-filled sack still tied to his side. I mourned his death one last time before I followed Kernel Ofelia out of the tent.

"What's your problem?" I asked as soon as I stepped through the tent's flaps.

"Problem? Problem?" She screamed at me. "Everything is my problem! The war! The overabundance of patients! And now? A disease that I can't figure out and can't beat?! I can't take it!" She faced the sky and screamed. "SON OF A BITCH!"

Her voice echoed before her heavy breathing took over, or maybe my same scream moments before echoed back instead.

"It's my fault," I said.

"Stop saying that." She emphasized each word in a deliberate, calm manner. She no longer screamed, whether out of breath or finally calmed down. "I'm so tired of that. You fought in a war using something you didn't know that well. You did something drastic in a life-or-death situation. You saved so many people. It's unfortunate that this disease was born from it, but you didn't intend to create a deadly disease. Right?"

I looked past her into the tent filled with patients. "Right."

"Serendipitous sight," she simply said, nothing more.

"Huh?"

"Seeing the unexpected leads to the unexpected. That is how your whole life has been recently: a lot of the unexpected. Serendipitous sight."

"And I don't want it." I shook my head. "I want it taken away."

"Well, it won't be. So you can admit defeat, or you can keep on fighting. Finding a cure for a disease won't happen if we don't try. Errors will happen. Mistakes will be made. But as long as you are careful not to repeat the mistakes, that's the best you can do. Maybe some more serendipitous sight will come from it."

"My mistake caused someone to die faster than any of us expected." I looked at the ground.

Kernel Ofelia stepped forward and poked me in the chest, my chest still sore from her earlier volley. "That man was going to *die* either way. What if you *had* saved him? What if what you tried to do *had* cured him? You thought it possible for a moment. We both did. I can guarantee you that he wanted to be healed. You *had* to try. It was the only hope we had. So, you tried. It didn't work. He died." She started pacing around me. "It's shit. It's pure shit. But now we know for next time, right?"

"Right..."

She stopped pacing and closed in on me. "So, what went wrong?"

I wasn't ready to think about it so soon. "What went wrong?" I lingered on the question. "I tried to hold the disease, but this time I didn't remove it. I knew if I did, it would eventually fly back to the patient. I knew my hands heated up when I held it for a long time. That is how I amplified disease." My fingertips tingled at the recounting. "I thought maybe if I held it for longer, it would eventually, I don't know, burn out? So, I tried. It did. The tumor shrank. It was out of that area."

"I saw the tumor shrink." Kernel Ofelia nodded. "Then, what happened? It suddenly grew at a quicker rate. What did you see?"

"Well, the rainbow flowers in the other areas rushed to the tumor area."

"It came from other areas?"

"Yeah..." I paused again. "It came from other areas...but what if it was only in one area?" A chill rushed through my brain, settling the pressure plaguing me.

"What do you mean?"

My cheeks warmed. "What if it was in one area? That's it!"

I ran back into the medical tent. The harsh light struck my eyes. After my eyes readjusted, I looked around at the patients with rainbow flowers. My head moved back and forth as I searched.

"What are you looking for?" Kernel Ofelia walked next to me.

Scanning the room, I found the patient I was looking for. "Follow me."

Kernel Ofelia followed me across the room. The younger patient perked up as I approached. Her lighter brown hair shimmered just like her light brown eyes. Wrapped in bandages, her left leg stuck straight out. Antibiotics dripped from the IV bag into her arm. A few rainbow flowers gathered near her shoulder. Maybe about ten or so.

"Hello," she said while trying to sit more upright. "Here to check on me?"

"Yes." I nodded and turned to Kernel Ofelia. "Does she…" I hesitated as to not alarm the patient.

"Have it? No." Kernel Ofelia's face lit up before she analyzed the warrior.

Glancing back and forth between Kernel Ofelia and me, the patient squinted. "Have what?" They looked at their hands and then at their arms, searching for whatever we mentioned.

"A small…infection," I said with a reassuring smile. Though I saw the few flowers, Kernel Ofelia saw no sign of infection. It had to be something I could handle. "I see one forming on your shoulder. Mind if I look at it?"

With a great sigh, the patient's body relaxed. "Please, go ahead. I don't want to deal with another."

"Please turn that way," I instructed.

I reached out just above her shoulder and grabbed the rainbow flowers. I held them and my hands warmed up. The flowers grew brighter in vibrant colors.

"Tell me about yourself."

"Me?" My distraction worked as she stopped turning. "Well, I'm eighteen. My name is Kira. I'm from Blanche. My father was injured about a month ago and couldn't serve. My mother is still breastfeeding twins."

"You have siblings?" I asked in a high-pitched voice. My hands hurt the more the flowers glowed.

"Yes, eight," she said. "We are a big family. I'm the oldest." She turned a little. "I feel something…itchy. But only a little."

"I'm just using some antibiotic," I said as fast as I could through my rapid breathing. The pain became greater, but I focused on my targets. Then, the rainbow flowers shrank. One by one, they faded away. Just as the last one disappeared, I let go and took a deep breath. "That's it." I straightened my spine and put my foot forward to avoid falling over.

She felt her shoulder. "Was there something there?"

A sudden rush of dizziness came over me. "Not anymore. Let us know if you feel anything else. We will check on you later."

My pace quickened as I moved as fast as I could toward the tent entrance. I stepped back out into the moonlight and fell to my knees, exhausted.

"Did it work?" Kernel Ofelia asked, stepping up behind me.

I glanced up at her. "I think it did."

"You do?" A genuine smile curled up her cheeks. "That's great. How did it work?"

"There was just...less." I yawned. "But I'll have to keep an eye on her."

Overwhelming weight swept over my body, making me want to rest my head. I blinked slower and slower.

"Of course." She caught me by the arm before I fell forward. "You look tired."

I yawned again. "I am." Each word I tried to say felt slower.

Kernel Ofelia helped me up and walked me into my nearby house and into my room. "Let's get you back into bed."

My eyes shut. The dim light of my room glowed through my pink eyelids, but I didn't open them. My body was lowered into a bed, my head resting on a pillow. I yawed again before drifting to sleep. I pictured a rainbow flower for a moment before it faded.

CHAPTER 14
THE FUTURE

I checked on Kira every moment I could. If it weren't for her actual injury, my visits would've come off as obsessive. I pretended to readjust her bandages and check the wound while I surveyed her body for rainbow flowers.

"You don't have to check on me so often," Kira said with a smile. Her youthful optimism settled my angst. "There are so many other sick people here. I really am fine."

"We have to be careful of recurring infections. They can get worse before you know it." I pretended to check her blood pressure.

"You are good at your job." She began picking at her shirt. "I wish I could say the same about myself."

I turned to her and saw her face darken. She was young, probably close to the lower cutoff for the drafting age.

"How did you end up here?" I asked.

"I drafted myself. My family has little money, and the guaranteed income they get helps a lot." She straightened, looking me in the eye.

"You haven't been here for long?" I took her arm and pretended to check for marks.

"About a week," she said with a nervous laugh. "And I'm already hurt." She looked down at her shirt again.

"I wasn't the best when I started. I was actually pretty bad." Lowering her arm back down, I grinned.

"Really?" The brightness returned to her eyes.

"Oh yeah. Terrible." With a soft grin, I shrugged. "But now I'm better at my role. I practiced a lot and didn't give up on myself. You should do the same."

I finished looking her over and didn't see any rainbow flowers. It was the third day since I had healed her. A deep relief flushed over me. Though I cursed her with the sickness, something good had come from my gift, and Kira was a testament to this.

"Everything look good?" she asked.

"You look great. Take a nap." I patted the side of her cot. "Now, I'll finally go and check on the other patients."

As I walked away, Kira said, "Thank you, Ciro."

Kernel Ofelia stepped up next to me once I was a few cots away, something she did every time I checked on Kira.

"Well?"

"There are still no rainbow flowers." I leaned on one of the tent's center posts.

"That makes it day three," she said. "You told me after day three you would try this on someone else."

Kernel Ofelia had been pushing me to heal more people since the first success. But I wanted to make sure it worked—I didn't want to treat more people who ended up dying quicker because of me. Three days of no more flowers with Kira meant success. Success meant I had to try healing someone else.

"You're right," I confirmed with a sigh. "I will try on someone else."

"Great!" With an uncharacteristic skip, she coughed and settled back to a firm stance. "I would help you figure out who needs help, but I can only tell who has the disease the worst."

I searched the tent for anyone with a less advanced infection. But rainbow flowers covered all the warriors around me.

"I don't see any smaller cases."

"Should we maybe try on a medium case?"

"No, I'm not ready for that." I shifted my feet, a sudden discomfort climbing up my right leg like there was something stuck to it. I itched at the spot, thinking I'd find something stuck to me. All I found was my leg. Then, the itchy sensation moved across the rest of my body. "It's definitely based on how much I can handle. I could barely handle a very, very small case. If I lose focus or lose my grasp, then it will just make it worse."

"We will have to work you up to it then. It's like a muscle. You have to train a muscle to make it stronger. So, let's keep training it." She seemed so confident.

I didn't share the feeling. "What if medium cases don't exist? I think I'd see one around this room." With one more scan, a dense forest of rainbow flowers encompassed me. "I only see severe."

"It has to transition at some point. Unless the growth is exponential. There must be a threshold...a no passing point."

"Kernel Ofelia," one of the medics said. "Patient Rico just passed."

"Dammit." Kernel Ofelia let out a firm grunt. She looked over at the bed the dead patient lay in. "He had fought the disease the longest."

"I know," the medic said. "I did all I could." Her face crumpled as tears formed in her eyes.

Kernel Ofelia placed her hand on the medic's shoulder. "Don't forget that—you did all you could. You *are* a spectacular medic who needs to keep fighting this disease. Maize needs you."

The medic's face brightened a bit.

"Of course, I'll keep pushing," the medic said. "For Maize and for health."

"Por Maize y por la salud," Kernel Ofelia echoed in the native tongue.

The medic stayed there, lips pressed together before finally popping. "I also think we should name this disease," the medic said. "It would help with differentiating it from others."

Name the disease. Name the infliction I brought upon our citizens.

My insides flipped. It was as if my intestines were wrapped around my lungs. I made my way to the doors of the medical tent, unable to breathe. My eyesight went foggy as I stumbled between patients and medics. I needed to get to the brightness of the outside world. I pushed through the tent's flaps and gasped in fresh air. The air was hot. It burned my lungs as the auburn sun cooked the sky, and I put my hands on my knees for support.

"Are you okay?" Kernel Ofelia's voice reverberated behind me.

"Not at all," I said. "Stop wasting your time on me. There are too many patients who need your help."

"They need my help with something I don't know how to treat. This disease is complicated. You are my best bet."

"*This disease* is complicated?" I started laughing. "*This disease.* That is vague. Just name it already. Name it what you want to name it."

The twisting in my gut burned away. Rage pushed its way up my throat.

"What are you talking about?"

My hands flailed in the air as I spoke. "You know you want to name it after me. The disease's creator. Its father." I gave a low, bitter chuckle. "How does *Ciro Disease* sound? Or *Ciro's Kiss of Death*? Or *Enfermedad de Ciro*? Oh, that's good. Use the native tongue. It adds more punch to it."

Sweat pooled on my forehead. It burned my eyes. Saliva flung off my tongue as I spoke. I was like an Anguila Terrestre. I slithered across the hot ground, spitting venom from my vile mouth. I pictured its black scales covered in bright green arrows running along its limbless body. I was poisonous.

Kernel Ofelia stared blankly in my direction. Her tan skin glistened with sweat as well. Moisture pooled on her black eyebrows. My gaze fell into her fierce eyes as they locked onto me, piercing me like a needle. I normally faltered, but I instead stared back. My Anguila Terrestre eyes met her self-righteous attitude.

"The fact you think I would *ever* name this disease after you is beyond me." Her eyes softened and tears formed. "I would *never* do that. I know being here is hurting you. I want to do everything I can to help your mind find peace. I'm responsible for all that is happening."

"You're responsible?" My cracking voice echoed in the barren city. To our luck, no one was near to hear our conversation. It was just us. The idea made me laugh. My laugh grew louder. I forgot Ofelia was there. She looked like she pitied me and tried to make it all about her. "In what world would this weight be *yours*? You did *nothing*!"

"I pushed you into doing something you pleaded not to do." She paused. "And for what? For you to lose your mind?"

"I thought this was all so *we could save Maize*?" I mimicked her self-serving voice, using her words against her. The release caused my tense muscles to relax, but it only allowed me to focus more on striking her down. "I thought this was all done to *protect our people*?"

"At what cost?" She stamped so hard on the ground, a small dust storm kicked up below her.

For the first time ever, I witnessed something I never thought I would—Ofelia wept.

Tears cascaded down her tan cheeks. Most evaporated in the hot sun, others made it all the way down her face before falling off her jaw. Her eyes remained brown, but the yellow twinkle they once had was gone. It was as if the positivity she held had evaporated.

The tension in my face lifted. The Anguila Terrestre I personified moments before slithered back underground. I stood before her in a barren city as myself under the scorching sun.

My insides flipped again. Breathing became easier. My body lightened. There was something else stirring inside me...compassion. Her last question echoed in my mind.

At what cost?

"The cost of me." I paused. "A cost I wasn't ready to handle. You aren't the reason I chose this. I chose to do this for my family. To keep them safe. Now? We have a new enemy to fight. A disease. Enfermedad Floreciente." The words tickled my tongue. "A disease that looks so beautiful from my end. Flowers of so many colors dancing along our bodies with their only purpose to inflict suffering and death."

I took deep breaths, both of us standing in silence. The silence threatened me. I forced myself to pace around. Dust kicked up below my feet, and my steps echoed in the deserted city.

"That's it," she said.

I turned to Ofelia, her face brightening a bit. After such a dark conversation, there was somehow light remaining.

"What's it?" I asked.

"Enfermedad Floreciente. The Blossoming Disease. That's the name."

Enfermedad Floreciente. She's right. That's the name. Born in victory, flourished in war.

A cold breeze moved within me before moving out of my mouth. I hummed, crossed my arms, and held my hand under my chin, nodding.

"Enfermedad Floreciente." I paused. "Enferflor, for short."

"Enferflor," she said. "Named by those who first diagnosed it."

We stared at one another. I witnessed the disease's birth. Ofelia watched its first death. Though it made this disease feel more real, it needed a name.

Fatigue clashed with a sudden chill prickling across my skin. My eyes caught sight of the small fountain in the city center. After all this time, the fountain still sputtered. The taller waterspout shot straight to the sky as the smaller spouts surrounding it angled toward the center with smaller streams. It reminded me of the first day of training. Aameen had changed, Kernel Ofelia had changed, and I had changed. But the fountain was the same—a careless stream in the hot sun.

"Kernel Ofelia?" a soft voice asked as we looked over. A younger man wearing the Maizean colors stood before us, but he didn't come from the medical tent. What he wore came from the battlefront.

"Yes?" Kernel Ofelia returned.

"The Krown Kernel requests the Kernel and the Co-Kernel's presence," he said. "They are coming into town as we speak."

Kernel Ofelia and I exchanged a quick glance. That meant only one thing.

"Have we...won the war?" My words felt foreign as they left my mouth. "Is it over?"

The boy smiled even bigger. "It isn't my news to share."

"We'll meet him now," Kernel Ofelia said. "We just have to clean up."

"I'll alert the Krown Kernel." The boy nodded. "Kernel. Co-Kernel." He started running toward the northwest edge of town.

"It's over?" My eyelids became heavy, and tears broke through. "The war is over?"

Kernel Ofelia embraced me for a deep, soul-lifting hug. She pressed her wet cheek against my own. A conglomeration of laughter, sobs, and screams each fought its way out of my mouth.

I was going home.

We separated, still simultaneously laughing and crying. "Can we tell the others?" I asked.

"Not yet. We need to talk with the Kernels first."

She was right. We went to the washing station in the medical tent and scrubbed our hands, arms, and faces. Avoiding eye contact with the other medics, I dipped my head before exiting the tent and walked to the city's edge.

The Maizean warriors came into town with an abundance of smiles covering their faces. Some were singing. Some were laughing. I still remembered the day the warriors first left for the battlefront. So much fear. So many shaking bodies. Now, happiness resounded. Joy had returned to our nation.

We walked up to Krown Kernel Fernando, Kernel Aameen, and the other Kernels.

"Kernel Ofelia," Krown Kernel Fernando announced. "Co-Kernel Ciro. We bring great news! The Coalition has retreated. We have successfully defended our land from their tyranny. Maize is safe." Various warriors who walked by cheered. The Krown Kernel let out a deep, belly laugh. He patted his gut. "Co-Kernel, Maize has you to thank for ending this. We are indebted to your service."

The Kernels all nodded. I caught Aameen's eye, who smiled before nodding.

"It's all for Maize and my family," I said, only half smiling. The weight of what the victory cost pulled me down. A sudden inclination to bring up Enferflor boiled within me until it became too much to bear. "But I'm afraid the new disease is becoming a new problem."

The Krown Kernel's smile dropped for a moment. "A matter we can address another time. Let our warriors enjoy this moment. Let's return home, and let the residents of Husk return to their homes. Today is a great day for Maize!"

"For Maize!" the other Kernels yelled, fists raised in the air. Kernel Ofelia did the same while glancing at me. I raised my hand, but I didn't feel the invigoration the rest of the group felt. One thing I knew for certain: I was ready to go home. The rest of me swirled with doubt.

"We will need to get the final patients treated and arrange transport home for those that cannot walk," Krown Kernel Fernando said. "The medical tent will need to be dismantled. It should be a quick endeavor. We want to return Husk to some semblance of what it used to be."

Kernel Ofelia exchanged glances with me. "Krown Kernel, we still have a good number of patients infected by the new disease. It is likely death will find them, but we want to keep them as comfortable as we can."

"How are they not being treated?" the Krown Kernel asked. "Kernel, this is *your* job."

My chest burned, wanting to defend Kernel Ofelia. She sacrificed so much of herself to keep the medical tent running. The Krown Kernel had no right to tell her to do more. I wanted to shout at him.

"With respect, Co-Kernel Ciro was trying to tell you that this new disease is causing issues," Kernel Ofelia said.

"What disease?" the Krown Kernel questioned.

I sighed. His inability to listen left me irritated.

"We are calling it Enfermedad Floreciente, Enferflor for short," Kernel Ofelia responded with patience. "Enferflor is like nothing we have ever seen before. The infection causes tumors, and its spread builds up to a point that it causes tumors to explode. Death comes quick after this."

"We noticed some odd sicknesses after Ciro's victory," the Krown Kernel admitted. "I wondered what it was. But those that didn't die were brought back to Husk."

Aameen's attention remained on me no matter who spoke.

"And we did our best to treat them," Kernel Ofelia said. "More contracted the disease. It's very, very contagious. We lost one of our medics to it."

I surveyed the incoming warriors. Dread crept up my spine. I saw little rainbow flowers dancing along some of their bodies, the beginning, treatable stage of Enferflor.

"What are we to do about it?" the Krown Kernel asked. "Ah, never mind. This isn't a decision I make. I've done my job. Stena Mezca will have to be informed on the matter."

"But Krown Kernel—" Kernel Ofelia began.

"Kernel Ofelia," the Krown Kernel interrupted, "the matter will be discussed back in Cornia. Not here. Not today. Now, finish your work here and we will begin our trek back home."

"Yes, Krown Kernel," Kernel Ofelia said, gritting her teeth.

"Now, let's get this town back together and head home!" the Krown Kernel yelled.

Despite the fire growing inside of me, the weight inside my head pushed the flames down. The Krown Kernel deserved to be told off, but it wouldn't fix anything. I gritted my teeth and grumbled at his turned back.

The Kernels all broke in different directions. Aameen oriented his attention straight at me. "Ciro, my friend." He embraced me for a hug. "I'm proud of you. Thank you for saving Maize."

I hugged him back but kept my eyes on the infected warriors walking past, unaware of what was to come. I counted twelve infected. I didn't want to lose track of them.

"Thank you," I said. "Aameen, we're going to need your help. I need to grab some of these warriors. I see something that I need to fix. Just tell them we're checking random warriors for infection."

Aameen looked behind himself. "Are they infected?"

I looked over at Kernel Ofelia and nodded. "Yes, they are. It's just the beginning, but I can treat them."

"You can?" he asked.

"I'll explain more later, but we need to do this now," I said.

I pointed Aameen in the direction of a few and Ofelia to others. I chased down the ones that were further away, more men who chatted like close friends.

"Excuse me," I said. They turned and smiled.

"Co-Kernel Ciro!" one of the men yelled. "The Hero of Maize!"

"Yes…" I said with a smile. "I'm sorry to rush, but we are checking some random warriors for infection. It's part of the return home. Do you mind following me?"

They exchanged confused glances. "Whatever you need," another warrior said. "We trust you with our lives."

With their lives.

The weight of their trust sat heavy on my shoulders.

"Follow me," I said. They trotted behind me as Aameen and Ofelia walked up with each of their four gathered warriors, totaling twelve. "Thank you all for doing this."

"We're just taking extra precautions," Kernel Ofelia added.

Approaching the stable where Ofelia first saw my gift in action, Shapples shifted out of the stand to make room for us. My Shapple friend was among them, and reached out with its wooly extensions and grabbed my wrist before pulling away and backing up. A strange confidence transferred from the beast to me.

"Sit here," I gestured, and the first man sat down. "Kernel Ofelia will help me inspect." I widened my eyes in her direction. She started observing his body, allowing me to focus without the patient watching me. "Just relax."

Three rainbow flowers sat on his neck. I grabbed them and held on as my hands warmed up. I kept holding until it felt like a similar burn level to what I felt with Patient Kira. The flowers dissolved, and I let go. The treatment made me stumble. Kernel Ofelia nudged me forward.

"Looks good," I said. "Thank you for letting us check you."

"Thank you for checking," the man said before rising from the bench.

I moved on to the next warrior. Then, the next. One man had five flowers, the largest infection in the group of warriors. Exhaustion took over, but I kept pushing. The Shapple reached out here and there to touch my arm. The interaction befuddled me, but I welcomed it each time.

I kept healing. Kernel Ofelia could tell that talking had become tiresome. She spoke for me, allowing me to do what I was good at. One patient remained. A man about thirty to thirty-five years old. It was just one more, but I wanted to rest my head. I grabbed the disease, held it, and the burning wasn't as strong. It was numb to me.

"That's it," I whispered. My throat felt dry.

"This means everything looks healthy," Kernel Ofelia said. She helped the warrior to his feet. "Thank you for serving Maize."

The warrior smiled and departed. I sat down, and Kernel Ofelia reached over to Aameen, pointing to his water bottle. He opened it and handed it over. I aggressively drank the water, streams coming down my cheeks. The Shapple rubbed my back with its wooly extension.

"You can heal the disease?" Aameen asked, eyeing the beast but remaining focused on me.

I looked over with fatigued eyes and nodded. Kernel Ofelia responded for me, "Ciro can heal Enferflor in its beginning stages. Other medics can't diagnose the illness at the moment, but Ciro can see it, so we know who to heal."

"This seems like a solution!" Aameen proclaimed. "Problem solved."

"Not quite," Kernel Ofelia said. "Do you see how tired he is? That was twelve people, which is the most he's done yet. I'm fearful of how quickly it spread within our warriors. Imagine its ability to spread throughout Maize. Cornia has a large population and Ciro is only one person. What about the other cities?"

"I see," Aameen said. "I'm sure our health officials will figure something out."

"We will need to get our resources together," Kernel Ofelia added. "Before it becomes a problem we can't overcome."

"We can bring it up to Stena Mezca," Aameen said. "He is wise and will listen."

"Nosotros solo podemos esperar," Kernel Ofelia said. "I hope he will listen."

"I think I need to lie down," I cracked out.

I found a thicker portion of hay to be my makeshift bed. As I rested, the hay poked my ears. I looked up and found the Shapple rubbing against my head. It let out a moan and widened its round eyes at me. I swore it smiled. Maybe it was a sign of good things to come.

With that hope, I found a brief peace within the chaos and rested my eyes.

CHAPTER 15
THE DAUGHTER

Despite what the Krown Kernel wanted, our devotion to the patients in Husk remained. Aameen was the only other Kernel to stay in Husk besides Kernel Ofelia, and most of the warriors who served under Aameen stayed back to help as well. Whether it was their dedication to him or the fact that I served with them as well, we needed the extra help. Even the citizens of Husk who served in the war helped. Without Aameen's leadership, organizing the extra people would've been impossible. Aameen proved a better leader than the Krown Kernel.

More warriors arrived in Husk from the further battlefronts, and more rainbow flowers covered many of them. For every warrior I tracked down, I treated, but I feared how many I missed.

The infection moved into Cornia and the other cities, no matter how hard I tried to prevent it.

As I continued treating Enferflor, my endurance increased, just as Kernel Ofelia expected. My ability was like a muscle that needed training. But I still didn't think I'd ever be able to treat the more severe cases.

Kernel Ofelia and the other medics loaded the uninfected patients onto wagons so they could be hauled back to Cornia. Some would need further treatment and rest, but it was better to have them treated at the capital's medical center. Kira left with the rest of the group, still flowerless, still safe.

The remaining patients were severely infected with Enferflor. The goal was to make their remaining moments in our world as comfortable as possible. Instead of treatment, the healthy warriors engaged in conversation and played card games with them. I kept an eye on these healthy warriors to make sure they didn't get infected, burning away flowers if they appeared. We did anything to distract the infected from their excruciating pain. I found the relaxed conversations and games to be more difficult than treating the sick. Scanning the healthy warriors and burning away any rainbow flowers kept me distracted, but only went so far.

My diligence kept away any new cases of Enferflor. My diligence allowed for more time to watch the severe cases. And my diligence let me watch them die, eaten by the disease from the inside out.

Beautiful, terrified faces etched themselves in my mind.

An older man named Eron, with mountains of wrinkles and gray, wispy hair, commanded a quiet, wise presence whenever I came near him. A Cornian native, his laughter, always ending with a croak, moved small earthquakes across his face. Married to his wife for thirty-five years, he talked about her as much as he talked about his own life. At each mention of his wife, his face lit up and made me forget he was dying. Soulful mahogany eyes with tan flecks and taupe streaks reminded me of a dim, warm fire, still bright even as the dreadful reign of rainbow flowers infested his wrinkles. He went unfazed by the death rampaging toward him.

Counteracting the old wisdom of Eron was Irena, a younger girl who reminded me of Kira. The Enferflor flowers flowed in rainbow waves across her body. The unfortunate beauty of the flowers complemented her fair skin and her shiny, pitch-black hair. Freckles emphasized her cheeks below her sunken eyes. She feared death, even though she tried to hide it.

Eron formed a close bond with Irena. I don't know if he was just good at hiding his fear for her sake or if he truly wasn't afraid. Either way, he kept talking about life beyond—Gaia's realm. His description painted the realm as a beautiful forest with every color you could imagine. Irena had many questions for Eron, especially about his belief of life after death.

"Belief is what fills our first breath, carves our essence in our younger years, and challenges our existence in our older years," Eron said. "Without belief, we are but leaves on a windless day."

Irena died first.

With every tear Eron shed for Irena, an etching was carved into my heart. Right before Irena died, and even while in excruciating pain himself, he rose from his bed and held her hand as the last bits of her life faded away. The fear in her eyes met the love in his. Not a single word was exchanged, but her eyes brightened as she smiled in her last moments.

Eron picked up her hand with a great tremor and kissed it. "May Gaia guide you into the forest of colors, sweet Irena. Like a leaf in a soft breeze, may you live more there than you ever lived here."

Eron died later that day. He wrote a final letter to his wife with help from Kernel Ofelia. Aameen promised he would deliver it as soon as we returned to Cornia. His promise reminded me of my promise to Eduardo. Someday, I'd visit Blanche and tell his wife and daughter of his unwavering love for them.

As a citizen of Maize, our bodies were born from the stalk and returned to the stalk. Dust to flesh and flesh to ground. Husk's cemetery was small when we first arrived. Post-war, it had tripled in size. Aameen and his team of warriors labored to make sure every warrior received a proper burial. Mound upon mound of dirt freshly packed down terrorized my mortality. Dirt upon dirt, flesh upon flesh.

One of the warriors still in Husk was a woodworker from Blanche. For each warrior, he created small triangular headstones, names carved in thick letters. Below each name, he wrote *SFDFM*, which stood for *Served, Fought and Died for Maize.*

After countless hours, sleepless nights, endless tears, ceaseless guilt, and complete dedication to treating every patient, our last patient passed away. The strangest silence overtook the medical tent for about an hour. The last time the tent had been that quiet was when we first set up the cots. The cots were now stained with blood, pus, vomit, and shit. I preferred the ugly stains over the rainbow flowers no longer present.

Each warrior, medic and non-medic alike, had aged by ten years. Heavy bags, harsh wrinkles, and battered postures crippled each of us. Some wept while others just stared blankly ahead. For a group of people who were about to make their way home, not an ounce of joy was present. Just grief.

After being disinfected, the cots were stacked and placed near some of the houses. Without question, the bedsheets, blankets, and pillows were burned. With the tent empty, the epicenter of Husk was dismantled. With the final remnant of the war gone, the city looked almost as if nothing had happened. Just a pile of cots and an imprint where the tent had stood. And the graves. The hundreds of graves.

Once the cleanup was finished, we left Husk. I looked at the fountain one more time before leaving it behind me. I hoped to never see that fountain again.

Aameen made conversation most of the way home. He captivated the warriors and medics with every word he said, which was necessary for the two-week journey. Joy slowly crept into the group.

"I still remember my greatest battle," Aameen said. "It was on the northern flank. We were outnumbered. I commanded the Blanche riders to fly further north to draw their army in the other direction. Then, we had a smaller, skilled team come from behind and quietly take them out one by one."

"Did you defeat them?" a warrior asked.

Aameen smiled. "We not only defeated them but used this tactic several more times throughout the war."

"That is genius!" another warrior exclaimed. "You are a true leader."

"I only do what I can for Maize." Aameen smiled and patted his comrades on the back.

Kernel Ofelia and I walked further behind the group. Something about their joy didn't sit well with me. I couldn't stop thinking about the rainbow flowers and feared what we would find once we were back in Cornia. Something told me it wouldn't be good.

"Are you thinking about Enferflor?" Kernel Ofelia asked.

"Yes. I can't stop," I admitted.

"Me too." She looked up at the sky. "I know the war is won, but I have a sickening feeling that the real war is about to begin."

"A new war." I sighed. "A war that I started."

Her silence made me think it was because she agreed with my statement.

She shifted the conversation. "Are you excited to see your family?"

I thought about Valeria and Isabella. A smile found me. "That, I truly am excited for. I can't wait to hold them. Kiss them."

"And I assume more than kiss a certain mujer." She elbowed my arm and raised her eyebrows up and down.

It had been six months since I'd seen Valeria last, and all our time had been spent in the medical tent. Blood rushed to my cheeks as I thought about my wife.

"Con muchas ganas." I elbowed her back and grinned. "I would be lying if I said otherwise." She laughed. "What about you? Is the great Kernel Ofelia excited to go back home?"

"I think by now you can just call me Ofelia. You have more than earned it."

My mind shifted back to the first moment I met Ofelia and the absolute disdain she had for me and I for her. I wanted to run away. Now, I left Husk at her side. My spine straightened from the honor she bestowed on me.

"Are you excited to go back home...*Ofelia*?" I methodically said her name. "That feels weird to say. Makes you seem...like a human." I wrapped my arms around myself and pretended to shiver.

"I'm a human." Ofelia smiled as I laughed. "I am!"

"If you say so," I whispered.

Her gaze moved forward. "I don't think I'll be returning to Blanche. Too much history. Too much hurt from my ex."

Air rushed into my lungs, forcing an arrogance I leaned into.

"Am I allowed to ask about your ex?"

"Nope." She clapped her hands together. "Some of us don't over-share our lives."

Ofelia had only mentioned her ex one time before. The last time she had been angry when I pressed about it. I wouldn't make that mistake again.

"So if not Blanche, where?"

"I've decided I'm going to move to Cornia. I have a feeling my services will be of better use in the capital."

"You are moving to my home city?" I exclaimed.

"You can't get away from me that easily." Arching her shoulders up high, she smirked.

"I'm glad. You've become a good friend of mine."

"As you have been a good friend to me. I don't have anything back home. It was an easy decision. Plus, you would be lost without me." An evil grin grew across her face.

"So lost." I chuckled.

Trotting steps came from behind.

"Looks like I'm not the only one who is following you back to Cornia," Ofelia said.

Glancing back, the Shapple I saved marched up to us, little tufts of wool bouncing as it ran. Though I didn't expect the beast to follow me, its presence just felt right.

"I'm glad it's here. Isabella will love the beast." I paused. "But I'm not sure what I'm going to tell Valeria."

"Tell her you found a new passion for sock knitting using Shapple wool." She slowly turned her head to stare at me.

Looking down at my new Shapple friend and back up, I replied, "What?"

"I need to get assimilated back into regular society." She sighed. "My jokes have lost their edge."

Moving past Ofelia's tired joke, my mind drifted back to the rainbow flowers. "What is our plan with Enferflor?"

"Ah, yes. Reality." A great sigh escaped Ofelia. She raised her hand and started counting each step of her plan. "Assess the situation first. Maybe it didn't spread. Maybe it's done, but I'm not that optimistic. We will have to obtain counsel from Stena Mezca. We are going to need resources and a smart team to figure out how we can treat the severe cases. We will also have to push for the containment of those who are sick."

"Containment?"

"It's contagious; we have to figure out ways to keep others from being exposed."

"Are you talking about sequestering the sick from the others?"

"I don't know." She shrugged. "Maybe that's a bad idea. But we have you to treat the sick, and you are only one person. That's why we have to find some type of treatment or cure. We have to talk to other doctors, herbalists, or whoever might have creative ideas to try. I have a feeling that standard medicine won't work."

The whole time I'd been worrying about the disease, Ofelia had been thinking through a plan. Feeling a bit guilty about my lack of preparation, I admired my friend for her obsessive nature.

"I'm sure the Stena and the Maizean council will cooperate. We will figure it out."

We have to figure it out.

My thoughts drifted to the passing farmland. The harvest season would begin soon, and the crops glistened bright green with hints of yellow. A light breeze provided some relief from the burning sun. The tall stalks swayed in the wind, almost whistling. It made the foliage look like a giant, freshly washed sheet being thrown in the air before falling upon a bed. Birds chirped overhead. My Shapple friend's breath heaved in and out from behind me. Some of the birds perched on the crops' stalks. Heads twisting, they kept us in sight, either casting judgment or indifference.

We walked along the dusty road from Husk, the dryness following us. The road firmed up with each step closer to Cornia, coarse grass weaving into the dirt in sporadic patches. I had forgotten what it was like to walk without kicking up dust. The crops grew larger and the soil more fertile. I was almost home.

The sun approached the horizon, and the air became just a little bit cooler. A thin mist formed where the sky met the land. Then, a city peeked through the haze—Cornia. Home.

Buildings stretched for miles in each direction, with Pastel Castle standing tallest in the center. Though the sky darkened as the sun set, the pastel roofs shone bright, oranges, yellows, pinks, and teals lighting up the city and my heart. I hadn't seen Cornia in so long. I walked up next to Aameen, who stopped with slouched shoulders. We both just stared ahead.

He put his hand on my shoulder without looking at me. "We are going to see our families, my good friend."

A wave of emotion came over me as a tear fell down my cheek. Cornia frequented my dreams. Though I had lived there for so long, I had almost forgotten that the city was real. I wondered if the city before me was just another cruel dream, and I would awake again in the medical tent surrounded by disease and death. Reaching over to my left forearm, I pinched myself. A sharp pain traveled across my skin. What I saw was real. I couldn't believe it.

Reality settling in, a punch of fear struck me.

Will Isabella still recognize me? Will I recognize her?

Caught up in war, creating a disease, healing a disease, and grappling with the inevitable death my disease often caused, I stayed distracted from all else in my life. A foreign fear that I often thought about but always got drowned out by all my other problems rose to the surface. The fear of my daughter not recognizing me far outweighed all else. I clenched my chest, my heartbeat becoming so heavy.

"Do you think our kids will remember us?" I asked.

"Of course, they will, Ciro." Aameen turned his gaze upon me. I returned the stare. His eyebrows settled above his warm, russet eyes. "They are our children. Our better halves talk about us to them."

No matter if his words held merit, it didn't stop the building tension in my chest. "She was only three when I left." My voice became shaky as I stuck my hand in my pocket and gripped her drawing.

Turning his whole body toward me, he grabbed my other shoulder. "Hey, Isabella loves you. She always has. It might take a second, but she knows the love never left."

"You're right." I took a deep breath and patted one of his hands, and we faced Cornia again. My Shapple extended a section of wool and caressed my hand. "Well, let's go hug our families." A smile engulfed my face.

The remaining venture to Cornia was the quickest, longest path I had ever taken. I tried not to run, but I accelerated my pace. I pictured my front door. Was it still the same color? Would I remember which streets to take? My pace transformed into a run.

The transition from crops to buildings happened as soon as we entered the city. So many people walked around. I forgot what a big city was like. The citizens stopped and stared as we entered, some even applauded. Gratitude and shouts of praise echoed in the streets. I acknowledged many with smiles, but I didn't care about them. All I cared about was seeing my family.

Familiar streets appeared as I recalled the route. Ofelia followed close behind before I rounded the corner and saw it. Stucco walls called me in. The turquoise roof brightened my heart. And the orange door. *My* orange door. My home.

I stopped running. I didn't know why my eagerness to run home disappeared. After all these years, all the suffering and sacrifice, I stopped short, suddenly filled with trepidation.

What if Isabella hates me? What if Harper doesn't remember me? What if my home doesn't feel like my home anymore?

Ofelia looked ahead and then back to me. "Is that your home?"

"Yes." I took a deep breath.

With a couple of steps forward, she faced me. "Well, what are you waiting for?"

"I...I don't know." Frozen in place, I didn't even turn my body to face her. "But I need to go there. I *want* to go there." Melting in the hot sun, I marched forward before stopping and turning back to Ofelia. "What will you do?"

"I'm going to talk to Stena Mezca. Then, hopefully, find a place to sleep." She put her hand on my shoulder. "Get in there, estúpido. Tu familia está esperando. Don't let them wait any longer."

I hugged Ofelia. "I'll find you later. You can stay at our house."

"We'll talk tomorrow. Don't worry about me." She looked toward my house and tilted her head upward. "Give your family the time you all need."

After a brief hug, my orange front door beckoned me forward. My body gravitated toward it, my feet floating like they couldn't touch the ground. I reached out and grabbed the handle with closed eyes and pushed the door open. A loud bark made me jump, something I hadn't heard in so long. I looked down, and my three-legged Talonhound let out a low grumble with narrowed eyes. Then, Harper's tail wagged as she leaped in the air and hit my legs with her one front paw. She breathed heavily with little barks of joy.

I got down on my knees and scratched her head with aggression and laughter. "Harper, my baby girl." My long-lost Talonhound voice had returned. She licked my face as I kissed her nose. "How have you been?"

She panted in response. Her fluffy face and splotchy colors accentuated her clear smile. With a startled look, Harper growled past me. I almost forgot about my Shapple close behind.

"Easy now." I petted Harper's head. "This Shapple is a friend."

The Shapple groaned in response before reaching out with its wool, letting it hover just above Harper's head. She observed the fur, then the Shapple stroked Harper's head like I did.

Rushing footsteps came from around the corner. My heart fluttered. I looked up to a not-so-little girl, stopping and intently staring at me. I lost my breath. Her braided black hair hung to the side. With curious honey eyes, the girl observed me and then the Shapple petting Harper, trying to find something she knew but had lost. Her lips pursed, and for a moment, I thought a smile formed, but her lips just shifted. My Isabella looked so old.

"Isabella," I whispered, love gushing through my heart. "Mi hija." My skin tingled.

Three years had passed without seeing my daughter. For three years, I tried to picture what she looked like or how she would act. Without realizing it, I had reached into my pocket and fiddled with Isabella's drawing. I pulled my hand out, my dream and reality coexisting as one right in front of me. Reality stood before me. Isabella stood before me. Yet, the joy I imagined...no, dreamed about, held no place.

A face popped around the corner behind Isabella. Valeria's hair waved behind her like a tail, tied back into a single braid as she rushed next to Isabella. Valeria put her right hand to her mouth, and her left hand rested on Isabella's head. Little teary fireworks shot out from Valeria's amber eyes.

Lowering Harper back to the ground, who remained entranced by the Shapple, I jumped up and rushed over to them. Falling to my knees at the same rate Valeria did, we embraced one another with Isabella in the middle. I gripped them, fearing that if I'd ever let go, I'd never see them again. My heart ached and inflated at the same time. Feeling their skin against mine sent overwhelming shivers across my body. I kissed them each on the head. With the faintest grip, Isabella hugged me, or may have just patted my back.

When I stood back up, Isabella's little brown eyes looked up at me. Her lips still showed no emotion. She moved her glance over to Valeria.

"Mamá, can I go play in the backyard?" she asked.

Valeria looked down at Isabella. "Isabella, your father is home and wants to—"

"It's okay," I interrupted, though my heart shattered as I said it.

"But—" Valeria began again.

"Seriously," I said, my voice cracking from being so dry. "Go and play, hija."

I was graced with a small smile as she ran off to the backyard. Harper followed, and the door shut behind them. My Shapple sauntered up to my side.

"I'm sorry she is acting like this," Valeria said, eyeing the beast.

"Don't be. She hasn't seen me in so long. She needs some time." I noticed her staring at the Shapple. "And we may have a new pet." I smiled.

Valeria tilted her head with an open mouth but turned it into a smile before pulling me in for a kiss. The electricity from her lips stunned me at first. Once I became used to the zap, I met her intensity with a passion locked away for too long. At first, the electricity coursed through my entire body. Then, the heat built in my chest and at my hips, a longing for her body to be wrapped up with mine. As we parted, the spark and heat were replaced by a different feeling.

Everything hit me at once. My muscles tensed, my eyes widened, my head throbbed, and my skin tingled. It all climaxed into tears erupting from my exhausted existence.

She wrapped me in her arms and squeezed as if to contain my sudden sadness, joy, or whatever was going on. The Shapple extended its wooly fur and rubbed the part of my back that Valeria didn't touch.

"Shh," she said, scratching my back and petting my head simultaneously. "It's okay. You are *home*."

Everything crashed into me at once. Being used as a weapon, creating a disease, watching hundreds of people die, and everything else in between needed to be voiced. A great and terrible guilt finally cracked me.

"V," I began in between sobs, "I did some *terrible* things."

"I know." Her voice cracked within strained cries. "That's part of war. But you're alive, and we're safe. That's what's most important."

"For now..." The Shapple continued to rub my back. "But all the things I did beyond this are truly terrible."

She pulled away from me and stared into my eyes while holding my shoulders. "What do you mean?" My mind went foggy and my body felt woozy. I didn't reply and just stared ahead. She guided me to the couch while my breathing became more rapid. "Come, sit."

My body lowered to the couch. My breathing slowed back down. The Shapple sat next to me and placed a tuft of wool on my left hand. A cloud of pillows consumed my body in one gulp. I forgot how comfortable our couch was. It was the softest thing I had sat in for so long. The tension in my body subsided, and I took one deep breath, letting the air out of my mouth as slowly as I could.

"I did what you all wanted me to do before you came back to Cornia," I said. "I was able to move disease and infect the Coalitionists. It was getting too easy for me to do. Then, a wave was coming to strike the battlefront. It was going to be a wave that all of our warriors would have died from. Aameen left to recruit Solara's aid."

"Solara's aid?"

"Yes. It involved politics I didn't understand. But the wave ended up coming to an area that only I oversaw. We were doomed. La muerte estaba cerca. I was running out of diseases to inflict on Coalitionists." I paused, recalling one of the most terrifying moments of my life. "Then, I saw what you had. The purple flowers. I had no choice. I took these flowers and other diseases and fused them into a big ball. I let them burn in my hands. I knew this amplified them. Then, I released it toward the incoming Coalitionists. It…it…exploded." My throat became very dry, and I swallowed hard to keep my voice going. Valeria put her hand on my thigh. "The disease changed into rainbow flowers. It struck both Coalitionists and Maizeans alike." Locking eyes with Valeria, my chest ached. "It was a new disease."

"A new disease?" Her hand lifted from my thigh and lingered in the air, unsure of where to go.

"I didn't mean to do it. I shouldn't have done it." I started hyperventilating. "It was the only choice I had, or our warriors would have died. I would have died." The Shapple gripped my wrist tighter. "They would have probably made it to Cornia and attacked the city. I had to protect our family."

Leaning forward, I hid my undeserving face in my hands, trying to hold back further tears. The air buzzed around me, my head throbbing.

Valeria's hand touched my back, recoiled, then came back. I wanted her comfort, but didn't feel like I deserved it. Then, her soft hand pushed me. She embraced me. It was a familiar touch, and it broke down my mental barrier and made my body collapse toward her.

Valeria started singing:

Mira dentro para verte a ti mismo.
Encuentra la comodidad.
Descansa la cabeza.

Siente el amor a tu alrededor.
Siente el amor bajar tu plumón.[1]

The song mesmerized me, drawing my head into her chest like a magnet. Even the Shapple loosened its grip at her melody. After a deep breath, the tears subsided. She sang the song to Isabella every night when she was a baby. I wondered if she still sang the song to her. I hadn't been around for so long. Her voice rang in my head, each word carrying some semblance of peace. It accomplished its lyrical goal—to rest my head.

She switched to humming the song, running her hand over my head with just a hint of scratching. I looked at our table in front of the couch. It was covered in drawings, with a scattered pastel box next to it, colors of every kind popping their worn heads out. I raised my head and grabbed a nearby drawing, one of Isabella's masterpieces. A picture of Harper missing a leg and what looked like Isabella throwing a ball to her captivated me. Another was of Isabella holding Valeria's hand as they walked into the market.

"She's pretty good." My voice became shaky as I struggled to regain the ability to breathe. I kept looking through the drawings while I wiped the tears from my eyes. It was a heartwarming distraction from my grief and guilt. I reached into my pocket and pulled out the tattered drawing, unfolded it, and showed it to Valeria. "I kept this from the day I left." My hands trembled as Valeria reached out to steady me. Taking in the red drawing of us on the couch from years ago, I drifted to the new drawings again. "So much has changed, yet stayed the same."

"That it has, esposo. She likes to draw." Valeria continued to scratch my back. "She does it most of the time."

I came to a drawing of Isabella, Valeria, Harper, and a man.

"Is this...?" I couldn't finish my question.

"It is you, el amor de mi vida. She talks about you all the time."

My heart recharged. She remembered me. Though she put a beard on my face, and we all knew I couldn't grow a beard if my life depended on it. No matter if my facial hair came off accurately, she drew our family.

"She does?" I looked over to Valeria.

"She always asks what I think you are doing at various times throughout the day." She touched my face. "She asks me questions about what you look like. Do you still have longer hair on top of your head? Do you still wear your shirts half tucked? Do you still make people laugh like she remembers laughing with you? She still knows *so* much about you."

"She asks all those questions?"

"And many more." She lowered her hand to the drawings and touched one. "She remembers you. But apparently not your facial hair." We both chuckled. "I think she was scared to finally see you again. She will come around. This is a big transition for all of us."

"I know. I was afraid she wouldn't recognize me. I just want things to be normal."

"Normal means boring." She slapped my back a couple of times. "We are *far* from boring. We have also experienced a lot over the last few years."

I looked out the window at Isabella throwing a ball to Harper.

"I'm going to talk to her."

Valeria kissed me on the cheek. "Now there is the Ciro I remember." She looked at me with concern and a smile. "Go love on your daughter."

I stood up and walked out the back door. Harper turned and ran over to me as I bent over to pet her head, the Shapple walking up next to me. I noticed a small yellow cloud around Harper's ear, the same yellow cloud the Shapple next to me had all those years ago, though much smaller. It was the beginning of an ear infection. Nothing too serious, something I could address later. Isabella stared at me with pursed lips again.

"May I play with you?" I asked.

"Yes," she said. Without hesitation, she threw the ball to me. It came much faster than I expected. Holding the smooth ball in my hand, I smiled before tossing it back to her. We played catch while Harper wobbled back and forth between us, watching the ball with eager eyes. Harper adapted well to her missing leg. The Shapple just sat at my side, watching Isabella and Isabella watching the beast in return.

"Do you play with Harper often?" I asked.

"When Mamá lets me," she responded.

"I always liked playing with Harper as well. I missed her. I missed you."

Isabella smiled. "She whines a lot by the door. Mamá always says she is waiting for you to come through."

"I have wanted to come through that door for a long time." I nervously laughed. "I saw your drawings. You're really good."

"I know." She stood up straight with a half-smile. "I like looking at things." Her gaze drifted down to the Shapple again.

"You remember details well. This is my friend who came back with me from Husk. It'll be staying with us."

"Does it have a name?"

I eyed the Shapple. "You know, no, it doesn't."

"Can I name it?" Isabella tossed the ball.

Not looking up, the ball nearly hit me in the face before the Shapple caught it with its wool and brought it to my hand before nodding. "Sure. Go ahead and name it." I threw the ball back.

"That was cool." Isabella caught the ball while watching the Shapple bring its wool back to its body. Staring at the ball, she grinned. "What about Vito?"

"Vito." I looked down at the Shapple and thought about all we had gone through together. "I like that. It's very...full of life." My attention back to my daughter, I waited for her next throw. "Maybe you can add him to the family drawing."

"I could do that." Harper danced around at her feet as Isabella held the ball in the air. "But I'll need to add the new thing for Harper, too." She threw the ball back.

"New thing?" I caught the ball and scrunched my eyebrows and forehead. "What new thing?" I threw the ball back.

"With her ears." She threw the ball again. "The yellow, fluffy stuff."

I froze as the ball hit me in the chest. Isabella giggled. It was the first time a genuine smile had curled up her cheeks since I had returned. However, that didn't capture my attention as much as what she said had.

"What did you say?" My eyes looked down at Harper, reassuring what I saw. I observed the yellow cloud around her left ear again. It was there.

"I just saw it yesterday. I think it looks kind of funny."

My heart pounded so hard that my ribs ached. I couldn't believe what had just happened.

My daughter could see disease like I could.

Can she do what I can do?

The absolute worst thing in the world crashed into me and made me want to fall to the ground. How could it be happening? Why would Gaia do this to me? Did my daughter carry the same burden I did?

Could Isabella see disease?

PART 3

RECOVERY

CHAPTER 16
CORNIA

My first morning home raced along in a blur. I needed to get my mind off of what Isabella had said, and Harper's ear infection became the perfect one.

"I'm taking Harper to the vet," I said to Valeria.

Harper itched her ear and wagged her tail before I put her leash on and left my house, away from my daughter. Vito followed behind, as I expected him to. I still tried to digest what I had discovered the day before. A brief inquisition with Isabella took place in the backyard, but she was only seven years old. She didn't understand the gravity of what she could do, and I had to remind myself of that.

I should have told Valeria immediately, but I didn't know what to say. How could I tell her our daughter could see disease, probably move it, and, more importantly, hurt other people? It was too much power for one little girl.

If I couldn't involve Valeria yet, I could try to come up with a plan. I hadn't even had a chance to relax since arriving home. My focus was split between my daughter, Enferflor's unknown impact on Cornia, and adapting to normal life. I couldn't talk to Valeria about it; she wouldn't understand. But part of me wondered if I could trust her. She had gone behind my back and joined the war, unbeknownst to me. What else could she do? I shook my head, trying to rid my mind of these ridiculous ideas.

But was our relationship changing?

I will train Isabella. That's the first thing I should do. But how and when?

Walking down the street, I tried to clear my mind, but everything about Cornia distracted me as well. Everyone wanted to talk to me, congratulate me, or ask me about the war. I had no chance to breathe.

"Sorry, I'm late for a vet appointment," I said to everyone. Once again, the perfect excuse. Did I need to go? Not at all. I could heal the infection myself, but I wanted to talk to Victor.

Get the hell away from me and leave me alone!

I quickened my pace after each interaction. If I moved quicker, I could make it to Victor's without further conversations. I had a sick beast after all. This excuse worked until a terror stopped me where I stood.

Rainbow flowers danced along the shoulders of Maximo, the baker.

I froze. Harper yanked me forward before dropping to the ground and attempting to scratch her ear. Vito reached out and helped Harper with her scratch.

I didn't know why seeing Enferflor's flowers shocked me. But the reality of seeing the disease on Maximo made it real. He didn't even fight in the war, which meant the disease *had* spread to the city.

Three people lined up to pick up his baked goods at the small stand outside his home. The green wooden fixture with a small canopy overhang covered the most delicious baked goods. Loaves, conchas, and other pastries wafted their delightful aroma into the air. For the first time ever, the smell made me nauseous.

Harper barked, pulling my attention from the baker. "Sorry, honey." We continued walking. I would treat Maximo later. That became my next top priority.

Now isn't the time. But would there ever be a good time? I'm already late—he's already infected.

I opened the rounded door to Victor's office, and a bell chimed from above. The noise caught me off guard, something that hadn't been there before. Victor looked up from a serpent he was analyzing. The Eloterra, covered in golden yellow and mustard scales, coiled around Victor's hand and wiggled its long green ears and tail with similar green extensions. A green tongue vibrated from its mouth before it pulled it back in. Just above the beast's mouth, orange ribbons writhed in an odd pattern.

"Ciro!" Victor exclaimed, holding the Eloterra close to his chest. "It is good to see your face."

"Yours as well." I gave a quick smile. With eyes like emeralds, the Eloterra watched me as the orange ribbons moved all the way into the beast's left side of the mouth. "The left tooth is infected. Second from the middle."

"Ah ha!" Victor shouted as he yanked the tooth out of the serpent's mouth. The limbless beast hissed and recoiled. The ribbons twisted before fading, and the Eloterra's body relaxed in Victor's hand. "I was worried I would have to pull more out. I could have used your help all these years. You are quicker than before. You must have learned a lot." Eyes drifting down to Harper, they moved next to Vito. "And new friends?"

"I learned more than you know," I said more to myself than to him. "And yes." Pointing to Vito, the Shapple extended its wool and wrapped it around my pointer finger before I recoiled. "Vito is a new friend. But I'm here for Harper. She has an infection in her left ear. It's very mild."

Victor placed the Eloterra into a cage and walked over to Harper. Wagging her tail, Harper's tongue hung as Victor petted Harper and crouched to look into her ear. "Very mild. A little antibiotic will do the trick." Moving over to the shelves of vials and bottles, he grabbed a small tube. The bottle clinked as he flicked it twice, squeezed the bulb atop the dropper, tilted Harper's head, and dripped two drops into Harper's ear. He then massaged the ear as it made a squishy noise. As soon as he released, Harper shook her head and little droplets sprayed my face.

"Dammit." I wiped my face. Yellow mucus hung off the tips of my fingers.

"I'm sure that isn't the grossest thing you experienced during the war." With a little wink, he grinned. "Speaking of the war, how was it? How are you?"

What a loaded question—how was it?

A wave of guilt collided with the fear and grief surrounding my heart, but I swallowed it down for another time.

"It was...something." Such a simple statement was all I could offer. "I'm happy to be back with my family." I forced a smile. "I will admit I'm very tired."

"I'm sure you are. Getting adjusted to normal life has to be hard."

Normal life.

"I'm afraid there won't be much adjusting. Not with what I can do." My hands awkwardly swirled in the air like I did when moving disease.

Almost stumbling forward, he stood straight up. "So, this means you will be helping me?" His eyes pleaded.

Pressing my lips together, I shook my head. "I wish, but a new problem has come to our city, and my focus will be there."

"New problem?" He tilted his head.

What to tell him and what not to tell him. Of all people, he deserves to know. Maybe even provide some needed insight?

"There is a new disease—Enferflor."

"Enferflor?" Though he chuckled, he noticed my stern face. "Seriously? That's a terrible name. Why not just Enfer?"

That does sound better.

"Enfer," I repeated. "It does roll off the tongue easier. Anyway, it's a disease like necrotizing fasciitis, but slower and much more contagious. We believe it to be airborne."

Ofelia warned me to be careful with Enferflor...or Enfer and my knowledge about it. But Victor knew about my abilities well before most, and he kept it a secret. Well, I hoped he had.

"Airborne?" Crossing his arms, his smile faded. "Necrotizing fasciitis isn't airborne. How is that possible?"

"It changed. It's in the city already." I thought of Maximo.

"That isn't good." He put his hand on his chin and shrugged. "Well, that's how you will treat Harper's ear. One drop in the ear each day for about a week."

The shift in conversation forced me to take a step back.

"You brushed that off so easily."

"Brushed off what?" Victor squinted. "The new disease?"

"Yes." My tone came off a bit condescending. "You of all people should know that healing is *our* job. When a new disease pops up that we can't heal, it adds more weight on our shoulders."

Shocking me even more, Victor laughed. "You have that right."

"Why are you laughing at this?" I clenched my fist, debating punching him for his callousness. "This disease is *killing* people."

Hands up, Victor backed up. "Whoa, I'm not laughing at the disease. I'm laughing at your new discovery." He jabbed a finger into his chest. "I'm not a monster. I don't get a kick out of watching people die, though I did pick treating beasts instead of people for a reason. Nevertheless, the weight part. That weight is always there for us healers. But I can't let it bring me down. If I do, I'll be less effective at what I can do to help."

My hand relaxed at my side. His wisdom swept through me and left my heart lighter. He was right. "So, you just keep pushing?"

"I just keep pushing." He smiled.

The guilt and fear still pressed at me, but his new revelation made me feel inspired. If I let Enfer get me down, how could I hope to fight the monster I created? It was all we could do as healers—keep pushing.

"Thank you, Victor," I said. "For everything. You're an actual inspiration to me."

He smiled again. Harper shook her head, and some discharge from her ear splattered on Victor's face.

"Sometimes I forget that I can be." He wiped the gunk off his face. "I'm glad to see you're alive and making a difference for our country. I'm proud to call you my friend, Ciro."

I nodded. "I'm sure we will talk again soon."

"Adiós, mi amigo." He waved.

"Hasta luego." Harper, Vito, and I exited his office.

I debated heading home, but whether it was Harper who pulled me or if my subconsciousness drew me over, I stood back in front of the bakery, Maximo handing a concha over to another person. Smiles and money exchanged, Maximo exuded warmth and made everyone feel appreciated. A burly man, both in height and width, I remembered he said it was because of his family traits, not his diet. Though no hair sat atop his head, a thick mustache made up for it. None of his appearance mattered to me, just the rainbow flowers. They mocked me, rotating in place. The good news was that I didn't see that many. It'd be a quick treatment, but how was I to do it without raising any alarm? As if on cue, he grabbed his shoulder and stretched in pain—the perfect opportunity.

I hurried over to him. "Hola, Maximo. How are you today?"

He looked up, eyes widened. "Ciro? Is that really you?" I nodded as he clapped his hands. "It is good to see you back home, my friend!" He embraced me for a hug, wrapping his arms around me and lifting me an inch off the ground. My back cracked from the embrace before he lowered my body. "Thank you for serving in the war. Are you here for some concha? It's on the house. Mi concha es su concha."

"You don't have to do that."

"Don't be silly. I owe you more than concha for saving our city, for serving our country. Word has gone around about your involvement. You are said to be the savior of Maize." He snapped his fingers. "No, the Hero of Maize."

His words pierced my heart, especially as I stared at the rainbow flowers.

"You flatter me." He handed me two conchas. He grabbed his shoulder again. "I see your shoulder is bothering you."

"You're very observant." Rolling his shoulder back, it let out a loud crack. "For about a week now."

Pointing at his shoulder, I asked, "Do you mind if I look at it? I learned a thing or two as a medic."

"I don't want to keep you from your day."

"*Don't be silly.*" I mimicked his statement from moments before. "I owe you for giving me a concha."

"Always witty." He snickered and turned his back to me.

The rainbow flowers danced, and I returned their dance by burning them one by one. The burning on my fingertips intensified as I moved toward taking down the five targets.

"How is your family?" I asked as I worked on the flowers.

"It is good to have my daughter back from the war. She has grown so much since her involvement. She makes me proud."

"She wasn't in my ranks, but I heard good things about her," I lied. His eyes lit up when I said that. I shook my head. I don't know where that came from. I finished burning the flowers. "Well, I can't say much about your shoulder. I think it will get better with some stretching."

"That much I figured. Thank you for looking." He handed me two more conchas. "For your time."

"You're too kind. Keep stretching that shoulder." I patted the shoulder, which was now flowerless.

"Oh, I will. Hasta luego."

"Hasto luego," I echoed before departing.

I kept my head down and hurried home, either to avoid praise as the Hero of Maize or to avoid seeing more rainbow flowers. Harper and Vito trotted with me. Each house I passed was a step closer to my own home. Though difficult walking without looking up, my neighbor's house caught my attention. Just as I looked up to see my front door, I collided with someone.

"I'm so sorry," I said. My head wobbled with my arms trying to keep my balance.

"Watch it, asshole," Ofelia responded with a smile.

My scowl at the comment morphed into a mirrored grin. "Oh, it's only you."

Squinting, she looked past me. "Why are you running around without looking?"

"I'm apparently the new *Hero of Maize*. I also saw some rainbow flowers."

Her smile faded. "Well, since you know…things aren't great. I stopped by the medical facility today, and there were ten cases already at the breaking point."

My heart stopped beating before I released a breath I didn't realize I held in. "The Hero of Maize strikes again."

"Stop it." She stomped hard on the ground with her eyes shut tight. "We need to come up with a plan, and I have a time set up with the Stena and

Counts in about thirty minutes." Opening her eyes, she looked up. "Will that work?"

"Yes." I paused. "Let me get Harper and Vito inside and tell my wife." I opened my door.

"May I come in?"

"Please." We entered the house as Isabella popped up from behind the couch. I kissed her head. "Where is your mother?"

"In the kitchen," Isabella answered, glaring at Ofelia. "Who is this?"

The way that Isabella's honey eyes narrowed was so like Valeria's that it made me chuckle, but I also didn't like her abrupt question. Before I could tell Isabella not to be rude, Ofelia raised her hand in my direction without looking.

Snapping to attention, Ofelia saluted. "Ofelia. Ofelia Herrera." She leaned in close and put up one of her hands to her mouth and whispered. "I was the Kernel of the medics in the war. Your father helped me a lot." After Ofelia gave a little wink, Isabella giggled.

"She also helped save my life," Valeria said, rounding the corner. "A friend who is always welcome in our house." Strutting forward, she embraced Ofelia. "It is good to see you away from sickness."

"Well, war sickness," Ofelia responded. "You seem to be moving smoothly."

"The doctors here were impressed by your stitchwork." Valeria patted her leg. "They say there will barely be a scar."

"The signature of my work," Ofelia said, clapping her hands together and twinkling her fingers in the air. "Nothing."

"I'm Isabella." My daughter rose from the couch and looked up at Ofelia with her hands behind her back.

"I have heard amazing things about you," Ofelia said. "Your father talked about you *all* the time."

Isabella just smiled, sat back on the couch, and went back to drawing. She drew the puffy cloud around Harper's ear. Should I have addressed it? Maybe. Did I decide to just keep pushing forward on my current task at hand? Yes. I followed Victor's advice.

"We have a meeting with the leaders in about thirty minutes," I said. "To talk about Enfer."

Ofelia turned to me with furrowed eyebrows. "Enfer?" I just shrugged. Moving her jaw back and forth as if tasting food, she nodded. "That sounds better."

"Thank the vet," I said.

"Is it about finding treatment for...Enfer?" Valeria asked, trying the new name out.

"That's the goal," I said. "I'll probably be home close to dinner. I'm sorry I'm already gone so much."

Valeria smiled and kissed my cheek. "Don't be. Keeping Maize safe is important."

The last time we had spoken about keeping Maize safe, I went to war as a weapon. A dark cloud swirled in my chest, making breathing harder. I closed my eyes and steadied my breath. When I reopened my eyes, Valeria's smile dwindled. With a quick shake of my head, I broadened my smile and stepped toward her.

"You're too good to me. I love you." Pulling Valeria in, I pecked her lips. The normal electricity between us wasn't present. Moving over to Isabella, I kissed her head. "And you, hija."

Valeria cleared her throat and turned to Ofelia. "Join us for dinner."

"I appreciate the invite, but I can't tonight," Ofelia said. "I have a new place I'm getting situated in. A night by myself has been long overdue."

"I hear that," Valeria resounded. "Another time then."

Leaving my home too soon, we made our way to the capitol building. Having Ofelia in my house forced a little smile on my face, despite the odd interaction with Valeria. It was just a blip.

I focused on Ofelia again. Though she wasn't family, she integrated well with us. Aameen used to be that person. I wondered if our relationship would return. So many relationships had shifted since I left for the war. I dragged my feet as we moved along, a bit unsure if Aameen and I were the same as before. Or if Valeria and I were okay.

"How was your first night home?" Ofelia asked. "You seem on edge."

At times, I appreciated Ofelia's questions. At other times, they came off abrasive.

How was my first night home? What a ridiculous question. The truth? I haven't even had a chance to enjoy it. I'm terrified about Enfer. I can't go outside because I'm worried about seeing the rainbow flowers everywhere. I can't stay home because I don't know what to do about my daughter. Now, I'm not telling my wife things about Isabella.

An insurmountable guilt pressed on my chest, making it hard to breathe again. I needed a way to relieve myself of my stress. At least focusing on Isabella presented itself as a more realistic option. But I needed help.

I could tell Ofelia.

"Isabella said something interesting yesterday." A rush of air followed after I said it. "We were playing catch, and I noticed fluff on Harper's ear. Like the kind I see. Out of nowhere, Isabella casually mentioned the fluff." My heartbeat raged within my chest. "She sees what I see. She saw the ear infection."

"What?" Ofelia exclaimed.

"Shh," I hushed her. "Don't cause a scene."

"Your daughter has your abilities." Pacing around like the Felaize that prowl around the hills near Amar, she kept her eyes on me. She stopped. "This is good. Maybe she can help."

"She's *seven*." I shot the sharpest glare I could at her.

"Not now, but eventually." She paced around again. "I'm not into child labor, Ciro."

"I had the opposite reaction." Still appalled at what she said, my heartbeat continued its rampage within me. "What if she makes another disease or kills more people?"

Halting her prowl, Ofelia pointed at me. "Except she has you to teach her how to handle this gift. I tried my best to help you, but you had to teach yourself. You have experience that you can now share." Pointing to the sky, she jumped a little. "You should start writing a journal about what you learned and how you did it. It could be useful to her when she doesn't always want to ask you."

"That's a great idea." A confidence swelled inside me, warming my lungs. "I can be a teacher. That could be good."

"That is *monumental*. Es una gran cosa." Her shoulders slouched. "How did Valeria respond?"

My teeth clicked tightly together as I opened my lips just enough for her to see my tension. I closed one eye, hoping to avoid her reaction, and kept the other one open to see it. "I haven't exactly talked to her about it yet."

"And you told me first?" She yelled and shook her head. "Ciro, you need to talk to your wife."

"I was planning to, but the day got away from me. There was just an easier opportunity with you. I trust you and you're important to me."

"But not as important as the wife you whined about missing every day. All the protecting your family and shit. Ser inteligente, idiot."

"You're right." A deep sigh followed.

I had made up so many excuses for why I hadn't told her. She deserved to know. I had to find time to tell her.

To my relief, Pastel Castle came into view as we turned the corner. The cake-like building was a sight for sore eyes. I missed its ridiculous architecture and colors. It made my heart happy.

"Which door should we pick?" I proposed my lighthearted question, shifting the subject.

"Um, does it matter?"

"Ah, this is your first experience with Pastel Castle." I strutted forward.

"Not at all. I have been here many times."

"Well, each door represents a different mindset. You choose which door, or mindset, you want to enter with," I said, gesturing with my hands to each door.

"Ciro, I know. I'm native to Maize. But thank you for explaining my culture to me."

"Right…" I drifted. "So, why did you ask if it mattered?"

"I just wanted to see you light-hearted. You seemed excited, so I went along with it." She laughed and sashayed up next to me.

I was excited about explaining this mundane experience. "I guess I was…sorry."

"Don't be. It's okay to be happy again." She patted my shoulder.

We entered the same doors I had entered before the war—the orange doors, representing the spirit of timidity. Timidity would allow me to listen. It had worked for me before. Ofelia would do most of the conversation heavy lifting anyway.

Footsteps echoed around the curved walls of the castle and up the colorful stairs. Aameen walked ahead of us. I wanted to say hello to him, but he seemed very focused. I didn't want to break his trance.

We followed Aameen up the curved staircase to the third floor, or flavor orange. With few people on the floor, an uncomfortable silence filled the space. We followed Aameen through large orange doors, adorned with intricate carvings of corn cobs in a large circle meant to represent the sun. Inside, the Counts sat along a long brown table with Stena Mezca in its center. Only one chair at the table sat empty, Count Ariba's chair. The notion shocked me—Count Ariba was never late.

"Welcome, Kernel Ofelia and the Hero of Maize," Stena Mezca said as he stood and clapped. The other Counts joined in. Aameen rounded the table while clapping and stood next to Ariba's chair. I looked at Aameen, confused. He smiled and shrugged his shoulders. "Now, let us sit. It is good to have our vacant seat filled with Aameen on such short notice. Or I should say, Count Aameen."

My jaw fell. I turned my head to one side and then the next, analyzing Aameen's large grin. He looked over at me and smiled even bigger. We'd been home for only a couple of days and he'd become a Count? Pressure built in my chest. Why hadn't he told me?

"It is my pleasure to serve Maize," Aameen said.

With Aameen now in Count Ariba's chair, her absence was unaccounted for.

"What happened to Count Ariba?" I asked.

Stena Mezca let out a long sigh as his face softened. "Count Ariba passed away about two weeks ago." An uncharacteristic sheen glistened in his eyes. "The cancer she had took a dark toll. She had fought valiantly for three years. I will miss my friend and ally of Maize."

My heart sank. Count Ariba's disease was the first I had seen with my gift—the cancer had appeared as a translucent scarf around her neck. I know she fought. She promised me that she would.

Our conversation all those years ago made me hopeful for a future friendship between us. Would death ever leave me be?

"I'm sorry to hear about your loss." I gazed into Stena Mezca's eyes, only speaking to him. "She served Maize, but more importantly, I know how good a friend she was to you."

Stena Mezca smiled, tears building up in his eyes. "Thank you for your words, Ciro. They mean a lot." He blinked the tears away, recovering. "If I remember correctly, you didn't care for her. The war seems to have changed you."

"If for better or for worse, time will only tell," I said.

"Wise words," Stena Mezca said. "I was eager to ask Count Aameen to fill the position upon his return. His leadership, foreign diplomacy, and dedication to Maize during the war didn't go unnoticed." He slapped the table, the noise echoing all around. "Now, let's discuss the dilemma facing our great country."

"Yes, Stena Mezca," Ofelia took over. "The healing process during the war went smoothly with the assistance of my new friend Ciro. His ability to diagnose diseases is like nothing else I have seen before."

"Another accolade for Ciro," Stena Mezca praised.

"Certainly," Ofelia continued with a smile in my direction, "but something new came up at the end of the war. A new disease has...blossomed. We named it Enfermedad Floreciente, or Enfer for short. It mimics another disease called necrotizing fasciitis, caused by flesh-eating bacteria."

"Flesh-eating?" Stena Mezca asked.

"Yes," she repeated, "flesh-eating. Though Enfer is not as fast. It is slower-moving, but just as deadly. It comes to a climax when large tumors form in one or more areas. The tumor grows quickly, and eventually explodes. Death comes shortly after this."

"Correct me if I am wrong, but didn't Valeria have necrotizing fasciitis?" Count Bebida asked. Valeria's good friend had aged in the years since the war started; wisdom shone in the new wrinkles lining her face. "She mentioned this when we met after her return from the war."

"Yes," I said. "She did, and she survived."

"But hers came from an open wound transmission," Ofelia took over. "Necrotizing fasciitis originates from a bacterial infection of a wound. Enfer is different. It is contagious on a grander scheme. No wound necessary."

"Airborne," I said.

"Airborne..." Ofelia repeated. She turned her attention back to our audience. "A disease that keeps evolving and becomes deadlier by the minute."

"What was the death rate of those infected?" another Count asked.

"Over ninety-five percent," Ofelia said.

The Stena and Counts mumbled to one another. The soft buzz from their low conversation made my ears vibrate. I itched at the irritating tickle.

"And what are we to do about this?" Stena Mezca asked. "In your professional opinion?"

"We need to start searching for possible treatments and, better yet, prevention," Ofelia said. "A professional team funded by Maize should be formed to investigate the disease."

"You mean to pull citizens away from their needed roles...to find a cure?" Stena Mezca questioned.

The way he positioned his question made me uneasy.

"Yes..." Ofelia responded with hesitation. Pivoting, she analyzed the shift in the room and slowed down her words. "The disease will amplify and infect more the longer we wait."

"I see," Stena Mezca said. "Count Juan, I think this is a good time for updates on the Coalition."

We turned our attention toward the man in all black with a thick black beard. He held a firm gaze and thick eyebrows. Piercing golden eyes contrasted with his darker skin.

"Yes, Stena," he said in a rough voice. "The Coalition's surrender was good for us. My sources say the Coalition retreated due to Solara's involvement in the war."

"Thanks to Count Aameen," Stena Mezca said.

Aameen seemed to have a strong relationship with the Stena. It made me wonder if they'd been talking well before this meeting.

"Thanks to Count Aameen," Count Juan agreed with a nod toward Aameen. "I'm told the Coalition's tribes, which were united as one during the war, are restructuring. Johan, leader of the Fahir tribe, has been appointed Emperor of the Coalition Empire. A new weapon, one I'm told we should fear, is in development. More war may be on our horizon, either on the Maizean border or in Solara."

"Thank you, Count Juan," Stena Mezca said as Count Juan sat down. He seemed like he had more to say, but followed the Stena's command. "With the threat of more fighting on the horizon, it seems our resources should be directed toward defense, not...prevention. If that is what you want to call it."

"Prevention?" I asked. "Not to be rude, but that's bullshit." Ofelia and Aameen glanced at me. I didn't know what had come over me, but I had to say it. "There will be no war if we don't deal with this disease. It will *kill* us, and there will be nothing to protect."

"Ciro," Stena Mezca said, "know your place."

"Aameen," I continued past the warning, "tell them what you saw at the border."

Aameen widened his eyes. He shook his head in my direction. "What about it, Ciro?"

His tone came off condescending. My veins lit on fire. "How about Eron and Irena?" I asked, matching his patronizing attitude. "Did you forget about them?"

Aameen squinted. "Of course, I remember them. They died of Enfer. It was saddening, but they served Maize well."

Before I could scream at his callous attitude, Ofelia cut me off. "What Ciro is trying to say is that deaths caused by Enfer are very quick and very taxing. Count Aameen was there when it all happened. He knows the importance of finding a cure."

Stena Mezca turned his attention to Aameen. "Count Aameen, what say you? It sounds like Ciro has started to figure out how to use his ability to find a cure. At least according to your reporting."

My mouth hung open, and a high-pitched ringing sounded in my ears. He had told Stena Mezca about what I could do. Just like he had told Krown Kernel Fernando.

That son of a bitch.

"I believe the disease has made great progress," Aameen said, each word stabbing like knives at my chest. "But I believe we have as well. I think our resources would be better used in other areas."

"But—" Ofelia began.

"And the other uses of your abilities should be considered against the Coalition again," Stena Mezca interrupted.

My heart had been ripped out of my chest. Aameen told him everything. Every terrible secret.

"What..." My voice faded from shock.

"But Ciro is needed to help heal the infected," Ofelia pleaded. "His abilities will be better used in Cornia."

My world started spinning. I remembered creating Enfer. I remembered killing so many and infecting all those people at once. I couldn't do it again.

I had only been home for one night, and they were ready to throw me back into the fire.

"But war will kill us all," Count Juan said.

"The disease will first," Ofelia countered.

One Count shouted at another. Count Bebida shot a glance at Stena Mezca before sharing her thoughts. Ofelia continued her argument with Count Juan.

Panic pushed me back against a wall. Luckily, it was there to catch my body. I watched all these people argue about what my role would be.

Am I in charge of my own life anymore? Is my only purpose to be used by others?

Ofelia stopped arguing and turned her attention to me. "Ciro..." Her voice came off so muffled. My ears still rang. "Ciro, say something. Help me."

I took a deep breath and yelled, "Stop!" The room fell silent. I took another deep breath. "I see myself used best as a healer. That is what I'm meant to do. I have killed too many people already. This disease...this disease that was birthed during the war needs to be our focus. I will be better used in attacking it. Please, please let me stay here and fight it."

The room grew quiet. Each Count observed me.

"This is something to consider," Stena Mezca said. "We will have to discuss this...now."

"Let me stay and say my point then," Ofelia said. "Let me plead the case from the medical side. Your Counts do not properly represent my expertise. I'm seasoned in disease treatment and prevention."

"Fine," Stena Mezca said. "You are permitted to stay and discuss Ciro's purpose. Ciro, you are dismissed."

I looked at Ofelia, my panicked face stiff. She tried to comfort me with a nod. She would fight for me. I trusted her. Aameen, on the other hand, had betrayed me. I couldn't even look at him. His presence disgusted me. I said nothing more as I exited the doors and slammed them behind me. I left the castle through the orange door I had entered through. Maize's beliefs were true. The doors did decide what your attitude would be like.

I shouldn't have picked the timid door.

CHAPTER 17
FRIENDS AND ENEMIES

Hours later, I had my answer.

I owed the decision to Ofelia and Count Bebida. Ofelia convinced enough of the Counts of how important I was in fighting against Enfer. Still unsure, Count Bebida swayed enough for the remaining votes. After helping me twice now, once before the war and then after the war, Bebida's dedication to Maize and my family would never be forgotten.

Stena Mezca still wanted me as a weapon, but didn't go against his Counts.

"The only stipulation is that the Stena has issued a six-month deadline before they review the decision," Ofelia relayed Stena Mezca's message. "No pressure."

Ofelia wanted to talk through a plan, but I told her I needed some time to think more about my own understanding of the disease. Whatever our plan ended up being, I needed to face the disease I created head on. I needed to embrace it.

I walked through the streets of Cornia, trying to pull my thoughts together.

Though much had changed since before the war. I started with the buildings. Stucco walls and pastel roofs made up most of Cornia. Though much had changed since I left for the war, the buildings hadn't changed much. Some front doors had been painted a different color. Gardens and landscapes shifted. A few houses had new additions. Even with these changes, the city still felt the same.

The people of Cornia had a positivity that I hadn't felt since prior to the war. The terror of uncertainty and death removed, the culture returned to its previous glory.

People gathered on front porches and at outdoor tables. Conversation and laughter filled the city with light. Music flowed out of homes and echoed throughout the streets. Children played games and filled the sidewalks with murals made of chalk.

Seeing our city so full of life reminded me of the times Valeria and I walked Cornia hand in hand. Could my life be that peaceful again?

A large group walked by me, filling the street with conversation and laughter. Like a cruel punch to the gut, I noticed rainbow flowers on two of them.

My hopes for a peaceful life came crashing down. Cornia wasn't the same city it was before. I wondered if it would ever be again. It was stained by a rainbow smear. I questioned the past portrayal of happiness. Had I been living in ignorance?

I wanted to heal the infected citizens, but I couldn't just walk up to them and awkwardly say I wanted to heal them from something no one else could see. But I couldn't take my eyes off them.

"Watch out!" someone yelled.

I turned and dodged something that was about to hit my head. A short zipping noise flew past my right ear. All the air flew out of my lungs. The zip sounded just like an arrow.

A shadow enveloped the city. Buildings transformed into wooden barricades. Screams of pain echoed around me, punctuated by the zips of arrows flying through the air. I closed my eyes and opened them to my worst nightmare. I was back in the war zone.

Barricades lined the field. Warriors reached up to me, pleading for help, while Coalitionists charged at us. I looked at my hand and found the ball of rainbow flowers, ready to be thrown. I panicked and did what the ball expected of me. Rainbow flowers showered on all the bodies surrounding us, infecting everyone. I fell to the ground. But the ground wasn't the ground anymore; it was a pile of bodies. So many bodies writhed around within the soil. Rainbow flowers sprouted from the soil and grew.

One of the warriors atop the ground and covered in flowers looked up at me, terrified. Growths popped up along their body, enlarging by the second. The warrior's mouth moved as if they were talking, but I only heard screaming and the zip of flying arrows.

With a faint whisper, the warrior asked, "Are you okay?"

What a strange question.

"Are you okay?" It echoed.

I shook my head and blinked. The flower-covered warrior and the soil filled with bodies were gone. Children took their places, throwing a ball between them. An older woman had her hand on my arm as I breathed heavily against a wall.

"Are you okay?" she asked.

"Yes," I cracked out. "I'm okay. Sorry. It's just a headache."

"Are you sure? I thought that ball just missed your head, but did it hit you?" She reached toward my head. "Do you need a medic?"

A medic. I am a medic.

I pulled my head back. "No, I'm okay." Forcing a smile, she let go of me. I immediately walked in the other direction.

Why did the war zone appear? What's going on?

Clenching my chest, I focused on my breathing.

I have to keep pushing, like Victor said. Keep pushing.

I turned down a narrow street to escape the crowd. Aameen and I used to take this route as a shortcut to the market. The street was quiet, but someone with a few rainbow flowers on their body passed by. As much as I didn't want to see someone infected, it was a good distraction from whatever was going on in my head. I needed to figure out how to combat Enfer.

How could I heal this person? I couldn't easily explain what was wrong with them, and I couldn't force them to let me heal them. What was the best approach? By the time I finished my thought process, the citizen was gone. Indecision was a problem. I needed to be bolder. I needed to act quickly next time. But how?

I could use my title, the Hero of Maize, to instill confidence in those I pursued. But would I just wander the streets all day and heal people as I met them? I didn't feel like a hero, so how could I get others to trust that I was one?

If I could just get the infected to come to a space for me to heal them, it'd make my life so much easier. But how could you get someone to come in who wasn't feeling sick yet? Ofelia was better at ideas. I just knew how to heal. Well, at least heal less severe cases.

"Ciro!" someone yelled from behind me. I turned to find Aameen running up to me. "Can we talk?"

My heartbeat raged against my chest. Aameen had changed so much since returning. Hell, he had changed so much since before the war. The way he wanted to exploit me was like gasoline on the growing fire in my heart.

"We have nothing to talk about."

"You deserve an explanation. I should have talked to you before the meeting."

I laughed. "Are you fucking kidding me?" I pointed at him, nearly jamming my finger into his chest. "You literally told the entire council my secrets. I have nothing to say to you."

My head pounded like a war drum. Without any further words, I walked away from him.

"You are valuable to Maize," he said. "You are supposed to protect our country's freedom."

My feet stopped, and I turned back to face him. "*Freedom?*" I exclaimed. "Correct me if I'm wrong, but there wasn't *freedom* when citizens were commanded to fight in the war."

I felt eyes watching us from nearby apartments' windows and balconies. Others who were walking by slowed their pace. Aameen looked around and held out his palms as if indicating he spoke for everyone around. "You helped win the war. The people of Maize still need you."

Heads nodded around us. But did they even know what they were agreeing with? Aameen the people pleaser had struck again.

"I am helping Maize! I don't need *you* to tell *me* how to help." I turned away.

Why is he harassing me like this? He doesn't deserve my time. I have no reason to keep wasting it on him.

"And there he goes, the supposed *Hero of Maize* walking away..." Aameen said, sounding as if he talked to someone else instead of me.

Jolting to a stop, I clenched my fists so hard they cracked. A hot energy pulsed through my body, skin twitching. No self-control. No wisdom. Just emotion. I didn't know if it was the way he said it or if being called the Hero of Maize again prodded me, but a swell of rage bubbled inside. "What did you say?"

He paused for a moment. "You heard me."

I turned back in his direction. "Do you really think that's what I want to be called?"

"It doesn't matter. You don't *deserve* it."

His disgust for my title suddenly hit me. "And *you* deserve it? That's it! You think you should have that title."

He stared at me, the expression on his face communicating kindness and care. But, for the first time, I saw through it. I saw it as what it was, a face put on for the sake of others. A mask to hide his disgust.

"I fought for Maize," he whispered for just the two of us to hear. "I have given my life for Maize. Do you think you're the only one who wants to protect your family?" He paused. "You're selfish. Your gift could help protect so many families in Maize, but you choose *not* to. Stop being a coward and start using your abilities to help others."

My friend was nowhere to be seen in his brown eyes and smug face. Pure arrogance and pride oozed out of him. I hated him. I hated everything about him. As my emotions built, the street around us faded and the war zone came flooding back to me. The barricades. The scorching sun. The arrows. But Aameen still stood in front of me—my enemy.

Before I knew it, my fist launched forward and struck him across the left cheek.

Blood and spit flew from his mouth, and a sharp pain pulsated through my right hand. I had never punched anyone in my life, but it felt good.

It felt *so* good.

Aameen looked back at me while touching his cheek, shocked. Cold, angry eyes locked onto me.

He screamed as he lowered his head and tackled me to the ground.

My back hit the street and scraped along the dirt until my shirt ripped. I pushed my hands forward, trying to wrestle him off me. He began punching my sides. My ears started ringing while my eyes remained fixated on him.

I punched at his sides, but no matter how fast or hard I hit, he seemed unfazed. His experience in combat far outweighed my skills in trying to inflict physical pain.

The fight wasn't fair, but I kept pushing. It was all I could do.

I broke free of his grasp and stood up. He kicked both his feet forward, hitting me in the gut.

My body went numb, then I flew backward. I landed on my back again without my shirt there to absorb the scraping. Rocks and dirt cut at my skin and embedded into my flesh. Every bit of pain hit me at once. The ringing in my ears became stronger.

He jumped up from his back onto both feet in one attempt. His fuzzy voice pushed out, "Instead of fighting with me, how about you fight for your country. You won't be able to protect your family if the Coalition attacks again."

Rage consumed me. How dare he bring up my family? All the pain was replaced by adrenaline. I could feel my eyes swell as I surveyed my surroundings. Two-story buildings dotted with peeking heads gazed at me. The nosy citizens of Maize wanted a show. Did I want to give them one? I shook my head, unsure of where this desire came from.

I kept looking around but only found more curious Maizeans. They weren't what I wanted to find. But what did I want? My instincts took over.

Then, I saw it—a rainbow flower on a man watching the fight. He had two of them.

The flowers followed the commands of my swirling hands. They came to me and burned on my fingertips. I focused on Aameen.

"This fight has been unfair," I mumbled just loud enough for him to hear.

He could beat me. He could always outmatch me in warfare. But my warfare was different. I held something I could throw at him. By just holding Enfer long enough, I could amplify it and win in an instant. I had power. He had fists.

Just before I threw the burning flowers at him, I stopped. He had no idea what I was about to do, but his brown eyes reminded me of his daughter, Dani. In that moment, I remembered his family. I remembered my friend.

Who am I?

I stopped moving my hand, filled with a rainbow flower ball. Something came over me and I didn't recognize myself. I held the rainbow flowers tighter while they scorched my hand. They fizzled away and my hand stopped burning.

My head fell forward, and I stared at the ground.

Cool droplets trickled down my cheeks. My soft sobs echoed around the silent space. Some whispered, but my cries outgrew them.

"Are you okay?" Aameen asked.

"Just get away," I said.

"I didn't mean to hurt—"

"I said get away!" I screamed.

He stepped forward for a moment before turning and walking away. Other people whispered around me louder than before. Whatever scene Aameen and I caused, I just realized how bad it looked.

"The Hero of Maize was beat?" someone asked.

"Count Aameen beat him," another responded.

"How did he win this war?"

"He couldn't even handle one person. I thought he was one of Gaia's descendants."

Their words echoed through my mind. I was unworthy of my title. What made me worthy of a gift I didn't even want? Maybe if I were stronger, I would use it the way it seemed everyone else wanted me to use it as—a weapon.

But that wasn't me.

Firm footsteps moved toward me. I looked toward the footsteps, but my eyes were so full of tears that I couldn't make out who it was.

"Everyone, get back to your days and leave this place," Ofelia said. She kneeled next to me and helped me up. She lowered her voice. "I don't know what happened, but let's get you home. You look like shit."

My head hung low, and I watched the ground pass beneath my feet as we made our way home. The pain in my sides and back flooded back, but I didn't care. Ofelia didn't say any more, and I had nothing to say. I just wanted to go home. Before I knew it, we were at my front porch staircase.

I pushed away from her. "I can get myself inside."

"Are you sure?" she asked.

"I am." I cleared my throat and forced a weak smile. "Thanks for helping me get home."

She shifted her stance, hand on her right hip. "Don't let what he said get to you."

Just as I stepped onto my porch, Vito wrapped a wooly tuft of fur around my hand. I welcomed the support. My lips pursed together as I opened the door to my house, released Vito and ushered him away, shut the door, and leaned my back against it. I knocked my head backward, hitting the door three times while my mind went numb. The room faded into silence. My head pounding echoed in the living room.

Thud. Thud. Thud.

Harper barked before walking up and looking up at me with concerned puppy eyes.

"You shouldn't hit your head on things," Isabella said from the couch. I jumped. "Mamá says it isn't good for your brain."

"You scared me, hija." I put my hand on my beating chest. The beating was so intense it was as if my heart was trying to escape my body.

She smiled. She was the reason I had to keep pushing.

"You look tired," she bluntly pointed out. "What's wrong with your shirt?

I looked down at my bloody, torn shirt. "You aren't wrong. Where is your mother?"

"She's upstairs."

I kissed Isabella on the head and walked upstairs. Harper followed, hobbling up on her three legs. I was impressed with her ability to accomplish the feat.

Each of the other two bedrooms and the bathroom upstairs passed by me. The same brown tile covered the floor, just like the rest of the house. We had nice, thick rugs in each room, scattered with colors and abstract shapes. Valeria was in our room folding laundry. The smell of fresh flowers overcame my senses and filled me with peace.

Our room was a welcome sight. The bed took up most of the space, allowing for a couple of dressers and nightstands to fill the rest. The light on the ceiling fan illuminated the room and our light blue bedspread that was covered with scattered small stars. My mother-in-law had sewn the stars onto the blanket. Valeria's hair was in a messy bun, and she wore a loose-fitting blue sweatshirt. Though it was hot in our house, she always seemed to be cold.

She looked at me and smiled before squinting, reading me like a book.

"Your face looks...off," she said. Her eyes widened as she looked down. "Why are you bloody? What happened to your shirt?"

I walked over to the bed and pulled my ripped shirt off, wiped the blood off my back with it, and tossed the dirty shirt on the floor. My body plopped down, and my head landed on a pillow. Another wave of peace surrounded me. Pillows were a luxury I so missed when at war. Sure, we had makeshift pillows made of wadded-up sheets or clothes, but nothing compared to the fluffiness of my own.

"My head's pounding." A sharp pain launched along my back. After reaching back to massage the ache, my hand came forward with blood and dirt on it.

"Levanta los pies y di lo que piensas." She looked at my bloody hand. "Tell me what's going on."

Where to start. I need to tell her about Isabella.

"I should tell you this right away." I sat up. "I learned it yesterday and have been digesting it myself. Isabella can...well...see what I can see."

"¿Qué?" She dropped the shirt she folded on the bed while staring at me.

"Yesterday, I noticed Harper had a cloudlike thing around her ear, which is indicative of an ear infection. When Isabella and I were playing catch outside, she said she had to update her drawing of Harper to include the new thing on her ear. I asked her what she was talking about, and she described the yellow I can see only because of my gift." I paused and looked at Valeria, who had drawn her hand to her mouth in shock. "I was as stunned as you are."

She closed her eyes. "Gaia, por favor, cuida a nuestra hija." Her eyes reopened. "Are you certain?"

"Very, and I wish I wasn't. I'm planning to ask her how much she can see. I was just taken aback by this unexpected..." I struggled with the right word, "...discovery my first night home."

"Is she okay?"

"She seems unfazed by it, and I didn't make it a big deal when I asked."

"Gaia nos ayuda." She sat on the bed. "What about your torn shirt and bloody hands?"

I sighed. "When we addressed the Stena and Counts on Enfer, a couple of unexpected things happened." I moved my hands in an alternating, rhythmic up-and-down motion. "First, Aameen took the position Count Ariba used to fill. He's now a Count."

Saying it out loud sent a cool wave across my body. I hadn't acknowledged Aameen as a Count. It made it real. Surprisingly, it made it hurt less, like he was just an object I explained to another person.

Snapping her head back, she caught herself from falling off the bed. "How?"

"Count Ariba has entered Gaia's Light." I turned to Valeria. "Why didn't you tell me she was this sick when you were in the medical tent?"

"Really, Ciro?" She put her hands on her hips. "Do you think Ariba was my priority in that moment?"

"Well, no...I was just shocked." My cheeks warmed at the inconsideration. "Either way, clearly Stena Mezca had Aameen in mind to replace her. I thought there was normally a slow decision process. They must have been talking for some time."

"Why wouldn't Aameen tell you this?"

"He's a plotter." I grew angry. "Aameen told the Stena about my ability to see disease." Valeria's mouth hung open. My words became sharper and quicker. "He only wants to do things for himself. The Stena sees Aameen as a great leader and says we will need his leadership if there is another war with the Coalition."

"What? More war?"

"It's what the Council thinks. Aameen used this as an opportunity for himself—he told the Stena I could move disease, and that my abilities would be better used in attacking the Coalition."

"WHAT?" She stood straight up with fire in her eyes. "Ese traidor. How dare Aameen offer you as a sacrifice to benefit himself? He is dead to me."

"I know." I agreed. Though I hated him, the *dead to me* part came off a bit harsh. But my wife was right—he had betrayed me. "He has hurt me in more ways than one." I looked down at the bruises forming on my sides.

Her eyes widened. "Did he do this to you?" She touched my side as I winced.

"I started it." She squinted in disbelief. "I did. What he did during the meeting got the best of me." I thought about the rainbow flowers I almost infected him with. "He just sees me as an object now."

Valeria's soft touch on my shoulder made the built-up tension fade. The real truth settled in—my best friend had betrayed me.

She moved her other hand up to the back of her neck. "Does this mean you are going back to war?"

"No...at least not for now. Ofelia was able to get us six months to fight the disease. Bebida helped. We owe Bebida so much."

Valeria took a deep breath while lowering her hands. "Thank Gaia. Thank Ofelia and Bebida." She grabbed a pillow and screamed into it for a moment. My fiery queen then lowered her pillow, flames still in her eyes. "Aameen will pay for this. He calls you a friend. A friend! Cobarde. Pedazo de mierda. He is no friend."

"I'm afraid you're right." My chest collapsed with a deep sigh. "I don't think I can call him a friend anymore, but I don't wish ill upon him and his family. He thinks he is only doing what is best for Maize."

"Including selling his friend into slave-based warfare." Her words carried so much weight.

"This is why I fear for Isabella...that she could be used like I'm being used." A shiver ran down my spine.

"We can't tell anyone about her," she said. "We have to keep her secret. We need to teach her to keep it a secret." I looked down at the bed. "Who did you tell?"

She knew me too well. "I told Ofelia. I trust her."

She glared at me. "You trusted Aameen."

"True, but Ofelia kept my secret throughout the entire war. Aameen seems to be the one with loose lips."

With a low growl, she spat out, "El diablo."

"Easy now."

It was odd defending someone who had just attacked me, but no matter how hard I tried to detach myself from him, I couldn't forget all the moments we shared together. The Shapple barn moment replayed in my head. The laughter we had exchanged while trying to herd the Shapple back to their barn.

"He isn't evil," I said. "He's just selfish."

"If you say so." She casually started folding laundry again. "What a day." She stared at me for a moment.

"What?"

"Just...tell me things. Okay? You used to tell me things right away. I can't help but feel a distance growing between us." She placed the folded shirt down into a new pile.

"I was busy. I'm sorry. I was getting to it."

She eyed me. "Yeah, you're right. Life has been loco. There is too much to do." Her gaze returned to the laundry.

Valeria deserved my attention. I walked over and wrapped my hands around Valeria's waist. A sudden warmth tickled my fingers and traveled up my arms. Her eyes wouldn't look away from the laundry, so I pulled her closer.

"We'll handle it." I kissed her on the cheek. "We always do." I kissed her on the cheek again. My stress, adrenaline, and anger morphed into desire. Before I knew it, my lips traveled to her neck as my kisses became slower and deeper.

The softest moan came from her, and she pressed her body onto mine. "Shut the door," she whispered with a little push at my chest. I pinched her side, shut the door, and she pulled me close. Her desire met my own.

CHAPTER 18
NINA THE HERBALIST

Just as I expected, Ofelia came up with a plan. Using the medical buildings she now oversaw, she had an idea to draw people into them. Posters. Lots and lots of posters. The posters were bright and straight to the point. In big red letters, it read:

The war is over, but the fight is not. Learn about Enfer.

Right below this statement in smaller blue letters read:

Get tested today at the West Medical Building. Preventative screenings recommended for all.

Over the next few days, about ten people came in for screenings. Though we expected more, it was a start. The crowds grew as word spread and symptoms began. People were incapable of believing in something until they saw it.

To start, I limited the number of people I treated to ten a day, and increased it by one person per day as my tolerance grew. Though the number of people I healed kept growing, the number of infected people exponentially increased.

Then the first deaths happened. A dark shadow was cast upon our country, and it was only the beginning.

Ofelia began observing patients who were infected, allowing her to gather data on external and internal attributes of Enfer that were visible to a normal person. Toward the beginning of the disease, the patient's tongue would have a bluish tint to it. The blue tongue was on those with only a few rainbow flowers. We had our first indicator.

A fever followed the blue tongue. At that point, I would see about ten flowers. Next were rashes around the infected area. And finally, the growths. At that point, the number of flowers passed at least twenty flowers, often more, and the disease was beyond my ability to heal.

The last step was death.

The number of deaths started out small but grew quickly. After about a month, the total surpassed one hundred. Enfer's dark shadow grew larger and darker. The city's attitude shifted away from indifference to concern. The fear that once plagued the city returned, and people stopped interacting in big groups.

Yet, Stena Mezca ignored it. He was still more concerned about the war, even though the Coalition showed no signs of attacking again, at least from what Ofelia and I heard. We continued to request a team to specialize in finding a cure or a way to treat the disease, but the Stena wouldn't fund or allow it. It was only us and whoever we could convince to help.

Despite Aameen's attempts to talk to me after our fight, I kept busy, avoiding a conversation. There were times I should have given him attention—he was an important person to me—but my days became so full in the fight against Enfer. I truly didn't have enough time. My working hours started earlier each day and ended later into the night. Eventually, he ignored me, and I ignored him.

When I wasn't thinking about treating someone, I was thinking about new symptoms I noticed on people. When I wasn't thinking about symptoms, I was reviewing patients' charts. Chaos consumed every bit of my life.

But in the midst of the chaos, I was still able to prioritize Isabella.

When I was home, I spent a lot of time with Isabella. We would go on walks and sometimes head outside the city to observe beasts. It was the best place to openly talk with her about what she could see. The small forests outside the city allowed us to have our own space.

Like the ones I trained in with Ofelia, the trees stood tall and narrow with smaller bushes lining the ground. Beasts of different sizes and shapes used this forest as shelter. The creatures would take crops and bring them back to their little forest homes.

Isabella liked the Nostrangals best. The small beasts could run on all four of their legs, but also used their feet like hands when grabbing items. Their furry black bodies hid their bare gray stomachs. Bulbous eyes would be invisible in the creatures' black fur if not for the soft sheen on their pupils. Round gray ears topped their heads, also covered in fur. Their little mouths chomped as fast as they could when eating. Whenever one of their food choices, mostly corn, was nearby, the Nostrangals scurried toward the crops, methodically extracted the cob, brought it to their beds—a hole filled with leaves—and pulled the kernels off one by one.

One day, we saw a smaller Nostrangal with an infection. Green ribbons covered its right fingers, indicative of a bacterial infection under its nails. Though I knew this, I wanted to see what Isabella could see.

"See that Nostrangal over there?" I asked.

She giggled while she watched two Nostrangals fighting over a stick. After hearing my question, she surveyed the scene. "There," she said without hesitation, pointing at the Nostrangal. "He has green swirlies on his hand."

"Good catch. Do you remember what the green ribbons mean?"

"The green swirlies," she began, as she always refused to use the terminology I used, "mean he has something bad on his hand. Little bugs are climbing under his fingernails. Gross."

"Bacteria," I corrected. "An infection."

She loved to say what she wanted to say. Even though it may not have been the most professional way to say it, it was easy to understand. Why stop that?

"Little bugs." She acted as if I didn't just correct her. "In his nails. I know."

"You're stubborn, hija." I sighed. "Just like your mother."

She started chasing the Nostrangals who were fighting over a stick. Their heads focused on her before they scurried up a tree. As if projecting laughter toward her prey, the Nostrangals mimicked her laughter from up high.

"We should head home," I said. "Your mom will want to get you to bed soon."

"Can't we play a little longer?" She batted her honey eyes, knowing all too well how to manipulate me.

"Five more minutes," I conceded.

She cheered and started chasing other Nostrangals carrying crops. I walked around the forest while she did this. It was good for her to burn off some energy. A small pack of Furrowburrows rushed into a nearby bush. Their white fur rustled through leaves and branches. Two smaller Furrowburrows rode on the larger one's back. Their little baby heads intensely observed me before disappearing under the foliage.

An Eldo perked its head up from behind the bush housing the Furrowburrow family. The beast was a rare find in the outer forests around Cornia, often found further away from larger cities. About half my height, the Eldo used its long, elegant legs to prowl around while its thin neck, topped with a slender head, rotated back and forth. Bright green pupils observed its surroundings while its head moved about. Besides the brightness of its eyes, the rest of its body was covered in very short brown fur with small bright green dots matching its eyes. When it was darker out, the Eldo would run in small herds, and the bright green of its eyes and dots covering its body reflected the moonlight. They looked like bugs flying in a haphazard pattern, confusing any predator hunting them. They didn't normally travel on their own. The beast sensed my presence and darted away.

When I had time, getting away from the city helped refresh my mind. I enjoyed my time with Isabella, and it was nice not to think about Enfer, if only for a moment.

After a sigh of melancholy and exhaustion, I turned to Isabella. "Time to head home."

"Okay." She dropped her head and walked over to me. "Thank you for giving me more than five minutes."

I jostled her hair. "Anything for you, hija."

She looked up at me. "Daddy, what happens to the beasts that are sick?"

I avoided the topic for as long as I could, but the inevitable question finally came.

"Well, most of them will heal on their own. Some don't always make it."

"Oh. Like die?" Curiosity filled her little eyes.

"Yes, die." It was better to be truthful.

"That's sad." She looked at the ground. Something was on her mind.

"What are you thinking about?"

"Don't you heal people?" She glanced back up at me.

I clicked my jaw. "I do. I heal people every day."

"Why can't you heal the Nostrangal from the green swirlies? It is so small and would be easy for you."

"Well, I'm more of a people healer," I lied. "Victor, Harper's vet, is more of a beast healer."

"Oh. Maybe Victor should come out here to help it." She nodded, convinced by the logic.

"He could, hija. But he has a lot of other beasts in the city that he needs to help. Sometimes we have to pick who we should help and who we can't help. If we decided to help one beast far away from us while leaving a lot of other beasts that needed our help, so many beasts would be hurt by our decision."

"Oh." It seemed like most of what I just said went over her head. "Do you heal a lot of people?"

"Many." I let out one small laugh. "But they don't always know it."

"Why?"

I had rehearsed this conversation so many times in my head. What I would say. How I would say it. But I paused. Closing my eyes, I steadied my breath and chose my words carefully. Once I opened them, I knew I was ready.

"Because they don't always know they are sick. Remember when I told you that you and I are special?" She nodded. "This goes for seeing sickness in people as well. I know you haven't seen sickness in people yet, but when you do, you'll be able to help them."

Her eyes lit up. "You think I can help people?"

"You're going to help save the *world*, hija." I brushed my finger along her cheek. "Don't ever believe otherwise."

She grabbed my hand and squeezed it tightly. My heart lit up. She was one of the reasons I had done all I had. Moments like these only happened because of decisions I had made. But at what cost? I thought about all the people who were sick because of the disease I had created. Death crept closer and closer to them—I had to keep fighting.

"Hey, Daddy?"

I shook my head, focusing back on her. "Yes, hija?"

"What happens when something dies from being sick?"

Her thoughts were heavy that night. I admired her curiosity and loving intentions. She deserved real answers.

"Well, your mother believes we enter the Great Light of Gaia and enjoy Gaia's forest forever. Life beyond life."

"Do you?"

I paused. "Well, I do." I hadn't thought of it much in years. I'd had little time or energy to think about life beyond death. The more I pondered the question, the more I realized I did believe in something. I had witnessed so much and performed unbelievable things. "I have to. I have to believe there is more to life than this. It gives me comfort. It gives a lot of people comfort."

"I want to meet Gaia someday."

"Not too quickly." I squeezed her hand tighter. "I like having you around."

"Thanks, Daddy." She squeezed back.

"Can I tell you a secret?"

With the biggest grin, she whipped her head to face me. "I love secrets."

Reaching into my pocket, I pulled out her drawing and unfolded the gnarled paper. "You gave this to me when I first left for the war, all that time ago. I kept it with me the whole time."

She tilted her head as she observed the drawing. "I've gotten a lot better."

"That you have, but this one will always be one of my favorites. It reminds me why I fight to help people." I folded the drawing back up and put it in my pocket. "Especially when it involves my favorite people."

Gripping my hand again, she said, "You're my favorite, too, Daddy."

Returning to the streets of Cornia, I looked around at so many familiar faces. The number of people I recognized grew every day. Many I had treated, or they had introduced themselves to thank me for the war. It made walks more engaging, something I often disliked but tried to lean into.

Isabella pulled at my shirt. "Daddy, who's that?" She pointed at a crowd of maybe ten people across the street.

I crouched down to her level and looked behind the hand she pointed with. A hooded figure with their back to us stood taller than most of the group.

"Who are you pointing to?" I asked.

Before Isabella could respond, the hooded figure turned around. Sharp cheekbones and pale skin caught my attention. I stood up and let go of Isabella.

"It can't be," I whispered to myself. Stepping forward, I moved toward the crowd. The hooded figure locked eyes with me and began running down an alleyway. "Wait!" I yelled.

Is that Count Ariba? No. She's dead.

As much as I wanted to chase after the person, I had Isabella.

I turned around to take Isabella's hand again, but she was gone. Spinning around in circles, I searched through the crowd and didn't see her.

"Isabella!" I shouted. "Isabella!"

More people press into the crowd. My heart pounded as I pushed through them.

Why isn't she here? Did someone take her?

I wanted to scream. I wanted to swing my arms around and knock everyone over until I found her.

"Isabella!" I shouted again.

"Daddy," her faint whisper echoed from outside the group.

"Isabella!" I pushed through the crowd, her voice repeating my name. Breaking through the group, I gasped for air and surveyed my surroundings. "Hija? Where are you?"

"This way!" she shouted. I turned toward her voice, and saw her sprinting down the alleyway that the hooded figure had run down.

"Isabella! Come back here!" I bellowed.

Not listening, she followed the hooded figure around a corner to the right. I sprinted after her, moving faster than I ever had. Trash cans created an obstacle course. I sidestepped some and jumped over others, knocking over a bin.

I turned the corner, and saw Isabella several blocks ahead, turning to the left. I dipped my head and continued my pursuit.

What is she doing? Why is she chasing this person?

Despite all my questions and curiosity about the hooded figure, I cared more about my daughter's safety. Picking up my speed, I ran even faster, my hamstrings burning from the effort. With every turn, I closed in on her with another block. I rounded one last corner and nearly collided with Isabella, who had finally stopped.

I crouched down and took her by the shoulders, breathing so heavily. "What was *that*?" I shouted. "Don't *ever* run away from me like that ever again."

Isabella paid no attention to me. She just stared past me.

I pivoted, standing up, and looked in the direction she did. The hooded figure pulled off their covering and hung it on a post just outside a house. As the hood revealed their face, I swore the figure's face morphed from pale with sharp cheekbones to glowing wrinkles stretched out over a warm face. Rows and rows of cots surrounded her and the building.

After fully catching my breath, I realized we stood outside the herbalist's shop, though it looked different from before. Valeria visited Nina, the herbalist, often to pick up essential oils for our house. Nina looked over to us with a soft smile and a wave. Isabella waved back, and I nodded, narrowing in on the herbalist.

"A pleasant day, isn't it?" Nina asked.

"Yes…" I nodded. "A nice day for a run…"

"I do agree." She walked up to one of the cots and kneeled to check on one of her patients. Since when did the herbalist have patients? At least ten rainbow flowers covered each patient.

Is this an Enfer treatment facility?

"We should go." I patted Isabella's head and ushered her forward.

She hesitated but followed my request. Her little eyebrows scrunched up as she stared forward.

"Something on your mind?" I asked.

With a little shiver, she shook her head and looked up at me. "Daddy, what was she doing?"

"She was taking care of sick people." My forehead ached as I realized my eyebrows furrowed like my daughter's.

"Do you take care of people outside?"

"No." I shook my head. "I work inside."

"Oh." Reaching over, she grabbed my hand and looked ahead, eyebrows scrunched up again.

As we moved back to the city center, the crowd grew in size. Any anger I had with Isabella running away faded into my questions about Nina and her treatment center. Did she know more about Enfer?

Pushing my thoughts aside, I focused back on walking with my daughter. She deserved my attention, and I could think about Enfer later. I didn't always have to think about it.

I looked ahead and noticed a young girl holding her father's hand just like Isabella and I were doing. The father nodded as I smiled and looked down at the girl. She was Isabella's age, based on her height. Her black hair was braided and bounced as she skipped. She had on a bright pink shirt filled with rainbow flowers.

Rainbow flowers...shit. Those flowers aren't on her shirt.

"Give me a moment, hija." I released Isabella's hand and went over to the father and his daughter. "Buenas noches." The man stopped and smiled. I kept talking before he could respond. "I know this will sound forward, but my name is Ciro—"

"I know," the man said with a nod. "We owe you a lot, Hero of Maize."

I flinched at the title. "It's no problem. But I'm part of the medical team, and we are offering screenings while walking the streets now. For Enfer. Is it okay if I check you quick?"

"Of course," he said. "I have been meaning to come in."

"No worries." I checked him first. The routine involved feeling the glands on the neck, checking the patient's pulse on the wrist, and looking in the mouth. It was all Ofelia's idea to keep people distracted while I healed the infected. "You look okay." I moved over to the daughter. "Hello, my name is Ciro. What is your name?"

"Flora," she responded with a small smile. The rainbow flowers twirled near her neck.

"Well, Flora, I'm going to check you," I said. "I'll be quick. Is that okay?" She nodded. I started checking her with my left hand while I used my right hand to burn the flowers. One by one, the flowers disintegrated. To Gaia's blessing, there were only four. I was done by the time I checked the pulse on her wrist. "You look great!" I extended my hand for a high five as she smiled and slapped my hand.

"Thank you," the man said. "That will save us some time."

"Don't mention it," I said. "And remember to get checked once a month."

The more opportunities there were for me to see people, the higher the likelihood I could find and rid them of Enfer.

"We will," the man said. "Have a great night!"

I waved them away. Isabella turned to look up at me.

"What were the flowers?" she asked.

Sucking in on itself, my stomach twisted. "You saw flowers?"

"Yes," she said.

I wanted to vomit. I knew it was a matter of time before she saw Enfer, but I wasn't ready for the conversation.

"By her neck," she continued. "But then they were gone. How did they go away?"

I crouched down. I had practiced this conversation in my head. With a quick prayer to Gaia, I needed the conversation to go well.

"Well, the rainbow flowers are Enfer, the bad sickness Daddy helps fight. I check people for it, and I help make it go away."

"Oh." She blinked and grinned. "Thanks for helping her."

I stood back up. "I'll always help as long as I can. But remember to only tell me or Mamá when you see the flowers. Don't ever tell the person who has the flowers."

She grabbed my hand, and we started walking again. The conversation came and went with such ease. A sudden relief relaxed my gut.

"Daddy, thanks for making the flowers disappear. I didn't know you could do that." Her little thumb rubbed against the back of my hand. "I wonder if that other lady can heal the flowers."

I didn't respond. I wasn't ready to teach her about holding and burning away disease. I didn't want her to try it. And did she wonder about Nina like I did?

The entire experience kept me distracted until we arrived home. I needed to remember everything as best as I could. To distract Isabella, I sent her upstairs to brush her teeth while I journaled all I saw and experienced. Per Ofelia's suggestion, the journal became my daily habit. I added the day's encounter and gave step-by-step instructions on how to grab, hold, and burn a disease away. I found writing in the journal to be therapeutic while providing instructions for Isabella to follow someday. She had to learn how to heal disease at some point, but I would never teach her how to move it. Why would I want her to do such a horrible thing and risk her being used as a weapon?

I wrote on nearly every other page:

Do NOT move the disease, only hold it.

The door creaked from upstairs as Isabella walked out of the bathroom. Valeria and I put her to bed. Isabella's bedroom was a little bed covered in various stuffed animals. She liked Nostrangals most, so the stuffed little creatures riddled her bed in various colors. A small tray with spicy, minty oils wafted its frigid smell throughout the room. Notes of citrus and pepper tickled my nose before the mint cooled it away. Tucked in under her green blanket stitched with stars, made by my mother-in-law, Valeria sang her nightly song:

Mira dentro para verte a ti mismo.
Encuentra la comodidad.
Descansa la cabeza.
Siente el amor a tu alrededor.
Siente el amor bajar tu plumón.[1]

---

1. Glossary: Valeria's Song Translation

We finished off by going over our daily gratitudes.

"I'm thankful for Mamá, Daddy, Harper, Nostrangals, and...helping people," Isabella said.

She had such a pure heart, and I was thankful for that. We both kissed her and shut the door.

Pillow talk was one of my favorite things. Valeria and I could talk for hours.

"How was your day?" Valeria asked.

"The same old," I responded. "How was yours?"

She began going over her day, but I drifted off immediately. Sleep hit me almost instantly every night as soon as my head hit the pillow.

"Great talk..." she said under her breath.

I could've replied to her, but I was too exhausted. It was something we could talk about at another time. Though, I delayed talking to her every day. My role was very important. She understood. I knew she did. I had to fix Enfer. I had to talk to Ofelia about Nina.

CHAPTER 19
THE HERO OF MAIZE

"Just keep looking forward," I grunted and burned the last flower away on the patient.

By my fifteenth patient, I didn't bother trying to remember a name. "All set." Releasing a deep breath, I wiped the sweat from my forehead. "The front desk will tell you the next time you should come in."

"Thank you, Hero of Maize." The old man bowed and walked out of the room and shut the door.

With a great crack, I stretched my arms high into the air, bracing my back against the wall to avoid falling. I relied on this ritual after every patient to keep myself grounded, especially with where I was. The Northern Medical Building contained my least favorite medics to work with. Based on my weekly cycle, this was the eighth or tenth time I visited the location. Or maybe it was the twelfth. I'd lost track. Their sour attitude and impatience with patients didn't convey the hope we wished to bestow. I did my best to zone out while in their company.

The rediscovery of my composure involved a deep breath, a slap on my cheek, and a forced smile. I opened the door and made my way to the waiting room, filled with patients. The lights flickered, and the sound of rushing arrows filled my ears. The war zone towers and dead bodies covered the round. People reached out to me, begging for help as Enfer flowers climbed up their arms. Great growths flourished from where the flowers touched. The smell of dirt, blood, and metal rose to my nostrils. Within my twisting gut, I wanted to lean forward and vomit out the nightmares. Instead, I dipped around a corner, pushed my forehead against the cool wall, and tried to bring myself back to the present.

"I understand that you want to see a doctor, but you have to wait like all the others," the front desk clerk snapped at a younger woman. The woman was itching at the small growths and seven rainbow flowers covering her body. "Go sit down, and we'll call you when it's your turn."

Glaring at the clerk, I marched over and ushered the young girl down the hall. "We can help you now. Come this way."

The clerk rolled his eyes and looked down at a sheet he was filling out. I waited until the patient moved just out of earshot and tapped the counter until the clerk looked at me.

"Remember to smile and give them hope," I whispered.

"Yes, Ciro," the man replied, willing me to follow the patient, which I did.

I glanced back, and saw another scowl on his face. I didn't blame them. The death rate in the north outranked all other medical buildings. I carried so much responsibility. My mind always fell back to my conversation with Ofelia a few months before.

"We need to rethink our plan," Ofelia had said. "The death rate is always lowest in whatever building you're in. We need you to start rotating from one building to the next."

"And the severe cases?" I had asked.

"The southern building will be their home. At least until their end…"

And so began the endless, hopeless cycle of me moving from one medical building to the next. Every time I made progress with one building, I forced myself into another. There were so many infected patients. It was my duty to heal them.

"All done," I said to the young girl before me.

The girl felt her now smooth skin, the little growths gone. "Thank you, thank you." She bowed her head several times.

By lunch, it was time to classify the cases. Thirty patients had passed the breaking point. Thirty patients were guided to the carts, ready to be transported to the Southern Medical Building. Thirty patients would be dead by the end of the week. And I was the one who decided their fate.

"Be sure to come see me right after they're transferred to the south," I said. "I want to keep the medics safe."

As much as treating citizens remained my focus, making sure my medics were safe became the largest priority. Each night, the medics were required to come visit the Western Medical Building so I could check them on my way home. Though we didn't explicitly communicate why, every medic knew that not a single worker became sick. I knew the rumors about what I could do floated around the city, but I dismissed any conversation about it when brought up. Well, Ofelia did. No one liked to confront her.

"We will, Ciro," medic Antonio said. "After we deliver the ashes to the distribution center."

Next to the Southern Medical Building sat the crematorium. I visited the center once after the restructuring of our plan. All the growths, all the bodies, and all the rainbow flowers terrorized my every thought. One by one, the deceased patients were brought to the furnace and cremated. We couldn't afford to have the mutilated bodies returned to their families. The best way to prevent infection was to burn the corpses.

The cremation process resulted in the absolute worst smell I'd experienced in my entire life. In between the rotten egg aroma of the fuel, the sulfuric scent of searing hair, the metallic, repugnant odor of burning meat, and a stale, unsettling layer of soot atop all of it, I abhorred going into that building. Witnessing the flowers consume people from within was already too much for me to handle. Watching the dead burn away would push me over the edge.

Depleted of all my energy, I floated like a ghost from the Northern Medical Building to the Western Center. Ofelia had my whiskey ready at the front desk. The grainy scent burned my nose before I took a swallow and let the burn travel down my throat and relax my brain. The medics trickled in over the next half hour, none infected from the day. My body rejoiced in not having to heal another person. I took another drink of my whiskey to commemorate the small victory.

"Ciro!" Ofelia yelled from down the hall.

The whiskey stopped in the middle of my throat and part of it burned as it entered my lungs. I started choking but ran toward her voice. Was she infected? Was she in trouble?

Darting around the corner, trying to keep myself from throwing up the burning liquor, I found Ofelia sitting at her desk, holding a vial of brown liquid and grinning so big I wanted to punch her.

"Are you joking?" I kept coughing, clearing the last bit of whiskey from my lungs.

Her smile faded. "What'd I do?"

"Nothing." With a grunt, I moved closer to her desk and picked the vial from her hand. With a quick sniff, I coughed again and moved the vial away. A terrible mixture of musty grass and vinegar burned in my nose and amplified the remaining liquor in my throat. "What is that?"

"Corn essential oil." She snatched the vial back. "I've been working on the right amount of rotten corn to fresh corn and finally cracked what the right amount is!"

"You've been visiting Nina again?" I crossed my arms.

"Once or twice this past week." With a flick of her wrist, she waved away my snarky response. "Just to gain some insight into the oils."

Ever since I mentioned Nina to Ofelia, their number of interactions had increased over the past few months. Ofelia didn't believe in her "witchcraft magic" and often voiced her disdain about Nina's work, calling it the "improper way to treat patients." But that didn't stop her intrigue about what the unorthodox plants could do.

"So, what'd you figure out?" I asked.

"This," she raised the vial, "can slightly slow down mild cases when diffused within a room."

I lowered my arms to my sides. "It can? You confirmed this?"

Without a word, she stood from her desk, placing the vial into a wooden holder, and guided me down the hall toward a room with a light on.

"This case was problematic yesterday with the beginning signs. So, I kept them back here and diffused the oil."

As we neared the room, the terrible scent intensified. The smell aggravated my throbbing headache and tensed up my already tight back.

"Are you joking?" I scoffed. "You didn't tell me about the case?"

"I had confidence." She moved faster and into the room. "Hello, Darla."

A middle-aged woman looked over at us, six rainbow flowers covered her shoulder. "Buenos noches." She nodded and moved her eyes to me.

"Hi," I said. "Do you mind if I take a look at your shoulder?"

After going through my routine, I treated her shoulder before we dismissed her. I cracked my back and then my neck before I snapped my attention to Ofelia.

"You know you could've killed her, right?"

Ofelia raised her hands. "I believed it would work, and it did. How many flowers did you see?"

Moving my jaw back and forth, I grunted. "Six."

"Exactly!" She slapped her hands together. "This is very good news. This could allow me to treat patients." Covering her mouth, she shimmied her shoulders and lowered her hand. "We can save more people."

Though my irritation at Ofelia's recklessness remained, a little fire erupted in my core. I didn't know if it was the whiskey or something else, but a sense of hope found me.

"Maybe." I tried to suppress a smile. "What about her secret plant? Did you find out any more about it?"

A shadow dropped across her face. "No, but I noticed she keeps some patients in the back of her house. I do wonder about them." The tiniest spark flickered in her eyes. "And I hate to admit it, but I think her knowledge of plants might become useful to us."

With a sudden drop, my shoulders and back slumped forward. The moment utter exhaustion threw itself upon me each day made my body collapse all at once. I wanted to keep moving and healing, but I valued rest more and more each day.

"I think it's time I make it home," I said. "Today was brutal."

Ofelia poked at the corn essential oil vial. "Today provided some hope." With a perky twirl in her chair, she pointed at the calendar on her wall. "Did you see what tomorrow is?"

Exhaustion making its way up to my eyes, I blinked, trying to focus on what month it was. I had lost track of the days of the week, the time of day, and what month we were even in a long time ago. Each day consumed every bit of me. The only day I cherished was Saturday afternoon, which I spent teaching Isabella about seeing disease.

"Should I know something about it?"

"Six months." Ofelia moved back to her desk and leaned forward, resting her chin on her hands. "Our deadline is here."

A burst of energy pushed back the fatigue. My heart pounded against my lungs and forced out the little air they held.

"It's here?"

With a great groan, Ofelia nodded. "And we've accomplished so much. Now, we just need to prove this to the Stena Mezca. Keep fighting and keep pushing."

"Keep fighting and keep pushing," I echoed, though the words made me more tired than inspired.

CHAPTER 20
THE POLITICS OF THREE NATIONS

The time finally came, Stena Mezca's deadline for our Enfer endeavors. Six months since he set our expiration date. Six months of countless hours spent treating Enfer, saving so many lives. I expected him to be delighted with our progress, but for the last couple of weeks, he refused to offer us a meeting. It made me nervous that he wasn't happy with the results. But how couldn't he be?

The need to speak with the Stena grew into an obsession. Every time a door opened, I worried I'd be dragged off and sent back to war. Even Bebida was unable to help us. I needed someone close to the Stena. I needed someone who had his ear. I knew the one person who could help us, and it was someone I had been avoiding since our fight—Aameen.

Despite my constant fear, I pushed off the conversation with Aameen. Ofelia grew irritated with my lack of action. But fate eventually pushed us together.

Early mornings were the best time to travel, with the roads quieter and less busy. Aameen preferred mornings for the same reason. I may not have called him a friend anymore, but I still knew him like a brother. He approached wearing purple clothes made of very fine material—since he began his new role as a Count, he wore nicer clothes and had moved from our neighborhood to a bigger house near Pastel Castle.

As we passed each other, he glanced at me before looking away, which pissed me off.

Rather than blowing past him and matching his frigidity, I stepped in front of him. "Aameen, can we talk?"

He froze and looked behind himself, then back forward while pointing at his chest. "Oh, are you talking to me?"

"Yes, I'm afraid it has come to that."

He laughed coldly. "I'm sorry talking to me is so unbearable."

A burning cyclone swirled in me again, quickening my heartbeat. Avoiding him altogether had been my solution to avoid confrontation. His betrayal still felt fresh, like a knife in my back. "I just have to be careful around someone who *uses* a friend for his own benefit."

"Is that what you think of me?" Inferno eyes blazed at me.

At the rate we were going, we would soon be rolling around on the ground again. I couldn't risk all we had done with Enfer for my issues with Aameen. I hated to say it, but I needed him.

I took a deep breath. "It doesn't matter what I think. I'm coming to you because we need to talk to the Stena."

As soon as I said it, his attention drifted away. "I can't arrange this for you."

"Are you kidding?" There was my anger again. "You see him every day. It would be very easy for you to help us arrange a time to talk to him."

"It's out of my control." A gray gloom covered his face. It was a look I recognize well—exhaustion. "Why are you asking me and not Count Bebida?"

"She said she tried and failed. You're close to him."

"Bebida is good at politics," he said under his breath, but loud enough for me to hear.

"What did you say?"

"Nothing." He realized I heard him. "The Stena will call for you when he is ready."

"When the Stena is ready to use me as a weapon again. I can't let that happen. We have achieved so much."

"I cannot help you." He lowered his head and started walking past me.

I grabbed his arm. "Please, Aameen. I can't leave my family again. I can't handle going to war again. I keep seeing all the people I killed during the war. I keep seeing all the patients infected by Enfer. Just let us talk to him. Please. Do it for the friendship we once had."

He pulled away and kept walking. I let out a deep sigh, defeated. He stopped and turned his head just enough for me to see the side of his face. "I'm having dreams, too. I will ask today. I will send for you if it works." He kept walking. "Just promise you won't attack me again."

"Thank you, Aameen. My friend..." I whispered the last part to myself. Uncertainty clouded my brain. Though I said the word, I shook my head and remembered where trusting him got me last time.

He just needs to help me this one time.

A deep breath of relief came over me. I carried on with my morning walk to the western medical center. I entered through a red door on the one-story building covered in white-painted stucco. A line of fifty healthy-looking people had already formed to be tested for Enfer. It was much different than the early days when we had to beg people to come in. The city's mindset had changed, and Enfer was finally viewed as a threat, including the private funding Ofelia had been able to gather each month the disease continued.

"Buenos dias," Ofelia said. "How does the line look today?"

That was my cue to survey the line of citizens. I didn't see any signs of Enfer. Not a single rainbow flower.

"It looks thin," I replied in our code language.

"Good, because I wanted to talk. I already told Miguel and Florencia we would be gone this morning."

"And possibly afternoon." I smiled. She raised her eyebrows in suspicion. "I spoke with Aameen on the way here."

"You did?" She cocked her head.

"I did. I asked him to get Stena Mezca's attention. He said he will try to let us know this afternoon."

"Oh! That's surprising. A very good surprise."

"I know. I followed your advice." Before Ofelia could gloat, I waved a hand in the air. "I initiated our meeting, so he sees that we are confident in what we have done."

With a cocky grin, she didn't rub it in like I expected her to. "Let's hope that works. Walk with me."

We turned down one of the quieter streets. We passed a spice stand rich with sweet and savory smells, a man weaving intricate and colorful blankets, and two kids helping paint the walls of an older woman's house. Her stucco walls were being painted white, setting the house apart from the primarily tan and gray houses throughout the city. Ofelia turned down an even quieter street with low traffic.

"What's going on?" I asked.

"I wanted to talk about forming a team. In case we lose you, I'll need help figuring out this disease. People we can keep in the loop. It'll have to be kept secret, as I don't want the Stena to find out we recruited help without his approval."

"A team?"

"Miguel and Florencia have already agreed to join. I wanted to start with a couple of other professionals who can help figure out Enfer more. Any ideas?"

"Victor." I didn't even hesitate. "I know he will, and his understanding of beast medicine could help us think of things in a different way."

"I expected you to pick him. He will be a great fit."

Not only had Victor first noticed my abilities, but he also knew medicine. Covering our human and beast areas, I wondered about other areas. A potted plant not too far away caught my attention.

"And I don't know her well, but Nina the herbalist." Before Ofelia could say more about how Nina was only an herbalist and would never be able to understand medicine like she did, I cut her off. "I know, I know, you don't think her methods are ideal."

"She has patients sprawled around the outside of her house." She raised her chin. "That is not the way to treat patients."

Ever since that odd encounter where Nina ran to her house while Isabella and I followed her, I had tried to understand the interaction. When I told Ofelia about it, she went to analyze Nina's facility and wasn't impressed. I couldn't help but feel there was a reason I was pulled there.

"It would be good to have someone specializing in plants, providing some possible new ideas," I said. "I don't think it'd hurt to have her on the team."

Ofelia grunted before crossing her arms. "Fine. You think she will join?"

"I do. She is trying to help with Enfer just like we are." A minuscule burst of energy pulsed in my chest. "Who knows? Maybe there's a plant that could help."

Ofelia placed her right hand on her chin. "I did hear a rumor about someone living longer than normal."

"You did?" I perked up.

Shifting her stance, she swiped a hand in the air. "Yes, but it's probably nothing. If we did find out more about this plant and where to get it..." She stared ahead. "We could go on a little field trip to find the plant."

Lost in a daydream, I pondered the idea of another plant. I pictured rainbow flowers growing in a field, overtaking everything. Another small, white flower appeared next and grew over the rainbow flowers, their petals withering away while white flowers engulfed the field.

I wonder...

Shaking my head, I pulled myself out of my ridiculous daydream. Though Ofelia started as the cynic with Nina, I took over the role. Dreaming about a plant that could fix all the problems with Enfer only provided false hope. I didn't have time for that.

"When time allows us to." I scoffed. "There are too many people to heal."

"There are, but—"

"We can't afford any more deaths," I cut her off. "I started this, and I need to stop it."

"But the medical team—"

"The medical team needs me here. Without me—"

"Ciro!" she almost shouted. She took a deep breath and smiled. "Stepping away from a place where you are always needed wouldn't be a bad thing. I think you could use a break. You moved nonstop during the war and even more since we returned home."

I realized searching for a plant was just an excuse Ofelia was using. She just wanted me to take a break.

"I'm okay." The idea of a break made me anxious. Adrenaline pumped through my veins. My anxiety transformed into rage. I became angry at her blatant disregard. "I have to be okay. Maize needs me."

"Enfer isn't the only thing happening in our city."

"Maybe not to you. I'm taking this seriously."

She snapped her gaze to me so fast I swore a gust of wind blew across my face. "Excuse me?" She glared. The conversation took a turn that neither of us seemed to expect. "So now, not only are you the most important person to our cause, but you're also the only one serious about it?"

"If the shoe fits." I squinted my eyes and bit my lip.

"El asno..." She began pacing back and forth. "I'm trying to tell you to slow down. I'm concerned about you. I pulled you away to talk, but I also wanted to get you away from the medical building. Your whole life doesn't revolve around Enfer."

"No one asked you to do that."

"Yes, they did." She put her right hand to her mouth as if trying to capture what she had just said.

A sudden pause filled the void between us. She didn't want to say anything, and I was unsure if I wanted to ask. As slowly as I could, I asked, "Who?"

Another longer pause deepened the moat between us. The silence was unsettling. Her eyes looked deep into my own. I studied them. They pulsated, fluttering between sternness and compassion. Her mouth looked tense before it relaxed.

"Your wife did." Her words came out with a deep breath.

My brain pulsed like my heart, pounding against my skull. I stared ahead, eyes blank.

"Valeria did what?" I spoke slowly.

Ofelia's eyes widened, realizing she had shared something she shouldn't have. It was too late. Valeria was talking behind my back, to Ofelia of all people. The adolescent, immature side of me felt annoyed in a way I hadn't felt since primary school. I thought Valeria understood why I was doing what I was. She told me to keep fighting.

"Ciro, she is concerned about you. I'm concerned about you." She took a step toward me.

I stepped back. The constant pounding in my head continued. I didn't know what to do. "Well, stop it. You both can stop it."

"You're burning out."

"I'm doing just fine." I stormed up to her with my finger pointed at her face. "I thought *you* understood. I thought *she* understood."

"When's the last time you talked to her?"

"Valeria?" I laughed. "What a rude question to ask me. Every day."

"I mean, *really* talk to her?"

The question cut into me. I talked to her all the time. Flipping through my recent memories, I searched for the times we talked. Every conversation we had was short. Even our pillow time didn't last long before I passed out.

I spent a lot of time at the medical buildings. I spent time at home with Isabella. When I wasn't doing one of my main activities, I was exhausted and slept. Didn't I deserve to rest?

But what about Valeria? Is Ofelia right?

"I just have so much I need to do." A blistering pressure began at the top of my forehead before moving to the sides of my head, just next to my eyes. Surrounding my eyes, the pressure closed in and demanded relief. Tears formed, releasing the tension, but I held them back and embraced the terrible pressure.

I sputtered out in a shaky, quiet voice, "I have to heal people." The tremors moved to my hands. I formed fists to steady myself. "I have to teach Isabella." Panic swelled up, squeezing my neck. "If I don't fight Enfer, they'll make me fight outside of Cornia again." Tiny, wispy breaths trickled out of my mouth as I stared at Ofelia. My vision went blurry. I focused so hard that I could barely make her out. "I can't leave home."

With a slow, calculated step, Ofelia came closer to me, her face becoming focused. She tilted her head and arched her eyebrows in a way that made me uneasy. "You may be at home, but you're not around." Ofelia paused, letting the words stab right into my heart.

Ofelia betrayed me. Valeria betrayed me. Why was everyone betraying me?

"I'm telling you as your friend." Ofelia reached forward but retracted, unwilling to provide a drop of comfort after wounding me.

As a friend?

The shakiness subsided as a coldness swept through me. With each deliberate, harsh word she said, she did it all in the name of friendship?

Rounding my neck, I snapped my head up and leveled it back down, eyes locked with hers. "Stop sticking your nose in my life and stay out of my relationship." I turned away.

I couldn't look at her. Each harsh word she used passed through my head: "You're not around."

Is she right? Am I spending too much time away? It's almost as if I'm not actually home. Everything I do is wrong. That is all I do. I created this disease. It's all my fault.

"Ciro..." Ofelia touched my shoulder.

I yanked away. "Stop it. Please, stop it."

"Sorry, er, um, is this a bad time?" a girl asked from behind us.

A girl, maybe twelve or so, stood there awkwardly. It took me a moment, but I recognized her. She had grown up so much in the years since I saw her. It was Aameen's daughter, one of the twins.

"Dani?" I asked. With an expressionless look, Dani looked at me like I was a stranger. "It has been so long."

"My father sent me to tell you that Stena Mezca wants to see you," she said like a soldier on a mission. "Now."

"Now?" Ofelia asked.

"Yes, so please don't be late." Dani turned and walked away.

Aameen's daughter was cold and short with me. I remembered her as a baby. She used to take naps with me. Aameen called me *her comforter*. With the interaction, I realized my problems with Aameen had trickled into our families. I used to play with her as a child. Now, I was a stranger to her.

With awkward glances, I stepped forward, Ofelia at my side. I didn't want to talk to her, let alone walk with her, but there weren't any other options.

"Ciro, I—"

"I don't want to talk about this right now," I interrupted. "We need to focus on talking to Stena Mezca."

"Okay. You're right."

We headed to Pastel Castle, feet crunching on the loose pavement. From the corner of my eye, I watched as Ofelia kept looking at me and then away. Her mouth fumbled open and shut. A dash of empathy pushed at my anger.

"And you're right," I grunted. "I'll talk to Valeria." I gave her a quick glance. "I promise."

Below rosy cheeks, Ofelia's mouth curled up. "Good, that's all I was trying to say."

A less awkward silence filled the rest of our walk to Pastel Castle. The sun hit every color from Pastel Castle's roof in an abundance of tinted hues. My eyes gravitated toward the doors. I nearly ran to the purple doors. I needed boldness and courage. No more timid Ciro.

Moving up the stairwell and into the meeting space, the Counts turned to us all at once. Only one person was missing—Stena Mezca. The coward hadn't shown. I moved my gaze across the audience, glaring at each Count, except for Count Bebida. I gave a quick smile to her.

"Where is Stena Mezca?" I asked, focusing on Aameen. "I was told he would be here."

"I'm here," a feeble voice said from the right. A fragile man sat on a cushioned chair. He wore the Stena's headpiece with each of the brightly colored beast feathers, but this man didn't command the room like the Stena I knew. He looked frail. His face was gray. He let out a cough, and his body shook in violent tremors.

One last attribute finalized Stena Mezca's new look—rainbow flowers. Adorning the colorful feathers of his headpiece, Enfer moved across his body with rotating petals. A growth protruded from his left arm, about the size of my fist.

"Now," he sat up straight and let out a weak chuckle, "this is your time to gloat."

"Stena Mezca," Ofelia responded after I said nothing and only stared at him. "When did this happen?"

"About a week ago," he said. "I'm sure you can understand why my attention to our deadline was delayed."

"Why didn't you come to us?" Ofelia asked. "We could have helped."

"I shrugged it off," he said. "I will admit that. I did not feel like the affliction was worth paying attention to. Then, I noticed the damn tumor forming." He held his left arm up, the growth jiggling below. "A gross thing, if I must say." He lowered his arm back down. "I did seek medical care from the top doctor within the Eastern Medical Building. He did all he could."

I continued to stare at Stena Mezca as his eyes drifted to mine. Eyebrows arched high, he nodded once and lifted his hands, welcoming my response.

"I...I...don't know what to say," I said.

"Count Aameen said you want my attention," Stena Mezca said. "Now you have it, and you have nothing to say?"

"Right." Shifting my stance, I gulped and cleared my throat. "Well, we need more time to figure this..." I paused and watched the rainbow flowers move across his body. "...disease out. It's killing so many." Hesitating at first, I pointed at him. "*You're* even sick now. If we can find a cure...maybe we could help—"

"A cure?" Stena Mezca interrupted with a scoff. "Ha! I'm dying, boy. The cure is past my grasp."

"But there are others who need it," I said.

"New politics have entered our city," Stena Mezca said. "Which is why I called for your presence. Count Aameen and I thought it would do you both well to understand why we must make the decisions we must, especially with my limited time left. Potential openings will come up within the council. I'm past politics and politeness. *You* have been suggested as a possibility." He looked more at Ofelia than me. "Which brings me to the people I want you to meet," the Stena paused. "Our guests should be arriving soon."

"Guests?" Ofelia asked.

A knock came from the doors behind us. Aameen's daughter pushed open the doors and popped her head through the crack. "Stena Mezca and the Counts, our guests are ready."

"Send them in," Stena Mezca commanded before turning back to us. "My job is to keep Maize safe, after all."

Like the faint burn left on your lips after liquor, Stena Mezca's statements left me on edge about what came next. Did he convey a warning? What was to come through those doors?

Dani exited for a moment before opening the doors. A man adorned in a white and gold cloak stepped in, with another man at his side in similar attire, but with less gold. The first man was slender and tall, with the most golden hair I'd ever seen glistening in the room's lights. Even his bronze, hairless face shimmered with luster. Specks of gold lined his face, and piercing green eyes sharply contrasted every other part of him. The man next to him wore a white shirt with a sun and a moon on it. His dark face was stoic, in sharp contrast with his bright counterpart. His facial hair was perfectly groomed into a strong mustache.

An older woman followed the men, wearing a green and brown tunic with a dark green tree embroidered on her chest. Her black and gray hair was tied back tightly into a bun that sat on the top of her head. Long straight strands of hair hung outside of the bun, flowing down her head and framing her face. Her eyes and skin were a dusty hazel that analyzed every corner of the room as she entered. The men parted and she stepped between them, smiling at each person within the room, ending with Stena Mezca, to whom she bowed her head.

"Thank you for coming," Stena Mezca said. "This meeting is of utmost importance before my life takes a turn."

"Stena Mezca," the man dotted in gold said. "You do not look well."

Stena Mezca swiped his hand in disregard. "Counts, Ofelia, and Ciro. I present to you Spodnic Solareon, Sapa of Solara, Heir to the Solareon Dynasty, and Keeper of the Sun." Spodnic Solareon nodded his golden-haired head slowly with a soft, arrogant smile. "Next to him is Sol's foreign diplomat, Kuraka Amaru." Kuraka Amaru gave a quick bow before standing erect, indicative of formal military training, his sun and moon patches reflecting the light. "Lastly, we have Juniper from Conifera, across the sea. She is one of Gaia's descendants."

"Of what?" I asked, mouth hanging open.

To my utter disbelief, the literal children's story I grew up with stood before me in dark green. The offspring of Gaia, the Light of all light, shifted her gaze to me. Her eyes twinkled as they took me in. I knew the tales about her magic and wondered if I only imagined seeing it within her eyes. What powers did she possess? I had dreamed of having such powers when I was a child, but now, in the face of this Juniper, part of me just wanted my abilities to go away.

Juniper grinned and leaned a little bit forward. "Yes, I am one of Gaia's five daughters blessed with certain gifts." She winked in my direction before squinting. "And your eyes convey a story I once knew."

I blushed, my whole body warming up. Somehow, I both feared this stranger and felt like I'd known her my entire life. Falling into a stereotypical trope, I found Juniper...magical. I wanted to ask so many questions. Someone in the room understood me, understood the weight of my gift.

"Right," Stena Mezca said. "Now, this meeting is for multiple reasons. The first is in response to the Coalition's growth. We have word that the nation now has weapons that are able to fire rocks like arrows. They are very deadly. We believe the Coalition Empire will strike soon."

"What is your evidence for this?" Spodnic asked with a hint of condescension. "Solara has done more than its share in this war..." He glared at Kuraka Amaru before continuing. "And now we are seen as the Coalition Empire's enemy. I believe diplomacy is more important than responding with fire."

"Lack of action means the war will find you when you least expect it," Stena Mezca snapped back. "We believe the Coalition Empire will strike Solara first."

"And we will handle this the way we always do," Spodnic returned. "With grace and peace."

"My Sapa," Kuraka Amaru entered the conversation, "I know the choices I made may have put us in a...problematic position, but we need to respond in a way that both safeguards and strengthens Solara rather than endangering it. We *must* align with Maize."

My head swirled with so many questions. Why was I part of this discussion and why did it seem like Spodnic, the leader of Solara, wasn't the one making decisions here?

"We will find our way back to an alliance with both," Spodnic said. "We have many times in the past and will again."

"You are a *fool*, Solareon," Stena Mezca said. "We believed Maize was safe, and the Coalition struck us down. They will do it again, and they come with more fire this time."

Yelling erupted in the room.

"Cowards!"

"Reckless!"

The three men argued, but I couldn't follow or understand who was saying what.

After the name-calling died down a little, Aameen stood up and yelled, "Leaders!" They all turned their attention to him. "I am Count Aameen. I was a Kernel during our recent war. I witnessed all the bloodshed firsthand and convinced Kuraka Amaru to lend Solara's forces to end this war. I believe we have another option..." He looked at me, and I glared back. "This new disease could potentially be a favor to us all."

"Disease?" Juniper asked, breaking her silence.

"Enfer," Ofelia responded. "It is a highly contagious and deadly disease sweeping our lands right now. It is what afflicts our Stena."

Juniper looked over at Stena Mezca. "How would this favor any of us?" she asked Aameen.

"Who are you again?" Aameen asked.

Juniper smiled. "Company of Spodnic Solareon and an old friend of Maize. Here on trade business, more or less."

"Juniper sells herself short," Spodnic said. "She may be able to offer some *powers* to further all our causes."

"Possibly," Juniper smirked. "But I want to get back to...what was it called again? Enfer?"

"Enfer," Ofelia confirmed. "I believe Aameen is saying we have certain powers in Cornia that could use the disease as an asset, but this would also mean our own warriors would be further infected as well. It isn't something we advise."

"I'm still trying to understand this dilemma," Spodnic said. "I've heard of this disease, but there is also some way to attack others with it? Is that what you are saying? What are we talking about?"

Aameen was about to talk, but Stena Mezca cut him off. "We won the war with the Coalition creatively. We have other creative approaches on our side."

"*Creative.*" Spodnic laughed at the word. "Be vague, Mezca, for all I care. It does not matter. We will not be fighting, and we will find peace with the Coalition again. It is settled."

"Spodnic—" Kuraka Amaru started.

"*Sapa* Spodnic is my title, Kuraka Amaru." He turned his attention to Kuraka Amaru. "Do not commit insubordination in front of our allies."

The gold on his cheeks sparkled. An odd energy pulsed through the air, flowing from Sapa Spodnic. Did he also have some kind of ability?

"Yes, *Sapa* Spodnic..." Kuraka Amaru said with his hand on his sword's handle. Sapa Spodnic calmed down and turned back toward the group.

Kuraka Amaru ran his hand along his belt as he said, "I'm sorry for this..."

A stale energy numbed my brain and made me itchy. Something was off.

In a sharp scraping noise, a bright flash of metal blinded me for a moment. Kuraka Amaru thrust the sword forward, through Spodnic's back.

The shimmering sword poked out the front of Spodnic. A glowing crimson waterfall gushed from his chest. The sword disappeared in another harsh scrape.

For a moment, the blood looked golden before turning red.

"I'm only doing what is best for Solara..." Kuraka Amaru said before stepping back.

Count Bebida gasped. Ofelia tried to rush over to help Spodnic, but I pulled her back.

"Don't move," I whispered.

The energy in the room shifted. A sudden terror filled me, my life under threat. The council's faces reflected my own terror. All except Stena Mezca, who was unfazed by what had just happened.

Juniper leaned against a wall, covering her mouth.

Spodnic put his hand on his chest and took it off. It was covered in blood. Blood gushed out of his mouth as he looked up and fell forward, dead.

"What's going on?" Aameen yelled while the rest of the Counts stood and backed away from their chairs.

"The beginning of change," Stena Mezca said as he looked at Aameen. He turned to Kuraka Amaru and Juniper. "Though earlier than planned. Either way, to the new ruler of Solara and the descendant of Gaia from across the sea. A great alliance has formed today."

Kuraka Amaru nodded. Juniper looked around the room in panic, took a deep breath, and shakily responded, "An alliance, yes. I...I look forward to it." Uncertainty outlined her words.

"Now," Stena Mezca said, turning his attention toward the rest of us, "what has transpired today will *not* be talked about, or you will meet the same *fate* as Spodnic. Ofelia and Ciro, you may keep fighting this sickness.

You have learned what I wanted, and I know you understand our position. Consider this my last gift to you."

Did he just gift us this bloodshed? What's going on?

"This alliance will fight in the war," Stena Mezca continued. "You both will fight the disease. There will still be no further financial support as resources need to be put into the war. But Maize can still call for you, Ciro. Counts, we will concentrate our aid to Solara for the upcoming war, even after my death. Will my orders be fulfilled?"

Stunned, silent expressions bounced back and forth between the Counts. A body lay before us. Fear gripped the room. What would happen if they said no?

"Yes, Stena Mezca," all the Counts responded shakily.

"Good," Stena Mezca said. "I need to lie down now." He stood up and walked out of the room at a very painful pace. He nodded to Kuraka Amaru and Juniper before he left.

I looked at Ofelia. I looked at Aameen. What was I supposed to do next? I needed guidance.

"You may all leave," Kuraka Amaru said. "We will take care of the mess."

Motionless for a moment, Count Bebida moved first, and everyone followed toward the doors. I kept an eye on Kuraka Amaru and Juniper. An obvious darkness shrouded Kuraka Amaru and made me distrust his every move. Juniper, on the other hand, seemed as surprised as the rest of us. Juniper's hand started glowing once we left the room. Though I was curious to see what she was doing, I went straight down the stairs and exited through the purple door.

So much for boldness.

"What just happened?" Ofelia asked.

Aameen was right behind us.

"I'm sorry," Aameen said. "I didn't expect any of that to occur."

"Did we just witness the beginning of a civil war within Solara?" I asked.

"I don't know, but Stena Mezca and Kuraka Amaru seem to be behind it," Ofelia said.

"I will figure out more," Aameen said. "But please be quiet about this. Not even your family should know. Something dark just happened, and I feel like this won't be the last we hear about it."

Though I was still unsure about how much I trusted him, I agreed with his warning. The disease wasn't the only problem happening in Maize. Much more was going on. Foreign deals were made with a bloody signature. New blood was spilled, and I didn't know whose mess it truly would end up being.

At least I fought against something I understood. Aameen's battle was much more complicated.

An odd feeling came over me, something I used to feel for Aameen. Respect. Though bitter and unwelcome, I held onto this respect. I didn't trust him, but we were going to need one another.

CHAPTER 21
MARRIAGE

Kuraka Amaru and Juniper left Maize the next day. They loaded a large box into their wagon as they left. No one told me, but I believed Spodnic's remains were within them. Only Stena Mezca and some of the Counts were able to bid them farewell. Most of the council didn't show up, except for Aameen and another member. I was annoyed with Aameen's constant politics, but Ofelia told me he had to keep a good relationship with them.

Solara was powerful, and powerful entities should be kept close. As for Juniper, she could do things like I could. A sense of ill-placed wonder had teased me each day since she left. Did she hold the answers to why I could do what I could? Some day I'd find her again. I'd ask her all the questions I had. Until then, the realities of Maize and Enfer haunted my every thought and action.

Stena Mezca died within the next week. The disease he thought wasn't important became so important that it ended him. Had Gaia punished him for lack of action? He was a devoted follower. Was it worth following a deity who would punish you when you faltered?

With the passing of a Stena, tradition requires the body be burned in dry crops outside the religious building, a modest, stone building with four colored doors. A grand blaze reached high into the sky with the building's silhouette behind its glory. A black and gray smoke filled the air, and the whole city prayed and watched until the fire went out. It took four hours to die off. The citizens adored him. Cornia was awash in tears and grief—the first native leader of Maize since the country's formation had served his country and joined Gaia's Light.

I had trouble grieving for him. The respect I once had for him shifted after the assassination of Spodnic Solareon, the leader of Solara. The explanation I deserved was never given. Aameen kept telling me he had his reasons, and they were all for Maize, but I found it hard to believe.

A week after the Stena's passing, I had a surprise visitor at the medical building during my lunch hour. I squinted, looking down the hallway.

"Aameen?"

I wondered if my eyes deceived me. It was the first time he had ever been in the medical building. Surrounded by twenty empty chairs in the common waiting area, I began walking in his direction as I passed private rooms on each side of me. Most of the rooms were empty during lunchtime. I rarely had time to eat, but our staff needed to. A sterile scent encapsulated the building, a combination of fresh air and a hint of bleach. We had to keep the rooms clean to prevent contamination and the spread of Enfer.

"Can we talk?" Aameen asked. His eyes were surrounded by dark circles. His normal high energy was subdued, and his bright eyes were dim.

"Yes." I stopped by one of the sinks and washed my hands.

"Somewhere private?"

The room I took him to was one of the patient rooms. I shut the door behind us. It had a picture of a big leaf on the wall. We wanted pictures of life in this space to subconsciously promote hope in fighting Enfer. A low table with a cloth sat in the middle of the room where patients would sit. Two chairs sat opposite one another, facing the table. Tucked back in the corner were a few cabinets and a sink.

"You look exhausted. What's going on?" I asked.

A deep sigh preluded his words. "So much. The Counts received word two days ago from Solara. The entire Solareon family was killed."

I gasped. "Wait, for real?" Since meeting Spodnic, I read up on the very large Solareon family. Spodnic had three children himself and at least ten cousins beyond him with their own children. "Even the children?"

The way his face contorted answered my question. Trying to hold back tears, he closed his eyes, pinched the bridge of his nose, and opened them after a deep breath.

"Yes, the entire family. The city is in an uproar." Aameen looked at the ground.

Despite the chaos of the situation, my mind remained clearer than it normally did. Calamity had followed me everywhere I went for years now. My thoughts found the space easier to think within. If I could figure out diseases and their secrets, I could understand soulless politics.

"Kuraka Amaru did this. Just like he killed Spodnic Solareon in front of us."

He looked back up. "Kuraka Amaru has been named the leader of Solara."

Dumbfounded, I wondered how such a terrible man acquired such power. Just when I thought I understood politics, the truth left me a fool.

"What? How could the city name the killer of the Solareon dynasty as its leader?"

"Because the city doesn't believe he killed them. They don't believe he killed Spodnic."

"Then who?" I asked. Aameen gaped at me like I knew the answer. Only then did I realize what he implied. "Do they think Maize killed Spodnic?!"

"It was the last place he was seen alive. Word went around their city that an assassin was hired in Solara to kill the rest of the Solareon family. The city believes Maize is behind it."

"You're joking."

"I wish I were. Ciro, Kuraka Amaru has promised to avenge their family after the Coalition Empire is addressed."

I stepped back and fell into the chair behind me.

We brought Solara into our war with the Coalition, but they are shifting their attention to us? Was that the goal the entire time?

"They are going to war with us?"

Aameen shook his head. "Kuraka Amaru wrote me yesterday. He believes he will be able to distract the city from its thirst for vengeance. He apologized for blaming this on us, but it was his only way to power. Solara is going to keep the impression that the Solareon dynasty still controls the country when discussing with other foreign nations. They worry it will impact trade if their country is in unrest."

I sat up straight. "You can tell the truth about Solara to its citizens. You have his letter. They will believe you. If they don't, we will tell the other nations about this. They will stop trade."

He shook his head again like a parent tired of their kids' ideas. "I think that to be unwise. I may as well write my own death sentence by doing that. And Kuraka Amaru is close with Juniper. I'm sure they will take her word over ours. We are in a tricky position."

Silence occupied the space between us. I didn't know what to do. He just stared at me. The steps to healing Enfer made sense. Politics shifted every time you thought you had an answer. I understood why he looked so tired.

Despite my shifting mood, I stood from my chair. "So, now what? We just sit here and trust him?"

"I don't have any other options for now. I believe another opportunity could come from it."

I watched his relaxed state. "You are too calm for this, Aameen." My distrust of him returned. How could someone be this calm after such a betrayal? Was he impressed? Was he scheming himself? "It makes me scared for you."

He stared at the ground. "I scare myself as well."

I drifted back to trusting him again. Was I supposed to trust him or not? He just sounded like my good friend Aameen from before the war. Then...he smiled. The smile sent a chill down my spine. He wasn't staring at the ground in embarrassment; he was staring at the ground like he was proud, even calculating.

"Why are you smiling?" I asked.

"The last part of my news." He straightened his spine and raised his chin. "I have been selected as the next Stena."

He widened his shoulders and puffed his chest out. With his chin raised high, he looked at me like he was waiting for something. I didn't know what to say. The smile across his face seemed malicious. The most powerful person in Maize stood in front of me, and he basked in it.

"Congratulations on getting everything you ever wanted." My voice went monotone.

He lowered his chest. "You sound unhappy for me. I came to tell you so I could share my success with my best friend."

My voice shifted back to its normal octave. "I'm happy for you. I truly am." I tried to force a smile, but it hurt my cheeks. "But it has long scared me how much you wanted political power and how quickly you have gained it. I guess I thought you wanted good for Maize, not power for yourself."

"I *do* want good for Maize. I want the best." He shifted like he wanted to embrace me but straightened his back again. "If anyone thinks otherwise, I don't care."

"I'm happy for you." I pushed out another weak smile. "This is what you wanted, and you got it."

There was a pause of silence; his face shifted.

"You're a jerk," he said.

"Excuse me?"

"You heard me. You're an *ass*. You act like you know everything about everyone and that you know what's best for them, but you don't. You're caught in your own delusion. If it doesn't meet your expectations, it's bad. No matter what."

"The best for me? My own delusion?" A harsh laugh came out of my mouth. "You're so self-involved that you forget the terrible things you did to *me*. You told my secrets like they were your own to tell. You were willing to sell me down the river to further your political career. Everything you've done, you've done for yourself!" I stomped hard on the ground. "*You're* an ass!"

He scoffed, running his hand over his mouth. "You're a terrible best friend, Ciro."

"You haven't been my best friend for years now, Aameen."

His face softened before it hardened again. I hurt him. "That is *Stena Aameen* to you."

I walked over to the door and opened it. "Have a good day, *Stena Aameen*." With a bow, I extended my hand as a gesture.

Aameen stormed past me, down the hall, and out of the building. I watched him from the hallway outside the office we'd been in.

"You *certainly* have a knack for dramatic encounters," Ofelia said from behind me before slurping her morning tea. "At least you didn't attack him this time."

"Just stop," I said.

"Okay, but only if you agree to talk to your wife." Tipping her glass back, she downed the last bit of tea and clinked the cup down on the counter.

In the weeks since Ofelia had confronted me about my relationship, I hadn't had time to take a break. Distractions always popped up.

Ofelia's daily reminder to talk to my wife became rather exhausting. No, more like downright annoying. But I welcomed the distraction this time if it meant I didn't have to think about *Stena* Aameen. Valeria and I had been drifting apart more and more. I had every intention to talk more intentionally with her, but distractions always popped up. Thus, the daily reminders.

Stop making excuses.

"Understood." I nodded. "I'll get to it."

"Sure." Ofelia scoffed with a dramatic eye roll. "What was *that* about anyway?" She gestured to the door Aameen had walked out of.

I peeked out of the examination room before pulling Ofelia in and shutting the door. "Aameen is the new Stena."

"What?" she exclaimed.

"Quiet." I hushed her.

With a hand over her mouth, she lowered her voice. "Sorry. They just selected him so quickly."

I told her all Aameen told me, including about the assassination of the Solareon family and how Maize was blamed.

"Wow." Her mouth hung open. "That's a flat-out lie. The people of Solara are buying this?"

"Not only that, but they are backing Kuraka Amaru as the new leader. Well, their unannounced leader. Their plan is to pretend as if the Solareon dynasty still runs the city."

She laughed. "And I'm sure he has people to back this claim. I bet Juniper is backing his claim, so Kuraka Amaru's words sound legitimate. It's a master web."

An alliance within an alliance turning on the other alliance member.

"You're smarter than me. I didn't connect those dots while Aameen told me."

Ofelia squinted like she figured out something. "Why did Aameen tell you all this?"

"He thinks we're still best friends. Well, maybe not now. I think he wanted someone to be happy about his new position."

She nodded. "And maybe you should be happy."

I let out one short laugh. "Are you kidding me?"

"He's the most powerful person in Maize now. If you befriend him again, he might back our goals. You should keep him close."

"I can't lie like that. I'm bad at this political bullshit."

"Then get better at it." She paced in circles. "We're fighting against Enfer. We need resources. This is important."

I didn't understand how, from hearing all the same things I did, she pulled out so many important details and opportunities. I just got angry and sad.

"You are better at this than me."

"You'll get it someday." She winked.

"I don't know what I would do without you."

She opened the door and hummed. "You'd probably fall apart, hombre loco. It's time for us to get back to our jobs." Stepping out, she shut the door. Then, the door opened again. "Oh, and talk to your wife." The door clicked shut.

Though my nosy friend was intense, I appreciated her wisdom. And I knew she nagged me about my relationship because she loved Valeria and me. Valeria deserved the same investment from me.

No matter how I went about it, I was the problem. Of all the problems in my life that I blamed my faults for, I was my own biggest issue.

I rubbed my temples, already exhausted from thinking about what to do with Valeria. Down the hall and in the waiting room sat patients waiting for me with a problem I understood. Dealing with Enfer seemed so much simpler. At least simpler than relationships. I walked to the waiting area to get my next patient.

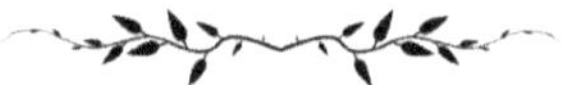

Much-needed redundancy filled the remainder of the day. The tedious distraction of holding and burning the rainbow flowers let my mind drift. I treated about twenty people a day, which meant my stamina grew. So much so, I was barely tired. On my way home, I even treated two more infected citizens.

By the time I arrived home, it was nearly nine o'clock. Another late, chilly night. Vito woke from a deep sleep on the porch. I leaned over and scratched his scaly skin below his ears. He caressed my arm in return. Inside, Harper wobbled to greet me at the front door. Isabella sat on the couch, drawing.

"Hi, Daddy," she said without looking.

I kissed Isabella on her head. She drew a winged beast colored in shades of red. "Is that a Talladia?"

"Yes, I learned about it in school today." She looked up proudly. "They live on the beach and prey on *invasive* animals. This allows the sandworms to live and keep the beaches white."

The thought of sandworms creeped me out. A shiver ran across my body, picturing their strange bodies wiggling on the sand. I had only been to the beach a few times growing up. The sand was soft, but those sandworms were very unpleasant when accidentally touched.

"Our little biologist." I made my way to the kitchen, where Valeria sat at the table, reading a book. She didn't move or acknowledge my presence, a normal response lately when I came home late. A plate of noodles and a cooked meat leg of some kind sat on the counter. "Sorry, I'm late. I had a wild day."

"Mhm." Valeria didn't look away from her book.

A frigid air filled the room, and it wasn't the temperature.

"Aameen told me some *interesting* things today." I tried shaking off the irritation that was overtaking me.

"Didn't know you were talking to him again."

Iced again. She gave me nothing but her words. No glance and no engagement in conversation.

"Well, not exactly." My attempt to talk to her more, like Ofelia suggested, seemed pointless, but I kept trying. "He said Solara's new leader is Kuraka Amaru and the Solareon family is no more, but they are keeping it a secret."

She likes to gossip.

"Cool."

But apparently not anymore. An intense pounding slammed at my brain. *Why am I even trying?*

"I'm trying to talk to you."

"Great." Another page turned, though I didn't believe she was actually reading.

"V," I walked over and put my hand on the page she pretended to read, "I want to talk to you." I tried to keep a positive, engaging attitude even if she wasn't.

"Oh, you're finally noticing me?" She pushed my hand to the side and started reading the book again.

"Of course, I am. I'm talking to you now."

"I'm glad you're in the mood to do that again. Sadly, I don't feel like it tonight. Maybe another time, but make it *earlier* in the day."

I sat at the table across from her. "You haven't exactly tried to talk to me much either. I found out you were mad at me from Ofelia."

"Because I knew you'd listen to her. *She* listens to me. Funny how that works."

My brain ached. If I just left the room, I could find some peace from her frigidity. But I couldn't. I needed to stay.

"It feels shitty when your wife can't talk to you and talks to your best friend." I scowled at her.

"Good to know. I'll try to remember that next time you remember to give time to me."

"I'm doing a lot. I'm sorry that my saving people is such an inconvenience to you." My voice grew louder, not quite yelling, but close.

She slammed the book down. "Ciro, it's great that you are helping people to make yourself feel better, but you're neglecting your family. El asno."

"I'm training Isabella as well," I added. "Don't act like I don't do anything for our family. I'm doing so much to help—"

"You're neglecting me!" She slammed her hands on the table, breathing heavily. I could smell her minty, floral breath from an essential oil candy. Normally, the smell made me want to kiss her, but tonight it made me nauseous. Her amber eyes pierced me in a way they didn't normally. Such pain burned in her eyes. "You're obviously so bored and tired of me that you're doing everything you can to stay away. I don't even feel like you love me anymore."

A wave of reality crashed against my heart. She meant what she said. She sincerely meant it. I stared at her with my mouth open. Harsh tears pooled in her eyes. I knew I had hurt her, but seeing her physically react to it made it real.

"I'm going to bed," a soft whisper came from behind me.

Valeria flicked the tears from her eyes, pushed her chair back with a loud screech, and walked over to Isabella. "Goodnight, mi amor." She kissed Isabella on the head.

"Sleep well, hija," I said in a strained voice as Isabella went upstairs.

Valeria moved back to her chair, screeched it back, and plopped down. An unnatural silence hovered around us. We waited to hear her footsteps upstairs and her bedroom door shut.

"V, I love you with my whole heart. Siempre tengo," I immediately assured her.

"No, no lo tiene. It doesn't feel like it. It feels the same as when you were at war, but here you have the *choice* to come home. It's like you want to be where everything is happening. You like to be around pain. I would know…"

My heartbeat pounded so hard my sternum moved up and down. My breathing grew heavier, and the air became difficult to inhale. I just wanted to run away, not deal with my problems.

"I don't like being around pain." My voice cracked. "I *hate* being around it. But I have to fix this. I made this problem."

"I can't help but feel like we aren't the same anymore," she said, pausing as if looking for something in my expression. "And there it is again." She rolled her eyes.

"There's what?" I asked.

"You don't care," she said, resigned. "Ciro, do you even like me anymore?"

"Of course I do." It was meant to be reassuring, but the words came off monotone, an uncertainty behind them.

"Then why do you spend all your time away from me?" she exclaimed. "You spend all your time at the medical center. When you're home, you barely even look at me."

Her hardened glare threw swing after swing of slicing judgment. I only blinked, feeling as if I should respond but barely caring to do so. What was wrong with me?

"I...I have so much to fix."

"That doesn't mean you can't enjoy your life!" She slammed her hands on the table as a few tears shot from her eyes onto the table. "Ciro, you were hurt by this war. You haven't let yourself process it at all. You're trying to do things that keep you in this constant stressed state. It helps you avoid your problems. This war shattered you. It shattered me. Estoy roto. Estaban rotos. We need to heal. And don't think that I don't still love you. I love you with every ounce of myself. Eres mi todo. It hurts me to see you hurt. For so long after you came home, I sat by the door every night waiting, desperately waiting for you to come home. Each time a person would walk by, casting a shadow through the window, Harper and I turned to the door, willing you to walk in. Then, when you did eventually come home, you'd pet Harper's head and walk to bed. Me?" She shook her head. "I was lucky to get a hello."

I heard her words as clear as day, but my mind went foggy. I didn't want to have this conversation. It was too much. I didn't have these problems when I was away. It was why I wasn't coming home. It was why I wanted to be back at the medical building. The obsessive, abrasive pounding in my mind hit its peak at home. Home was supposed to give you peace.

It hit me. She was right. Everything she said was right. She sat by the door, ready to talk to me. I shrugged her off. My hand covered my mouth while my mind kept trying to escape the conversation and its hard reality. My head pulsed with a rhythmic pain between escape and presence.

"Ciro. My love. Look at me." I tried to look into her eyes, but the world was so foggy. "I know you. Something just came to you." Though tears glistened in her eyes, they were eager and bright. They saw something. "Please tell me. Don't push it away. I can't take it anymore."

My brain and heart collided. Everything I felt and everything I knew fought with one another. The pulsing in my head stopped like built-up pressure finally releasing. My heart slowed down. Reason and compassion clashed with my brain like a giant wave to a rocky cliff. The fogginess in my eyes lifted, and I saw my wife. Her amber eyes shimmered with passion, power, and tears. I didn't deserve her. I wasn't treating her well. Then, the words started flowing. Nothing was going to stop them.

"I'm just not worth loving." I paused and took a shaky, frail breath. It wasn't enough air, so I took another, deeper breath. My heart pounded in my ears. "Why would you love me? All I do is hurt people. All I've done is hurt people. And I know you and everyone else say I didn't mean to hurt people, but I still did. Everything I've tried to do to stop that from happening is still happening. So many people are dead because of me. And I know I didn't mean to do it. But I feel it." I paused and took another breath as tears rushed down my cheeks. "I don't deserve to be here. I don't deserve to be loved. I don't love myself. And I don't know how to get rid of these feelings. V, I don't know what to do."

I sobbed. My body gave out. My head fell forward, heavy with pain and emotion. Valeria stood from her chair and embraced me before my head hit the table. I pushed my head into her right shoulder.

"You're loved." Valeria cried with me. "You're wanted. You deserve to be here." I grasped her shirt as she said this. The words ricocheted off my ears. "You're loved. You're wanted. You deserve to be here." She repeated the same statements four more times, almost sensing that I wasn't hearing her. Then I heard her. Her voice was slow, a low whisper in my ear. "You're loved. You're wanted. You deserve to be here."

The tension in my body let off. She held me, and I fell silent, my sobbing subsided.

"Say it," she said. "Say it now."

I lifted my head from her shoulder and gave her a puzzled look. *Say what?* It then hit me. I realized what she wanted me to say.

"I'm loved," I cracked out the simple words in an insincere, unconvinced way. "I'm wanted." My heart jumped. I sensed a shift in my tone. "I...I deserve to be here." I let out a deep sigh. My body caved in on itself as she caught me again. A sensation prickled across my skin. Our bodies were one, a familiar energy flowing between us. We were linked like we had always been before.

Valeria lifted my head, and her pooled eyes looked into mine. Her face glistened from the tears and the kitchen's ambient lighting. I missed the face before me. It had been so long since I looked at it with true awe. She kissed me before I could kiss her. Her minty breath invigorated me. Something missing rushed back in an explosion—sparks. I held her face and kissed her more.

Our faces parted, and she smiled. "Ahí está mi esposo." I inhaled her words like my life depended upon it.

"There is my wife," I echoed.

She sat on my lap with her legs to the side, the bare skin of her mid-thigh visible in the kitchen's light. The scar from her arrow wound was white against her tan skin. My hand rested on it.

One of her hands sat on my shoulder while the other wrapped around my neck as she stroked the back of my head. Harper walked up and put her chin on Valeria's lap while looking up at us. I patted Harper's head.

"Harper is happy to see you again," Valeria said. "Now, let's stop growing apart. Let's grow together." I grabbed her hand and nodded in agreement.

Together, we will grow.

Harper barked and began wagging her tail. I snapped back to reality. It was time to stop drifting away from what had happened and rather integrate it into my actual life.

"We should get away," I said. "Take a break away from the city."

"El hombre de mis sueños. My dream maker." She surveyed my face, thinking it was a joke, but saw my sincerity. A pure grin lit up her face. "But when?"

I thought about the rumored plant that Nina used to help treat Enfer.

"Ofelia and I have been talking about looking for a plant that might help fight Enfer." Valeria raised her eyebrows. "I know, it's about the disease. But it would be a journey more than anything. We could go look for it and make it a trip."

She squinted. "You promise this will be a real break for you?"

"I promise. The population is smaller outside Cornia. And honestly, my hands hurt from healing so many people. It could do me well to recharge."

Valeria eyed me down. "Talk to Ofelia. Figure it out." She pecked me with a kiss before standing. "I'm going to lie down. You know I don't like to cry." She touched the bottom of her eyelids with her pointer fingers and flicked the tears away.

I grabbed Valeria's hand and pulled her back. I kissed her once more, taking my time with it. Taking in every inch of her. We parted in ecstasy and static.

"I love you," I said. "Thank you for loving me."

She smiled before leaving the room. It was just Harper and me left, sitting in the kitchen. I put my hand on her head and stared around my home. I wasn't healed. I didn't know if I would ever be fully healed. But I remembered I had my partner in life. I needed Valeria.

The kitchen glowed. It was the most beautiful the kitchen had ever looked to me. The dishes sat on the drying rack. The cupboards looked humble in the dim light. I still smelled the lingering scent of dinner and Valeria's minty, floral breath.

I needed more time for relaxation. I forgot how good it felt and I deserved it.

CHAPTER 22
ISABELLA

To secure what we needed for our trip, one task rose above the rest: a visit to Nina the herbalist.

Ofelia didn't hide her reluctance, but she came with me all the same.

Entranced by Nina as she nodded and listened to Ofelia's speech about why we need her help, I tried to find any clue to why I thought she looked like Count Ariba when I saw her in the crowd. Isabella followed her, captivated for some reason as well. But why?

With a slow blink, Nina fixed her honey-eyed gaze on me. Such familiarity filled her stare. Almost like Isabella's...

"Right, Ciro?" Ofelia asked.

"Yes, sure." My neck strained as I nodded quickly, agreeing to who knew what. I kept my attention on Nina. "Can I ask you a question?"

"Go for it." Nina placed one hand on the chair she stood next to, leaning.

"Are you...well, were you related to Count Ariba?"

"No." Nina snickered. "Why do you ask?"

"Oh, no reason." I shook my head, putting to rest what I thought I had seen.

"Right..." Ofelia drummed her fingers on the table. "Can we get back to the topic at hand?"

Every bit of Nina's quaint house was filled with shelves of dried plants, potions, and other empty containers. The scent of herbs and essential oils wafted through the air. The cots lined up outside her house only made sense after you saw how full her home was. Since the last time I came to her property, the twenty or so cots outside had filled with patients.

Ofelia spoke at length about the Enfer group we had assembled, and Nina's importance in it. Though I hardly spoke, Nina kept her eyes on me.

"You want me to join a group whose sole purpose is fighting Enfer?" Nina lifted her hand from the chair she leaned on and crossed her arms. "Why now?"

"Because of your knowledge of the medicinal uses of plants." I elbowed Ofelia. "Right?"

"Right." Ofelia rubbed her arm, shooting a glare at me. "You may have convinced me of their importance."

Nina paused, thinking, until her face lit up. "When do we start?"

"That took a lot of convincing." Ofelia snorted.

"I will do anything and everything I can to beat this disease," Nina said. "Especially if it means joining the two people who are fighting it more than anyone else in Maize. What purpose do you see me serving?"

"I asked this before," I said. "Don't you know of a plant that can potentially help with Enfer?"

"I do." Her eyes lit up. "I appreciate your love for plants." With a smile, she pointed at my eyes. "I can see it in your eyes. You *know* plants."

Do I know plants? What an odd thing to say. The only one I know is one that others can't see.

"I know a thing or two about plants," I glanced over at Ofelia. "But mostly about flowers." With several rapid blinks, I stopped myself from saying more, but that didn't stop Nina from leaning forward and looking deeper into my eyes. "Do you have more of this plant?" I asked.

"Yes, but I used up my small stash months ago," she said, backing off. "I found it one time while venturing near Blanche. I thought nothing of the plant since it served little purpose before. When I tried every other combination of herbs and potions I could muster, I thought trying something new wouldn't hurt. The people I used it on had fewer symptoms for a few weeks. Then, the symptoms returned but didn't get worse. They are still alive but have been continually sick."

A little burst of air swirled in my lungs, making me catch my breath. Could it be true? Was there a plant that could help us? Help me? I imagined not spending every minute in a medical center healing people. My chest warmed.

"Where are these patients?" I almost yelled.

Without a word, she stood and walked toward the back of her house, waving us over. Ofelia and I exchanged a concerned glance, but I stood first and followed Nina, Ofelia soon after. Through a back door, we entered the alleyway behind several homes. The houses in this part of Maize were much smaller than my neighborhood. Many of the farmworkers lived here.

Ofelia leaned over to me as we followed Nina and whispered, "How the hell does she look this young? She has to be at least ten years older than me, but she looks ten years younger. What am I doing wrong?"

"It's probably all the wine you drink," I whispered back.

Ofelia rolled her eyes, shoved me, and stepped forward. With a soft chuckle, I followed along.

We came to a small stucco hut with a wooden roof. As we entered, a younger couple looked up from their beds with beads of sweat cascading down their faces. Wearing only underwear, small growths covered each of their bodies. About fifteen rainbow flowers covered each of them.

"This is Ramon and Claudia," Nina said. "As you can see, they are still sick, but the plant has kept them alive for a few months."

Ofelia asked me, "What do you think?"

"It's a lot, but I think I can do it," I said.

"Do what?" Nina asked.

I walked over to Claudia and said, "I'm going to inspect your growths. Just relax."

Claudia nodded and lay back. She didn't even question me. I recognized her desperation. Starting with the four flowers near her shoulder, I burned away the flowers. The other flowers near her right ribs and on her leg gravitated toward the shoulder flowers I burned away. Being far enough away from her shoulder, it allowed me to work before they collided and multiplied.

One flower burned, then the next. I moved faster as the other flowers closed in. Three, four. They were gone. Still full of energy, I moved down to her leg. One, two, three. The flowers near her ribs raced faster toward the leg. They split into two extra flowers. After the last flower by her leg vanished, I rushed to her side. Claudia's body no longer had a single rainbow flower on it. The tumors started shrinking, though not as fast as they normally did, and newfound brightness returned to Claudia's eyes.

"What...what did you do?" Claudia asked.

"What just happened?" Nina asked.

I ignored Nina and moved on to Ramon. I repeated the same pattern, though his growths were in five different spots with fewer flowers at each growth. His eyes lit up once I was done.

"How..." Nina whispered, a wondrous sparkle in her honey eyes.

"Come with us," Ofelia said as I stood up, feeling woozy for a moment. Ofelia handed me water, and I chugged the bottle while exiting their home.

"Get some rest," I croaked out to Claudia and Ramon.

Ofelia walked ahead, shushing Nina each time she tried to talk. My head steadied and I watched Nina continue to look back at me with furrowed eyebrows. Once back at her home, she held the door open and rushed us in.

"Speak now," Nina commanded as soon as the door shut.

I finished another gulp of water. "I can see disease. I can also heal it." If she were on the team, she deserved to know my truth.

"What?" Nina exclaimed. "That's absurd. And if you can, why is this disease still running rampant across Cornia?"

My throat clenched. I had decided to tell Nina everything about what I could do, but my body tried to suppress it. Swallowing, I cleared my throat.

"You saw what just happened to your patients," I said. "It's absurd, but it's true. And I only have so much energy in a day to do so, and I can only treat mild cases. I have tried healing those who are very infected and...it speeds up the symptoms instead."

Nina's mouth hung open as her eyes shifted back and forth between us. My heartbeat intensified. What if I had confided in the wrong person? Would she use it against me? Flashbacks of the war and attacking others with disease taunted me. I shook my head—Nina wouldn't ask this of me.

"This plant you found, and your knowledge about it, are very important for the future of Enfer," Ofelia said. "You found a way to halt this disease's symptoms. This allowed the overall infection to decrease and allowed Ciro to heal what was unhealable before."

"I have no words for this," Nina stated.

The pounding of my heart echoed in my ears. My brain followed along to the haunting rhythm.

Thump. Thump. Thump.

"That's okay," Ofelia said. "We need to know what the plant looks like and where to find it. We plan to gather more of it, come back home, and have you work with us to eradicate the disease."

Nina stared. She smiled. "Okay." She walked over to one of her notepads and flipped through it before coming to a drawing of a plant. She ripped the page out and handed it to Ofelia. "Here. It's called a Sunset Cone-flower. I know it's just an outline, but the flower is yellow and brown with hints of purple on its petals and dark green leaves, narrow and long. At least you have the flower's shape." The flower's cone-shaped center was surrounded by drooping petals. "I found it growing on the prairie hills around Blanche. It isn't very common. I suggest asking locals there about it."

All at once, the pounding ceased in my head, ears, and chest. A wisp of a cool breeze filled my lungs. I stared at the flower. Each swoop of its petal brushed against my heart. Hope stood before me.

Ofelia was from Blanche. Eduardo was from Blanche. The nightmares of his death replayed in my mind, his eyes fading as he died because of me. I promised him that I would tell his family that he loved them. I kept postponing visiting there. It was something I wanted to do, but just as I had done with Valeria, I was avoiding my issues because of how busy I was. Maybe it was a sign from Gaia to fulfill the vow I made.

"Thank you," I said.

"From one plant expert to another," she raised her eyebrow, "I share my expertise just like you share your own."

Why does she keep stressing my expertise in the invisible plants only Isabella and I could see?

"What *plant* did you see?" she asked.

I shook my head. Was I missing something? Leaning toward her, I couldn't help but grin.

"I'm sorry, what?"

With a small laugh, she casually replied, "What plant did you see being the answer to Enfer?"

Pulling back, my mind went cold. "Oh." I'd misunderstood her question. "I guess I didn't know. I honestly thought there wasn't anything that could help."

"The world is full of terrible things causing death, but the world is also filled with wonders that sustain life," Nina said. "It's up to you whether you want to believe in only one."

"You should come with us." I smiled. "We could use your wisdom."

Eyes twinkling, Nina leaned forward before frowning and looking out her front window. "I'm afraid I can't. You saw all the citizens I'm helping. There is no one else skilled enough in the art of healing through plants. I can't leave them. I would've tried to gather more of this plant myself, but I can't find anyone who can get it for me. Blanche has ceased trade with Cornia since the disease has taken over. We need to figure out a way to get more. I know you will figure this out for us. But I do wish I could come and help."

"That's fair," Ofelia said. "Thank you for joining our cause. Please keep it secret. We *will* come back to you upon our return."

"Gaia's speed," Nina said as we exited her home.

The patients lying on the cots surrounding her home had larger growths and were riddled with Enfer's flowers. Green mud covered the growths. I wondered if it soothed the sores. I wanted to heal them, but with at least twenty flowers on each patient, it was well beyond my capabilities.

"We should leave tomorrow," Ofelia said.

"That's a good idea," I said. "I'll let Valeria know so she can get ready to come with us."

Ofelia froze. "What did you say?"

"Oh, well, I may have taken your advice." I held her shoulder. "Valeria and I spoke last night."

"Yeah? And how'd that go?" She started walking again.

"*So* good." I squeezed out a smile. "We both thought it'd be best to take a break from the city and from all the work."

"Even though this trip is about Enfer?" Facing me, she raised one eyebrow. "You know, the thing that is causing you to overwork?"

"I promised her it wouldn't be. Though we are looking for a plant to help in our fight, I'll be away from the medical centers, away from long hours with patients."

"Good." She faced forward. "Then I don't have to go."

"Please do. I'll need help finding the plant."

"Are you sure?" Shifting her jaw, she rubbed the back of her head. "I want you to have your time."

"Positive. Valeria and I will be fine. We'll find some time for ourselves. I imagine you want to see your home city again."

"And I'll make sure you get time alone. I promise." She twisted at the waist, cracking her back with the momentum. "It'll be nice to visit back home."

"I wanted to do one other thing before we left. Would you be okay if I brought Isabella to the medical building for the rest of the day?"

"Certainly. Why?"

Nina's wisdom from earlier repeated in my head. It was time I started focusing on the positive instead of the dread.

"I talked to Valeria this morning. I want to start teaching Isabella to heal Enfer."

Ofelia froze again. "Seriously? Are you sure?"

"It needs to be done at some point. I noticed her poking at an infection during our last encounter with some beasts. I'm worried she may try playing with a disease and accidentally move it." I shivered. "I'd rather she know what to do and what not to do. It's time to see the good within the bad."

"When you put it that way, it makes sense." She started walking again.

"I know. It's been heavy on my mind."

"You're a good father, Ciro." She noticed the look I gave her at her sudden sincerity. "I mean it with my entire existence. I don't know how you balance all you have going on. Even your daughter handles the same complexities you do. I can barely handle myself at the end of the day."

"I just spoke to my wife for the first time in weeks." I let out a little chuckle. "I wouldn't say I've handled things well."

"True." This time, she gave me a half-smile. "Actually, very true. You've been pretty terrible at it." Her little smile morphed into laughter, which I joined. "But you have been great with Isabella, at least."

"I'm glad you think so."

Ofelia turned toward the medical building while I went to pick up Isabella from home. She had just gotten home from school, and her excitement grew with each bounce she accomplished. Her hair, tied up in a ponytail, bounced along with her.

"Are you sure you're ready to go to work with me?" I asked.

"Yes, yes, yes!" Isabella exclaimed.

Valeria smiled as I kissed her. "We'll be back before dinner," I said. Valeria raised her right eyebrow. "I promise." I kissed her again. "And we're leaving tomorrow for the trip. Can you ask your mother to watch Isabella?"

"Tomorrow?" Valeria exclaimed before lowering her voice. "I'm sure my mother will be able to drop everything she's doing." Widening her eyes, she scoffed.

"I'm sure she will as well," I joked as I walked away. "Love you!"

"Hombre loco...I love you, too," Valeria said. "Have a fun time, hija!"

"¡Adios!" Isabella exclaimed. She turned her attention to me. "Where are you going?"

I put my arm around her shoulder. "Mamá and Daddy are taking a small vacation. Daddy has been very tired from work."

"That's a good idea. Sleep is important for living." She raised her chin. "It helps you poop better, too."

"What? Who told you that?"

"My teacher told us that. You need to do important things to live." She started counting on her fingers. "Rest is important. So is pooping." She stopped at two.

"I'm so happy you're educated." I giggled. "Speaking about life, do you remember how we've been going over how to see sickness?"

"Daddy, do you really think I forgot about this? We just went over it three days ago."

"I know. Well, do you know how you saw me heal the girl from the flowers that one day?"

She smiled big. "It made the boy happy."

"Right. Well, this one thing I can do is very important. I need you to keep it a secret." I lowered my voice as her face lit up. "I...I can heal people from being sick."

Her smile faded. "I know. You made the flowers disappear. I haven't told anyone about it. I keep promises."

"You're intuitive, hija."

"Hehe, toot." She giggled more.

"You're very smart," I corrected. "Well, I think you can do what I can. We're going to Daddy's work so you can try it out. How does that sound to you?"

"Hmm, okay." She kept skipping with her ponytail bouncing along. "I think I can try that."

Her swaying ponytail came to an abrupt stop once we arrived at the medical building. Isabella waved to the line of patients as we walked in, her infectious joy spreading through smiles and waves. The maximum number of rainbow flowers I saw was ten on one person. It would be a tiring day, but we would get it done.

When we entered the building, Ofelia was talking to the front desk receptionist. She saw us and waved.

"I'm so excited to have you here today, Isabella," Ofelia said.

"There are lots of people here," Isabella said. "Do you help them all day, every day?"

"We do," I responded. "That's our job." I turned my attention to the front desk. "Give us a moment before we come and get the first patient."

The receptionist nodded.

I held Isabella's hand as we walked back to the observation room. I closed the door behind us while she explored the small room.

"It isn't very big in here," she said.

"It's all the city would give us. We don't need too much room. Now, did you see the flowers as we walked in?"

"Yes. Most of the people had flowers on them."

I nodded. "I'm going to bring the first person back and I want you to watch what I do. You're going to see me hold a flower like this." I pinched my pointer and middle finger together with my thumb. "You can feel the flower in your hand. All I do from there is hold it. Your hand will start to get hot. You can't let go, or it will make the flower nastier. We don't want that."

"How long do I hold it for?" she asked.

A soft hum tickled my lips as I smiled at my daughter. Her understanding and patience with learning the ways of our gift never faltered. I never kept a level head like she did. Rubbing the back of my neck, I willed away the odd jealousy. I reminded myself that Isabella had a teacher while I taught myself it all. And I needed to keep teaching her.

"I count to ten at a slow pace. One, two, three...do you see how fast you should go?"

"I can count, Daddy."

"I know you can, hija. Then, when you let go, the flower will go away. You then will move to the next one until they're all gone. Watch me this first time, okay?"

She nodded as I stepped out of the room and called my first patient.

"Mariana Flores?" I asked in the waiting room.

An older woman with wrinkly skin and short, curly black hair stood up. She wore large, round glasses and a cardigan covered in cats.

"Hola," Mariana said, walking with a limp.

"Hola, my name is Ciro, and I will be checking you today. I see you have a limp. Is that new?"

"No," she said. "Bad knees and ten grandchildren will do that to you."

"Ten, wow." I led her into the room. "You're a lucky lady. This is my daughter, Isabella. She's observing me at work today."

Mariana smiled at Isabella while Isabella waved back.

Mariana sat on the patient table, and I inspected her and the rainbow flowers across her right shoulder. I moved around Mariana, out of her sight, while pointing to the flowers. Isabella nodded as I pointed at each one. Just as I always had, I pinched the first flower between my index and middle finger on my thumb and let it burn while I mouthed counting to ten. Using my other hand, I acted as if I were feeling and analyzing odd marks or lumps on Mariana. Then, I moved on to the next flower, and then the next. I finished the last flower.

"You look good, Mariana," I said. "Nothing to worry about."

"Thank Gaia," she said. "My family couldn't take losing another to this dreadful disease."

"I'm sorry you lost someone," I said. "Make sure you hug your grand-children extra tight tonight."

"Oh, I will," Mariana said as I opened the door for her. "Thank you. Have fun today, Isabella."

"Bye," Isabella said.

"De nada," I said. "Check out at the front desk on your way out. Adios."

I turned to Isabella after shutting the door. I made a couple of notes on Mariana's folder. "Did you see what I did?"

"Yes. Ten seconds. Poof, no more flower." She made her hands look like an explosion. "I get it, Daddy."

"Good, I want you to try with me. I'm going to say you're helping me check for symptoms during the next patient. When you feel ready, grab a flower and hold it. I'll watch over you."

Isabella's legs started swaying with nerves, but her eyes remained fierce like Valeria's.

I brought the next patient back, who had six flowers across his left arm. While going over my normal speech with the patient, Isabella walked over and began inspecting him with me. Isabella watched me take care of the first flower. I nodded to her, and she reached forward to grab the next flower.

The patient was very talkative, going on and on about recent politics. I paid no attention to his words but fixated on my nervous daughter holding the flower. Her face shifted while burning away the disease and the heat it produced on her hand, while the chattering patient kept talking as if nothing was going on. After a smile and a nod from me, she kept holding. Her mouth moved as she counted. Once she counted to ten, she let go, and the flower faded.

"Very good," I said.

"I know!" the man responded.

Isabella burned away one more flower, and I finished off the last three. As soon as he walked out of the room, still talking, I shut the door.

"Muy bien!" I exclaimed. "You did so good!"

"It hurts a little." She shook her hands like she had touched something hot.

"You'll get used to it," I said. "Take little breaks whenever you want, but remember to make sure all the flowers are gone before you take a long break. Take it easy. It makes you tired."

We worked our way through the rest of the patients. She was getting faster and could handle a lot more than I could early on. My walkthrough about taking breaks and when to let go helped, but she was doing it all on her own. She made me proud.

By the end of the day, she looked tired, so she just observed the last patients. I had more energy than I normally had since her help relieved me.

"You did so good today!" I exclaimed after I shut the door behind the last patient of the day. "How do you feel?"

"Tired and hungry," she said.

"I bet. The last part I want to go over with you has to do more with holding the disease. Did you notice how we helped people with only a small number of flowers?"

"Yes."

"That's on purpose. I've tried to do more before, and I didn't have enough energy for it. When you don't have enough energy and let go, the flower flings back to the sick person and makes the other flowers to grow faster. It does terrible things to people when that happens."

She stared at me with large, round, brown eyes. "Do they die?"

The question came so naturally. "Yes, they do, hija. And I don't want you to deal with that, ever. You have to be careful with this gift. Don't tell anyone about it. Keep it secret when you're doing it. This is very important to keep you and the patient safe. Okay?"

"Okay."

"And make sure you remember to take breaks." She was about to say I already told her that. "I know I've said this, but it's very important and it's easy to forget. Daddy isn't very good at this and will get better. I want to make sure you are always feeling okay."

She nodded. "Have you ever...moved it?"

I expected this question to come at some point, but not this early.

"Yes." I sighed. "I have. I don't ever want you to do that."

"Why?"

"It only does bad things." I was coming off harsh, so I took a deep breath. "Don't ever do that. Promise me?"

"I promise."

I could have told her the real reason not to move the sickness, but I was terrified. The giant ball of diseases I mashed together and pushed toward the attacking Coalitionists haunted me. It was a ghost I would forever deal with.

How could I tell a little girl that she held the power to create disease and inflict pain and suffering on so many people?

I started breathing hard.

Valeria's beautiful face appeared in my mind. My muse. My heart. Her words she made me say repeated.

I'm loved. I'm wanted. I deserve to be here.

A cooling sensation swept over me and relaxed my limbs. There would be opportunities to tell Isabella about the dark side of our gift. I had written in my journal about all the reasons why not to move disease and what happens when you do. I had already taught her so much. When she was old enough, I would give her the journal and talk her through it. For now, she was still young.

I kissed Isabella's head. "Let's go home and get some dinner." Tugging at her hand, we left the building.

On our walk home, the kids played and laughed in the streets. A few of them said hello to Isabella. She told me they were friends from school. She went on and on about why she liked some of them and why she didn't like others. She was just like her mother.

The setting sun made her black hair look auburn. The way she talked was so precise. It was like watching a tiny adult explain the mysteries of life. Then she would gossip about something, sounding her age again. She was perfect.

"I love you," I interrupted her at one point. She looked up at me with a smile. I pointed up to the sun that was in the last part of its day. "I love you more than the sun. Eres mi sol, hija."

"I love you, Daddy." She smiled so large while looking up at the sun. The light made her tan skin glow.

I was grateful to have my daughter. I was grateful to be her father. My life was becoming more like it used to be, with a little more spice. It was a weird feeling to live with this spice, but I learned to adore it more and more. I couldn't wait to spend more time with Isabella, but right now, I had to focus on Valeria. It was time to mend our relationship.

CHAPTER 23
BLANCHE

Mountiffs made the journey to Blanche take just over a week. The spacious wagon pulled by four of the crimson beasts provided plenty of space to haul back all we would gather. The Mountiffs' curly, short hair kept the beasts' skin feeling cool rather than hot. Something about the insulation kept heat out. Longer, curly hair extended from the beasts' manes and stuck out in all directions from their thin faces.

The hilly, vegetated fields of Blanche beat the flat, trauma-filled land of the Husk in terms of beauty. Though both areas bordered other countries, Husk's proximity to the desert dried out its land. The sea had the opposite effect on Blanche.

Melons and squash were the main crops, and their vines weaved up and down the hills in waves. Ofelia educated us about the local horticulture. The hills were the foundation for the crop's growth, supporting its immense root system.

The further east we traveled, the closer the ocean came. Trade winds reached far into Blanche's territory and cooled us as we rode. Small flowers covered the hills in between the melons and squash. Coming to Blanche in the heart of spring meant we entered the peak opportunity to witness many blooms, according to Ofelia. Dots of honey yellow, vermilion, crimson, and vibrant white painted the emerald green landscape.

The view, Ofelia said, had been her favorite part of living in Blanche.

"But I don't miss home. I prefer Cornia." Ofelia had repeatedly noted the thought throughout the trip.

When we were close to Blanche, Valeria finally asked, "You have said you don't miss home, but why?"

"Let's just say I had a bad breakup with my girlfriend about a week before I left for the war."

"Girlfriend?" Valeria asked.

"Yeah," Ofelia responded.

The oddest crackling noise came out of my mouth before I cleared my throat. "I didn't know you...had a girlfriend." I tilted my head so far to the right, I almost fell over.

Ofelia laughed. "You never asked, *again*. I don't like going around and advertising my love life."

"Pretty sure the two times you mentioned your ex, you got angry when I asked questions."

Palms facing upward, Ofelia teetered her hands up and down. "You always picked the wrong time to ask. Some people ask their friends questions when they notice they are down or lonely."

I recalled how often Ofelia asked how I was doing and what she could do to help. I neglected to find examples when I'd done the same in return.

"I'm sorry I never asked," I said. "I've been—"

"Distracted," Ofelia finished my sentence.

"Self-absorbed," Valeria added. "Pretentious. Rude."

"This is fun," Ofelia said. "Moody. Dazed."

"Okay, okay," I said. "I get it. I've been unlikable lately."

"But we still love you." Ofelia grabbed my head and rubbed my scalp with her knuckles.

Valeria and Ofelia laughed with boisterous, echoing cackles.

We came to the top of a hill covered in bright green melons and crimson flowers growing from thick vines. In the distance, a city stretched across a valley to the base of another hill, much vaster than Husk but quainter than Cornia. A stream surrounded the outside of the city. A lone bridge was the only way to enter the city. The wooden bridge had railings on each side with crisscrossed wood rungs. The bridge ended in a steel gate into the city that you could see through. Steel was uncommon in Maize, so the gate was out of place among the homogenous wooden city walls. No stone or stucco covered the walls of the buildings inside the city. Instead, wood paneled houses and roofs made of thin black and gray rocks dotted the city.

"Welcome to Blanche, the city of melons and squash," Ofelia announced, raising her hands and shaking them.

The home of Eduardo. I reminded myself. If time allowed, I would find his family. He deserved it.

"It's pretty," Valeria said.

"Sure, it is," Ofelia joked. "Let's go eat some *real* food. I'm tired of camping meals."

After finding a stable to tie up our Mountiffs, Ofelia marched forward with her water bottle swaying from her backpack, thudding with each step. We followed her path to the bridge over the babbling, light blue stream. Freshwater streams were rare in Maize. In Cornia, a water table ran under the city, which we accessed using wells. This stream in Blanche contained so much liveliness. It smelled pure, a contrast to the soil-rich well scents of Cornia's water.

The wooden walls surrounding the city displayed carvings in various places, mostly initials or years of some significance. We walked through the arched metal gate. People roamed the city in every direction, but little conversation occurred between the citizens. The purple feathers of the Zapa fluttered from above. The immense wingspan of the beasts cast shadows along the city streets. Three Zapas perched atop the wall, the sun reflecting off their purple feathers and shimmering beaks in a metallic haze. A few of the beasts fought over scraps littered on the street, while a shop owner scared them away with a broom.

"Damn birds," the shop owner said.

The Zapa fought like a great warbird during the battle. The natural Zapa picked from the trash.

"Are Zapas pests here?" I asked.

"Depends on who you ask," Ofelia said. "Shop owners don't like them because they are notorious for stealing things. They like to build nests out of the prizes they take. But if you don't mind the occasional theft, they are excellent at flying and riding."

"It's interesting to see the warbirds in a relaxed state," I said.

"I'm just happy their population is doing okay after how many died in the war," Ofelia said.

"Ofelia? Is that you?" a woman's shrill voice asked.

Ofelia paused, sighed, and forced a smile as she turned. "Beatrice. It's been so long."

A woman waving in our direction with her hair tied up like a nest became more animated as she came forward. Yellow ribbons twirled around her brown hair, and yellow eyeshadow overpowered her face. She wore a flowy dress covered in green flowers. She charged toward Ofelia and nearly tackled her with a hug.

"We've missed you here." Beatrice released Ofelia from her grasp. "I was sad to hear you moved to Cornia."

"I needed a change of atmosphere," Ofelia said.

Beatrice looked past her, eyeing us. "Who are your friends?"

Ofelia turned from Beatrice in relief. "This is Ciro and Valeria." An amusing grin was plastered on her face. "Ciro worked with me in the medical tent. This is his wife, Valeria, who fought in the war."

"You are both *beautiful*." Beatrice ran over and hugged us. "I am Beatrice. If you could not tell from the oozing chemistry, Ofelia and I are ex-*lovers*."

"I see," Valeria said.

I gave Ofelia a wide-eyed glance mixed with a silly grin. Beatrice threw her hands back from our hug, as if releasing a caged bird into the world. Ofelia shrugged with a great sigh. I couldn't tell if Beatrice was being serious, but Ofelia was certainly flustered, acting in a way I hadn't ever seen before. Ofelia always spoke the truth and let people know exactly what she thought. Beatrice did the same, but in a different way. As Beatrice overshared, Ofelia's face lit up. I couldn't find the animosity Ofelia spoke about her ex with anywhere.

"I take it Ofelia did not talk much about me," Beatrice said. "We were *madly* in love, you see. For a long time. Then the war happened, and we drifted. I still get emotional thinking about it." She flung her right hand up to her forehead as she sighed.

"You dated each other?" Valeria cocked her head, analyzing this mysterious woman making claims neither of us believed.

"I know. We were *perfect* together," Beatrice said.

"No, we weren't," Ofelia corrected. "We were terrible together."

"Always such a pessimist." Beatrice glared before returning to her bubbly state, a brief shadow behind the light. "Well, anyhow, why are you all in Blanche?"

"We have been combating Enfer, the disease sweeping through Maize," Ofelia said. "We are looking for a plant that may help."

"A plant to fight a disaster?" Beatrice asked. "Curious."

I scanned the crowd while she gave her opinion. Despite all the people, not a single rainbow flower covered one of them.

"How is Blanche handling Enfer?" I asked.

"We just haven't been impacted much by it, to be honest," Beatrice replied. "But I know a person who might be able to help with your search. Come with me."

Beatrice turned in the most dramatic way I had ever seen, hands flailing in the air and body wriggling with the wind. She continued to walk forward, hands still in the air before letting them fade to her sides. Her dress flowed behind her like a cloud.

Ofelia gave us a tired look, but her eyes followed Beatrice in a trance.

"Seriously? Her?" I asked.

"Shut up," Ofelia said.

With a burst of laughter, we followed Beatrice, who was surprisingly agile.

Blanche's buildings stood at a maximum of two stories, but most of the homes were one story. The people didn't acknowledge one another much, very different from Cornia, where everyone said hello to strangers and friends alike. We tried to extend the same hospitality, smiling at a few people, but they averted their eyes as quickly as they could.

The buildings' motifs followed the same pattern—square windows and square architecture. The more I observed, the more I realized Blanche wasn't as exciting as I had hoped it to be. The buildings lacked charisma, the colors across the city fell flat, and the people remained in a preoccupied state, all things Ofelia warned us about.

"Sorry, this isn't very exciting," I whispered to Valeria.

"It's okay," she said. "I like the temperature, and we have each other." She reached out to hold my hand.

My cheeks warmed first before heat blazed through my chest and across all my arms, making me grip her hand tightly.

"Here we are!" Beatrice announced, halting her stride and pivoting to face us.

We stopped before the brightest house in the city. It was painted a vivid yellow and had a multicolored garden around the front and side of the house. It made my heart flutter.

"I thought you were bringing us to someone who could help. This is your place," Ofelia said. She looked around and sighed. "And you grow flowers now? Great…"

Beatrice laughed louder than the situation allowed. "Oh, Ofelia, much has changed about me. I am a plant person, you see."

"Wait, so were you referring to yourself earlier?" I asked.

Beatrice smiled with her hands angled beneath her chin. "Why, yes."

"Gaia help me," Ofelia groaned.

"What is this plant you ask about?" Beatrice asked.

Ofelia pulled the paper Nina gave to us out of her pocket and handed it to Beatrice. "It's called the Sunset Coneflower."

"I am aware, Ofelia," Beatrice said as Ofelia rolled her eyes. "What a strange flower to seek."

"We need it," I said. "Do you know where it is?"

"I know of a place," Beatrice batted her eyes in Ofelia's direction. "But what will *you* do for *me*?"

"You're joking?" Ofelia asked.

"My services are not gratis," Beatrice said. "I make a living off my plant knowledge. You are not exempt from my fees."

Ofelia blushed, and the pink slowly crept down her neck.

"Then, what would you like?" Valeria asked.

I leaned in, waiting for her answer. Beatrice fluttered her long eyelashes and tapped her right pointer finger on her chin. With each tap, my heartbeat quickened.

"Hmm," Beatrice eyed us. "Money seems so droll to ask for...I have it! Dinner. And drinks." Her eyes shifted away from Valeria and me. "With Ofelia."

"Absolutely not," Ofelia said.

I whipped my head toward Ofelia so fast that my neck cracked. After all we had done, this was the line Ofelia wouldn't cross?

"Then I am sorry, I cannot help." Beatrice handed back the sheet. "Such a shame. It is a difficult flower to find."

I enlarged my eyes in Ofelia's direction as she rolled her own. Making sure I cleared my throat as loudly as I could, I gained Ofelia's attention again. With a slow dip of my head, I silently begged her to concede.

"Fine," Ofelia said, raising her middle finger at me before turning to Beatrice. "I find your lack of respect for the dying ridiculous, rude, and selfish. I will counter your suggestion with another request. Can we grow this flower in Cornia?"

"Yes," Beatrice said. "With proper instruction."

"And you can provide this instruction?" Ophela asked.

"Yes."

"I will take you out for dinner..." Ofelia said.

"*And* drinks," Beatrice added.

"*And* drinks," Ofelia continued. "But show us where the coneflower is and teach us how to grow it."

"We have a deal, Ofelia." Beatrice reached out her hand as they shook. "Pick me up in an hour." She walked up to her house and shut the door with a dramatic slam.

"Not what I expected," I said.

"It's everything I expected," Ofelia growled, rubbing her hands on her face. "I need to get ready. Come and eat at my family's restaurant while I grab some things. I'm afraid you will be on your own after that. She expects an extravagant meal. Are you okay on your own?"

Valeria squeezed my hand. "We'll make do."

We followed Ofelia for a few blocks until we came to a one-story building with five sets of tables and chairs set up outside. Ofelia's cousin was working that day—she was warm with Ofelia but couldn't care less about us. None of that mattered as the food left me more than satisfied. Their chiletentas were warm with the perfect amount of crunch. The cheese, pork, and corn tortilla danced around in my mouth with each bite. A spicy and sweet smell wafted through the air.

After we finished our meal, Ofelia stopped by our table. "Dinner is on my family. I'll see you around eight in the morning. We'll meet at Beatrice's." She sighed and walked away without any further interaction.

"Okay, thanks for the meal and bye," I said as Valeria and I laughed. "She doesn't like it here at all, does she?"

"I'm sure there are *some* good things," Valeria said, raising her eyebrows. "Let's go find them."

She took my hand, and we strolled into the city, wandering the streets as the sun began to set. Two-story apartment style buildings with balconies hung overhead. Along a narrow street, the buildings blocked some of the fading sun. The balconies, lined with metal barriers, twirled in circular designs. Chipped black paint along the railings exposed oxidized turquoise metal that gave some color against the bland buildings.

Kids played on the street, and a man fiddled with a guitar on one of the balconies. Another man and woman argued near a wall. Three kids kicked a white and blue ball. Many of them at least smiled in our direction.

"Excuse me," I said to one of the men sweeping his doormat, nervous of an unfriendly response. "Where is your market area?"

To my surprise, he pointed in the direction we were heading. "Phantom Court is three streets in the direction you're going. Make sure to stop by the Folly Hall. The best of Blanche is found there."

"Gracias," Valeria said as we kept walking.

The streets on the way to Phantom Court widened. Many people filled the streets—couples walked slowly, hand in hand, people on individual missions zipped around and children ran up and down the sidewalks. We rounded the corner to market stands lining the road. The stands were held up by sticks with canopies covered in leaves. People argued, bartered, and purchased everything from food to shovels.

"This is just like home," I said. "But the citizens and shop owners seem to be arguing more."

Valeria giggled as we surveyed the stands. Cut and cooked melons sat in elaborate displays. One had a melon sculpture of a great beast. They used the green shell of the melon to form the body and its soft, red flesh to make eyes, ears and a nose. Isabella would've loved to see the creations. The only thing rivaling the display was the taste of the melon, a sweetness unmatched by any other. I recalled Eduardo telling me about Blanche and the marketplace.

"It's just like what Eduardo said it'd be," I said.

"Did he live around here?"

I shrugged. We made it to the Folly Hall that the man had recommended. It wasn't a stand but a storefront. As we entered, the smell of lemon and herbs filled the air. Wooden carvings of animals, humans, and plants filled the wooden shelves. A busy woman in the back worked on a carving. I imagined Isabella running around in delight.

"Hello," I said. The woman with white, wispy hair tied back with a purple bandana glanced up. "This is our first time here. Your work is amazing."

"Gracias," she said. "I've worked on perfecting my skill." She pointed to the front of the store. "Your child will like the toys up there."

Valeria and I looked at each other. "How'd you know we have a child?" Valeria asked.

The woman just laughed and continued carving. Following her instructions, we walked to where she pointed.

"We look like we have kids," I said.

"Must be the bags under our eyes," Valeria mused.

"Not yours, mine," I corrected. "You'll never look a day older to me."

She pushed me and grinned.

Wooden carvings of local beasts covered the shelves behind us. Ones with four legs, winged beasts and even limbless beasts looked up at us. Then I saw it. I reached to pick up the carving about the size of my hand. It was a Nostrangal, Isabella's favorite. It stood on four legs with beady eyes.

"Pull the tail," the lady said from the counter.

Following her instructions, the toy perched up on two legs, moving just like the beast did.

"She'll love this," I said.

"Her favorite beast," Valeria responded.

Returning to the counter, I paid the woman. She took the money, stuck it somewhere below, and went right back to carving. Her focus wouldn't waver, but her eyes didn't match her intensity. They were soft and reminded me of Eduardo's eyes. I needed to find Eduardo's family. My promise from long ago echoed in my mind.

"Excuse me, but do you know where Eduardo Ferria lives?" I asked. The woman stopped carving in an instant. "I served in the war with him."

Her gaze moved up to me, looking like she had seen a ghost. "Yes, Alexandria lives above here. She's my tenant."

I tried to say more, but I just stared at the woman, stunned and perplexed by our fateful encounter.

"Is she home right now?" Valeria asked in my stead.

"Yes." The woman stood up. "Their door is this way." She shuffled her feet to the back right of the store. We exited the shop into an alley where a brown door was carved into the wall. "Here. This is where she lives." She touched my shoulder, gave me one look, and went back to her shop.

The door was before me, but I only stared. "I know this is something I should do, but I don't think I'm ready for it."

"Then do it later," Valeria said.

"No. I have avoided this for too long. I owe him."

I reached my hand up to knock, but froze. Valeria smiled to reassure me and helped me knock on the door. Shuffling steps came from inside from someone walking down the stairs. The door handle twisted and a woman with curly black hair and large brown eyes looked up at us, a puzzled look across her face.

"Hello," she said. "Can I help you?"

My mouth hung open. No words came. I took a deep breath.

"My name is Ciro," I said. "I was a friend of your husband, Eduardo."

She gaped at me. Tears formed, and she put her hand on her cheek. "You knew Eduardo?"

I thought of Eduardo lying on his cot. Rainbow flowers danced along his body before consuming him. Life faded from his eyes right in front of me. His wife was in front of me instead. Tears dripped down my cheeks.

"I'm...I'm so sorry it took me so long to come here. I was supposed to come here long ago. I promised him."

The lady cried with me, launched forward, and embraced me for a hug. "It's okay," she said. "You're here now."

I didn't hug her back at first. "He...he loved you." My arms reached around, and I squeezed back. "He loved both you and your daughter so much. He wanted me to tell you."

She pulled away from me. "I know," she said. "We both knew this. He was our heart." Soft cries occasionally rose from her. "I'm sorry. I thought I'd grieved enough."

"Don't be sorry," Valeria said. "This was an unexpected visit."

A little girl, the same size as Isabella, walked down the stairs. Her black, curly hair was tied to one side.

"Mamá, who are these people?" she asked. "Are you okay?"

The mother turned to her daughter. "I'm okay," she said, wiping the tears from her eyes. "This man was friends with your father during the war."

The little girl looked at us and gave us a small wave. I waved back. "Hi," I said. "I have a daughter the same age as you. Your dad and I talked about how we wanted you two to play together someday."

She looked past us. "Where is she?"

"She isn't here right now," I said. "We aren't from Blanche."

"Oh," she said. "I'm going to play with my toys then." She ran back upstairs.

"I'm so sorry," the woman said. "She isn't trying to be rude."

"Don't worry about it," Valeria said. "Our daughter would do the same thing."

We all laughed a little.

"I would invite you in, but I can't," the woman said. "We have somewhere we need to be, and we were just getting ready."

"Don't feel like you have to," I said. "I just wanted to fulfill the promise I made to him."

The woman smiled. "My name is Alexandria. You're welcome to our house whenever you are in Blanche again. Mi casa es su casa." She touched her hand to her chest.

"Gracias," I said.

We stared at one another for an extra short moment. She smiled and shut the door. A deep breath escaped me as the door shut, a mixture of relief and satisfaction.

"Are you okay?" Valeria asked.

"Yes," I said. "I am." A peaceful presence calmed my steady heart. I know my actions caused his death, but I didn't do it on purpose. I didn't even know it happened. For the first time, I believed it. I believed it with all my heart.

Valeria grabbed my hand, and we walked out of the alleyway into the commotion of the crowd, pulling me out of the emotional state I was in. The oddest feeling came over me, like I still needed to feel worse than I did. But I didn't. I did something right. I gave Alexandria something she didn't expect, and her warmth reminded me of the way Eduardo always treated me. The moment wasn't what I expected. Far from it. Part of me thought she would've blamed me for his death, cursed me. The other part expected immense guilt to force a confession of my true gift and what I had done to end his life. Instead, she showed love and shared in my grief. It was exactly what Eduardo would've done.

I had blamed the war for all that had happened. I'd blamed Krown Kernel Fernando, Stena Mezca, and Aameen for forcing me into doing something I didn't want to do. It was easier to say everyone else pushed me to the decisions I made. But really, it was me. All the dark, the light, the good, and the bad were part of my life. They were part of who I was, of the decisions I had made. Just as Nina had said.

Eduardo loved his family so deeply that it endured beyond death. He was attentive and caring, things people used to associate with me. But these traits were slowly coming back. My moments with Isabella before I left for Blanche showed them. She saw them. Valeria deserved to see them again. It wasn't that I owed her, but rather that I wanted to show her. I longed to vocalize my love.

Valeria looked up at the sky, closed her eyes, and breathed in the fresh air. The evening sun brightened her tan face and black hair. Wisps of rogue hair glowed so brightly they looked golden. An overwhelming sense of pure devotion made me fixate on her and her alone. She was beautiful, there was no doubt about that, but something greater consumed me. Her intangible beauty drew me in like a bird to the sky, like a winged beast to a sunrise. Valeria was genuine, good-hearted, brave, and passionate. She was a cornerstone in my life. All the dark things weighing me down seemed lighter because of her. She made my heart leap, my skin tingle, and my mind race. I fought for her, I loved her, and I'd die for her. She was everything I wasn't and everything I wanted to be.

"What is it?" she asked. "Why are you staring at me?" A smile expanded across her face.

Everything I believed about her radiated from my heart, but I couldn't figure out how to say what I wanted to say. How to tell her how much she meant to me and how much I didn't deserve her unrelenting love. Her smile, her eyes, her hair, her smell, her touch, and everything else about her was something I could easily vocalize, but she deserved more. She deserved the best of me and my thoughts, something genuine.

"You are..." I paused, "...everything to me. You're my heartbeat, my joy, my support, my sun, my moon, my horizon, my day, my night. You make me stronger. You make me confident. You keep me grounded. Valeria, I adore you. I adore every ounce of you, and I'll kick myself every day for forgetting this." I took her hands into my own. Her soft fingers caressed my callous palms. Her amber eyes moved back and forth in the smallest way. If I died lost in her eyes, all would be okay. "Valeria Sinsal, I love you." My voice cracked. "I love all the inner, all the outer, and all the in between of your essence."

"Mi amor."

She pulled me in and kissed me. The passion between us passed in a quiet, breathless rhythm. The tighter she pulled me in, the more I had to grasp her back from the impact. The intangible beauty crashed into the tangible. The collision sent a shockwave down my spine, making my legs shake. We pulled apart, electricity sparking off our bodies. I smiled, taking in the beauty of my wife.

Then, something odd filled my mind. I thought of Eduardo's family again.

"Thank you for being yourself again," Valeria said. "I've missed this side of you." She stared at me, realizing my distraught mood shift. "What are you thinking about?"

Saying nothing would have been easy. It was what I had been doing for so long. I wanted to tell her.

"I'm thinking that I need to stop blaming myself for Eduardo's death. He wouldn't have ever wanted me to do that. Seeing his wife's face reminded me of this."

She squeezed my hand. "Eres una buena persona. He knew it, I know it, and everyone else thinks this about you. You forgot about it for so long that you started becoming something you pictured yourself as, something you are not."

Instead of the image based on fear and pain, I tried to imagine the one I often reminisced about while I was at war. It was an image I tried with all my might to protect. I pictured our couch with Valeria leaning against my shoulder, and Isabella sleeping in my arms. Harper was sitting near me, and I petted her with my spare hand. It was the reason I joined the war as a medic. It was the reason I made all the choices I had—to protect my family.

I chuckled. "I have something to admit to you."

"What?" Her fiery, yet welcoming eyes gazed into my own.

"I joined the war to protect something. I felt like I succeeded in protecting it. But now...I realize I actually failed. I thought all I had to do was fight and do my job. But I lost myself. I was the reason for my own failure." I took her hands in my own. "Valeria, I'm sorry for ripping our family apart. With everything I have, everything I am, I *will* change this. I *will* dedicate my life to our family. Mis coronas y mi impulse."

She placed her hand on my chest and paused. "I have to admit something to you."

"What?" I asked.

"It started with my jealousy after you returned." She pressed her lips together. "Your title—the Hero of Maize—made me feel things against you that I despised." Before I could remind her of my hatred of the title, she raised her hand. "I know. I know. You hate the title, but that doesn't stop people from saying it all the time." She sighed. "I loved being called the Hero of Husk." Eyes bright, she looked up. "But when I returned to Cornia, no one knew this about me. When you returned, *everyone* knew that about you."

"V, I didn't—"

"Let me finish." She pushed her hand forward. "I hit a point where I started believing it myself. I saw you as someone I didn't recognize. I blamed you for our family falling apart. I blamed you for every problem that had entered my life. Your coldness was just fuel to my fire."

I stepped back and averted my gaze. There was guilt again.

"You did?"

She nodded, stepping forward and grabbing my right hand. "But then someone told me something I needed to remember. Isabella kept telling me all the great things you were doing together. She never called you the Hero of Maize. She kept telling me all the things you were teaching her. How to be careful with what she can do. How to help people. All the real parts of you, those hidden parts, were very evident in how you treated her. You were pouring yourself into our daughter. You wanted to do good. You are *her* hero. Isabella reminded me that you are a good person. Eres una buena persona."

Tears formed in my eyes. A warm wave gushed through my chest. I was overtaken by love. Not only the love I rediscovered with Valeria, but the unwavering love I had for Isabella. The two people I did everything I could to protect loved me. They believed in me. Isabella saw my pure heart even in my darkest times, and Valeria didn't give up on it. I was a good person. I had to remember that.

"Thank you," I said. "Thank you for not giving up."

"Isabella and I will *never* stop loving and believing in you, Ciro. From now and until we enter Gaia's light."

We kissed in the middle of Blanche's busy street. Flowing between us was the unwavering, intense spark we always had, sending a surge pulsating through and out of my body. I loved my heroic bride with every fiber of my being. I needed to start treating her like it, every moment I could.

CHAPTER 24
SERENDIPITY MEETS ZEMBLANITY

The small inn we were staying at was an old apartment converted for travelers. It was quaint and musty, with an aroma of old leather, and had dusty pictures of Blanche's history.

Though the inn was cozy, we didn't get much sleep. Our time was spent twisting around in the sheets, keeping our bodies busy. For the first time in a long time, there was no possibility of a child interrupting us. Our emotional reconnection fueled our passion—it was as if our bodies and souls were one for hours on end.

Despite Valeria's faults during the war and my struggles after, the wall that had built up between us fell. With the tension gone, all our inhibitions were set free. My heart burned for her. My skin desired her. My brain loved every bit of her.

After we'd spent hours in bed, I found myself walking the streets with Valeria. Wherever Valeria went, I followed. She was my leader, and I was her council, waiting for her command. She was the sun, and I was the moon reflecting her glory.

A morning mist covered the dusty roads, our hands intertwined, and Valeria hummed while we walked to meet Ofelia. We took our time as the morning came so close to midday. A cool breeze brought the smell of freshly cut melons from the nearby market. It was just us, and that was all that mattered.

The Blanche citizens bustled around the city on their various morning missions. They still gave uninviting scowls and glares to those they passed, but Valeria's humming transformed each of their scowls to smirks. She made them smile. She made *me* smile.

As we approached Beatrice's floral front yard, Ofelia tapped her foot aggressively on the street. "I said the *morning*."

"It is *technically* still the morning," I replied. Valeria and I giggled. The sun was about an hour away from its highest point in the sky.

"I take it last night went well," Ofelia stated. "It's about time you two...rekindled."

"You are polite." Valeria grinned.

"Yeah..." Ofelia squinted. "Good, whatever. Now, let's complete our mission and get some coneflowers." She clapped her hands together. "Follow me."

Moving away from the city center, we left Blanche from the east with the wagon and Mountiffs at our side. The city, its people, and even Ofelia were mere distractions I had no trouble ignoring. I couldn't keep my eyes off Valeria. Ofelia sighed at an obnoxious volume, walking backward while facing us.

"How was your night?" Valeria asked.

"Painful," Ofelia said, hiding a grin. "Thanks for *finally* asking. I needed a reminder of why we broke up. But I got the reminder I needed, and now I know how to transplant the coneflower so we can grow it in Cornia. Come to find out, it was very easy to do. She just wanted to make one more shot for my affliction...I mean affection."

"I'm sorry you had to go through that," I said.

"Don't be, it's all good." Ofelia looked toward a hill and pointed at a tree covered in pure white bark. "The Palo Blanco. A large field of coneflowers should be at the base of the tree."

She marched ahead while Valeria and I followed, entranced by one another again. Once we arrived at the tree, its white bark reflected the sun. Taking my eyes off my wife, I had to shield my eyes from its brightness. A breeze pushed a floral aroma through the air. Blue and yellow dots covered the sides of the hill. Once we were closer, I noticed the blue flowers were in the shape of stars. The yellow flowers were made of smaller flowers sticking off the sides. It resembled a tree up close. Atop the hill, we found our target. Covering the ground were yellow and brown flowers with drooping petals and dark green, pointed leaves—the Sunset Coneflower.

"We need to scoop up the dirt below them and make sure the roots come up in a ball," Ofelia said as she opened her bag. "They should last the journey back home before Nina can show us a good, partly shaded space to plant them."

She reached down and scooped up the dry dirt. Some of it fell to the ground between her fingers while the rest clumped in her hand, small roots dancing in the air. She placed the uprooted plant into her bag. It looked easy enough.

Valeria and I opened our bags and dug our hands into the dirt. It was moister than the dirt near Cornia but still dry. The narrow roots intertwined with my fingers and the dirt cooled my hand. The flower came up easily with the roots. I stuck the root ball in my bag and kept going until the bag was filled and loaded onto the wagon.

I dusted my hands off and asked, "Now what?"

Ofelia let out a deep breath. "We go home. The quicker, the better. We have people to help and flowers to keep alive."

After briefly returning to Blanche to gather food and water, we headed for the south gate and the road home. I hoped it wouldn't be my last time in Blanche. The city wasn't as bad as Ofelia made it seem. Maybe they weren't the most positive people, but the atmosphere had left a lasting impact on me. A sudden wanderlust inspired me to want to see more of Maize.

"We should travel more," I whispered to Valeria.

She snapped her head to face me. "For real?"

"For real." I grinned. "Next time, let's bring Isabella."

"Joy of my joy." She tickled the back of my neck.

Making our way down to the southern gate, Beatrice ran into the streets in a nightgown as we passed her house, waiting expectantly for Ofelia's presence. Ofelia kept the conversation short, but Beatrice still tried to give her a kiss goodbye. Ofelia dodged it, and we nearly ran out of the city.

"We will see each other again!" Beatrice yelled at us. "Just you wait, Ofelia! I will sweep you off your feet!"

Without looking back, Ofelia raised her right hand and waved. Cheeks flushed in pink clouds, the slightest smirk curled up. I opened my mouth to make a jest, but stopped once I saw the twinkle in her eyes. Instead, I just hummed to the tune of Valeria's nighttime song to Isabella.

"What?" Ofelia narrowed her eyes at me. "Wait. Don't say anything."

I just raised my eyebrows once, looked ahead, and kept humming as we left Blanche.

Our first leg home was speedy and uneventful. Rejuvenated, I was ready to bring long-awaited hope back to Cornia. When we camped, I expected exhaustion to take over after a day of hiking. Ofelia revealed that she hadn't gotten much sleep the night before. She had stayed at Beatrice's home, and they had drunk too much. A mischievous, subtle grin crossed her face as she said it, once again revealing a relaxed, happy Ofelia. Just as I had thought earlier, she didn't find all of Beatrice insufferable. She dismissed the rest of the conversation when we questioned her.

"Get a fire going," Ofelia said, laughing. "I'm tired of your shit."

Once the fire was constructed, Ofelia pulled out a surprise bottle of wine.

"I stole it from Beatrice's," Ofelia said with an evil chuckle. "She may be annoying, but she has always had good taste in wine...and women."

She poured the wine into our travel mugs. Valeria raised her glass.

"Salud to the Sunset Coneflower," Valeria said. "Let it bring hope back to Cornia and let it bring defeat to Enfer."

"And..." Ofelia said before we took a drink. "Salud to my two best friends. I'm thankful to have you both in my life. And Ciro, thank you for never giving up on fighting Enfer. Even with all the foolish guilt I know you feel about its creation. To good people and badass parents."

We clinked our mugs together and had a drink of wine. It was a basic red and dried once it hit my tongue. Just a hint of melon lingered. To my surprise, the melon mellowed the wine.

"Melons and wine, who would've thought," I said.

"Some lunatics in Blanche, that's who," Ofelia said. Her eyes shifted to Valeria. I turned to see her staring at me.

"What?" I asked.

"Can I ask you something?" Valeria paused and took another sip of wine. I nodded. "What does it look like? Enfer?"

The question caught me off guard. "Oh, well, like flowers. Rainbow flowers."

"I've heard that, but do they move?" Valeria asked.

Her dedication to learning more made me feel seen, like asking an anxious person what is making them anxious or a depressed person what is keeping them down. It made me love her even more.

"They do." I took a sip of wine. "The rainbow flowers float, their petals waving in the air. It's like a leaf blowing in the wind until another flower appears next to it."

"They sound...beautiful," Valeria apprehensively said.

"They are." The words were rough on my lips. "Hauntingly beautiful, but beautiful nonetheless."

"I can't imagine what it's like to see something that's so deadly but looks so harmless and beautiful," Valeria said. She squeezed my hand and rested her head on my shoulder. "Just know we both love you and will fight this terrible thing until it's gone."

"I love you. I love both of you." Ofelia and I exchanged smiles.

Our circle became silent. The firewood cracked, and a puff of smoke traveled upward. Its smell relaxed me and irritated me at the same time. Valeria's question was abrupt but satisfying to answer. Vocalizing the attributes of the flower that haunted my every thought took some power away from it.

"Not to change the topic," Ofelia said with an awkward grin, "but I think we should make the rest of this trip as quick as possible. If the Mountiffs can handle it, I think we should try to shave a day or two off our journey. The coneflowers are looking a little wilted."

"If that is the proposal, I'm off to bed," Valeria said. She finished her wine and leaned over to kiss me. Her lips were wet with sweet fruit, followed by a pucker of dry aftertaste. "Don't stay up too late."

"I love you," I said.

"Mi amor," Valeria replied. She turned to Ofelia. "Buenas noches, mi amiga."

Ofelia nodded, and Valeria made her way to our tent. Branches of the trees we camped in formed silhouettes against the moon's bright light. The air was fresh and cool, and filled with the sounds of bugs chirping and buzzing.

"You're happy again," Ofelia said.

"I am." I looked down from the sky. "My life feels right for the first time in a while."

"Who would've thought Blanche would be the key?" Ofelia let out a short, sharp laugh and gulped her wine.

"I visited Eduardo's house. Well, his wife's house," I said. Ofelia choked on her wine. "It was good. She seemed happy with our interaction. I felt his love through her. And I thought to myself, he wouldn't blame any of this on me. Not for one second. So why do I keep blaming myself?"

Ofelia grinned, and her eyes glistened with tears. "Ciro, you don't know how happy it makes me to hear this."

"I still feel guilty. I can't stop that. But I'm trying to focus on the people I'm surrounded by and the support they give me. I'm remembering that instead of the guilt. The people who love me."

"The reason you went to war and did all you did."

I nodded. "Yes, exactly." I took another drink, watching the fire leap into the air before disappearing. "Do you think war will come again?"

Ofelia paused for a while. She acknowledged me with a nod but continued to stare at the fire, just as I did. "I do, but not sure in what way."

I perked up and turned to her. "What do you mean?" Something churned in my friend's brain, and it told me she didn't think it'd be with the Coalition again.

"Just some interesting conversations with Aameen. I know he hurt you, but he's smart. He would be a powerful ally."

I tried so hard to dislike Aameen. He had given me every reason to hate him. But I kept gravitating back to him. Though our friendship would never be the same, some of our ideals lined up. And he was powerful.

I sighed. "I think you're right about Aameen. I need to talk to him."

"Politics." She smiled. "You can either play the game, or it will play you." Another pause; her lips quivered. "Speaking of that…Aameen asked me to be the newest Count."

"He did?"

She nodded.

"That's great!" I pictured stubborn Ofelia sitting on the council, forcing her candid reality on the others.

"I haven't said yes yet. I told him I'd think about it."

"Seriously?" She didn't respond. "You need to. Ofelia, you are good at this. You always have been. You would be so good for Maize, and it would give health and wellbeing a stronger voice in the government."

"That's almost exactly what Aameen said." A menacing grin covered her face. "You're right. I'll do it."

I laughed a little. Ofelia would never stop fighting Enfer. I knew it with my entire heart. But there was something else heavy in my heart. A subtle snore came from our tent, so I knew Valeria was asleep.

"Can I ask you something?"

"No, I didn't steal another bottle." She laughed. "But seriously, ask me anything."

"If anything happens to me, I want you to watch over Isabella."

"Whoa." She stared at me. I held a stern look. "That's dark. I haven't had enough wine for that." She looked at me with clear eyes. The most genuine form of herself was present. "Nothing is going to happen to you."

"Eduardo's family lost him. I don't think he and his wife had a plan for death. Their place looked worn down. I've just been thinking since then, and I want to make sure I have some kind of plan. It isn't that I don't think Valeria is capable; I just think her hands would be very full, and Isabella would need someone to guide her. You helped guide me. I trust you would do the same for her. So many things could happen. Aameen could call me to war. I could get sick. I'm in a good place right now, and I trust you. Can you help Isabella if something happens?"

"I would do anything for you." She cried. Another very rare occasion to witness from my good friend. I didn't know if it was the wine, the trip back to her home, or if I truly hit a chord. "I'll help her as much as I can."

"I took your advice on journaling about my abilities," I said. "It's in the drawer next to the fireplace." Ofelia gave me a confused look. "Valeria knows where I put my things. Just know it's there."

"Okay. Now, can we drop the dark conversations and just enjoy the night?"

"Absolutely."

We talked for ten more minutes before Ofelia passed out, slumped over by the fire. I learned she was a bit of a lightweight with wine. I tucked a blanket around her, poured water on the fire and watched the last bits of it leap into the air before disappearing in a cloud of white smoke. I kicked some dirt on the remaining soot and made my way to my tent, where Valeria already slept. I scooched close to her and watched her breathe. She looked so peaceful. Her face followed me into my dreams.

We arrived in Cornia two days earlier than planned, thanks to the Mountiffs. As we neared the city, the land shifted again, but from hilly to flat. As we approached Nina's house, her patients tossed and turned upon their cots. At least ten more cots surrounded her house than when we left. I knew our absence would have a negative effect, but I was only one person. I had to keep reminding myself of it—the entire world couldn't rely on just me.

"I'll take the coneflowers to Nina," Ofelia said. "Go see your daughter."

"Are you sure?" I asked.

"Absolutely," Ofelia said. "I want to give Beatrice's planting instructions to Nina while my mind is fresh. Go on."

I took Valeria's hand, and we walked. For traveling so far so fast, a light energy bounced between us. Just the two of us walking the calm streets reminded me of the days we used to do the same thing when dating. So much had changed since those awkward years of figuring out love and life.

"We're back in Cornia," I said as she glanced over at me.

"We are," she said with a sigh. "Promise me something." I nodded. "Promise we will keep growing with each other. I don't want to go back to what we became postwar."

"We'll grow together and become even stronger than prewar," I said. "Cornia better watch out. Our family is about to kick some Enfer ass while being relationally sound." She laughed.

When we came up to our house, my mother-in-law sat on the porch drinking coffee. She waved as we walked up, looking just like Valeria, but shorter and with gray hair. There were also wrinkles on her face, but I never mentioned those to her. They not only looked alike, but they were just as fierce as one another.

"How was your trip?" she asked.

"Great," Valeria squeezed my hand. "It was greatly rejuvenating."

"Thank you for doing this," I said. "Thank you for all that you do."

"It was my pleasure," my mother-in-law said with a smile directed toward me. I think she knew more about what was going on between Valeria and me than she let on. Just the look she gave me made me think about it. "I do love my Isabella. She's still sleeping. She was insistent on talking to you, Ciro."

"I'll talk to her when she wakes up," I said.

I still didn't feel very tired, even after walking all night. Harper wagged her tail while looking up at me. Our backyard had to be a mess. I hadn't cleaned up her droppings in a couple of weeks. It was something I could do until Isabella woke up.

"I'm going to pick up Harper's shit in the backyard," I said. My mother-in-law scowled at my language choice. "I mean, droppings. I feel energized. What better way to spend this energy?"

"Now?" Valeria asked. I nodded. "Okay. I'm going to talk to my mother for a little bit." I leaned over and kissed Valeria. She looked so beautiful with the sunrise warming her face. I touched her face and caressed her cheek. "Ciro, I'm not going anywhere."

"I know," I said. "I just wanted to touch your beautiful face again."

After grabbing her bag, I walked through the front door with Harper and Vito following behind. I took off my backpack and stretched my arms and back. Lemon essential oil wafted through the air. My beasts continued to follow me to the back door as I grabbed the scooper and looked over the yard. Dew twinkled on the blades of grass. The yard just warmed up. The same piles of shit looked up at me in agony, just as they had so long ago.

"Thanks for this," I said to Harper, who wagged her tail. I scratched her ears and began my work.

My green wooden fence lit up as the sun stretched out its rays. Harper walked around the yard until she found a spot to pee. She made direct eye contact with me as she did this. I averted my eyes.

Birds chirped, and people began their morning walks. I looked at one of the piles. My life had zipped by over the past few years. Harper's amputation. The drafting for the war. Learning how to properly identify diseases. Valeria's near-death and Eduardo's untimely death. Using disease as a weapon. Creating a disease. Returning home and learning that my daughter could do what I could do. Fighting this disease. All of it because of seeing white fluff on my Talonhound's shit. I laughed. It was an odd feeling, being joyous after all that had happened, but it was what I felt. An inner peace and hope for the future.

Vito let out loud groans from near the back door. I turned to find his silhouette next to another's.

"Daddy," Isabella said next to Vito.

My heart leaped. More joy.

"Morning, Isabella," I said, squinting in the morning sun behind her.

The sun made her black hair shine. It was a little overpowering looking at her. I took a step to the side, where the sun was blocked by a faraway tree. My eyes readjusted, and her sun kissed silhouette revealed her little honey eyes and her bedhead. She wore her favorite white and pink polka dot pajamas, wrapped in a new robe. My mother-in-law must have given it to her. It was bright blue and covered in flowers.

I paused and squinted.

Covered in flowers?

I stared, body frozen, dropping the scooper. My world started spinning and my stomach flipped. The flowers were...rainbow. The rainbow flowers spun around with the world. At least twenty-five flowers covered her little body, mocking me.

Isabella had Enfer.

"Daddy, I told Abuela I needed to see you," Isabella said. "I told her I needed your help. I didn't tell her why, like you told me to. Only you and Mamá could know. Daddy. Do you see them?"

I didn't know what to say. My mouth hung open. My heart stopped and the chirping birds faded. I wanted to cry. I wanted to give up. Peace and chaos collided. Hope and despair fought.

Her legs trembled. Her little body fell forward. I ran over and caught her before she hit the ground. Her frail body hung in my hands, looking up at me with a soft glance.

"Daddy..." she said in a soft voice. "The flowers...they hurt."

I stood up, cradling my daughter. Chaos overtook peace. Despair destroyed hope.

"VALERIA!"

CHAPTER 25
UNCONDITIONAL LOVE

Harper barked, sensing my panic. Vito tried to comfort me with his wool, but I pushed it away. Valeria was at the door the moment I ran up to it, whipping it open so fast a gust of wind blew her hair back, ripping out the hair tie holding her ponytail together. Strands of hair came off her head like fire before falling back down. Her eyes fixated on Isabella, and her hand reached out to touch Isabella's face.

"What happened?" Valeria's eyes begged me for an answer she didn't want.

"She...she...she..." I tried to speak, but I instead hyperventilated.

"Ciro!" Valeria exclaimed, demanding an answer.

I gathered my breath. "She has Enfer." Simultaneously, a pit formed in my throat and a knot in my stomach. Saying it out loud made it real.

Valeria covered her mouth. Her hand trembled.

"My mother just told me Isabella said she wasn't feeling well," Valeria said, her mother standing behind her.

"Mamá," Isabella said. "I did what Daddy told me to do. I waited to tell you about the flowers."

"Shh." Valeria kissed Isabella's forehead and looked back up to me. "What do we do? Can you fix it?"

"We need to get to Nina's," I said. "Ofelia is still there with the coneflowers. There are too many for me to heal."

I nearly ran my mother-in-law over, Valeria at my side. The front door was our objective, and anything in my way would be trampled. We needed to save our daughter.

"I'm sorry," my mother-in-law said. "I didn't know..."

"Please watch Harper," Valeria said.

We rushed out the door and ran as fast as we could to Nina's. More people filled the streets. Each of them stopped and stared at us as we ran by. The worry on their faces was of little concern to me. Isabella took all my attention. Her little face was calmer than I expected, observing the streets and their occupants. The rainbow flowers sat on her shoulder, reaching down her left side.

How did this happen?

Panic kept trying to take over my body and its functions, but I wouldn't allow it. I couldn't lose her. Not to Enfer of all things.

Valeria muttered a prayer in the native tongue. She cried, but tried to hide it with rapid breaths. We were holding hands just moments before, casually walking down the same street we were now running on. How could my day change so quickly?

Nina's house came into view. Rainbow flowers pulsed on the patients surrounding her building. They begged to be saved, but none of them mattered.

"Ofelia!" I yelled. Ofelia popped out the door right as I beckoned her, eyes widened. "We need space in Nina's house!"

Ofelia, without hesitation, turned around and rushed back in. Valeria tackled the door open. Ofelia cleared the table in the center of the room, and I placed my daughter down on it. Another rainbow flower had already formed.

"What happened?" Ofelia asked.

"She has it," I whimpered. "Ofelia, she has it."

Ofelia looked across Isabella's body. "Where?"

"The left shoulder and down the side." My hands gravitated to the back of my head, allowing me to breathe better.

"Hi, honey," Ofelia said to Isabella, keeping her voice calm. "I'm going to look on your side. Is that okay?"

Isabella nodded. For the first time since arriving home, her soft honey eyes darted around and her body trembled. Little soft breaths quickened before transforming into whimpers.

Valeria came to my ear and whispered, "We need to calm down. She's terrified." She grabbed my hand, and I squeezed it back.

She was right. I needed to get it together. I focused on slow breaths while Isabella observed us. Her face relaxed seeing us calm.

As Ofelia examined Isabella, a growth protruded in a small dome like another deltoid. Ofelia felt it and glanced up at me.

"Can you?" Ofelia asked.

"I don't think I can," I said. "It's too much. I'll amplify it."

"What about the coneflowers?" Valeria asked.

Nina walked into her house holding a black stone bowl where she crushed something. "I'm working on it now," she said. She took a milky substance from her shelf and mixed it with the crushed coneflowers. "Isabella, is it?"

"Yes," Isabella responded.

"My name is Nina. I'm going to put this cream on you. It'll be a little cold, but I promise it won't hurt you."

Nina took the cream and rubbed it on the growth and up Isabella's side. The rainbow flowers vibrated. One even seemed to start fading. A burst of hope steadied my unsettled heart, but Nina looked grim.

"Is it working?" Valeria asked.

"Can I talk to you?" Nina asked.

Hope went stagnant. I nodded and followed Nina and Valeria. Ofelia stayed and tried to distract Isabella with casual talk.

"What is it?" I asked.

"Her growth is further along than when the coneflowers would normally have an impact," Nina said.

"I saw it fluttering," I said. "The rainbow flowers. It was petering out."

Nina scrunched her eyebrows. "I have seen before where the growth seems to stop for a moment, but then it comes back more aggressively. At least at the state her growths are in. It's like the disease feeds itself at a certain point. We may be at that point."

Hope evaporated like spilled water in the midsummer sun.

"What if you fought the flowers while this happened?" Valeria asked me.

"I don't know," I said. "It might get worse."

"It'll get worse soon, no matter what," Nina said. "I don't mean to be harsh, but I've seen it before. I don't know if I have the right combination of plants to use yet. My expectation was to experiment a bit more. I only used it in some cases I showed you, which were minimal. Your daughter's infection is growing too fast."

It's fine. It has to be fine. I walked over to Isabella and looked at the rainbow flowers. There was another one.

Shit. It isn't working. Panic eclipsed hope. The flowers flickered, taunting me.

Is that all you got? Try to beat us, Master, the flowers seemed to say.

Ofelia looked up at me, "Her fever is increasing. The growth is hardening. Ciro, I don't know if it's working."

Isabella looked scared again. "Daddy, what's happening?"

"Ciro, we have to do something," Valeria said.

"I can try more cream," Nina said.

All the words and expectations crashed against me. There was no way I could defeat so many flowers. I was too weak. The panic in the room was overwhelming. Isabella sensed it.

"Daddy..." Isabella said.

"I have to try," I said. I kneeled next to my daughter. "Honey, we are going to give you a little medicine to make you sleepy. This will keep you calm. Daddy needs to try something, and I know you can see too much of what I'm going to do. Is that okay?"

"Daddy..." she said with worry.

"I've got you, hija," I said. I placed my hand on her face. "Trust me. I will fix this. I love you so much." I kissed her on the forehead.

Isabella nodded, and I looked to Ofelia. Ofelia grabbed a cloth and dabbed a clear liquid on it—Sleeping Nectar. She placed it on Isabella's mouth. Isabella kept eye contact with me before her eyes fluttered shut. As soon as they shut, tears rushed down my cheeks. The confidence I wanted her to see didn't need to be displayed anymore.

"What are you doing?" Ofelia asked.

"I'm going to burn it away," I said. "I'm hoping the cream will diminish the growth as much as it can."

"Are you sure?" Ofelia asked. She knew better than anyone about the risk I took. She had been there the first time I amplified it Enfer instead of healing it.

My hands trembled at my side. A high-pitched buzzing burned in my ears. A great ache formed in my chest and my heart slammed against my sternum. All these sensations needed to go away. With a long, shaky breath, I closed my eyes, steadied my body as best as I could, and shot my eyes open.

"I have to be," I said.

Valeria embraced me for a hug, placing her cheek against my own.

"Save our daughter," Valeria whispered before letting go. Her stare was haunting, placing every bit of hope she had in me. "Please, Ciro. Please."

I kept eye contact with Valeria. Her presence gave me strength. Isabella slept peacefully on the bed. The rainbow flowers slowed their motion after additional cream was added. My chance was there, and I had to take it.

The trembling began again, but I shook my hands as hard as I could. Forming fists, I cracked my knuckles and reached out to grasp the first flower with my right hand with a tight grip.

It burned before it disappeared.

My left hand worked on the next one. I moved as fast as I could, one flower after the next.

The other flowers gravitated toward the area I attacked. More flowers blossomed each time I made some disappear. For every three I burned, another appeared. I was winning. I just had to keep going.

My breath became heavier. My hands were on fire. I pushed down the pain and exhaustion. I had to. I had to save my daughter. Protecting my family was the reason why I did all I did. My lungs filled with cool air and my mind focused on only my daughter. I believed I could do anything.

I would do anything.

The flowers kept burning and disappearing. One by one.

But then, it changed.

For every three flowers I burned, three more appeared.

I moved faster. Exhaustion pushed back harder than my effort.

"No, no, no," I said.

My hands trembled again. The intense pounding in my chest returned.

"What is it?" Ofelia asked.

"I was doing so good." I looked at Ofelia and Valeria.

"Keep pushing," Valeria said. I heard her start to cry. "For Isabella."

I grunted, burning the flowers more than I ever had. My grunting morphed into screaming. It hurt so badly. I had to push through the pain.

Five flowers remained when my eyes became blurry, and I fell to my knees. I could barely breathe. I wanted to keep going, but I couldn't. My body had hit its full capability. I burned one more flower before my hands fell to my side.

"NO!" I screamed. Twenty flowers suddenly appeared.

Falling to my knees, I reached forward, every muscle in my body tight. My mind disappeared in a cool cloud. Time slowed as I focused on the rainbow flowers.

In slow motion, I saw the tumor expand.

The final stage of Enfer had arrived.

"CIRO!" Valeria screamed.

My daughter's growth was too big. It was inevitable.

I lifted my hands, but the flowers slapped them away.

The room slowed down again. Rainbow flowers riddled her body.

Every pump of my heart made my arteries pulse.

Is this the moment? Is this the moment my daughter dies?

I closed my eyes. I couldn't take it.

I have to save her. I have to protect her. I can still move it. I can move it to another person...

My eyes reopened as I surveyed the room and looked at Nina.

I could move it to Nina to save Isabella...

Lifting my hands, they hovered toward Nina, fingers dancing to a hypnotic rhythm. I stared at Nina.

Forcing my eyes shut, I shook my head and retracted my hands.

Who was I? Time was running out.

I looked at Ofelia. She slowly pointed to herself. She could see what was going on in my head.

My heart ached as I stared at her. I couldn't take it and forced my eyes shut.

Ofelia is asking me to save Isabella. I could do it.

The memories of my friendship with Ofelia filled my mind. The first time she scolded me. The moment I helped her treat Vito in that shed. The deep conversations and hard talks she empowered me with. She had done so much for me. She was my best friend.

The pressure in my chest pushed upward as I growled, eyes open again.

I can't. I can't do it. I won't hurt another person. I made this disease.

Something came to me.

I should take it. I should save my daughter.

As soon as I thought this, my heart pumped faster. An odd sensation filled my veins. I leaned into the feeling. A return of energy, though different energy, coursed through my body.

"I have to protect her." I opened my eyes.

I reached out one more time with both hands. I grabbed the flowers. They froze. They turned to me. My heart raced, the sensation inside me growing. It was like a windstorm, but felt intuitive, like something I had always been able to do. Something I always knew about. I leaned further into the instinctual feeling. I brought my hands to my chest and pushed forward. The wind from inside me pushed toward Isabella.

The first rainbow flower lifted off Isabella's body and rushed to my chest and latched tightly to me. Then, another followed the same pattern. The flowers all floated away from Isabella and gravitated to me. I was becoming their new host.

Tears of joy cascaded down my burning cheeks as the growth shrank on Isabella. It was working. Whatever I was doing was working. There were five flowers remaining, just as before.

"Ciro..." Ofelia stared at me in shock. But she wasn't looking at me; she was looking at my chest.

I looked down at a growth forming, just like Isabella had. A numb space occupied my chest. The last five flowers floated off my daughter's left shoulder and landed on me.

Enfer returned to its master, its creator. Poetic justice. It was only right that I took it. There was no more pushing disease on others, burning away my decisions.

I created Enfer. I was the one who needed to take it.

A terrible pain formed in my gut. My body swayed, gravity becoming too much. Before my body hit the ground, Valeria caught me. She breathed heavily, her eyes assessing the situation before her.

"Ciro..."

Another look at Isabella revealed my accomplished goal—the flowers were gone. Every single flower. The growth shrank away. She was okay. My daughter wasn't infected anymore, though a small scar remained on her shoulder.

"Did you...?" Ofelia asked, but grew silent.

"She's okay," I said. I looked back at Valeria. "Isabella is healed."

"No, no, no," Valeria said as she touched my face. "Ciro, you're sick."

I smiled. "I know," I said. "It was my only choice."

"We need more cream!" Ofelia yelled before she grabbed it from Nina and ran over to me. She ripped my shirt open and started rubbing the cream on my chest; a sharp pain came from her touch. "We need it to shrink. Then you can burn it."

I grabbed Ofelia's hand. The soothing cream on her fingers transferred over to mine. It made my growth feel better, but the flowers were growing one by one. It wasn't doing anything.

"Ofelia," I said, steadying my voice. "It's okay. Save it for the others."

"I can't lose you," Ofelia said, snot dripping from her nose. "How am I supposed to do this without you?"

"You formed a team, remember?" I asked. "You have help. You will figure it all out."

"Stop it, asshole," Ofelia said. "We've been through too much together. You can't give up on me now."

"Remember what I said all that time ago?" I asked. "I would do anything to protect my family." I touched her arm. "This is it. I did everything I possibly could."

"But..." Ofelia began. She cried harder and harder.

"Keep burning this disease away," I said. "I know you'll figure out a cure. I have no doubt about it. And please help Isabella." I looked at my daughter peacefully sleeping. "She's going to need it."

I could feel my skin stretching as the growth grew. I turned to Valeria as time slipped away.

"Mi amor." I tried to keep a strong voice, but just looking at her made me cry. She looked so beautiful. Her tears reflected sparks of light on her tan skin. Though there was fear in her eyes, I didn't want to see it. I needed to see her love. Her fire.

"Mi amor." She touched my face. My skin tingled, the electricity still there. "Don't give up. I *need* you. Isabella needs you."

"I'm afraid Enfer is growing too fast," I said. "I don't have enough energy left. And even if I did, I'm not going to infect someone else with it."

"But we just fixed us. We fixed our love." She paused. "We were supposed to go see all of Maize. We were supposed to find a cure for Enfer. We were supposed to raise our daughter together. You *promised* me this war would give us a life together. You have to keep fighting."

"Valeria, I fought," I said. "I fought as much as I could. I fought enough to save Isabella. I don't have any more fight left." I became lightheaded. I felt like I could feel the flowers growing. "Can we have the room?" I asked the others.

Nina nodded and exited. Ofelia stared at me. She opened her mouth, but nothing came out. She shook her head.

"I love you!" Ofelia blurted out. "I'll keep fighting. I'll keep fighting in your name. Until I die, Ciro. You hear me!"

"Thank you." I smiled. "I love you, Ofelia."

She smiled and hastily left the room.

"Ciro…" Valeria said.

"Help me over to Isabella," I said.

Valeria stood and tried to lift me up. My body felt so heavy and my so legs weak. I pushed forward, grunting in pain. It was only a few steps, but it felt like I was climbing a mountain. I grabbed Isabella's bed and looked at her precious, gorgeous face. She looked so calm, unaware of the chaos surrounding her and the death about to change her life. My heart broke piece by piece.

"Isabella, mi hija bonita," I said. My words became heavier and heavier. "I'm sorry this happened. I'm sorry this disease is what it is. I'm sorry you got sick from it." I took a deep breath. "I'm sorry you have this curse. I love you more than you will ever know. I'll keep loving you when I meet Gaia. Watch over your mom for me. Grow together." I looked over at Valeria as I said this. "Because growing separately is too much for anyone to handle. Someone beautiful helped me learn this." I pulled out Isabella's old drawing and gripped it tightly as I leaned over and kissed Isabella on the forehead. She moved for a moment before settling down again. "Te amo, Isabella."

My body lost all muscle control, falling to the side. Valeria caught me. "Take it easy, esposo," she said. She lowered my frail body to the ground.

The truth hit with a sudden force. I saw more and more flowers take over my body, consuming me like the dreams I had during the war. Waking up wasn't an option. There was nowhere to go. I couldn't escape them.

"V, I'm scared," I said with a shaky voice. I wanted to cry but didn't have enough energy.

"I know," she said. "I'm scared too." She tried to keep her voice calm.

"What if we are wrong about Gaia?" I asked. "What if there is nothing?"

"I know Gaia is real," she said. The normal fire returned to her amber eyes, believing every word she said. "She has to be. Away from all this sickness and pain."

The world became blurry. I gripped Isabella's drawing tighter and tighter, wishing to have my moment again on my couch with my favorite people.

"Valeria," I said. "My eyes are getting fuzzy." I looked for her. Her eyes found me. I could only make out her amber eyes as the world around her faded. "I'm not ready." I reached up for her. She grabbed my hand. "I'm not ready to go."

She kissed my hand. "It's okay, Ciro," she said. She tried to be strong for me. She started singing the lullaby she sang to Isabella:

> *Mira dentro para verte a ti mismo.*
> *Encuentra la comodidad.*
> *Descansa la cabeza.*
> *Siente el amor a tu alrededor.*
> *Siente el amor bajar tu plumón.*[1]

---

1. Glossary: Valeria's Song Translation

Her eyes disappeared, but the fire in them remained. Two flickering flames warmed my pain. I couldn't see anything else. The pain went numb as the flames burned. My breathing weakened. Her song remained strong. She had it started again, but the words became harder to understand.

The flames finally faded, but I still heard her voice.

Then I saw it. A bright light. Not flames, but something greater. I started reaching for it. It was marvelous. Every color imaginable came from it. The light shimmered like the rainbow flowers, but instead joy pulsated from it. Not pain or suffering. Joy. It drew me in.

"Ciro..." Valeria's faint whisper moved around me. It sounded distant. She cried, soft and faint. "Te amo, mi amor..."

"Te amo, V," I whispered back, pressing the drawing against my chest.

Isabella's red, faded drawing lingered in my mind. I thought of Valeria and Isabella sitting on the couch. My arm wrapped around them both as Harper sat by my feet and Vito rested her wool on my arm. Everything I ever wanted. That's all I wanted. To keep them safe.

The light pulled me in. My last breath reached out into the feeble world.

I love you, Isabella. I love you, Valeria.

EPILOGUE
NEW BLOOM

I raced to the Northern Medical Building, another load of treatments ready for the infected. Maizeans zipped by, some trying to talk to me, but my mission served one purpose only—to fight the disease that killed my husband.

A great crowd filled the street I often used to get from the Western Medical Building to the Northern. That meant I had to take the route I hated more than anything. If I just kept my eyes down, I'd avoid the eyesore that had been erected near the city center. Moving faster than ever, the water feature surrounding it caught the corner of my eye. Yellow tiles glistened under the water's surface. I wanted to peek, but it hurt my heart too much.

"Valeria." A pair of expensive leather boots blocked my path. Deep purple clothes made of fine silk accented with yellow stitching made up the rest of the man. "It's good to see you, my friend."

"Stena Aameen." I gulped. Once a man admired, interacting with Aameen now filled me with dread.

To make matters worse, he wrapped his arms around me, forcing me into an unsolicited hug. The contact forced my head in the direction I avoided at all costs. All the air left my lungs as I just stared at the statue of Ciro. The artist had captured every detail of his lovely face, from the patchy facial hair, faint freckles, and combed-over, straight hair. What they failed to capture was his kindness. Instead, they had his hands on his waist and one leg raised, mounted atop a pile of coal. Below the terrible statue shone a gold plate reading: "The Hero of Maize. Never forget Ciro Sinsal."

Pulling away from me, Stena Aameen turned to face the statue with me. "It feels good to pay tribute to my best friend."

I shot a harsh glare at him that he didn't notice. The statue had been dedicated to my family, but I never asked for it. Ciro would never have wanted it. But Stena Aameen had insisted. I despised him for doing it, but politics were politics, as Ofelia often said.

"I wish he were here," I said.

Stena Aameen turned to face me. "Me, too. I miss him dearly."

Before I punched Aameen square in the face and fated myself to imprisonment, I stepped forward. "I'm sorry, but I'm in a bit of a hurry."

"Of course." Stena Aameen stepped to the side, letting me pass. He grabbed my arm. "You should come by sometime so we can catch up. It's been too long."

I pulled my arm away, cringing at his touch. "You know me, busy fighting Enfer."

Before he could say any more, I marched forward, putting a healthy distance between us. The rest of my trip moved in a blur. I dropped off the treatment at the Northern Medical Building and took the long way home, around the city, to avoid Ciro's statue and Stena Aameen's disgusting presence.

Lying at my front door, Vito sat up, not moving as fast as he used to. Stretching out his wooly extensions, he caressed my arm, always aware of my discomfort.

"Hi, old boy." I crouched and patted his scaly head, looking into his beady eyes. This beast would always hold a special place in my heart for his true dedication to Ciro. "I assume she's home."

The front door creaked open and Isabella stepped out. "Mamá. I thought you were running a delivery."

"I moved quicker than I normally do." I stood, grabbed my beautiful daughter and hugged her tightly, her head brushing against mine. "When did you get so big?"

"Stop," she groaned before I released her. "I'm a bit old to ask that question."

The little freckles dancing underneath her honey eyes reminded me of Ciro. So much of her reminded me of my late husband. Ten years later, it still broke my heart and warmed it at the same time. I admired her black hair, which she had tied back, and skin scattered with tattoos. Poking at her left arm, I pinpointed a new rainbow flower tattoo, a bit different than the others. "Is this new?"

She pushed my hand away and covered the tattoo with her hand. "Yes, and ow. It's still fresh."

As she moved her hand away, I took in the pointed petals riddled with rainbow hues. The flowers, invisible to me, had wreaked havoc on my life. Now, they sat as art upon her skin. I frowned at the artwork.

"Did this one capture what you wanted?" I asked.

Rolling her eyes, she covered it again with her hand. "Not quite. But it's another dedication to Dad. Even though you hate them."

I hummed. Though I didn't love the tattoos, I appreciated their meaning. The disease that Ciro created, that had almost killed Isabella and that had ultimately killed Ciro, taunted me each time I looked at her.

"I hate Enfer," I corrected her. "I'll never hate anything about you. After all, you're an adult. You can make your own decisions."

"Speaking of that," Isabella said, "I want to talk to you about Enfer. I think I figured out something new to fight it."

EPILOGUE
THE LEGEND OF GAIA

The legend went that there were four sisters named Juniper, Palma, Marlowe, and Acacia. Juniper, the oldest, brought a very patient and steady maternal air to the family. Palma, the next oldest, was energetic and likeable, always humming and singing. Marlowe's birth happened in the rain, and her temperament personified it in her easygoing and reflective state—she was often found alone. The last of the sisters was Acacia. Blunt and withdrawn, she did not fit in well with the rest of the family.

On Acacia's sixteenth birthday, an intense argument took over the family. Her sisters wanted her to be more like them. Out of rage, Acacia left the family, never to be seen again.

One by one, each sister went out to look for her. Instead, they each found a place to call home. Each raised their own families and found their own voice.

Each sister is said to have brought life to wherever they stood. Juniper brought greenery and fresh air. Palma brought biodiversity and humidity. Marlowe brought water and sun. Acacia never had the chance to figure herself out.

Why should anyone care about this family? Well, each sister holds a secret power, blessed by Gaia. Gaia gave them life, and in return, life is given to the world.

As Juniper's grandson, many taught me about their stories and their importance. Our family's history was rich, and I didn't see how big a part we would play, but that changed when a new threat came into existence. My grandmother and her sisters were divided—our only hope was to bring them back together. But there was still no sign of my Great-Aunt Acacia.

To understand what needs to be done, I need to tell you how we got here. The issues began during my Great-Aunt Palma's birthday. A joyous occasion became so messy so fast…

PRONUNCIATION GUIDE

PEOPLE/TITLES

CIRO: SEER-OH

VALERIA: VAH-LE-REE-AH

AAMEEN: AH-MEEN

OFELIA: OH-FE-LEE-AH

STENA: STEH-NUH

MEZCA: MEH-Z-KAH

ARIBA: AH-REE-BAH

BEBIDA: BEH-BEE-DAH

GAIA: GY-AH

KERNEL: KUR-NUHL

VITO: VEE-TOH

SAPA: SAH-PAH

SPODNIC: SPAHD-NYK

SOLAREON: SOH-LAH-REE-AAN

KURAKA: KOO-RAH-KAH

AMARU: AH-MAH-ROO

BEATRICE: BEH-AH-TRYS

PRONUNCIATION GUIDE

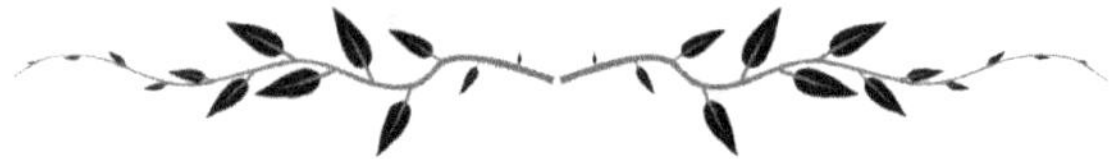

PLACES & THINGS

MAIZE: MAY-Z

CORNIA: KORN-EE-AH

PASTEL CASTLE: PAH-STEHL KA-SL

ENFERFLOR: EN-FEHR-FLOHR

ENFER: EN-FEHR

BLANCHE: BLAWN-SHH

AMAR: AH-MAHR

SOLARA: SO-LAHR-AH

SOL: SOHL

CONIFERA: KAH-NUH-FR-AH

Valeria's Song Translation

ORIGINAL:

Mira dentro para verte a ti mismo.

Encuentra la comodidad.

Descansa la cabeza.

Siente el amor a tu alrededor.

Siente el amor bajar tu plumón.

ENGLISH TRANSLATION:

Look inside to see yourself.

Find comfort.

Rest your head.

Feel the love around you.

Feel the love settle down upon you.

AUTHOR NOTE:

The lullaby was inspired by soft, nostalgic melodies I love—something between comfort and melancholy.

MAIZE HIERARCHY

STENA MEZCA
(COUNTRY LEADER)

COUNT ARIBA

COUNT BEBIDA

COUNT JUAN

COUNT PEPE

COUNT MARGARITA

SOLARA HIERARCHY

SAPA SPODNIC SOLAREON
(COUNTRY LEADER)

KURAKA AMARU

COALITION HIERARCHY

UNKNOWN

BEASTS

TALONHOUND

(ta-luhn-hownd)

Habitat: Hilly areas or cities
Abilities: Can dig through any surface, Can survive without air for an hour at a time

Height: 4'6" Weight: 75 lbs

CAPYNX

(kahp-eenx)

Habitat: High-grass fields or city streets
Abilities: Can alter the vestibular system & increase clumsiness

Height: 10" Weight: 10 lbs

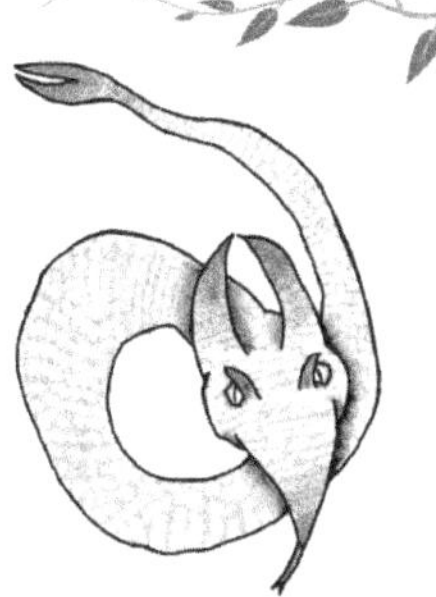

ELOTERRA

(eh-loh-teh-ruh)

Habitat: Highly vegetated fields
Abilities: Can alter temperature, Can alter skin texture & hardness

Height: 3'3" Weight: 15 lbs

MAIZEAN CHICKAROO

(may-zee-ahn cheek-ah-roo)

Habitat: Open fields & farms
Abilities: Can produce deafening
screech, Can vibrate feathers &
overstimulate nervous system of others

Height: 2'3" Weight: 10 lbs

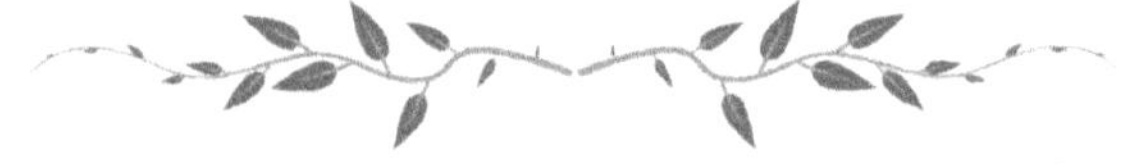

SHAPPLE

(shapl)

Habitat: Forest edge near fields
& farms
Abilities: Can extend wooly masses
into functioning limbs without
sensory function but with regrowth

Height: 5'1" Weight: 110 lbs

Height: 6'6" Weight: 295 lbs

MOUNTIFF

(mownt-if)

Habitat: Open fields
Abilities: Able to slow down
time for brief moments, can
go long distances without
nourishment

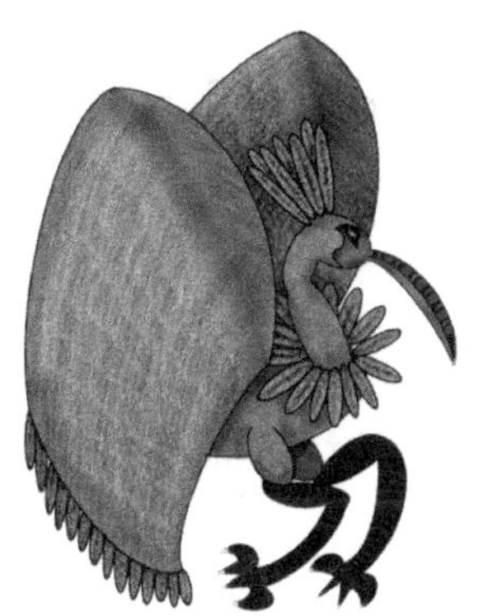

ZAPA
(zah-pah)

Habitat: Trees near hills or cities
Abilities: Can impair vision, Can create intense gusts of air, Can rapidly alter speed & dexterity while flying

Height: 11'3" Weight: 175 lbs

NOSTRANGAL
(no-strahn-gahl)

Habitat: Forests near dry fields
Abilities: Can evoke worry & doubt, Can go invisible for short stints

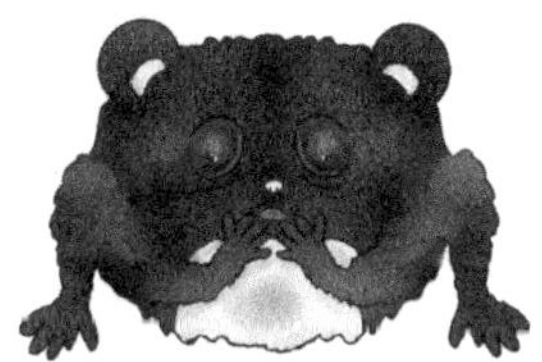

Height: 9" Weight: 3 lbs

FURROWBURROW
(fur-oh-bur-oh)

Habitat: Forests near lush fields
Abilities: Can evoke comfort & trust, Can slow down decision making & critical thinking

Height: 1'1" Weight: 8 lbs

ANGUILA TERRESTRE

(ahn-gwee-lah teh-reh-streh))

Habitat: Dry fields

Abilities: Can create illusion where markings across body keep moving when the beast isn't, Can inject highly toxic venom that makes one go mad

Height: 2'3″ Weight: 30 lbs

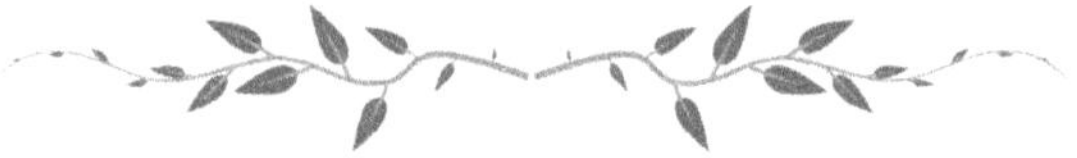

www.ingramcontent.com/pod-product-compliance
Lightning Source LLC
Chambersburg PA
CBHW070847160726
48004CB00003B/963